CLIFFORD'S GHOST

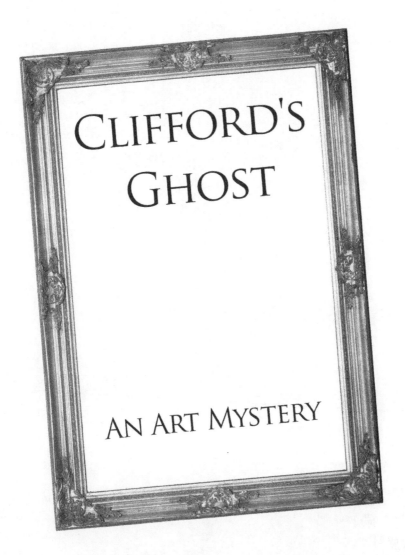

Clifford's Ghost

An Art Mystery

Cynthia Lang

Mill City Press

Mill City Press, Inc.
2301 Lucien Way #415
Maitland, FL 32751
407.339.4217
www.millcitypress.net

© 2019 by Cynthia Lang

All rights reserved. No part of this publication may be reproduced, stored in a retrieval system, or transmitted, in any form or by any means, electronic, mechanical, photocopying, recording, or otherwise, without the prior written permission of the author.

Printed in the United States of America

ISBN-13: 978-1-54565-694-5

For Sylvia

CHAPTER 1

Emeline's misjudged. With New York's forgiving air after the summer heat and cabs scarce on Seventh Avenue, it seemed a sensible move to walk east along 41st Street to Madison; if no cab came along, she'd take the bus uptown before the traffic grew brutal. She felt quite jaunty when she set off, swinging her cane like Fred Astaire and relieved she'd worn her low-heeled shoes. Only she forgot how long the blocks run from west to east. Just as her energy lags a September shower is making it tricky to manage her cane and open her umbrella.

Emeline is hardly the person she used to be—biking from 95th Street to the Cos Club on 66th without a second thought. Delivery trucks thunder past. It's quite an effort to make her way against the pedestrians pushing by her so when a particularly rude person elbows her from behind, yanks her Coach bag from her shoulder and out of her hand, and knocks her sideways into an alley, Emeline is face down on the stinking cement before she understands. Not bad manners. A mugging.

Xavier pushes through a canopy of umbrellas and the aroma of onions and *kimchi* from a Korean restaurant to stop in front of a shop window offering Posters for Sale. He tosses his cigarette on the sidewalk and steps on it, twisting his toe back and forth. Transfixed by the Italian statue, a dude in the nude except for a large leaf, he hears the traffic slow, then stop as the light up ahead turns red. In the hush, Xavier hears a moan from the alley.

Looking down the alley toward the sound, he sees a woman slumped between trash bags and the restaurant's gritty wall, her forehead bleeding, her skirt over her knees. He means to keep walking, though he isn't late yet, he left early to get out of the apartment. Is she a bag lady?

No signs of alcohol or slowed wits. Her hair, though mussed, looks clean. More likely she's been mugged. On the pavement, damp from rain and slick with some rank stream oozing out of a trash bag, he sees only an umbrella and a shoe on its side. No sign of a handbag.

Xavier hesitates, checks his watch, he needs to keep going, get to work; he can't afford to attract by-standers, or, God forbid, the cops. It wouldn't be the first time a white lady screamed she was mugged by an unknown *puertorriqueno* who'd only tried to help.

When Xavier hears her cough he stubs out his cigarette, and bends over her. "Miss? You okay?" Her eyes open, close again. On one scratched hand she wears a sizeable diamond ring. "Miss, come on, getup." He holds out his hand; shaking, she holds out hers and lets him hoist her to her feet. Not sure what to say, Xavier asks, "You been attacked?" Eyes closed, she nods. "Did you see who it was?" She shakes her head. Xavier picks up the scuffed shoe and reads the label inside—Ferragamo. "Afraid they got your bag, too."

Her thin hand trembles in his. "Everything. Wallet, glasses, some letters—"

"Can I call anyone? Your husband, maybe, or your kids?" Dizzy, she leans against the wall for balance. "Or I could get you home, even. First I have to call my gym."

As he is speed-dialing she opens her eyes, and grabs his cell. "Not until I know who *you* are."

Right then Xavier's ready to change his mind about stopping in the first place. Except he needs his cell and snatching it back might draw attention. Still shaking, the woman barks questions into the tiny phone, holds it at arm's length, sniffs with contempt, and snaps it shut. "No answer."

Xavier could have told her that. Ditzy *chiquita* at the front desk never answers in under eight rings. Too busy gossiping with her friends, she prefers to let customers work their way through the menu: "touch one for weight loss."

"Guess they don't want customers. Not that there's much left you could take, if you do turn out to be a thief." Xavier's eyes slide to her ring, a nugget of sharp splendor set in gold and flanked by brilliant, faceted stones. "I could manage on my own, I suppose." He doubts it; she is still shaking, holding his arm as she puts on her shoe. "Still, if you would be willing? I'll reimburse you and pay you for your time. I'll even pay the cab to return you to . . . to wherever it is you were going. Emeline Hughes, by the way," she thrusts out a free hand.

Her voice is commanding if unsteady, her accent familiar from the PBS his sister likes to watch. Like many Anglo ladies she has blue eyes, pale skin with almost no make-up at all, and grey hair. Xavier guesses she'd once been blonde.

"Young man? Or, am I to start hailing on my own?"

Another upper-east-side lady with more money than God and little purpose to fill her days, Xavier can tell the woman staring out the cab's smudged window sees nothing. As the cab heads east, he calls the gym, says he's delayed on the subway, then sits back to watch the midtown scene play out—tabloid-size papers blow against the lamp posts, lost men in hoodies, sporty dudes in Jamaican dreds or tight fitting caps in African colors shuffle toward a thousand destinations—until the cab turns north on Madison. Then he sees slender women in skin-tight jeans, stiletto-heeled boots, and sleek pony tails.

Xavier shifts uneasily, avoiding the curious Pakistani's eyes in the rear view mirror staring at his passengers. Knowing no Urdu, Xavier still gets what the driver is thinking: these two, not speaking, what are they doing together on a Thursday morning?

The woman's shoulder must hurt where she'd been slung against the wall. Her hands are scratched where she tried to break her slide. Gingerly, she pats the back of her left hand which is bleeding again. Xavier pulls a wad of tissues from his pocket. With the delicacy of a surgeon he extracts one and hands it to her. She looks at him then, expressionless, her papery eyelids hardly flicker. He knows: letting on how you feel, revealing fear, sadness, envy, or expectation leaves you unarmed. Each of them is counting the minutes until free of this unwelcome pairing.

The cab moves uptown through the midday traffic, turns east, and stops in front of an awning building just off Lexington. The woman allows the doorman to help her out, steadying her when she seems about to lose her balance. Shaking off his white-gloved hand, she says, "Gregor, this gentleman will be keeping the cab. He'll need forty dollars, if you have it?" Of course he has it; of course he will not hand it to Xavier, it has to go first to Mrs. Hughes.

CLIFFORD'S GHOST

Xavier watches her turn and put her hand on one awning pole so she won't totter. He waits for her to bend so she can see through the open cab window, say something. She doesn't and when he calls out to her, only pauses, then plows on. The cab shoots forward. He rides a couple of blocks, imagining what his brother Ramon would do. ("Crazy, *Broki*, give up a ride in a cab? How often you get to ride in a cab?")

Instead at the next light he gets out, pays the driver, and pockets his unexpected windfall, his conscience hardly flicking. He's out of place in this part of town, and it's faster to take the express downtown. At 59th he hears the shriek of metal on metal far underground and elbows past a man climbing the stairs, his bike over one shoulder. Good for him, Xavier thinks, good for the pecs.

His mother has tried to teach him: "New York is not San Juan. Here people rush, they make themselves crazy, even when they aren't late they're afraid they are." Last year for *Navidad* she bought Xavier the handsome watch; smug, he strapped it on, eyeing Ramon eaten up with envy. Minutes ahead of his client Xavier walks into the gym on West 41st Street. Only then he realizes: he is still holding that woman's umbrella.

If he's not talking, neither am I. Riding in the cab Emeline expects she owes the young man more courtesy, a drop or two of small talk. Her unknown companion has shortish hair, longish sideburns, white teeth and high cheekbones hinting at native Arawak ancestors as well as Spanish and African. Puerto Rican probably, though lately people from all over the Caribbean have been moving to the city.

His hand was what she'd noticed first. If bonier and younger than Jacinta's, his were the same *cafe au lait* color as the young woman's hands that made her breakfast, cleaned up her kitchen, took messages, even helped her dress on mornings when she felt too stiff to do it on her own. Jacinta, who's left for Barbados, dropping everything to help her ill father, and leaving Emeline to count the days until she returns.

Once out of the cab, Emeline is heading toward the lobby when a voice more amused than resentful calls out to her: "You're welcome!" He speaks with no accent, she realizes while her elevator glides upward. Either he was born here or he moved to the city very young. Clean, well-spoken, more than a little vain. A man with a kind heart, or a flair for deception?

Emeline steps onto the pristine black and white tiles of the hallway she shares with 7A and unlocks the door of 7B, more relieved to be inside her apartment than usual. On automatic she goes to drop her handbag on the small, inlaid mahogany table before she remembers: no handbag. Another unknown person has her wallet, her credit cards, her keys. She tries to remember what else was in her Coach bag. Letters with her address? The invitation to Muffy's benefit? Relief turns to new waves of worry. She'd call the police only she knows it's pointless. She never saw a face, she wasn't seriously hurt, and the police will never find the mugger.

Each time she unlocks the door to her new apartment Emeline feels air currents in their invisible dance pause and grow still. Like the Auden poem her daughter insisted on reading at Clifford's memorial service: "Stop all the clocks, cut off the telephone, prevent the dog from barking with a juicy bone."

Three books lie on the table, ready to go back to the Society Library on 79th next time she's up that way: *Above Suspicion*, a Helen MacIinnis and a taste acquired from dear Aunt Mildred, a fan of spy stories and suspense. *The Girl with the Dragon Tatoo*, with twice the violence of MacIinnis and none of the charm. *Bleak House,* Vol. I, because Dickens always soothes Emeline's soul.

The mugger, the attack, the uncertainty of the ride home: more than usual fatigue engulfs her. Returning books will have to wait. So will popping out again to d'Agostino's for English muffins and yogurt. Emeline longs to click her heels and be in the courtyard at the Frick Musuem; she knows today her feet can't take her there.

With a single *miao* Scaramouche tiptoes out from whatever cranny he's been hiding in, his black and white paws edging forward. Bending to pat the cat, she avoids looking in the mirror. She knows what she'll see: a face hardly more cheerful than the dour Kathe Kollwitz sketch Deborah took with her back to London.

Once a petite Brit with sandy hair and freckles, Emeline's a thinner, faded version of the girl Clifford Hughes met one summer afternoon. Coming ashore from a boat race on Long Island Sound, he'd lured her onto the East Hampton tennis court and laughed, intrigued, as she danced across the net from his aggressive serve. The same evening he managed to crash the dance at the Maidstone Club; tireless, she waltzed him around the floor and changed the poor dear's life forever.

Though Clifford was hardly poor, *Nouveau* as they come but *riche,* maybe richer than Aunt Mildred, whose income and pedigree-by-marriage, thanks to sweet Uncle Ray, had gently ushered the young Emeline into private school and the Social Register.

Today's mail brings requests from the Democrats, buzzing about like friends she loved but would like to see less of. A note from Tram (who does not, even in 2012, do email and hates the phone). Without opening the mauve envelope Emeline senses another uproar over change in the wedding plans of Tram's son.

Like all her friends Emeline owns her apartment, and not one of them calls it a condo. She hasn't yet adjusted to her reduced scale: two modest bedrooms, a ridiculous excuse for a dining room, a kitchen with barely room for the red, glass-topped French bistro table and two metal chairs. There's her tiny den off the kitchen, her previous, paneled study replaced by a room designed originally for a fairly short maid. In the den there's a compact marquetry-inlay desk holding her business files, it has three stacked drawers and a lock on the horizontal drawer that shutters them all.

The living room's not too bad. It would look bigger if she hadn't filled the walls with their framed treasures when she moved from her 95th Street apartment with its Central Park views. She clicks a switch, and on go three lamps perched like guardian angels over the best of the oils, even though no one else is coming to see them. Art and music are her companions now.

Deborah had been the one to push for the move: "There's a hot market in Carnegie Hill; Ma, you'll come out ahead. Start over in a smaller place, more convenient to manage, less stuff."

Stuff, Em soon realized, Deborah had her eye on. Flying in from Heathrow for a fast weekend of realtors and bossy as ever, Deborah cherry-picked her way through her parents' lifetime collection, her decisiveness taking Emeline's breath away. Deborah did have the grace to back off the one time Emeline raised a counter bid: "No. You can have the Kathe Kolwitz if you want. I'm keeping the Bridget Riley, the Emil Nolde sketch, the Rembrandt restrike, and the little Boem birds. They'll be yours after I'm gone; for now, they're mine and they're staying with me."

"You think you'll have the space, Ma?" After living in a ten-room duplex, Emeline knew she'd find her new classic six snug.

"I will have two bedrooms, so when," she did not say *if*, "you want to visit you'll have a place to stay." A charade really: once grown, Deborah had rarely stayed with them in the spacious old place.

With Jacinta's help, in no time Deborah boxed up her chosen pieces, called Gregor on the house phone, asked for a large cab, and transported her loot to Kinko's to be properly packaged and sent to London. Faintly mollified when Deborah insisted on treating her to dinner at the Four Seasons, Emeline spent a peaceful night with her daughter, for once, sleeping nearby in her childhood bedroom.

The peace didn't last. Halfway through their last breakfast in the old apartment, Deborah insisted on checking that her mother's power of attorney was current and sent Jacinta out to copy it along with Emeline's medical directives.

"Honestly, Deborah," Emeline was exasperated, "you act as if I'm about to cork off." Deborah, wordless, folded her copies of the papers into her monogrammed briefcase. Emeline understood: once back in London, Deborah'd have documents at the ready if she needed to make a decision regarding her mother's care or imminent demise.

Shortly after Clifford died one of Emeline's younger friends, meeting her for lunch at *Sel et Poivre,* stared earnestly over her blackened mahi-mahi and suggested Emeline install a new electronic toy called Skype. "You'll have to deal with the time difference between New York and London, of course. At least you and Deborah can see each other while you chat." Chat? Emeline and her daughter, rarely on the same page when in the same room, emailed intermittently and spoke less. Deborah didn't really want to talk to her mother, why would she want to see her on a computer screen?

Emeline presses buttons on the black stereo and Elgar's Cello Concerto in E Minor picks up where it left off. She smiles at the silver-haired man in the silver frame, sweeps her hand across the glass. It's the only dusting she's done since Jacinta left.

Since Emeline had been the one to teach Cliff behavior suitable for the Upper East Side, how he'd have mocked her for her lapse of courtesy with the Puerto Rican boy—insufferably rude of her not to thank him. Then, hinting at his being a thief, had she sounded racist? Clearly the attack has damaged her wits and erased her manners.

If Clifford were here . . . More than one friend has tried to explain the stages of grief: denial, anger, bargaining, depression, and acceptance. So at least her mind would know what is going on; only none of these friends can tell her when one stage will morph into another in her heart, in her entire body. Stages should at least come with a strict timetable, like the LIRR taking you to Greenport. May Sarton's is the only voice that helps: "Here is one door to the garden," said the salty poet, "that is forever closed."

Grief, like a partial eclipse of the sun, makes the world unexpectedly dim; except history so far says the sun will come back in a matter of minutes. Lately, though, Emeline has begun to find the finality—odd, painful, and unreal as it is—if not comforting, at least possible to entertain. Until she sees a man in a camel's hair coat and fedora on the street ahead of her, or hears at the Gilbert & Sullivan intermission an over-loud English voice say, "To my mind it's all a bit twee." Then it is May Sarton she summons to her aide, imagining the grand old girl hovering beside her.

Emeline makes her way slowly to the kitchen and plugs in her tea kettle. She could hardly invite that young man into her home; she doubts he'd expect her to, or come upstairs if asked. A young man with a busy day ahead—she was unclear about his connection with the gym: a client, an employee? What gym?

She thinks her phone will have the number; but no, it was his phone she'd used and blast, now she'll have to go buy a new one. Thwarted and embarrassed (a common enough state of affairs lately) Emeline feels a rush of tears as the electric tea kettle mounts its insistent whistle—a dubious house-warming present from Deborah, who worried her mother would grow vague and let her Le Creuset kettle burn dry.

On the answering machine are a monotone reminder from the pharmacist and a breathless call from Muffy. Her friend is worked into a state over the annual music benefit she chairs, now that she's coupled the benefit with Luca Bevilaqua's fashion show.

"Yes, fine. Although, to be honest," Emeline tries to get in before Muffy can take over. "No, not a cab in sight so I thought I'd walk from Seventh to catch the—what? Yes, Luca's clothes looked fabulous. No, I don't see us wearing piazza pants. No, not even on Long Island. Yes, I have the benefit on my calendar. Listen, Muffy? The strangest thing happened this afternoon, I really don't know what to make of it."

Nice try, but no, it has to be all Muffy, all the time, a woman who lives largely inside her own hula hoop. Nevertheless, Muffy is a friend who stood by her when many did not. Emeline, who could have used a minute more of air time, realizes she's lost the mike. Defeated, yet polite, she rings off.

She could boot up her computer and send an email to Deborah, only she sent an email last week and really, it is her daughter's turn. The gremlins are back, Emeline feels them gathering around her. Muffy's playful word for demons helps her some days. Not today.

Retreating to her bedroom, Emeline picks out a pill from the 21 compartments of a plastic box. More than her trembling and grey hair, or Cliff's absence from their bed, it's the plastic box that makes her feel she's grown old.

So ironic. On her own so Emeline can do exactly as she likes—and she can no longer do exactly as she likes.

She imagines herself in a few more years: that much stiffer, shuffling to d'Agostino's, trailing a wire grocery cart. The last thing she'll want is a live-in caregiver. She sees a fight of major proportions with Deborah looming. No, the agency will have to send someone in the daytime if it comes to that. Or she'll move again, to a place even smaller than this one, where she can reach everything she needs with her cane, or use one of those contraptions with a handle at one end and a claw at the other so she can retrieve her glasses or the large-print book she's dropped. She can hardly wait.

As for email, Emeline knows texting with thumbs is taking its place. If Jacinta stays away perhaps she'll look for a housekeeper with strong technical skills.

Emeline knows what he was thinking, this young Latino: another pampered, well-dressed matron. Scratch well-dressed, to be frank, though she does continue to wear Clifford's diamond on her left hand. Absently she turns her ring around and around. It's grown loose as she's lost weight, yet it holds below the knuckle.

This Puerto Rican kid would have her pegged for sure, "Privileged and protected," Emeline once overheard someone's maid say on the bus, "that's what the two *p*'s stand for in *upper*. Those folks just don't know it." Imagining, she is ready to create a scenario in the young man's head . . . when likely he'll have forgotten about her by tomorrow.

Why is she obsessing, and why does she care? Because for a few minutes in the cab she'd gotten a sense of something familiar, along with the strong and fairly tacky scent he wore: a whiff of a memory.

CHAPTER 2

F luent as Xavier is in both languages, his mother's convinced his real knack is with numbers. "*M'hijo,* you would make a very good accountant, no?" Though, paying her taxes on the short form, Flavia has no need of an accountant.

"*Mai,* just shoot me now."

Giving up the dream her first-born son Ramon will ever bring honor to her family, Flavia insisted her second son enroll at La Guardia; the community college, not the airport. If Flavia can hold a steady job, exchange her reddened hands for a Ralph Lauren tote, her cleaning tools for juice boxes, and open a bank account (most *El Barrio* women, if a long way from catching island rain in water drums for washing, would still rather walk into a check cashing place than a bank), what couldn't Xavier accomplish?

With long rattling rides underground from the 103rd Street station to Long Island City and back, LGCC did change him. Xavier found himself seduced by glimpses of another world, peopled by coders, programmers, MIS experts, and computer scientists—seduced as well by a stunning man from Barbados, his first real affair of the heart.

The day Xavier told Alejandro he had to drop out ("money problems at home"), Alejandro played hooky from MIS 101 to buy him a *cafe con leche grande* and bring Xavier again to his rented room to console him. Honeyed hours they'd spent in the room. Afterward, lying on his back, smoking, Xavier had listened to Alejandro talk about the florist shop where he worked for cash under the counter and learned the old-fashioned language of flowers.

"It's like *cryptografia*," Alejandro said.

Ten days later Alejandro caught a west-bound bus to try his luck at stardom in the City of Angels. Alejandro's parting gift (Xavier thought at the time, applying ointment for a case of crabs) was an introduction to Gabor Nagy, manager of a gym on West 41st Street. Good-bye to love, good-bye to computer science. Xavier thinks of the kid he'd once been, summer evenings, sitting out on the fire escape, dreaming of a job other than dishwasher, porter, or bus boy. At least he isn't spending his days up to his elbows in hot suds.

Sweet, Xavier thought when he got his first check. Maybe he could purchase an iPad? No, there was the new leather jacket and he'd already put down cash on an iPhone, his life back to alphabet letters, four years old and Flavia prepping him for kindergarten. All his buddies have iPhones, they use them to set up sports dates, complain about the rain, exchange class notes, and rate the girls they've scored the night before. Even Flavia has an iPhone. Like her tote bag it's a "gift" from Mrs. Wells. His mother's employer likes to keep in touch with the nanny, check on how the day is going or change plans for the children.

Xavier can sleep through the sirens and the Friday trash truck but when pigeons land on the window sill to broadcast their daily talk show he wakes up. He reads the digital numbers: 9:27 a.m. His mother will have left hours ago and his sister Rocio gone out with the baby.

It wouldn't kill him to stop at 63rd Street on the way to the gym, and return Mrs. Hughes' umbrella. Xavier's kinda curious to see where the lady lives and he's never been in one of those grand East Side apartments. He surfaces from the subway at 59th and strides past a cement construction barrier, a green boarding marked World Class Demolition. A flapping canvas tarp half hides the "Siamese Connection" standpipe in the building wall.

He walks four blocks up Lexington, turns east, and finds the green awning. "Mrs. Hughes." He holds out the umbrella to the doorman.

"You the plumber? Go around the service entrance."

"I am not the plumber. Mrs. Hughes, I need to see her." Suspicious, the doorman insists on telephoning upstairs first. Xavier follows him into the lobby and past the clubby leather chairs.

"Stop!" the doorman commands, rigid with distaste: "Service elevator," and, into the house phone, "Yes, Mrs. H., young man asking for you. No, not the plumber, this one's at the front." Xavier waves the umbrella back and forth, hoping hand signals will work. "I don't have his name—stop waving that thing in my face. What? Light brown."

What color? Affronted, Xavier thrusts the umbrella toward the doorman. "Listen, mister, I don't have the time."

"Mrs. Hughes, he say he's gonna leave—"

"Then get his number!" Xavier can hear her tinny voice. From his faux-leather man-bag he pulls out his card with the gym logo, *Xavier Escudero, Personal Trainer,* skips it like a stone so it falls short of the bigot's gloved hand, and leaves. Halfway to the subway he realizes: Maybe she meant the umbrella? It is, in fact, a pale tan.

Making it to the gym in time, he passes the front desk where the receptionist whispers on the phone, he studies the schedule on the bulletin board. He passes a room rocking with the Gypsy Kings where a dozen women, busty in tank tops and bulging at the hips, struggle to complete reps as prescribed as dance steps and sweat off the years.

One after the other, his appointments follow: unemployed ladies in the morning, secretaries between twelve and two. After that, come the young mothers who pack in a quick workout before racing off to pick up children from Dalton or Horace Mann. Xavier knows their children's names, their schools' names, knows way too much about each client. They confide in him as they work the machines, no matter how often he says, "Save your breath, okay? Kick it up a notch." They come for his company as well as lessons on crunches and curls, techniques for improving pecs, delts, and abs.

Today's last client is a man, thank God. Men mostly talk about the game, their paunches, or their mothers. Xavier's learned plenty at the gym, besides how to carry Gatorade to refuel electrolytes. In May, when Mother's Day sprang up like a demanding daffodil, other guys seemed as zealous as he felt to stop on the way home for a bouquet or a plant. The men talked about fifteen-inch pots versus twenty-six-inch pots, complaining how the price goes up three times for every pot inch; their mothers must live in apartments with a flow of sun coming in the windows.

It shocked Xavier, the casual way men dissed their mothers in public. They'd drop disparaging hints about the game they'd miss in order to schlep out to Great Neck or Westchester to put in an appearance for the sibling gathering in a restaurant one of the families had remembered to reserve.

Ramon and his followers had no trouble talking dirt about the women they slept with. Yet even the toughs who make up Ramon's posse, skip confession, and sleep in on Sundays, wouldn't be caught dead speaking that way about their mothers. If no longer intimidated by priests in their cassocks, they feared these middle-aged, made-up women who to this day wield unholy influence over the boys they've brought into the world.

By four o'clock Xavier's finished the training appointments and one of the taekwando sessions he's bartered in return for looking over the other trainer's taxes. While not on board with Flavia's vision for the future, Xavier doesn't plan to rely on Ramon's dream of boxing, either. Taekwando can help him build up his street chops.

Like a cold draft from childhood on, Xavier's known danger, known the feel and smell of trouble, and learned to be vigilant. Ramon had taught him to how to protect himself at the playground, at PS 171, and on the streets. Xavier's grateful, even if it was a case of self-interest, Ramon grooming him to be his wingman.

He's in the men's locker room, with the familiar smell of sweat and socks, when his cell rings. "Mr. Escudero? Emeline Hughes here. Sorry I missed you. Gregor can be a bit, hmm, protective. I wanted to thank you for dropping off the umbrella. Perhaps to make up for my bad manners I could do you a nice English tea?"

The silent elevator glides to the seventh floor and lets him out into a small hallway with doors to only two apartments and no smell of urine. Alerted by her stick of a doorman, Mrs. Hughes stands in the open door of 7B and extends her hand. She's wearing a dark linen skirt, pale pink shirt, and no lipstick. He's used to Flavia, who smothers her fear of poverty under plum-colored lip stain. Closing the door, Mrs. Hughes struggles with the clasp of a short string of pearls. Are they real? If he said, here, let me do that for you, would she call the cops?

As Mrs. Hughes waves him along, he says only, "How's it going?"

"I do appreciate your coming." Wrinkles under her eyes and around her mouth, sure, but her face doesn't look as weathered as some of the older *señoras* he knows; or as sculpted as the clients whose faces appear immobile from Botox.

Xavier's never set foot in such a large apartment (except for his mother's employer's, more palatial than real). High-minded music plays softly. To the left is a living room, formal, immaculate, and blah. The walls are not quite white, and the heavy curtains on either side of the windows half drawn. On the coffee table a scalloped silver dish that might have once been an ashtray, a set of matching boxes; easy enough to bundle them into his knapsack and hustle away, he's seen enough stolen goods pass through the bedroom he shares with Ramon. On a sideboard sit two photos in silver frames: a good-looking older man and Mrs. Hughes as a young mother holding a baby girl. And down at his feet a cat, staring with suspicious eyes.

Past the living room there is another hallway so as not to hurry visitors straight into the mess of family life. Except here he sees little mess and few signs of life. In a formal dining room, the table top is a square of gleaming, dark wood without the piles of magazines, catalogues, bills, junk mail, and pacifiers found on his family's table.

In the kitchen a window to the air shaft lets in warm September air though no Latino music or loud arguments. Track lights in the kitchen ceiling look recently installed, no one has repainted the ceiling. Mrs. Hughes doesn't strike him as the sort of woman who'd allow the ceiling to go unfinished for long.

She has ankles as slim as a girl's and a habit of looking up from under her bangs as though all her life she's been surrounded by taller people. Kind of a cute dame, and friendlier today. Following her lead, he sits on a red metal chair and feels an obstacle behind him.

"Dear me, my stick, it's right in your way. Hand it to me, why don't you." She takes back her smooth, stained cane and props it against a wall. She studies him as he helps himself to the "biscuit" she's laid out, sweet enough for her maybe, but he's used to seriously sugared pastries.

"And what about your name? Unusual, I think, not like Carlos or Pedro."

"I'm the second son so this time my mother got to choose. She picked a name that sounds like hers. Flavia."

"And you live...uptown?"

Was she trying to be tactful? "In El Barrio, yes."

"I was there not long ago. The Museo del Barrio, such an unusual exhibit, Rafael Ferrer. I don't suppose you happened to see it?" Maybe he's made a face; she seems to know that's a non-starter. "Tell me, what do you do at your gym?"

"Personal trainer," he says, trying not to sound proud.

"Do you have to go to a tech school to be a personal trainer?"

He smiles. "You thinking of taking it up?"

"Of course, the balance beam, my specialty. How do you come to be doing that?"

"Long story."

"I'm not terribly busy." So he simplifies, culling through his life to pick out some points, like Gabor, and leaving out others, like Alejandro.

Past sixty, Gabor, promising to lay out the options for getting Xavier PT-qualified in quick time, had invited Xavier to his East Village town house for supper. Ringing the bell, Xavier was caught between curious and anxious. What might he have to exchange for this one-on-one career counseling?

Xavier relaxed when the door opened to a compact man with grey hair, an aggressive moustache, and a partner much older or ill or both. "Gabor," he said, shaking Xavier's hand, "and this is Ryan. And this little devil wagging his tail is Diogi."

Their place is all mid-century modern. The fridge door has no photos. Xavier is used to Flavia's gallery, studded with pictures of family and friends. The men bring out wine, beer, olives, and small stuffed grape leaves. The only thing aggressive about Gabor, Xavier soon sees, is his moustache.

Ryan, a documented immigrant with an Irish accent Xavier barely understands, is an ex-Sinn Fein follower turned peace activist with a diagnosis of his own, casually revealed; though Xavier already guessed, he recognized the thin frame and palid skin.

No, Gabor explained, Xavier didn't need an associate's degree to be a personal trainer. No, he didn't have to be licensed. He did have to show he was knowledgeable about physiology, muscle groups, respiratory systems—all the systems, really—how they interact, how they respond to exercise.

Once Xavier took the weekend courses and joined the AFAA, he made the mistake of bragging to Ramon.

"American Faggots After Ass?" jeered his brother.

"Aerobics and Fitness Association of America," Xavier hit Ramon a mock blow to his shoulder, "muscle groups, body-fat composition." A harder blow to the jaw. "Muscle strength." A serious blow to the gut. Gone were the days when Ramon had to let him win a bout. "Flexibility. Aerobic endurance."

"Okay, okay!"

"Put ice on that, *Broki*. And if Mami asks," Xavier lifts a threatening fist, "tell her you were in a street fight."

Mrs. Hughes is staring up at the ceiling. Thinking, or, was she thinking about a paint job?

"If you wanted, I could take care—" he's pointing upward when the house phone rings.

"We'll see. For now, if you could get that?" She waves a half-eaten biscuit toward the red house phone by the back door; it probably leads to the service elevator he refused to ride.

"Mrs. Hughes. Plumber's here. Do I send him up?"

Xavier, covering the receiver with a slender hand and attempting an accent that mimics the doorman's, repeats the message. Mrs. Hughes switches into the solid PBS English he's heard on the TV. "That will do very nicely."

"Do send him up." Xavier imitates her accent.

"Mrs. Hughes, everything all right?" but Xavier hangs up.

"You're an actor, too." Mrs. Hughes is trying to keep a straight face. "I should have known."

Xavier undoes the chain on the back door and turns the lock in the knob. A heavy-set man stands in the back hall, lugging a tool box as if towing the weight of the world. Xavier swings the door wide to let in the plumber, then closes it and puts the chain back in place. Uncertain what sink, toilet, faucet, or errant valve calls for a plumber's attention, he glances at Mrs. Hughes.

"Good of you to stop by." Mrs. Hughes maintains her rigid pose and poker face. "It's the loo off the hall, if you don't mind," and, before the plumber is halfway there, she gives in to a series of snorts Xavier realizes would be Mrs. Hughes laughing.

"Absurd, utterly absurd," she snuffles. "Desperate for an audience, the two of us. Me, it makes sense, I'm alone most of the time. You, though, handsome fellow, young—"

"Want me to keep an eye on him?" Flavia would never let a workman wander unattended.

"He's known in the building. Time for one more cup?" She is swinging the leg crossed over her knee as if building up momentum to rise. "You can tell me what you are up to all day when you're out and about."

Emeline's calendar, if rarely exciting, used to be full. She sat on many worthwhile boards. To show she appreciated all Aunt Mildred had done for her? Or because she felt guilty about the family she'd left behind in Peckham? Other women came out of the closet or studied for a Master's, traveled to Nepal or filed for divorce. Emeline felt herself too uncertain or uninspired, to branch out of the world she'd grown used to.

Each time she was asked to join one of the good causes in health, education, music or art, she knew it wasn't only Clifford's money they were after. She was asked because she knew how to behave. Some of the city's boards were getting overloaded with "newcomers." As one of the old guard confided, "All these 'bold face' names, these svelte wives of ambitious men new to finance and naive in deportment. Really, have you noticed the way some of them hold a fork?"

Clifford appreciated the doors Emeline could open, the contacts she helped him make. Besides, Emeline liked these young couples arriving from Little Rock and Tacoma, Miami and Cleveland. Anxious to fit into a world they'd read about in Vogue or seen on television, were they so different from she and Clifford, when they began? Emeline saw it as her turn to play Aunt Mildred, explain the silverware, and offer subtle hints against wearing sequins in daylight. In spite of their nannies and personal trainers, private chefs and publicists, she knew that often the women were lonely, even when their husbands were being faithful.

One of these women, whose husband seemed to be, at least for now, wept uncontrolled tears in the privacy of Emeline's living room one night. "It's not only about the money, about all he's done for us. I love him, really I do. But I'll be forty in a month and I can't stop thinking: if he left *her,* though she was a piece of work, how do I know he won't leave *me* for a newer model?"

Emeline could only hum in sympathy. She'd stopped keeping track of the women who swore they'd only lucked out as a second wife because the first had been, "quite, quite crazy, you can't imagine." If true, there wouldn't be a vacant room left at the Institute of Living in Hartford.

When her days grew too busy and her mind buzzed, Emeline would hop the bus down Fifth to sit in the courtyard of the Frick. Ever since Aunt Mildred first took her to the old mansion, introduced her to its paintings, statues, outside gardens and inner courtyard, Emeline's loved the Frick. Strangely, the museum's courtyard reminded her of home—not her own South London home, the stained wallpaper, the shabby stairs, the hallway smell of cabbage and onions. The courtyard brought back vivid memories of visiting Kew Gardens, holding her mother's hand as they walked past spring tulips, daffodils, dogwoods, and in the fall, chrysanthemums.

Is it a coincidence her new apartment is only a walk away from the Frick?

Painful to remember how well she'd been doing before Cliff died. This self-protective, uncertain woman she's become, more vulnerable even than the distant child who sailed from London, Emeline's afraid she'll never regain the sense of her old self.

After Xavier finishes a third biscuit and leaves, Emeline wonders if she's being quite, quite crazy herself. An unknown person mugs her, an unknown Puerto Rican finds her in the alley. At his mercy for money and wheels, she allows him to hail a cab and discover where she lives. Then she goes and invites him into her apartment? If Deborah hears this story she'll have her guts for garters.

Emeline clears the tea things, scooping tea leaves into the trash and wishing, again, the building allowed a disposal. Fanciful, in any case, when what she longs to dispose of are the shadows that follow her every day, the unanswered questions flitting into every nook and cranny of the Mayflower van arriving minutes after she did when she moved.

She's improved, compared to four months ago. If not a whole lot, at least she's not the stranger she was then, sitting in St. James for Clifford's memorial service and molten with grief. Any minute she expected Cliff, late as usual, to slip into the pew and whisper: "Lilies? Good God, Em, what were you thinking, you know how I hate lilies."

Even more herself than the day she came home to the old apartment to realize a potential buyer had been going through Clifford's desk. That set her back, that began chapter two of what she calls "the troubles."

Emeline empties the young Puerto Rican's cup into the kitchen sink. She'd been the immigrant once, an unwilling child setting off on an old, slow ship ploughing its way between Southampton's harbor and New York's.

Enough. A practical task at hand, that's what she needs. She'll sort her pills. Maybe next time she'll ask him in for a coffee, buy a can of, what's that name? Café Bustelo. Then she catches herself. There isn't going to be a next time. Unless she wants him to paint the ceiling.

CHAPTER 3

Spanish Harlem is its own world, wedged into northeast Manhattan between the East River and the elevated walls that carry commuter trains north to greener pastures. Downtowners, eager to sound cool, may call it "SpaHa." Not the Puerto Ricans who live there. To them it's El Barrio. Brick and masonry row houses, often no wider than twenty-five feet, rise three, four, five floors on the east-west streets. And the north-south avenues, too, except on the avenues shops take up the ground floors. Half hidden between storefronts, narrow doorways lead to midget's foyers littered with flyers. Brass name plates, tarnished, outdated, or empty, display apartment numbers and sometimes names.

A century ago, when affluent white owners moved out to Port Washington or Yonkers, landlords bought up the houses, converted single-family dwellings into tenements, and lured outsiders to move in. First came immigrants fleeing famine in Ireland or upheaval in Germany, next the Italians, and after World War II, Latinos. Whether hopeful families or men determined and desperate, most of them came from Puerto Rico. Even now a volatile mix of poverty, racism, drugs, guns, and crime prompt suspicion and discrimination from the residents below 96th Street, and not without cause. Too often the Latin Kings seem to be winning against the efforts of the city's Empowerment Zone.

Xavier's mother seldom talks about her life before they left the island. Flavia has passed along a few details about her grandfather, the mayor of a small town outside of San Juan; hinted, only, how *la familia* has come down in the world. She hugs this secret—treasure or shame—close to her heart yet draws on it for strength when she needs to; strength and another quality Xavier realized as he grew older. A gentleness of manner she'd use with a store clerk, a polite demeanor, a way of speaking that set her apart from many in El Barrio.

Barely awake, Xavier thinks of none of these things. He's been dreaming of Mrs. Hughes' pale green walls and soft carpet, the framed paintings and robust light in the living room. Not every living room in the city looks out on a fire escape's black, angled iron.

He's back in the fourth-floor walk-up; crammed into what *los antiguos* call a railroad flat, Xavier and Ramon sleep in one bedroom. Flavia sleeps in the other along with Rocio and little Jomar, hoping to tame her teen-age daughter's combustible blend of need and insolence.

Unless an aunt fed up with her husband comes to stay, or a nephew in trouble in the Bronx or a cousin from Santurce; then Flavia moves to the couch. Knotted as Xavier is to all of them, he'd love them more if he had more distance from each. He's about to switch on Tato Laviera, *en clave* songs in the key of the people, when his cell phone rings.

"*Quien habla?*"

"Mr. Escudero? Really, no need to shout, I am not deaf. Emeline Hughes. Why are you asleep?"

"Wednesday," he manages. "Day off."

"It seems I may need your help again. It's Luca Bevilaqua, the designer. Nobody I'd give the time of day to, though my friend Muffy is infatuated. And right now hysterical. I feel I must get down there and help her. I'll pay you, of course."

"Pay me for what?"

"Luca Bevilaqua." She repeats as if to a three-year-old. "The fashion designer. You've heard of him, I suppose." Xavier wonders why they are even having this conversation, at this hour. Does the old girl need to buy a dress or does she have *la demencia?*

"Xavier. Are you there?" He is, if not for long, his thumb an inch from "off," macho pride warring with a low bank balance. "Luca's been murdered in his studio. I find I can't face getting back to the garment district on my own.

"Awright."

"You will? Splendid. Don't be dawdling on the subway, either—catch a cab."

Xavier pulls on black jeans, a black tee, and his new black leather jacket. He checks his hair in the mirror, dabs on a light pomade, clasps on his watch and a heavy, forged-metal bracelet, forgoes the cologne. So much for his free day, and why? He tells himself it's the money, unwilling to admit he kind of likes the old girl with her pearls and her PBS accent. He'll do what she asks, today.

Cabs at midday in El Barrio will be scarce as peacocks. Walking to Lexington, then three blocks south and over the sidewalk grate, he feels hot metallic air rise from deep in the ground and hears the pulse of the train. He catches the express. Across the way a Chinese girl wears a red-mop like a Raggedy Ann wig. More Asians are moving to El Barrio, if not usually dressed like dolls. Above ground at 59th, he decides a power walk will be good for the quads. Xavier sheds his jacket, swinging it over his shoulder with one thumb, and strikes out for 63rd. Street.

Under her green awning Mrs. Hughes leans heavily on a cane. A different one, it's black, with a metal duck-head palm grip and an expression as snooty as the woman's. Her doorman whistles up a cab and hands two Styrofoam cups of coffee to Xavier.

"Yours will undoubtedly be cold by now, what took you so long?" Mrs. Hughes scolds as their cab lurches west toward Central Park. No sign today of the impish humor from before. "Thank you for coming. I thought, after the other day . . ."

Right, thinks Xavier. You've lived in New York years, you know half the city, a gay fashion designer is dead, and that's the reason I'm here. He inhales her expensive scent, glances down at her feet: she's shined her low-heeled designer shoes. Traffic clogs the West Side: cabs, limos, bike messengers pedaling against the one-way street and courting death, buses fuming and farting. Half a block ahead a bus shudders to a stop with a violent honk. A grey sedan swerves from the curb, cuts off the outraged NYTA driver, and speeds away.

Off Seventh Avenue and close to suppliers of thread, snaps, buttons, belts, zippers, and trim, the driver stops his monologue in Haitian French long enough to take their money. Emeline steps out, avoiding a lump of chewing gum on the sidewalk. Xavier takes her arm to push her through a line of anorexic Vogue wannabes bent as if in prayer over their cell phones. "Will you look at those girls," Emeline says. "All three have *the* new bag, the one with all the zippers."

Ignoring the stunned receptionist on the 6th floor, they push through a show room to the studio in back. The small space is nothing like the design studio Xavier remembers. When his grandfather died back in San Juan, his mother dragged him by his small hand all the way to Seventh Avenue to tell her sister of their loss. Xavier pictures again the vast, open loft, startled faces—Hispanic, Asian, African-American—the narrow aisles and racks of garments, their plastic covers swaying in his mother's wake.

Aunt Koka tells him garments these days are made overseas; only samples are sewn in the city. No machines buzz like locusts in Luca's studio, as if all sound has died along with the man on the floor, hidden under a lavish length of cloth. Emeline draws a sharp breath and reaches for Xavier's hand. It must be her first, he thinks, unless you count her husband.

A short fellow in a blue smock covers his face with gnarled hands. A thin, tearful woman, looking from the back much like Mrs. Hughes, is comforting two Latina workers, one wearing a measuring tape around her stout neck. A trio of policemen stand around the man in the smock, as still as the nude, molded mannequins lining the walls. Only the police photographer is in motion, darting and snapping.

"No, no, this is how I found him." The man in the smock uncovers his face and reveals reddened eyes and a big voice. "Eight-t'irty, I get here. Luca, he always late. Me, I touch nothing." He slides his eyes toward the covered mound; only the top of a head shows and a brush of sand-colored hair. "How this happen, what you t'ink?"

"Inspector Flynn," barks an officer with a face like dressed stone, "and I'll ask the questions," but before he can, Emeline and Xavier bear down on his crime scene. With the cry of a wounded pigeon, the thin woman rushes forward and throws her arms around Mrs. Hughes. Like many of Mrs. Hughes' friends she has defeated hair once grey with silvery hair color. Not the solid chestnut Xavier's own mother applies every six weeks.

"Thank you, darling, thank you for coming. It is so terrible."

"Hey! Outta here," growls the inspector. "Who do you think—"

The studio door opens again. A slender man with leonine hair touching his shoulders extends his arms like the Pope on a balcony. "What the devil is going on?" His voice is soft, and angry. "You cannot come into my atelier like this. Out, out—all of you. At once!" The woman wearing the measuring tape screams. The stocky Italian crosses himself twice.

"Luca!" Abruptly the thin woman transfers her embrace to the newcomer and weeps copious tears. "Luca, we thought it was you!"

"Really, Muffy," the designer holds her off, maybe to protect his investment in wool. Keen on clothes himself, Xavier calculates the cost of the shawl-collared, cashmere sweater. "I cannot have these hysterics. My opening is in three days. Arnie, who are all these people? And who the hell turned up the heat? It's only September, for God's sake."

Muffy and the woman in the tape measure glare at the inspector as if he's misled them. The inspector points a finger to the floor. "Then who . . . ?"

Luca strolls by Emeline, takes in her outfit with indifference and leaves a fog of cologne, passes Xavier without a glance, and bends over the crumpled form. Before the inspector can stop him, he lifts a corner of the printed fabric, and sighs dramatically.

"How he did like to copy me. It's Bay, of course, my assistant. None of you noticed?" Luca looks disappointed, as if his clique has shown questionable judgment. "Poor fellow." The two-word eulogy is all he has to offer. "Someone—and I have a very good idea who—wants me dead. Only he got Bay instead. Was he here, Arnie, snooping around? You know who I'm talking about, that ingrate. Takeshi. The Japanese Judas who betrayed us."

"I'll need that piece of cloth." Upstaged and not pleased about it, Inspector Flynn moves forward to reclaim his crime scene but before he can his cell rings. He answers, grunts, hangs up. "Mike—you're with me, we're needed. LeRoy, you deal with the dead faggot." Xavier hears Mrs. Hughes inhale sharply. "Look around. Whoever it was used something sharp."

The inspector halts in front of Xavier, his nose inches away. "LeRoy? Start with this other one here . . . see what he knows." Xavier's foot jiggles, he balls his fists, he's minutes from erupting. Mrs. Hughes lays a hand on his arm and grips his metal bracelet.

Signaling with every step that he has more important things to do, the inspector departs. Officer LeRoy, whose people skills are slightly better, herds the visitors to one side of the room, "Ma'am? Sir? Over here, please." Luca, Arnie, the pattern maker, the seamstresses, and the receptionist who's scuttled in by now are waved to the other side.

Twenty minutes later, sharp questioning and note taking over, the officer tells Xavier and Emeline they are free to leave. Not Muffy, not yet. "A tragedy," she bleats, as she walks Emeline to the elevator, leaving Xavier to trail behind. "Poor Luca."

"Bit hard on this Bay fellow, too." Mrs. Hughes's voice is sharp.

"You heard that inspector," Xavier says. "You think he'll care?"

Muffy seems not to hear. "Terrible publicity. What am I going to do about the benefit? And Luca, poised to show his break-out collection."

"As well as funds for your young musicians," Emeline reminds her.

"Luca's right, it'll be that Japanese upstart Takeshi—do you know, he brags his name means warrior? He's been gunning for us since the day he left. You know how they are, these Asians. *Very aggressive.*" And that, thinks Xavier, takes care of one continent.

"Luca's worked so hard," Muffy goes on, "those difficult years in Italy, getting a start over here, on the brink of becoming, well, someone. A temper, okay. And yet a genius. I've felt honored," a ringed hand comes to rest on her modest bosom, "to be one of his backers. And a friend. Oh, you have no idea, Emeline, the pain, the pain."

"What?" Her voice cold, Emeline takes a step back.

Briefly Muffy seems to focus on the friend standing in front of her. "You'll get a cab?"

"Xavier will see me home." Mrs. Hughes gives him a glance of private complicity. "And, Muffy? Come by and see me later. We need to talk."

Briefly, Muffy looks alarmed then rallies. "It's up to us to support the next generation, especially when there's such genius . . ." the elevator door closes on Muffy, extolling.

CHAPTER 4

Emeline's furious. She knows Muffy fancies herself Emeline's opposite: a romantic. "You're so practical," she'll observe, draped on Emeline's couch to describe a new infatuation. "I wonder sometimes if you have feelings at all." Right now I feel I've had about enough of you, Emeline's been tempted to say and never does. Because old friends glow with a patina newer ones lack.

Too many others, aware of the mire and mud of the past months, when they ask how she is doing look at her with pitiful eyes and even a quiver of illicit excitement. No wonder Emeline has backed away, pleading fatigue or appointments, and relied on Jacinta for company.

She grips Xavier's arm hard as the taxi swings and sways. The nerve of the woman, "The pain, you have no idea," as if Emeline knows nothing about death. Faced with the murder of an upstart designer she's known a year, Muffy managed to forget about Clifford. That, even for Muffy, was a gaffe of stupendous proportion.

Jacinta would never be so tactless. Thinking of her copper skin, her lilting voice and gentle understanding, Emeline sends a quick prayer that the ailing father will soon get well, or else . . . Emeline stops herself in mid thought. Wishing for the only other outcome that will bring Jacinta back to New York makes her as bad as Muffy.

"It's upsetting to see a dead person," Xavier says as the driver makes a wild turn that slams her against his shoulder. "You can stop shaking now."

"*Ojala que*." She sees his face, reads his thoughts: yes, the appalling accent he'd expect from a Brit.

"If only? He does speak good the English, this Nuyorican. *Ahora,* we have double the chance of misunderstanding each other." He lights a cigarette.

Emeline rolls down the window. "I wasn't seeing this as long term. Though if you did have the time?" She cocks her head to one side like a curious bird. "I could make you a nice omelet and you could tell me what you make of that little drama."

"The murder? Or the genius?"

"Genius? Please. Luca Bevilaqua's a complete prat. Let's see, sixteen dollars times twenty percent . . ."

"Give him sixteen dollars, Mrs. Hughes."

"With the tip?"

"You really think he needs a twenty-percent tip? Give him seventeen. Here's two bucks, come on." He hands her out of the cab and guides her around the spindly plane tree growing in a square of dirt. "Mrs. Hughes," he says in the elevator, "you sure there isn't someone I can call?"

"My daughter lives in London." She knows her voice is icy. "My helper, she's . . . away. Omelet?" She turns, catching her balance with one hand against the wall, then shuffles to unlock her front door.

Xavier may be starving but first she must brew tea. From a shelf holding pale blue-and-white china, a vase with a frieze of dancers, and a pair of silver candlesticks, she takes down two cups and saucers. When the tea is ready, Xavier takes a sip of the hot but smoky brew. "Sorry, do you know your tea tastes like ham?"

"Lapsang Suchong, an acquired taste. I'd never trust him, what can Muffy be thinking? The way Luca carried on. So conscious of his image; you noticed it, too, I was watching you. He's a type: whatever the conversation was before, once he walks in the room it's all about him. And depriving that poor fellow Bay of his due, even in death."

"Very like my husband's first partner." Emeline is working on the omelet. Rye bread in the toaster soothes her with its earthy smell. "That man entered a room and minutes later you're wondering if there's any air left to breathe."

Disturbed as she is over Luca's behavior, she sees Xavier's still simmering over the inspector's callous indifference. Distracted, she lets an egg slip to the floor, splat. "Oh, hell's bells, help me clean that up, would you?"

After he does she watches him fingering the cigarettes in his shirt pocket. "A personal trainer who smokes? Great advertisement for health you are. Oh, all right, go into the spare bedroom, close the door and stand by the window." She disapproves, of course, though the break gives her an idea.

"I was thinking," she says casually once he's back. She puts the omelet and toast on two plates, sliced pears on another, "It would be helpful to know what's on his mind; that fellow in the smock, Arnie. If someone could get him to talk—some fruit?"

"*Excuse* me?" Xavier looks offended; it hasn't occurred to her he'd know the old-fashioned slur.

"Or there might be cherries if you don't care for pears. You might be able to talk to him, man to man."

"Mrs. Hughes. I do not know every gay man in New York."

"Are you gay, then?" She's pleased when she sees he can't tell if she's joking, "Arnie, yes. He'll know who'd stand to gain if Luca died."

"Or, how about we let the police do their job and we get on with our own lives?"

"Secrets, secrets. Everyone's busy keeping secrets. Take Muffy. Didn't she look frightened to you? I'm quite worried about her, the way Luca has her under a spell." She lifts her teacup to stop it clattering on the saucer. "Clifford's first partner cost my dear man $50,000 and six months before Clifford felt we could marry. The money I can forgive, even if $50,000 was a lot then." Xavier chokes on his Lapsang.

"But we never got back the six months," she goes on. "Luca's the same. All Luca's idea, turning his opening into the benefit for Yorkville Young Music. I know he's made her break one of Clifford's cardinal rules: use your money to leverage other people's money. Now it's not only her money Luca's after, either. He wants to get his paws on Muffy's contacts. More tea?

"So you see, Luca's not the victim, even if he insists on acting like one. His apartment, it shouldn't be too difficult. Would you know how to get in?"

"You think," Xavier's voice is cold, "Because I'm Puerto Rican, I'm clever with locks?"

And here she's thought he was starting to loosen up. Very tense, this young man. She's leafing through the Manhattan directory, heavy as a door stop. "No. Because you're curious, too. Besides, I saw how you reacted to that inspector. For a minute I thought you were going to, oh, here it is, 26 Prince Street."

"Don't you have anything else you should be doing? A benefit to plan, a tennis game?"

"I find benefits ferociously boring and my tennis days are behind me, I'm afraid. That insufferable inspector didn't look all that bright to me." Tucking her elbows onto the table, she rests her head in her hands and offers her most engaging smile.

"Look, Mrs. Hughes—"

"For heaven's sake, do try calling me Emeline. Honestly, I could use your help." Swiveling in her chair, she lifts two silver-handled lobster picks from a drawer. "These might be useful. If you decide to accept this commission, we'll call it. I'll pay you, of course, I have ruined your free day."

She lets the silver lobster picks jitter and dance in the palm of her hand. When he takes them both from her, she gives a soft sigh. She was right, for Xavier it's a chance to confront a personal nemesis. It's the bigot with the badge he is after. And she has to admit to herself: she's kind of thrilled to be part of an adventure.

"One more thing, Xavier, if you get caught—"

"I know. You've never seen me before in your life."

"I was going to say," Emeline succeeds in sounding quite hurt, "you must call me at once."

Beside private school, Aunt Mildred opened doors to subscription dances, *the Hols* and *the Gets*, no one called them the Holidays and Get-Togethers. The dances where girls met "nice" boys who'd arrive at the door wearing well-fitting dinner jackets; to say "tux" was not top drawer. The boys brought square boxes with cellophane window panes in the lid. Inside was a gardenia, to be pinned on the girl's right side where it was less likely to be squashed when the foxtrot began. An enviable life, yet over the years Emeline felt herself growing smaller and more constrained.

Not at all how she'd felt boarding the SS *Caritas*. In spite of her tears she'd felt then a sense of adventure. America! Who knew who she'd be in ten years: a famous actress, her name on a marquee, a stateswoman, her face on the cover of *Time?* Anything was possible, now that Aunt Mildred with her generous heart was opening her arms to her sister's child.

Having herself won a spot on the Upper East Side, Aunt Mildred's goal was to ensure Emeline had the same opportunities, demanding and narrow as the standards of entrance seemed to be. And, perhaps, Aunt Mildred hoped for maternal a do-over after her own daughter's betrayal. Meeting a young actor from Cleveland in a Lexington Avenue bar, she'd dropped out of Vassar after her freshman year. Defiant and beaming, she walked down the aisle at the elegant if small wedding at St. James her mother arranged on short notice, and promptly moved clear across the country.

"Los Angeles." As a child Emeline overheard Aunt Mildred tell a friend, "who does any of us know who wants to move to Los Angeles?"

Through her teen years, keeping her hair tamed and her grades high, Emeline could see her aunt holding her breath. When four Seven Sister colleges sent fat acceptance envelopes and she chose Wellesley, next door to that bastion of good manners, Boston, Emeline hoped now her aunt could exhale.

Hoped, too, that her own restlessness, building up as she earned A's in classes on Milton and American History and listened to Harvard dates carry on about tennis and sailing, finance and law, would melt away. All too clearly she could see the path that lay ahead of her.

Clifford had seen it, too. "If you marry one of those blokes, Em, you pretty much know everything that's going to happen. If you marry me, you won't have any idea at all."

This time the studio receptionist hardly glances at Xavier when he heads back to the studio. The crumpled form on the floor is gone, the colored cloth with him. No sign of Luca. Only Arnie is there. And he's not a bit happy.

"Luca's out. The *grand formaggio* hired a body guard, can you believe it? He gonna give interviews. Maybe by now he booked on the Today Show. Leavin' me to manage the clothes, the models, the press. Or, *Madonn!* Maybe his big day Friday will just happen — pouf! — by itself. Our women, they walked out. We employ only documented. Still, police make our people nervous, they worry about immigration. Now you gotta show up, give me the needle?"

"Maybe I can help."

"I don't need a frien.' I need a seamstress — whattaya doin'?"

"Calling my aunt, highly experienced seamstress, and legal. *Tia Koka? Te habla Xavier. Que tal?*" A spritz of rapid Spanish and Xavier pockets his phone. "Eight-thirty tomorrow, she'll be here. Okay, Arnie, time for you and me to have a talk."

Arnie talks. Xavier takes a cab downtown to Prince Street and remembers to get a receipt; it's time to start keeping track of expenses, certainly the old girl is good for it. When a woman walking her dog leaves the building, he is through the street door. Up three flights and after a minute or two with the lobster picks, he's inside.

In the fading light, Luca's apartment looks like the set for a magazine shoot. Nothing at all like the cluttered room Xavier and Ramon share where body-building posters of Anibal Lopez are taped on the wall next to Selena Gomez and Ramon's back issues of

Sports Illustrated stand in piles along with old *GQ's* snitched from the barber's.

Xavier takes in Luca's apartment: white linen sofa, butterscotch leather chairs, and a standing lamp like a metal giraffe; framed abstract prints on the walls, except for the large poster over the sofa. It's the same nude man with the fig leaf Xavier admired on 41st just before he heard Mrs. Hughes in the alley.

What he doesn't see: file cabinets, photographs, books, bills, letters, magazines, or newspapers. The closets are almost bare. Where are Luca's expensive sweaters and custom-made pants, a black cashmere blazer he might wear to an evening benefit? Xavier's leafed through Ramon's copies of *GQ,* he knows how Luca should live.

In the kitchen the only signs of life are an empty yogurt carton and crumpled paper from a Zabar's muffin next to the sink. In the bedroom hangs a large framed mirror. Xavier, standing on his tiptoes, remembers how tall the designer seemed, strolling around his studio. On the bedroom floor lie expensive silk pajamas, in the bathroom, a razor and a bottle of cologne. Envious, Xavier unscrews the cap, sniffs, and files away the name against the day he has more cash. And since he's in the bathroom . . . he lifts the seat, and used to living in an apartment overrun with family, out of habit kicks shut the door.

"Now I've seen it all," are Xavier's first words when Emeline opens her door. "Wanna tell me why an old woman—"

"Older." Emeline feels herself stiffen

"—gets off the elevator and asks your doorman to unscrew a jar of prunes?"

"That would be 10B." Emeline pulls him toward the living room. "Terrible arthritis and, frankly, rather odd, but on 9/11when all the subways stopped? Gregor says she was the only person in the building who thought to invite him to sleep on her couch. Xavier, you know Muffy." Her tea untouched, Muffy sits on the sea-green brocade couch, her knees tightly together, face drawn. Xavier might not have been in the room.

"Muffy's been explaining the financial side of the rag biz. I had no idea: in New York it generates $10 billion a year in wages. More tea for you, Muffy?

"And the backing, so unreliable. Investors can float a couple of million on a whim, then shut it off just as fast." Emeline hands him a blue-and-white tea cup. "Backers come from Hong Kong, Miami, Manhattan, all sorts of people with access to financial institutions. And occasionally," she smiles at Muffy, "even taste." Muffy fails to preen, her expression closer to panic.

"With Luca determined to expand, Muffy's been exploring some business arrangements. Here's the sugar." With only one hand holding, the bowl vibrates.

Xavier takes the silver bowl and weighs his options. "Business arrangements."

"Yes." Muffy finally speaks. "My husband and I prefer to invest in worthwhile cultural opportunities."

Dropping into the wing chair, Xavier sends Emeline a long and challenging look. "Worried you won't get your money back?"

Muffy's cheeks go pink. So much for tea-time manners, yet on a hunch Emeline decides to see where this rudeness leads. Or perhaps not rudeness, Xavier meant to provoke. "Young man," Muffy draws herself up. "If you're going to take tea from Wedgwood you should learn there are a few things one just doesn't—"

"Doesn't talk about, I know. Money," Xavier takes a deep breath, "and of course sex."

"Xavier!" protests Emeline. That really is a step too far.

Flushing a dangerous red, Muffy rises and presses her Kate Spade bag against her thigh. "If you ask me, Emeline, you'd do better to call an agency and get in some proper help."

"Proper. Let's see. You mean help who won't tell your good friend Emeline how you've been—" In Muffy's bag her cell phone rings.

"—more than just a patron to Luca? How you already suspect what's behind the killing? And that's what has you frightened out of your skin?" With obvious relief Muffy takes out her cell and stumbles from the room.

"Xavier?" Emeline's trying to hide her disappointment, disapproval, "I do hope you know what you're doing."

"You must think so. You could have interrupted, you were curious, too." He gulps the rest of his tea, repressing a shudder. "Matter of fact, Arnie had plenty to say."

"Responding to your charm, I suppose. Or did you threaten him as well?"

"Bribed him. The studio was short-staffed even before Bay's murder, the *gran formaggio's* temper driving employees out is my guess; whatever Arnie claims, I doubt all the employees carry papers. Anyway, he needs a seamstress, since his have melted away, and for last-minute fittings Arnie's in a jam. I called my Aunt Koka, she's gonna step in. She's union," Xavier finishes proudly.

"Ah. Do you think she'll learn anything?"

"*Caramba,* recruit my whole family, why don't you."

"I only meant, smart move."

"Maybe we can start with what I learned? The maestro's heavy accent, that's just Luca being . . . a prat. Turns out the men grew up together, part of a tight, Italian community in New England, not Italy. If it weren't for Luca, Arnie would be seine fishing off New

Bedford. He's a partner in the business by the way. Arnie manages everything."

"Leaving Luca out and about," sniffs Emeline, "swanning around."

"Arnie deals with creditors. Hires a new bookkeeper when Luca screams at the old one and she walks. Keeps Luca's 'admirers'—who sometimes turn up after hours—from bumping into each other. Generally cleans up the messes."

"Enviable job. You learned a lot."

"A year ago the assistant designer Takeshi leaves to start his own line. Luca throws a fit, carries on about betrayal, threatens Takeshi, Takeshi takes out a restraining order. Luca hires a new designer. Bay. Fresh out of the Fashion Institute."

"Ghost designer, I bet. Luca takes the credit?"

"Naturally. Bay begins to imitate Luca. Wears the same Roma-style clothes, even gets the same hair color so they'll match."

"A crush? Or, was he just—?"

"Kissing up? Point is, Emeline, anyone going after Luca could make a mistake in a bad light. Luca claims Takeshi's behind the murder. Like Arnie says, the rag business can kill you."

"Certainly can. You heard of the Triangle factory fire, know how many people died?"

He looks sorrowful. "Did you know any of them?"

"No, Xavier, I knew none of the victims. I wasn't born yet."

"I didn't mean—"

"Just go on."

"Arnie worries about Luca's plans to expand if his opening is a success. As it is, Arnie doesn't have much of a life. Works all day, then rides the train back to Jersey and watches TV, evenings. With me so far?" She nods.

"Here comes the good part: I went to Luca's apartment."

"So I was a help. Tools, please. " She puts out her hand and Xavier places the lobster picks on her palm.

"His place is bare, Emeline. The man's a designer, a clothes horse, so where's he keeping all his fancy threads? And there's another thing, you'll love this."

Her smile fades. "I'm pretty sure I won't."

"Almost missed it myself: the nightgown hanging on the back of the bathroom door."

"Nightgown," Emeline coughs.

"Silk, lacey at the top, with an embroidered initial: *B*. Luca's a piece a work, all right, but I don't see him as a cross dresser. I'm not even sure he's gay, it might all be an act. Anyway, this nightie's too small for Luca, and too big Muffy, for that matter."

"*What?*"

"Are you surprised?"

"I thought you were just, you know, trying to shock."

"I bet you Luca's been sleeping with your friend. Part payment for her generous investment, maybe." Emeline holds her hands to her temples. "What's the matter, upset with my bad manners? Or Muffy's repayment plan?"

"All of it."

"Sorry. If it makes a difference, you've made me break *my* golden rule: don't try to figure out who's sleeping with who."

"Whom," corrects Emeline, preoccupied. "Suppose the *B* does stand for Bay. That might mean Luca was never the target. If someone was jealous of Bay, if he—she—was the cross dresser—"

Muffy walks back into the room, her face ashen. She sinks onto the couch and reaches for Emeline's hand. "That was the inspector," Muffy mumbles as though, Xavier, two feet away, might not hear.

"He says it was not a knife. They think it was cutting shears, only they can't find them. They're trying to track down the women who worked there. And the inspector wants to talk to me again. He says, oh Emeline, I have been such a fool. Bay was not entirely successful in imitating Luca, Bay was really . . ." Muffy breaks into unbecoming tears.

"I know, dear. Bay was a woman. Xavier, stop smiling like the Cheshire cat and tell Muffy what you found." Staring down at the rug so he won't see Muffy's face, Xavier tells her, as gently as he can. Emeline is impressed.

"My God!" wails Muffy, "you're going to tell all this to the inspector?"

Emeline raises innocent eyebrows. "Tell him what? It's a hypothesis, that's all. Not our job to run down leads for the NYPD. You go on home, Muffy. Have Gregor call you a cab."

"A cab? It's only seven blocks."

"Because I'm not sure you should be out on the street alone until we know more. And stay in for the night. Truthfully I'm worried for you." Bewildered and defeated, Muffy nods. "One more thing, Muffy? Take my advice and do not talk to your dear old husband about any of this."

Emeline closes the door behind Muffy and, done in, sinks onto her couch. Xavier says, "You sound as if you feel sorry for her."

"You know how it is, older women developing a pash for a younger man; not that it's a problem for us." Embarrassed, Xavier turns away, stares absently at the old clock ticking on the mantle. "Seth Thomas," says Emeline after a minute.

"Muffy's husband?"

"The clock. It's an antique. Clifford loved that clock." Turning toward the mahogany end table, she takes a tissue and blows her nose, then looks with longing at the silver-haired man in the picture frame. "You know, you remind me a good deal of my Clifford."

"British, straight, very successful . . . *Claro*."

"Brash, spunky, hard-nosed, and clever. I suppose you'd best be getting home, too. Unless you'd feel like staying over in the guest room. You could help me get some supper together."

"If you really think—"

"That I could use a hand? I confess, I have been struggling a bit. I have rib eye in the fridge and a nice Merlot, so if you're up to broiling I might manage a salad. Besides, you're not bad company. Beats watching television, nothing on except wannabe chefs and police shows. What do I owe you so far?"

"I'm running a tab."

"Please yourself. You're right, of course. Our designer has to have another life somewhere. Maybe you can get more out of Arnie tomorrow."

CHAPTER 5

Tempting. On the IRT uptown Xavier imagines spending the night in Mrs. Hughes serene apartment, only he can think of no excuse good enough. Flavia's children come home, even if the sky's growing light over the East River when they do.

The Escuderos had a chance to move into one of the new buildings: tall, red-brick public housing named after white presidents like Taft and Jefferson. Flavia wouldn't hear of it. "I won't know anyone. How I make friends? I'm too busy to make new friends. Maybe later on."

"Later on, *Mai?* By then you'll be too old," teases Ramon, "your kids too big and making too much money."

"My kids too big?" As always, Flavia ignores any mention of wages, money being the one piece of her life she's managed to keep private. "Look around, *m'ijo*. You notice any my kids getting ready to move out?"

Not Rocio, the youngest. When Hunter High School turned her down was the only time Xavier saw their mother sob. "I'll go live with my boyfriend, *Mamacita*," Rocio threatened, blinking back her own despair, "if I'm such a disappointment." Little sister had bought into Flavia's dream of success at the school for gifted teens."

"Over my dead body! You live at home. Do your homework. And no running around at night, you hear?" As if that had kept his sister safe; months later, with a new reason if less enthusiasm, Rocio repeated her offer.

"If that boyfriend," Ramon smirked, "he wants to marry our little Rocio? Let him take her off our hands." Ramon had left once himself; soon as he finished his time in juvi, back he came.

"Marry that fool? No, no, no!" Flavia was shouting. "Only aisle she walking down is in Patrick Henry gym. You gonna graduate high school, Rocio, I'm gonna see you in that black hat if it's the last thing I see on this earth." Keeping silent, Xavier doubted escape had been Rocio's dream, her baby the result of afternoons spent at her boyfriend's before his mother got home.

"Meantime?" In a torrent of directives Flavia recalculated her daughter's future, baby Jomar so far not even a curve below Rocio's fake-alligator belt. "You will not spend your days watching Oprah or *telenovelas*. You gonna go back to school. You gonna work from three to nine at whatever job you find. I talk to Renata upstairs, she like babies, maybe she help out."

Perfect, thought Xavier, with Renata's cousin linked to the Genovese crime family. Protection racquets, gambling, extortion: the staples; newer activities, too, like drugs, money laundering, arms trafficking.

"I thought maybe you could stay home?" Rocio tried.

"You crazy?" screamed Flavia, not one to forfeit a paid job to be the unpaid caregiver of a grandchild.

"Yes, girl, you crazy," Ramon snorted. "*Mamacita,* how you get such an obstinate girl, tell me that! Rocio, you called her, dew, dainty dew? Or maybe your spelling is off, you really named her *roca*. Like you she is, both unyielding as a rock."

Rocio had barely begun her familiar complaint, *"aburriendo,"* when her mother slapped her cheek. "Boring with pay is better than boring without. You can work evenings after I get home. I go talk to that nice lady at Krispy Kutz. Tomorrow we go up to 115th Street, the clinic has pre-natal care and for after," Flavia lowers her voice, "contraceptive."

Rocio played her ace. "What about the priest?" Flavia, unmoved by evangelicals setting up shop in nearby storefronts, attended Our Lady of Mount Carmel Church.

"The day Father Alfonso get up two, three times a night with a howling kid I be happy to hear what he has to say on the subject."

As Xavier stood behind his sister, resting a steadying hand on her shoulder, it never crossed his mind he'd be the first to break away.

True to her word, Tia Koka sits at a sewing machine, exceeding the speed limit and frowning at fabric. Xavier kisses her on each cheek and tackles Arnie.

"No one is gunning for Luca, are they. It was Bay all along. Though God knows, must be plenty of people ready to kill Luca, Italian designer who's not Italian."

"He Italian." Arnie looks deeply hurt. "We all Italian."

"You might have told me the apartment is a sham."

"It wasn't me sent you down Prince Street!"

"You resented Bay being here. Or maybe you had your own thing going with Luca?"

"Never." Decades of disappointment swim in Arnie's eyes. "All our years together, never that. Only frien's. Home town boys. And Catholic."

"But you were jealous of Bay."

"*Una relazione amoroso?*" Arnie pulls away from Xavier's grasp. "It meant nothing. No, I was the good, like, wife. Manage the accounts, the schedule, the meetings, deal with creditors, hire the workers. Stay with him through t'ick and t'in. You imagine Luca ever make a success of the business on his own? The man refuse even to wear a watch."

"Inspector Flynn may not see it that way."

"You workin' for the police, now?" Wiping his nose on the shoulder of his smock, Arnie looks wary. "You should at least bark along the right . . . here, come to the office."

Arnie opens the door to a room barely larger than a broom closet. Taking a key from the loop clipped to his belt, he unlocks a cabinet, pulls out a manila file, and lays it on the table. A six-by-eight-inch colored photo falls to the floor.

Grabbing it before Arnie can, Xavier sees a woman like a Madonna, a dark-eyed, olive-skinned beauty with big hair, lacquered lips, and stubborn eyes. She's seated on a rose- velvet sofa, on her lap a boy not much older than Jomar. Flowered curtains frame the window behind them and outside stands a leafy tree.

"Luca has a *family?*"

Dismayed, Arnie reaches for the photo. Xavier waves it over his head. Arnie gives up; his stubby fingers riffle through papers in the file. He draws out a page stamped 'paid' in big letters and hands it over: a landscaper's bill for an address in Jersey.

"Now he does. She my niece, Simone, used to live in Napoli. We arrange it, Luca and me, when my brother in Napoli gonna throw her and her baby out on the street. This way everybody be happy." Arnie's pained look as he reaches to take back the photograph makes Xavier heart ache.

"Luca has a family?" Sitting on the couch as Xavier tries again to like Lapsang, Emeline struggles to take in the story. "Luca, vain, egotistical, ambitious, and deceitful? The perfect father."

"No argument from me. According to Arnie, Catholic fear began to trump Luca's act as the gay *artiste* so Luca struck a secret deal with his God. He agreed to take in mother and child."

"Simone made a bargain of her own," Emeline points out, "marriage, warm bed, house with a yard, and a name for her son."

"Worried as he is about his share of the business, Arnie's more worried about his niece. Poor kid came straight from the old country, speaks little English, keeps to her Italian neighborhood in Jersey, never comes into the city. *Volando bajito*. Flying under the radar."

"Besides giving Arnie another set of eyes and ears on Luca's doings. Do have a biscuit."

"No, I'm good."

"Until Catholic fear faltered in the face of the yummy designer under Luca's nose day after day. Remember him whinging on about Takeshi? That's a bit rich."

Xavier drums his fingers on the kitchen table. "Afternoon I met you on the West Side—"

"Rescued me."

"Whatever. You were coming from Luca's studio, you'd been there with Muffy. Right?"

"How did you know?"

"East Side lady, what else would you be doing on West 41st. Taking tap dance?"

Amused, she shuffles her feet to imitate a waltz clog. "Yes, only when I got outside, no cabs. So like a fool I decided to walk east to catch the uptown bus. Wasn't it just a random mugging?"

"Let's look at in another way. Suppose Simone somehow learned about Bay. Maybe she left her boy with one of the *nonnas*, went to the city for once and found her way to the studio. Your attacker could have been Simone, following the wrong woman from Luca's studio."

"We have to tell Inspector Flynn, Not that he'll believe us."

"Lemme think it over, just for like a day."

"Now who's making bargains with God?"

"Italians," sighs Xavier, "they're like Puerto Ricans. Family is everything. And for some of us, it's hard to imagine we'll ever have a family." Emeline sees a rare, wistful expression cross his face. "You may not understand, with your daughter living off in London—" Now she feels herself glaring. "Sorry, sorry. You gonna kick me out?"

"Thinking about it!"

"These arrangements of convenience, they never really work, do they."

"We're still talking about Luca and Simone?"

"What else would we be talking about? Let's get through the benefit first. Then we'll tell the inspector. Hey, I gotta get going."

"You might as well stay here tonight." Emeline only plans to use her second bedroom as a staging area when, come fall, she shifts her wardrobe. "Be easier for you to get to the gym, then come back and get ready."

"Ready?"

"If you plan to escort me to Luca's opening I'll have to dig out one of Clifford's jackets. I'm not showing up for the benefit at the Montgomery with you in that black tee-shirt, I'll tell you that much for free."

"Okay. But—"

"I know, I know. Only the one night."

Fashion Week used to sprout in white tents in Bryant Park like fall crocuses. These days it's moved to Lincoln Center. More room and more panache, known as Lincoln Center is for conductors, orchestras, singers, and dancers whose names are household words—at least in some households.

The Fashion Week extravaganza isn't only for major designers like Hererra and Lauren. Events less luminary like Luca's break-out show, this year combined with Muffy's Yorkville Young Music benefit, spill over onto terraces, lofts, French restaurants, and art galleries. On lower Fifth the Hotel Montgomery ballroom offers vaulted ceilings, colossal chandeliers, and gauze curtains tied in graceful knots at the side of floor-length windows. On their way backstage, Xavier and Emeline pass a petite Chinese woman with long, stick-straight hair.

"You know who that is, yes?" Emeline whispers. He shakes his head. Emeline mouths a name he can't hear.

Xavier has to admit Emeline's looking smart. Before they left the apartment she let him fuss with her outfit, agreed to remove her sweater to show off her silk pullover. He did drape the cardigan around her shoulders with one sleeve, debonair, swinging beside her necklace of pale blue beads. Opalines she calls them.

"There, Emeline. Foxy."

"At my age? Not precisely the look I'm after."

In the overheated dressing room, Xavier mops his forehead. For a function months in the planning he'd expect less chaos. Hair stylists, make-up artists, dressers; half-dressed models circle the area and brush past racks of garments, making Xavier uncomfortable, until he realizes the skinny babes in push-up bras don't even see him. Bodies for rent, he realizes.

Dressed in one of Luca's more subdued designs, Muffy is being made up by a professional; her shaped eyebrows give her a look of perpetual surprise. "Muffy," Luca swings by to ask, "you did talk to Anna Wintour?"

"No one talks to Anna. I reached Tonne Goodman, though she made no promises. At least the rehearsal went well."

"Rehearsal?"

"Yes, Xavier, rehearsal." Forgetting she'll never speak to him again, Muffy seems willing to educate. "The models must have their routines down pat, or they'll knock into each other. And they need to practice quick changes so they'll keep up with the schedule." She looks at her watch, and pulls off her smock. "Almost ready to start. Time to keep visitors to a minimum back here, so if you don't mind?"

Out front they pass a small Japanese man dressed in white. "Takeshi!" Muffy hisses and cuts him dead. Then noticing the publicist has jumbled the front row VIP seating plan, Muffy abandons good breeding like yesterday's hemline and screeches in the voice of an outraged *abuelita*. Arne scurries toward her: "I deal with it, I deal with it."

Looking carefully around the room, Xavier follows Emeline toward free chairs next to a trio of well-dressed women. Emeline lifts a hand in greeting. One woman glances up, then away, and two begin to whisper.

"Friends of yours?" asks Xavier.

"I thought so once." Face pink, Emeline grips Xavier's arm and steers him the other way. They take seats on the far side of the runway that cuts through the ballroom. "What do you think of it all so far?"

"I'd expected more, you know, class?" Her laugh makes heads turn.

The air carries a mix of expensive scents; the devotees gathering are a mixed bouquet as well. Many are young fashionistas in obligatory noir, stiletto heels, and straight hair. Offering air kisses, they work the room like short stops in the minor league tryouts. Art by art and illness by illness, as benefistas they are striving for a place on a Division One committee: "The New York Philharmonic," Emeline explains, "or MOMA."

In contrast Muffy's coterie is easy to spot: confident women of a certain age wearing little eye shadow and no beads (unless very small and pearl), who've thrown on an Hermes scarf and called it a day. Although a few, well-coiffed, in jackets that honor Coco Channel if not actually run up in Paris, confuse the swarm of photographers dancing around. Who on earth is she? Or her?

Close to the runway sit clusters of serious pros—buyers, journalists, editors—holding electronic tablets open on their skinny knees and ready to take notes. Among a group of slim, sleek fellows Xavier spots one who winks at him: a brief, past encounter. Did he ever know his name?

Enters a woman so soignée she makes his teeth ache. Her bangs cut straight above the eyes of a sly kitten, she and her entourage sweep in to take front row seats. Curious, Xavier raises his eyebrows. Please, Emeline gives him a withering look, you must be the only one here who doesn't recognize *her*.

Suddenly it's show time. High school girls from Yorkville Young Music swing long hair out of their eyes, tuck violins under chins delicate or plump, and strike up a John Pizzarelli tango. If Muffy took the hill over music, Luca won the battle when it came to the models. Murmuring against the tango, Emeline says any debutantes Muffy proposed were rejected in favor of agency professionals, size zero.

The first prances out in a tailored pant suit with very odd shoulders, sashays down the runway ("from somewhere on Saturn, Xavier?"), pivots, and heads back. By a hair she misses the oncoming second, this one dressed in an Italian printed-silk wrap dress, its neckline by-passing a non-existent bosom to stop inches above her navel. A swell of polite applause builds. Muffy stands toward one side, offering a running commentary in Luca's ear. Excusing herself, Emeline gets up to join them.

Nervous, Xavier turns in his seat to scan guests still arriving. If it was Simone who mugged Emeline, took her bag, read the invitation to the benefit . . . has he made a mistake not telling the inspector?

He stiffens. He can't see her face, only the mass of black shoulder-length hair, wildly curly and totally out of place in this crowd. Xavier pushes past a dozen bony knees to get to the aisle, and moves fast toward the back of the room. The woman turns, scans the crowd, and fixes her eyes on Emeline. Xavier recognizes the full mouth, Madonna face, generations of Sicilian angst in her eyes. She raises her arm with a little gun pointing toward Emeline.

"Tay-NESS- kwee DA-do!" The accent's so atrocious Xavier isn't sure it's Spanish. Out of the corner of his eye he sees Emeline moving down the open aisle, arms swinging like a speed skater's, her cane knocking into startled guests. Just before he can reach Simone, he hears a shot and feels a searing pain in his arm. Operating on street instinct, he grabs hold of the black-haired woman with the gun, drops, and rolls.

Emeline is crouching on the floor beside him. If she's talking to him, there is no sound. What a sweetie, she really cares, he's thinking before he blacks out.

Hands are slapping his face after an uncertain interval, and Xavier finds he can hear again. Women scream, chair legs scrape on the polished wooden floor. When a familiar voice says, "Watch out for the fallen fag—" Xavier forces his eyes open to the unwelcome sight of a blue-serge crotch as Inspector Flynn steps over him to wrestle Simone onto her stomach.

A stranger's voice at his shoulder: "I'm a doctor." Xavier grinds his teeth against the pain as a well-dressed Asian *chiquita* pulls off his jacket and rips open his shirt sleeve. "Not much more than a scratch, he'll be fine."

He doesn't feel fine. Beside him Emeline chokes back a sob. Hardly a surprise: Clifford's cherished jacket is ruined, Xavier remembers her lifting the tweed to her face and inhaling deeply before she handed it to him. He tries to recall the name of the tailor his mother knows, the one who does invisible weaving and can mend a rip so it looks as good as new.

"Sorry about the jacket, Emeline." Hauled up, he is sitting in a chair and no longer looking through chair legs, he notices Luca has seized one of the models, clutching this tiny twig against his chest like a shield. Always the gentleman, Luca.

The front-row VIPs hold up fans, handbags, iPads and PDAs to protect their faces. No sign of the fashionable kitten, she must have sidled out with her followers. There's a rising buzz of disbelief, punctuated by discordant chimes of cell phones. In five minutes news of the shooting will spread across the city.

Two uniformed policemen hold Simone's arms behind her back. Tears hang on her heavy lashes like sequins. The inspector looks pleased. Until in a voice that begins as a growl and ends in a shout, Arnie plunges through the crowd. "No," he cries, pulling on the inspector's arm. "It wasn't Simone, she didn't do nothin,' it was me, me."

Now officers are holding them both, while Arnie can't stop talking. "It was accident. Simone, she came to the studio one evening. Luca gone. Me, working late. Bad enough Luca say he'd make Bay a partner. Bay was taunting me, threatening Luca would divorce the 'little guinea,' Simone mean nothing to him. That Bay—she think she gonna replace me at work and my niece in his bed?" The officers are reaching for handcuffs.

"Simone has the temper, you know, Sicilian temper. You understand, officer?" Arnie twists his head to peer at the inspector. "No pistol, no knife, she attack only with words, calling Bay names—and Bay deserve them, trying to take over the business, trying to replace Simone." As Arnie's voice grows louder, drowning out the hum of voices, people closest stop talking to listen. A wave of quiet spreads through the crowd as the buzz of gossip recedes to the outer edges of the room.

"Simone rushes at him, her hands out, only her hands. It's Bay picks up the cutting shears, she'd have used them, too. I couldn't let her hurt Simone, she my family. So I push between them, Bay and I we struggle." Arnie collapses into sobs. "An accident! I swear, it was an accident."

Xavier wonders if he'll ever forget Arnie's shattered look. A man who'd tried to rescue the only family he had managed to create.

"Speak to the inspector for me Xavier," Emeline whispers. "Tell him I have to take a pee."

"Not in my contract. Besides, it hurts like hell to move."

"The EMTs are coming," says the Asian doctor, "you hold on,"

"We'll see," the inspector, smug, says to Arnie. "Your niece did shoot this . . . gentleman." He points to Xavier.

"My dear Inspector," Emeline says in a firm voice, she knows she has a captive audience. "You are quite mistaken. Ballistics will tell, of course, though I saw exactly what happened. Mr. Escudero realized the danger, he rushed forward to stop this woman who, as you must have noticed by now, was carrying a toy gun. Best be careful!" A crafty smile. The inspector gapes. "It might be a water pistol. No, I'm afraid it was your officer who fired the shot. Overzealous, wouldn't you say? Yet another case of police assault. Of course, we'll know more once we take legal advice."

Luca, reputation unraveling, stands unmasked. The crowd he's failed to charm, the law he can't manipulate, his loyal, childhood friend in custody. Bewildered at his shower of calamities, Luca says out loud to no one in particular: "My God. How am I supposed to manage without Arnie?"

Self-important invitees complain at full volume, threaten legal action, flaunt close connections to the mayor, the police commissioner, and the press. Inspector Flynn, back in charge, is separating the players, a job that takes much longer this time. EMTs arrive. The inspector dismisses Xavier. Faced with Emeline's defiance and earlier threat, he releases her to go in the ambulance, too. Only then does she confess she may have hurt her ankle.

"Did you recognize Simone?" Xavier asks through clenched teeth. "Was it Simone who mugged you? If she'd been watching the studio, thought you were Muffy . . ."

"I never saw who mugged me. I have nothing to add to the case." She won't meet his eyes.

Parked in a small cubicle at the ER, Xavier downs painkillers and watches as his flesh wound is cleaned and bandaged. Emeline's ankle is X-rayed and pronounced sprained, not broken. An Ace bandage covers the damage. The patients are discharged.

If Xavier can hobble to the IRT he can make it home in twenty minutes. Except Emeline hails a cab by stepping directly into the traffic and raising her cane, then insists he ride with her, saying only. "London has the right idea, imposing congestion fees."

Xavier isn't seeing the traffic. All he sees is the wreckage of one man's dreams for his family. At least Xavier has a family to go home to. Looking sideways at Emeline's pale face, he wonders: if real trouble hit her again, would her daughter be there for her?

Pain killers are kicking in and Xavier, feeling generous, says, "Let's hope they're not too hard on Simone."

Emeline takes his hand. "Of course it was Muffy that Simone was after."

"Yeah? That's why you were shouting warnings in Spanish—to warn Muffy? If it even was in Spanish. Your accent *es horrible*."

"Suppose," Emeline goes on, "Simone did leave her son with one of the *nonnas* in the neighborhood, she knows they'll never give her away. She comes to the studio after work. Overhears Bay taunting Arnie, telling him Luca plans to divorce her, Simone means nothing to him, it is only a marriage of convenience, this is real love, blah, blah, blah."

"You're making this up, Emeline, you know that."

"You think so? Either Arnie picked up the shears and went for Bay. Or it was Bay, the way Arnie says. For sure it was Arnie who turned up the heat. He watches television, you told me so. He'd know that heat would throw off the time of death. Arnie could have dropped the shears in a sewer on his way home. Simone could get off with a lighter sentence. So nobody's really hurt, after all."

"Oh, thanks a lot."

"Be quiet, you're fine. Once Arnie gets out . . . if his lawyer can persuade a jury it was attempted assault, no premeditation? Arnie may even persuade Simone and the boy to live with him. We know Luca's done with her, she ruined his show."

"And we know how well that's gonna work. These arrangements . . ." his voice trails off. They ride some blocks in silence.

"So, Xavier, you did tell the inspector after all."

"What? No, what are you talking about, I thought you did."

"Someone told him or why were the police already there?"

"It had to be—"

"Arnie," they say together.

"In the end," says Emeline, "more loyal to that asshole than to his own niece. Arnie wanted to save Luca. Perhaps they'll send Arnie to Ossining. You know, Sing Sing."

"Here's Arnie, not even tried." Xavier won't admit he feels sorry for the guy. As the cab passes under a street light Xavier notices Emeline's smiling.

"We could travel up by train," she suggests.

"Tell me you're not planning to visit."

"Lovely views along the Hudson, and I have a dear friend in Poughkeepsie. She taught at Vassar. I'm sure she'd invite us for lunch. She does such a nice chicken salad."

Sing Sing. Vassar College. Chicken salad. Rocking in the cab, Xavier is at a loss for words. What began as their shared adventure has ended in something dark. Some partnerships, he reminds himself, are ill-fated from the start. He will miss the cab rides.

Paying the driver, Emeline figures out the tip with no trouble this time. With her gloved fingers resting on the door handle, she's studying the taxi license in its metal plaque. Trying to memorize the driver's long, Islamic name? Or concentrating the way you might if you're afraid you'll leave something valuable behind.

"Well?" she says finally, opening the cab door. "Are you seeing me upstairs, or what?"

Chapter 6

After Xavier recalls the tailor's name, he insists on taking Clifford's jacket, turns down her offer of hot cocoa, and leaves for home, Emeline hears nothing from him. She doesn't care about the jacket; she is distressed the friendship has been ruptured.

Ever since June Emeline feels she's been juggling colored balls like a circus clown. Three balls, one in each hand and always one in the air: they've become her obsession. If the order had been different? Diagnosis, scandal, accident. Blue, red, yellow. Or yellow, blue, red . . . would her life feel any easier that way?

Tingling in her left hand was the first sign and easy to dismiss; maybe she'd slept the wrong way. Next came tingling in her left leg. Maybe her new Cole Hahns were too tight, from now on she'd stick with familiar Ferragamos. She thought about going to the doctor, only Clifford needed her to meet him on Long Island with clients.

Until, one day Emeline knows. The tingle, the stiffness, the start of a tremor, she can't write these off as just stress or nerves. Nerves? She has to laugh. As though it isn't all about nerves, biased signals sent from the brain's cells to her outer limbs. She's learned more than she wants to know about neurology.

In her mind Emeline lets the colored balls drop to the floor. The order is what it is. At least for a while she had Clifford with her, putting her first. Counted on him, appreciated him. Here is where she likes to linger, savoring again the hours when their days were good, her walking okay, and even so Clifford liked to take her arm. (And even so she might complain or fret. Such a waste, she knows that now.)

Then in a night Clifford is gone. She's barely starting to accept her loss, her move, and along comes this Puerto Rican kid. Too young to be a proxy for the brother in London she doesn't know or the son she never had. Young enough to be her grandson, if she had a grandson. Must he always dress in black as if his allegiance lies with a gang of Goths? Emeline understands: he's trying to gain distance from one mother, what would induce him to saddle himself with another one even older?

Thing is, she has an unspoken problem of her own to solve and even if Clifford is gone, the problem is not. For the first time it crosses her mind the mugger may have done her a favor. The brutal push that landed her in the alley, the chance encounter—if she plays her cards right—may possibly have brought her an accomplice.

She waits six days before she calls. "Xavier? Didn't wake you, did I? Good. I know it's your day off. Only I have my regular doctor's appointment up at Columbia Presbyterian and my ankle is sore. No, no, I'm mending, only feeling a bit stiffer than usual. You have people who count on you, I know. Are you perhaps free?"

Standing outside, leaning on her best cane, eventually she watches him saunter up, sees his appraising eyes go to the metal duck head, thinking: any chance it's real silver?

"You're very good to come along," she says. "One likes to think one can manage."

After that, an awkward silence falls as the cab heads north to Columbia Presbyterian. Silence in the elevator and walking to the reception desk. "You can wait here." She points to a row of blue molded chairs. Too late, she realizes the waiting room must look like a club compared to the chaotic floor at Metropolitan General where his sister had her baby. She limps after the beckoning nurse and disappears behind swinging doors.

Forty minutes later, ready to leave, they wait on the street as the next free cab in the line pulls up. "Everything okay?" Xavier looks at her intently. She shrugs. He waits. She waits him out, then blinks first.

"About the same, could be worse. Anyway," she concedes, taking his arm, "thanks for asking."

"Good to hear. Then, how about a different ride back, more scenic."

"You kidnapping me?"

"You bet. Unless," he's grinning, "your ankle hurts too much," and Emeline realizes she's forgotten to limp. He takes her arm and they cross the street. When the bus arrives he helps her up the steps. When she fumbles for change, he slides his Metro pass through twice and as the bus wheezes away from the curb Xavier catches her arm so she doesn't lose her balance. Apparently they're friends again.

Near them a young woman, hair in a fashionable top knot, pushes down the window so warm air blows in fumes from the street and the oily smell of fresh tarmac. She smiles to herself as she presses a button on her cell phone. A boyfriend? Her mother back home in Mumbai?

Emeline watches Broadway glide by: store fronts, street peddlers, apartment buildings, if few doormen. A trio of pigeons spiral past the open window, the bus veers left onto 110th, then right onto Fifth. Out the window the show changes: A pair of boys or maybe girls, skateboard against green trees in Central Park. Arm in arm an old couple leads two grey-muzzled poodles on a red leash. At 105th Xavier presses the black strip and the bus hisses to a stop.

"Where we off to now?"

"Lunch," he answers. "You told me you liked the Conservatory Garden."

"Central Park's only formal garden, yes, but it has no restaurant."

"Who said anything about a restaurant?" Xavier leads her to a hotdog wagon she's never seen or at least noticed. Xavier greets the park-side restaurateur. *"Como te van las cosas, compra'?*

"Bien, bien. What'll it be?"

"Two with mustard—you good with mustard, Mrs. Hughes?"

"Yes."

"And two Cokes."

"Not so good with caffeine this time of day. And my name is Emeline."

"A Coke and, what else you got, *señor,* Sprite?"

"Si, si. Un nieto muy sympatico, no?"

They settle on a bench. Emeline is about to tell him the garden is divided into three areas, English, French, and Italian, then decides he'll think she's showing off. "What was that last sentence?"

"He says I'm a good grandson."

She laughs, *haw haw,* and bites through mustard into the juicy hot dog. "Truthful as well as a good grandson." Xavier looks surprised; she was testing him. "Yes, I speak a bit of Spanish."

"Mrs. Hughes—"

"Emeline, please."

"You know the garden, don't you."

Does she ever. "I used to come here with my daughter when she was young. Until, later . . . we don't often see eye to eye." Growing up away from her own mother, Emeline longed to be the mother she'd missed out on; not that she'd say as much to Xavier. "Deborah settled in London. She'd been there as an exchange student, next thing we know, she wants to transfer to university and read history of art."

"And your husband, did he come here, too?"

"When he could, on weekends," Emeline knows her face shows pain, she doesn't try to hide it.

"Can I ask how he died, your Clifford?"

Why do you want to know? That's what she tempted to say. Simple question, simple answer: car crash. Emeline's said the two words many times, yet she's having trouble saying them to this young man. She isn't sure when she began to question if it was an accident; maybe in a thought drifting through her brain when she was half awake, then an hour later not sure if it was ever there.

She'd best say something or he'll start to wonder. Luckily a dog comes up, off-leash. Emeline bends to pat the sleek head; as always, she misses the family dogs they once had. She watches as the creature trots away, careful to bypass two stocky men on a nearby bench.

"Automobile accident on the Henry Hudson." For the first time it occurs to Emeline: was that why she'd been so quick to run to Muffy's side? Luca Bevilaqua meant nothing to her. It was the mysterious death that drew her in, compelled her to try to do what she'd been unable to do about the death that mattered to her the most. Xavier is looking at her, curious where her mind has wandered.

To distract him, she says, "Before that Deborah would come home maybe once a year. Clifford sometimes flew over to see her."

"Because?"

"Because he missed her."

"I mean, why didn't you go?"

"I can't fly. I didn't at first, my husband and I used to go over quite often."

"To polish up your accent."

"Aunt Mildred did the polishing, once she moved to New York she talked like a Tudor. But then after Ma died . . . I found I couldn't get on an airplane." Emeline begins waving her ringed hand at a swarm of yellow jackets attracted to their lunch leftovers.

"Time to leave?"

"I think so. Thanks for lunch, as good as Le Bernadine. Xavier, those two over there," hiding her hand with her handbag, she points to the men the dog ignored. "Did you happen to notice if they got on the bus with us?"

Emeline didn't feel uneasy about strangers until she put the 95th Street place on the market. The realtor, Braydon Wheeler, said he'd prefer she stay away, it was the custom. So each time there was a showing Emeline would straighten up the apartment as best she could (for once glad Fritzy was gone or her friend Tram would hound her with advice: "always scrub the dog's bone"). She'd sit in the coffee shop on Lexington with a book until the all clear call came. Inconvenient maybe, but that was all.

Until coming back one afternoon, she went into Clifford's study to check a zip code in his address book and noticed someone had been there—not to look the way a buyer might, opening a closet door to gauge the size—but searching. Pen holder, leather-bound blotter, the photo Clifford loved of his wife and daughter on Fisher's Island: little belongings she'd left exactly as he'd left them, which was to say askew. Cliff, always in a rush, had left the blotter at an angle and so had she. Now the blotter was squared. The drawers were tightly closed, not staggered like a ziggurat. It could have been

Wheeler, straightening up before a prospect arrived, though he'd never done it before.

"Absolutely not," Wheeler said when she phoned. "You told me to leave things as they were, and I do."

Should she have called the police? They'd only want the names of the visitors, and that would upset Wheeler. In the end she only called her daughter in London. "No, I didn't stay," she told Deborah. "You're supposed to disappear when prospects visit. No, I have no idea what they were looking for. Yes, the realtor came along with them. He always does, he signs in on the sheet and leaves it on the kitchen counter." Three showings later Emeline received a full-price offer and took it, glad she hadn't made a fuss.

Only to see how Emeline is getting along, Xavier decides four days later to stop at 63rd Street on his way home. "Not very friendly, your doorman," he says when he arrives at 7B. Emeline is in the hallway, with a couple of d'Agostino's bags standing on the floor.

"Gregor? Doormen are very protective of women living alone." Xavier picks up her bags and carries them into the kitchen. She bends over to take out a yellow can of Café Bustelo along with a new espresso pot. "Want to try it? Since we seem to be making slow progress with the Lapsang."

"You didn't have to go buy—"

"You'll probably want sugar, too." She reaches for the silver sugar bowl but before she can set it down it tumbles from her hand onto the table.

"Oh damn, look. I hate this, I do!" She buries her face in her hands. Xavier's as unnerved as she is, seeing her cool confidence vanish.

"Emeline. Want to tell me what's really wrong?"

She peers at him through her fingers, her eyes wet, and traces a shaky finger through the spray of sugar on the table top to draw the letter: *P*.

Please? Pity? Pancakes? Ah. Parkinson's, like one of his clients at the gym. Lifting her hand, he holds it gently. "What did they say at the doctor's?"

"Not much. Stay on the same dose. Exercise more." Xavier pulls out his cell. "What are you doing?"

"Looking up an aquatic therapy pool near here."

"No. I am not going."

"Okay. We'll talk about it later." Xavier stands thinking, uncertain, finally smooths out the spray of sugar and draws three letters: *P O Z*. In case she doesn't understand, he adds: *H I V.*

Emeline rummages in her sleeve for a tissue and blows her nose while Xavier sweeps up the sugar. "Right, then. If you open that cupboard you'll see a package of cookies. Appallingly sweet, if you ask me, I suppose they'll suit you."

"Or you could come down to my gym," Xavier says. "Swimming would be good for you."

"Get serious."

"I have older clients." She bristles. "Yes, over forty. Maybe you need some help here, too."

"I have help. A grand housekeeper, Jacinta, honest as the day is long." Xavier feels a flicker of pride: like my mother. "Only her father is ill and Jacinta had to go back to Barbados," her voice trails off. "I do miss her. When you let someone into your life, you know how it is."

Xavier has no idea, he's only ever lived with family members and too many of them at that. They sip in silence, and Xavier eats three biscuits. Apologizing, Emeline heads for the bedroom "to put my feet up for a minute."

Xavier unpacks the d'Agostino's bags: chilly, raw chicken breasts, prunes, a bunch of kale, potatoes too tiny to peel. It all looks inedible. From the fridge he pulls tomatoes, onions—*Dios mio,* not even a green Poblano to be found, let alone a tiny hot Serrano. Frustrated, he stores the chicken in the fridge, tosses half a dozen potatoes into the microwave, cracks three eggs into a blue-and-white striped bowl and beats them with the odd, bulb-shaped instrument Emeline calls a whisk. It does go faster than the fork his mother uses.

Emeline appears, leaning against the doorway in her fleecy robe. "You don't have to do that."

"I was hungry."

"You're always hungry. Even for you that looks like a lot."

"Thought you might need to eat."

"There's a bit of sliced ham in the fridge if you want."

"Bribery? So I'll come by and cook again?"

"That's your price, is it?" She nibbles at his frittata, softer and spicier than the omelets she makes. Not too spicy, he hopes; if it is, she doesn't complain. Silence is a novelty for Xavier— companionable, really—until she suggests, again, that he might want to stay over. If it had been last summer he would have, if only to watch the Olympics on her 20-inch screen. Instead he'd had to battle Rocio, always fascinated with *telenovelas* and the candid sex on **PBS**.

It's obvious Emeline has no notion about the apartment on 105th or its magnetic pull. No doubt she imagines an overcrowded space and a young man's hunger to get away. He can hear her thinking: In his twenties and he lives at home? This is America, for God's sake, not Italy. He can't explain, and he doesn't try.

The Escuderos' cramped rooms, like their battles, are a world apart: Emeline would never see them as adequate, even safe. Never mind the turbulence in a household where cute kids like Jomar grow into tall, unpredictable creatures with their own dreams and disasters. The family calls it home, and each evening Flavia spends with hers marks her triumph over abandonment and the more fatal effects of poverty.

Xavier puts their dishes in the dishwasher just so, adding to her lonely cereal bowl and coffee mug from breakfast; he says a polite good night, and leaves. This time he stays away a week, days spent wondering how he'll make enough money to help his family. Also, from time to time, how Mrs. Emeline Hughes is getting along.

The next time Xavier stops in, it occurs to him, with Emeline trotting ahead of him to the kitchen, that her ankle is healing surprisingly fast. Though today it turns out Emeline has more bad news.

"Jacinta? Not coming back at all?" Xavier repeats. Did Jacinta write, telephone, Skype from Bridgetown? Emeline, clearly undecided how much she wants to say, looks up with watery eyes. "A few weeks ago, she called long distance, I thought I mentioned it."

So not as truthful as he'd thought, though hadn't he watched her twist a story or two already? "You didn't want me to think I was looking after an old lady," he says, deliberately blunt. She doesn't flinch. "With Parkinson's do you die, like fast, like pancreas cancer? My Aunt Koka's husband had the pancreas, gone in three months."

"Sad truth is you don't die at all," she says flatly. He raises his eyebrows, and she laughs. "Magic isn't it, live forever, shuffling along. No, you die eventually, from complications maybe or something else entirely. I'm not afraid to die. What frightens me is the freezing. Not being able to move anymore. Suppose I'd lied to you,

Xavier, never told you about the Parkinson's, might it have worked out? At least until I could replace Jacinta. I have been calling around to the agencies."

Agencies. He's sitting in the kitchen of a woman who finds herself, always, on the other side of the equation from his mother. Who doesn't, at the moment, look a bit happier than his mother, a woman who needs help as much as Flavia needs money.

He'd seen Emeline, at first, as a woman to dismiss or exploit; free cab rides might have been just the beginning. Today he's seeing a woman who needs protection, who can ask for help without loading every request with innuendo and guilt, who just maybe offers him a way out of Flavia's tightly snarled nest.

Emeline's fiddling with her tea spoon while he thinks, turning it over to check the, what did she call it? Hallmark. Also, he realizes as she gives him a measured look, a woman who may be equally clever at finding the soft spot in the hearts of young people. Who may not have called any agencies at all.

Even so it's a job lead he can't refuse to explore. "Work out, how?"

"Do some shopping, make some meals. I'll pay you what I paid Jacinta, plus you'd get room and board."

"I couldn't be here all the time. I have clients at the gym, and at home I have responsibilities." He can't confess his pay from the gym is too low to free him from other obligations; feels embarrassed, a man in his twenties, he has to run home and . . .

"Vacuum once in a while?" she asks. But she isn't reading his mind, only calculating what it will take to keep her life going without Jacinta. "Just the house, really, no personal care, no health care. I'm not that decrepit, thank God. And no contract. We could go along day by day. You're free to stop whenever you say so."

"Sure, okay. Your brains and my brawn."

"Or, who knows, possibly the other way around. Deal?" Emeline puts out a trembling hand and he shakes it, feeling the tremor subside as their hands meet. In not too much time they've traveled from friendliness to respect to trust. What kind of a risk is he taking? Is she?

"In the morning, then, I'll draw up an agreement." At that he laughs, thinking of the informal deals struck in El Barrio all the time with nothing in writing. "And perhaps," her voice is deliberately casual, "if you have the time, you might help me look into a few things."

"I'll be straight with you, Emeline," he's reassured when she has the grace to grin, "on one condition: no mothering. I get enough of that at home. Also, do we have to explain, you know, about health things? Your friends, I mean. Won't they ask you if I'm positive?"

"My dear, they're much too polite. They won't even ask me if you're gay."

Chapter 7

With that settled, over the next day or so the two of them begin scrapping. Emeline doesn't want him smoking in the apartment, even in the spare room with the window open. So Xavier climbs the back stairs to the 10th floor where he unbolts a door and finds the short stairway to the roof. Someone has planted a bit of a garden up here, he checks to see if the greenery needs watering. He remembers the summer he first smoked, a 12-year-old, scrambling out the living room window to perch on the fire escape, cigarette cupped in his palm like Ramon. Autumn came, day by day it grew colder, and by then he was hooked, either on tobacco or stepping outside their tumultuous apartment.

One evening he comes back late to find Emeline awake and armed with a new critique. "Do you care about any of them, your young men?"

He's frankly shocked. "Why do you care if I do or don't?"

"What makes you think I care? Only it does seem a shame to waste all that . . . energy on indifferent partners."

"You want me to choose different partners? But I do, almost every time." Looking for a face like Alejandro's, with his smooth back, his shoulders shaped by nature, not a gym. He never revisits the sites of gay bars from the eighties like the Palladium and Ninth

Circle. Even if most turned out to be a pawn shop or a parking lot, in his mind the evening they spent searching is too dear. "If you're worried about my health, Emeline, no need. That train's left the station, remember?"

"Maybe this isn't a conversation we should be having."

"Agree with you there. Did you buy milk or do I go out first thing and get some?"

He should have had the sense to dodge the next argument, though it didn't begin as an argument, it began with a question. "How is it you read people so well, Xavier?"

"If you'd grown up like me, you would, too. It's self-protection."

"You don't know what it's like," Emeline began, working on a stretch he'd taught her to loosen her muscles, "growing up in a world where you don't belong."

"I can't believe you just said that. What would you know about not fitting in? You're part of the ruling class. Prosperous, white—"

"A kid in a new country? When I started school my accent was wrong. My clothes would have been wrong, too, except we wore uniforms."

"You're Catholic? You never told me you were Catholic."

"I wasn't Catholic, it was a private school. And my hair."

"What was wrong with your hair? Too straight?"

"Too wavy."

"So you use these big foam rollers . . ."

"To smooth it out, yes. All the other girls had straight hair, as if their mothers ironed it before they left in the morning."

"Their mothers ironed it? Unbelievable."

"A maid, more likely." Xavier makes a note to ask his mother if she has to iron Sophie's hair.

"You're the lucky one," Emeline persists. "You live in a close community. Everyone looks like you, speaks the same language, you share memories of the same island."

"Until I step outside," he corrects. "To get anywhere I have to step outside."

"You think you have it tough," Emeline says. "We had a candidate's wife saying she used to serve supper on the ironing board."

His sarcasm rising, Xavier says, "As if people with no money don't also deal with—"

"Errant husbands, sick children, inept teachers, I was making a *joke,* Xavier. You, though, have a world in common. Make the same food for holidays—"

"What about your friends? Tasteless chicken for supper and cucumber sandwiches for tea. Try a little Tabasco once, what the hell."

"Your temper, mister, it's as hot as your food."

The news doesn't go down well on 105th, either. He's being kind, Xavier tells his mother, working to keep the excitement out of his voice. Mrs. Hughes needs help with vacuuming, grocery shopping, cleaning up. He says nothing about "looking into a few things," which Emeline hasn't brought up again anyway.

"This Mrs. Hughes doesn't have a husband to help her with these?"

"He died, in a car crash on the Henry Hudson."

"Maybe I read about it in the paper." Since Flavia started working as a nanny she's addicted to gossip about people downtown. "You watch out, son. The maid's up and gone because this *blanca* is difficult to work for. You're an easy fill-in. You'll see."

Ramon has ideas of his own. "Hey, the kid's moving up to a fancier zip code. Big condo off, where?"

"Lexington Avenue," Xavier says then wishes he hadn't.

"White glove apartment," sniffs Flavia. "Doorman."

"And it's my business where I sleep, not yours."

Neither asks what he's getting paid. Ramon does say, "A straight shot downtown, I'll have to drop by."

"Forget about it." Xavier isn't worried; Ramon prefers to stay close to El Barrio. "You won't be helping yourself to anything at her place."

"Meeting her friends, young people she knows . . ." Flavia hesitates. "You gonna knock up some poor girl, get her pregnant like your sister. Then what?"

"Trust me, Mai. Nobody's gonna get pregnant."

His new housemate, it turns out, knows quite a few friends or at least people Emeline seems happy to ask over now that she has help again. Tactfully, she's bought him a plain blue shirt, no stripes, no cufflinks. Diplomatically, Xavier wears it with his black jeans when she's having friends in. Once when Xavier starts to clear away his *Sports Illustrated* lying on the coffee table next to her *Vogue* Emeline says, "Leave it. Maybe they'll think I'm becoming a senior athlete."

Women guests, mostly, and usually dressed in black like elegant guests at a San Juan funeral. With smooth, smartly curved grey hair, their own color or varnished a delicate silver, pure white or subtle blonde. Definitely not the blue-rinse crowd. Emeline's friends tend to have English names: Hope, Margaret, Elizabeth, or else Taylor, Tucker, Putnam, or Colby. Like, it's a law firm coming for lunch, Xavier's not always sure he'll be opening the door to a man or a woman.

Mostly they're women, though the lawyer Carl Cooper comes around now and then. "Handsome," observes Xavier. Coop's just left, he'd come for a drink and to check on his client's widow.

"I guess."

Then the odd nicknames: Muffy is for Margot; Tram, for Tramontana, her real name is Felicity. Happiness? Hardly. First time Tram comes by with her supercilious smile and blunt nails, she sits on the very edge of Emeline's damask couch, gripping her scuffed Coach bag as if the sight of a Latino face so close to her own can only mean a mugging.

"She's a bit Aspy," Emeline admits afterward. "You know, Aspergers? Brilliant, and the only girl in our class to get a graduate degree in science." Xavier knows Emeline has a few friends who'd gone to graduate school, if not as often as their daughters did. "Except poor Tram's tone-deaf to the niceties of social life." Emeline shows him the old photo, a row of girls in school uniforms. Plaid, square-necked jumpers can't hide the distinction between the cold stare a twelve-year old Tram produced for the cameraman and the determined smile of the blond English girl to her left.

"Tram's not her real name, of course. It started when we were at summer camp. A very cruel cabin mate said she was like the Tramontana, the cold wind that sweeps down from the—"

"NISJ, Emeline."

"Not In San Juan, no."

If Xavier ever day-dreamed about a place as spacious as Emeline's he'd expect to see sweeping, dramatic paintings to hang on the wall, not these puny scenes with nearly no color.

"Yo, dude! *Canilla,* vanilla." That's Ramon's assessment when Xavier describes the pale green living room sofa and chairs, the walls a green lighter by ten drops of Sherwin Williams, the ancient chest with drawers and brass buckles. Maybe a TV footman in a ruffled shirt will be coming along to open the drawers?

"It's how it's done, *Broki*." Xavier sounds smug, if secretly he agrees. He figures Emeline spent all her coin buying the condo and had to make do with these dowdy hand-me-downs.

Until he overhears one of her friends saying, "Emeline, dear, your little place looks perfect. Weren't you smart to go to Hare and Co." Used furniture people, Xavier guesses, he'll have to tell Flavia. His mother knows how to pick through a thrift store; she'd have come home with nicer goods. Bringing in more cake, he sees Emeline look around with an expression hard to read. Wary? Wistful?

"Guy Hare," the guest goes on, oblivious to the dismay in Emeline' eyes, "he always knows just what to do when you're downsizing. I always say: a good decorator is an investment." Xavier nearly drops the cake plate. The living room, it was done up like this on purpose?

By now he and Emeline have fallen into an amicable routine. She refrains from asking where he goes when he goes out evenings. He never asks about her ankle, apparently–quickly—healed. Emeline likes to rinse her own dishes and put them in the dishwasher, often leaving her rings for hours in the miniature Chinese bowl over the sink.

She continues to do her laundry in the tiny machine off the kitchen. He continues to carry his in a bundle and a pocket full of quarters to the local laundromat when he's going to Flavia's. Until one day, Emeline offers: "You know, Xavier, you can wash your clothes here, if you want. Except don't go dying anything black in the machine." She hadn't said "my machine," it almost made him feel like he belonged.

Xavier goes back to Flavia's one afternoon a week for a brisk dance with the heavy, old, noisy vacuum, very unlike Mrs. Hughes' vacuum, as trim as she is. It has to be when Jomar is awake. A window of time, thanks to his work at the gym and off-the-books job with Mrs. Hughes, that shrinks to a few hours of tension with Rocio, of watching his mother try to herd the family into a destiny that meets her standards. He plays with Jomar, buying him alphabet cards so he can start to learn to read letters.

"He's only ten months," whines Rocio.

"Can't start soon enough," Flavia defends her son and his cards. "A is for Father Alfonso," she holds up the card with a bright red apple. A is for Alejandro, thinks Xavier, sadly. Stuffing the vacuum into the closet crammed with winter jackets, sneakers, outgrown clothes and unused toys, he's glad when it's time to go back downtown.

He knows Flavia has done everything she could for her kids. When Ramon was six and Xavier four, the big first grader was making her proud. Ramon breezed into the high reading group and got gold stars on his grubby little papers. Even after he began to bring home warnings and more warnings, Flavia kept her hopes high.

Meanwhile the anxious mother grilled her second son with alphabet cards and flash cards, then one syllable and two syllable words. Good enough with letters and even words, good at reading people, even then, Xavier suspected he could never equal Ramon's early, dazzling grades. He knows the pressure began then in the undersize boy, cramming for kindergarten. If he couldn't be Flavia's brightest son, he could be the best behaved.

Answering the door at 7B, Emeline gives him a chilly stare. He has a key, yes, and next time, sure, he'll use it and not bother her. He hoists three d'Agostino's bags to show his hands are full. He's surprised by the display of fruit and vegetables at d'Ag, compared to the bodega where Flavia routinely shops. Even the beef looks as good as the meat Flavia finds in the Casablanca Meat Market when relatives are coming. He's debated about shopping at a less expensive grocery and pocketing the difference. Only d'Ag is closer, and Emeline always pays him back.

"Brought some supper," he explains.

"I'm afraid I don't really feel like food," she says, unsmiling.

"Anything I can do? Heat up some chicken?"

"I think you've done quite enough." She's studying him as if he is a stranger, swinging her gaze from his eyes to the small diamond stud in his ear

Emeline pivots on her cane; with stately determination she makes her way down the hall to her bedroom and shuts the door. Xavier's stomach is rumbling, his mind still on the stupid argument with Rocio. He starts some onions and sweet potato shreds in a skillet, thinking the aroma may draw Emeline out of her room. Only after he's nuked the left-over barbecued chicken legs and wolfed them down, does he wonder: is Emeline acting strange?

Mentally he ticks through the boxes in their agreement. He made her breakfast along with his own, cleared away the delicate plates, two bowls, his matching cup and saucer and the coffee mug she uses because it's easier to handle than her Wedgewood. Loaded the dishwasher, ignoring the rings she's left in the Chinese saucer over the sink. Made the bed in his room; already he's thinking of it as his room. Trash doesn't go to the back hall until tomorrow.

On the kitchen table he sees a J. Crew catalogue, an unopened telephone bill, what looks like an invitation with an embossed return address, though if she's received bad news she might have taken private mail into her room. Side-stepping Scaramouche, he walks into the living room and sits on the couch, hands between his knees.

Even the living room is quiet, the stereo for once turned off. Emeline's coolness was not fatigue from the day or irritation with a friend; she'd admit to the first and delight in retelling the second. It was aimed at him. He scans the room. The clock is there, "ormolu," she calls it; the two china birds. There's something . . . and he remembers Gregor's greeting. "Thought you'd come in already."

Xavier jumps up, runs lightly down the hall, knocks on Emeline's door, and is in her room before she says, "What?"

"Ramon was here. Wasn't he?"

"He needed to find you. Said your mother's trying to reach you and you're not answering your cell."

"Juice ran out," Xavier explains. She stares, unblinking. "Slang for—"

"Don't patronize me."

"How long was Ramon here?"

"Twenty minutes."

"And he said, man, how hot it is outside for September . . ." she looks startled. "You went to the kitchen to get him water or even make him tea. Didn't you."

"He said he was thirsty."

"I bet he did."

"Xavier, it seemed only polite." Emeline's voice grows sharp. "You jealous, bit of rivalry among the boys? You don't seem much like brothers at all. He's much more . . ."

"Puerto Rican? Boom box and low slung jeans?"

"Look, I didn't mean . . ."

"I gotta go out."

"Again?"

"Change of plans."

"Very well." He's surprised when her eyes fill with tears. "I believe I will call Tram, then, see if she wants to come eat with me. Since you bought all this food."

He turns his back on her sarcasm, gathers up his knapsack, and on his way out slams the front door. Down in the lobby he marches toward Gregor and stops five inches away.

The older man bristles. "You are in my face."

"Look at mine. Memorize it, you stupid Slav. The man who came in before was not me. Get it? That other man, whatever he says? Do not let him up again."

"You giving me orders?"

"You betcha." He lifts one closed fist and watches Gregor takes a step back.

"I tell Mrs. Hughes . . ." but Xavier is already on his way, jogging through the late afternoon crowd toward the 59th Street station, seething still as he goes two levels down to catch the express. As the IRT hurtles through the darkness Xavier sees his face reflected in the lighted car. He imagines his brother's face, a few hours earlier, a different train, going in the other direction.

Ramon, of course. Had Ramon followed him to 63rd Street before? Xavier has to take a stand before Ramon decides to come back with his posse and raise the threat level from orange to red.

The apartment on 105th is empty and it takes less than ten minutes before Xavier is out the door again, the trio of monogrammed silver boxes tucked in his knapsack. Catching the local so he has more time to think, he rattles back downtown.

He rings the bell at 7B. After a tantalizing wait Emeline slides back the deadbolt and opens the door. "You change your mind again?"

"Unless Tramontana's on her way over." He turns into the living room with Emeline trailing him, unpacks the little boxes, and sets them on their shiny circles faintly outlined with dust on the table.

Emeline says only, "We've got to get around to dusting."

"We will. It wasn't me, Emeline. It was Ramon."

"Of course," she agrees smoothly. "How did you know what he took?"

"I didn't, I only knew something was missing. You, though, you notice everything."

"About things maybe, not people. Not like you."

"I know where Ramon hides things. I found the boxes wedged into the toes of his old boots. You gonna call the police?"

She acts as if she hasn't heard him. "What will Ramon think when he finds the boxes gone?"

"He'll think it's time he stopped messing with me and my friends."

CHAPTER 8

Scaramouche appears, yawning and kneading his claws into the sky-blue duvet cover where it hangs toward the floor. Awake but moving slowly, Emeline knows she should take her meds and work on getting dressed. She lingers, hoping Xavier will bring her tea again. What a treat to have morning tea brought in.

It's like a dance, all these decisions, but who is leading, she or Xavier? Emeline's grateful for his company, even if it's not the same as chatting with a daughter would be. Not her own daughter, of course, acerbic, critical, bossy. Emeline was relieved when Deborah's daily phone calls faded to weekly, then no more than once in August, with a desultory email or two in between.

A knock on the door, Xavier doesn't like to assume. Emeline pulls on her new jacket. Should her bedroom be part of their common area, or is that too personal? "Come in." Xavier places the little tray on her bedside table and drops onto the chaise longue across the room. In a black T-shirt, tight black jeans, gold chains, and coughing, he lifts her glass of water from her Italian tile side table, Adam's apple moving like a metronome as he drinks.

Emeline smooths the front of her teal-blue quilted jacket and her diamond flashes. "You sick?"

"It's nothing. Nice bed jacket."

"Computer jacket," Emeline corrects. Always stiff in the mornings, she twists her wrists in and out, moves her shoulders up and down. "Bed jackets are for old women. You wear this snappy little number while you check your e-mail." Happily, she sips the tea.

"Tea's okay?"

"Very good." If his tea skills are a work in progress she knows this is not the moment for lessons. "You know, Aunt Mildred used to bring me tea in bed if I was sick."

"Where is she these days?" When she glances at the ceiling, as if Aunt Mildred might live overhead in 8B, he shakes his head and looks sorrowful.

"I do miss her; I wish she'd been around this summer. But don't you be sad, Xavier. She lived a great life. Aunt Mildred met her husband when he was in England during the war. You've heard what we Brits thought about the Yanks? Over paid, over-sexed, and over here. My aunt was lucky; like me she got the husband she wanted." Emeline wipes her eyes with her napkin.

"But, and no one saw this one coming, after Uncle Ray died Aunt Mildred moved to the Virginia countryside and kept horses. After she got too old to ride she took up carriage driving and bought herself a Bellcrown Focus. Quite the dream, for a girl from Peckham, wouldn't you say?" Then prays he won't ask: what was your dream?

In one of those moments when he seems to sense what's required Xavier says only, "You plan on getting up?"

"Give me twenty minutes. Fancy new phone you got."

"So you're skipping the apricot scrub, the aloe mist—I helped you unpack from Evelyn & Crabtree, remember."

"I'm skipping everything. Any chance there'll be those toasted flat breads again?"

"Sure," Xavier pushes himself to his feet, "with eggs and cheese. Twenty minutes. I'll go start the coffee."

Xavier knows twenty minutes is optimistic, so once the coffee machine is set to brew he heads for the expansive living room, a major perk of his new arrangement. Pushing the table aside, he devotes fifteen minutes to the tai chi moves he's been learning at the gym: sparring, self-defense, breaking. Too bad there isn't a mirror where he can see how his positions are developing.

Twenty minutes turns into forty-five before Emeline appears in tan J. Crew Slacks, a navy cashmere sweater, signature head band, daytime pearls, and—surprise, surprise—silver nail polish. Makes Xavier wonder if she's been the model for other older women he sees in her part of town, the ones who'd avoid his eye on a bus at all costs. "Wow. Look at you."

"I have to go see Tram, she's in a state."

"Again." Xavier hands her the sturdy mug she prefers. "What's worrying her now, Tramontana," Xavier loves using the full name of the chilly wind, "the florist, the caterer? The fact it's her son's third wedding?" He's heard from Emeline how the lithe *fashionista,* swinging down Madison eight months earlier, highlighted and anorexic, caught Julian's eye fast and his mother's resistance faster. "If she's coming here, let me remind you. Consulting on wedding plans is not in our agreement."

Emeline takes careful sips of coffee. Thank God she can take a little caffeine in the morning. Delicately, she picks up the silver sugar tongs to snare brown gobbets of cat food from a crystal bowl and one by one deliver them toward the floor. Alerted by the plink, plink as they land in his shallow Camperes dish, Scaramouche drops from his roost on the bookshelf and pads forward.

"A different problem. When you were reading this article about the Asia Society opening?" Tactfully she holds up *Art in America*. Xavier stares as if she's suggested he parse Urdu. "It mentions other owners who own pieces from China. Mentions, in fact, Tram."

Xavier yawns. Art is so not his thing. "So this is one of those newspaper phobias you people have."

"Three dealers have called her already. It's made Tram extremely jumpy. She's worried," Emeline lowers her voice, "about theft."

"On the tenth floor of a Park Avenue building, doorman on watch 24/7. Who's she expecting, Spider Man?"

"But Tram—"

"Is your problem. You deal with her, I'm due at the gym. You'll sort your pills?"

"L-dopa, vitamin D, calcium, that little pink one . . . I think I can manage." Across the glass-topped table Emeline reaches a hand spotted from decades of sun to touch Xavier's slender wrist, the color of café au lait.

"And, Xavier, maybe an early night, for a change?"

That's the closest Emeline's come to asking about his health. If she's even heard the word anti-viral she probably thinks it's a flu shot. Unless she was just trying to change the subject, until recently Emeline's been as private about her meds as Flavia is about money.

Young, fit, and energetic, Xavier never gave health a thought until the postcard came that changed everything, and how Alejandro was that: too cheap to spend a first-class stamp yet honor bound to let him know. A photo on the front of the famous Hollywood sign, and on the back, written in the language of flowers: "A garden filled with Veronica, Crisantemo, Salvia. Code for *Vaya a clinic subito*" . . . get to the clinic. "Sage, Iris, Dahlia, Almond Flower."

Three impenetrable levels of code, unless the postman is Latino and knows SIDA is Spanish for AIDS.

Back when men like Gabor's partner Ryan were frisky young guys, AIDS was a death sentence. Xavier knows he's lucky. Not everyone who's "pos" feels they have the flu and sick enough to go to the free clinic. Too many put off a visit until they have herpes or shingles. Still, the new stats don't help when he wakes up in the night, frightened; and often he does, staring at a possibly long life ahead.

Only he can't see what to do with it. Training self-obsessed New Yorkers at the gym, helping out a woman with a disease of her own, a sharp manner, and good soul: is that enough?

Returning to Emeline's past midnight, Xavier savors the moment when the elevator door will slide open and he'll see the small antique table with the vase, the black and white tile. Steamed from the bath, well fed, sexually content, and a bit light-headed, he turns his key in the lock. The hallway dark, his fuzzy brain registers the rectangle of light in Emeline's bedroom door, interrupted by an agitated silhouette, a short pyramid topped with sunrays.

"Xavier Escudero," Emeline's irate figure practically flies down the hall, the pyramid growing larger as her robe flaps, the foam rollers in her hair wobbling under a cover of netting. "Where the hell have you been? You tell me I should get a cell phone and you can't bother to turn—"

"Whoa!" Xavier holds out hands so she misses barreling into him. "No mothering. You promised. What's that thing on your head?"

"Lace night cap. Xavier, not everything is about you, we have to get over to Tram's right away, she's had a burglary and whoever robbed her has murdered that handsome doorman."

When Xavier raps sharply on the heavy glass at 1088 Park, a reluctant, uniformed policeman unlocks the door. Yellow emergency tape stretches across the left side of the lobby, a cluster of cops huddle around a long shape nearly hidden under a sheet. One cop holds a tiny phone to his ear, barking expletives in a rhythm that sounds like *ska*. A woman in a navy blue Yankee cap snaps photographs, her flash punctuating the scene like strobe at a disco.

Through the sleeve of her Burberry raincoat Xavier grips Emeline's arm; she seems to be doing a convincing improv of a lady whose breeding exceeds her capacity. Swaying and covering her mouth with one hand, she gets the officer's attention.

"You all right, ma'am? You can see we've got a crime scene here."

"Lipscomb. Tenth floor," Emeline says in a slurred voice."

"You," the officer commands Xavier, "your lady's about to pass out, get her home."

The doorman, what had been the doorman, lies curled on his side as if succumbing to the nap he'd dreamed about for thirty years on his feet. One arm is flung out; even horizontal he seems to be hailing a cab. An oddly shaped crimson pool spreads under his body, darkening the hunter-green coat. Someone has undone a few brass buttons and unloosened his collar. No use, given the knife stuck at an angle from his lower chest; but below the tender hollow at the base of his neck Xavier catches sight of a tattoo.

"You don't look so good yourself, mister," the policeman gloats, "your first?" If only. Twice in El Barrio Xavier's come across a dead body.

The elevator door closes. Xavier asks, "You okay?" With a sniff Emeline shakes off his arm and punches the button for ten.

In a printed housecoat, on duty even when out of uniform, the haughty Mrs. Fairfax answers the door. Behind her, gawky and frowning, Tram clutches her plaid wool robe close to her belly and grabs Emeline's arm with her free hand. In formation they troop back to the kitchen. Mrs. Fairfax would never take a seat in the living room and tonight of all nights Tram needs her housekeeper.

"It's a disaster," Tram weeps, dropping into a chair and leaning heavily on the round oak pedestal table.

"You poor dear! What'd they get? Your jewelry alone, I'm guessing, two, three hundred thousand." In Emeline's circle the more the dollars, the less the bling. Tram would be an anomaly if she ever wore her stash.

"No jewelry, no cash, not the laptop, or silver. Only the statue: the Scarsdale Doxy. How I'm ever going to tell Julian I don't know. Although I suppose he'll be relieved I wasn't hurt."

Emeline glances at Xavier. Julian's airy disregard for his mother is no secret. "Julian was that fond of him?" Emeline says, reminding Tram of the real tragedy. "I never realized."

Fingering a small square of cardboard, Tram looks blank. "Her, you mean. The Scarsdale Doxy. Ninth Century, of course, she's been in the family since Grandfather Caldecott went with the Harvard archaeologist to excavate on the Silk Route. Foreign Devils, they called them, the westerners who trailed from Luong to Uigar. " Xavier yawns, hoping to get to bed before dawn.

"But why now, Tram?" Emeline asks.

"It's that horrible article, of course." Tram lays the cardboard on the round oak table. "I know Julian's going to say I should sue. You know how upset he's been about seeing my name in *Art in America*. It's Julian who insisted we cancel our plans and hold the wedding here," Tram lifts her hand in the direction of her expansive living room. Xavier holds back a smile. He's heard how the chic fiancée had hoped for the Colony Club, a Vera Wang dress, and at least a half column in the *Sunday Times' Style* section.

The kitchen door swings open. Swiftly, Emeline moves her hand over the small cardboard and slides it into her Burberry pocket. It's Julian himself, wearing a striped muffler flung around his turtleneck, mussed khakis, and loafers with no socks.

"I can't believe it." He sinks into the housekeeper's vacant chair, exuding an aroma of Musk even in the middle of the night. Julian nods to Emeline and ignores Xavier. "Who would want to kill poor old Kevin? You must have been scared out of your wits, Mother."

"I'm afraid there's more, Julian," Tram begins bravely, but her voice fails her.

"Is gone," Mrs. Fairfax begins. "She gone." Emeline stares at the ceiling; Julian has to turn to Xavier, who simply spreads his hands and shrugs.

"De shkouzel dozhy," supplies Mrs. Fairfax, accents of the Ukraine undimmed by an American husband and forty years in New York.

"What is she talking about, Mother?"

"Darling, I know what she means to you—and two days before the wedding."

"What? No. I just left her, she's asleep."

"Na, na, shkouzel—"

Tram covers her eyes with her hands. Julian leans forward. "She's not talking about—the statue? Mother, tell me nothing's happened to *her*."

"Da, da!"

"Oh, shut up, Valda," snaps Julian. "It's that article. Crap! I told you people would come sniffing around." Tram lets out a moan and thin streams of tears melt past her crumpled fingers.

"Bad pipples," Mrs. Fairfax intones, drawing on centuries of mournful prose. "Brek in. Shteal the dozhey. Keel dat nice Kyevan. Aie, aie, aie."

"You know, Tram," Emeline points out, "you're going to have to tell the police."

"With the wedding in two days? No way, we'll have a circus up here," complains Julian, adding a beat too late: "poor Kevin."

"It's a murder investigation, dear boy."

"Wait until Monday, Emeline. After that, sure, we can tell them we've discovered — what do you think *you're* doing?" Julian rounds on Xavier."

"Yes, Xavier, stop stalking the perimeter like a panther," Emeline says. "Sit."

"This door was locked all night?" Xavier asks Tram, who looks vaguely at Mrs. Fairfax. The housekeeper nods. "And the front door, too? I hate to rain on your party, *amigos*. But you do realize there's no sign at all of a break-in?"

When the front door buzzes everyone jumps. Recovering first, Mrs. Fairfax stalks off to do her duty and comes back with another visitor. Is it having the police in her kitchen or the six-foot man of color? Tram looks uneasy.

"Detective Percy Hill," he says. "I'm afraid, Ma'am, there's been a death in the lobby. Older gentleman, name of Kevin Shaughnessy." Out comes a PDA which he lays on the table and after it a small pad of paper, edges smudged with notes on the city's malfeasance. "He's been murdered."

Mrs. Fairfax covers her mouth, Tram gives a theatrical gasp. "Some addict, probably." Julian sounds nervous. "Terrible. Terrible."

"Just to get the picture here," the detective goes on. "Mrs. Lipscomb," his gaze swings uncertainly between Tram and Emeline.

Tram lifts a ringed hand off the table. "Then you're the son, Julian Lipscomb." Julian nods curtly. "So this must be Mrs. Fairfax?" For the first time a respectful smile. Good God. Has the detective got the whole building on his Blackberry?

"As for you two," the smile fades. "Not part of the family. Off to a good start, aren't we, lying to the police. What are you doing here?"

"Detective, your men questioned our coming in at such a late hour," Emeline's voice is silky, "my nephew and I. All I said was Lipscomb, tenth floor. They must have misunderstood."

Xavier puts an arm around Emeline's shoulder, tenderly strokes her cheek. "Darling, level with the detective, he's seen it all, I'm sure," and under the table stamps on her foot. Conveniently, her face turns red. "My name is Xavier Escudero, officer. And this is Mrs. Clifford Hughes."

The detective studies her face, frowns. "We haven't met, have we?"

"We have not."

"Thought I'd heard the name."

"Mrs. Lipscomb telephoned her because of the sirens," Xavier explains, "when she wasn't able to reach her son. Very old friends these two. We came right over."

"You arrived at," he consults his notebook, "two forty. And Mr. Lipscomb, you were where, sir?"

"My apartment in Soho. Ask my fiancée, she's there now, asleep. I came as soon as I picked up Mother's message."

"What time was that, sir?"

"I don't know, I got up to—I saw the light blinking on the machine."

"On your way to the bathroom," the detective suggests.

Tram looks outraged. Theft, murder, and now urination? "Detective, my son is getting married the day after tomorrow. We still have a great deal to do, so if you don't mind—"

"Any enemies?"

"He was a kind, kind old man," Julian steps in, "been here since I was a boy. But truthfully, you know how it is in New York. We knew nothing about him, really." Julian spreads his fingers eloquently: the city so large, our lives so busy.

"But he'd know you, wouldn't he," the detective fires back. "Thing is, as you'd realize living here for years and all, the front door is locked after midnight. So, either the killer had no trouble persuading Shaunessey to unlock the door. Or the killer was already in the building." This is met with a silence so complete that when the birdsong clock begins to chirp three-thirty, even Xavier gives a start.

"Excuse me," Tram murmurs and runs out of the kitchen. Ignoring the detective, Emeline follows to console her friend in her hour of great inconvenience. Xavier spells out their names and gives Emeline's address. No sense getting Flavia involved. More questions, some skillful bargaining (sleep deprivation, dear Emeline's health) and Detective Hill allows them to leave.

"How could you!" hisses Emeline as Xavier hails a cab out cruising before dawn.

"Jesus, your nephew? That detective's going to check our names, addresses. And what about you, what did you pocket when Julian came in?" Emeline hands him the piece of cardboard. Under the street lights pulsing as the cab speeds down Park, the black and white photograph reveals a statue of a Chinese woman wearing an enigmatic expression and a robe with pleats sharp enough to cut cheese.

"That's her, the Scarsdale dachsie? She's not even German."

"Doxy," she corrects. "In Britain a doxy means a woman who, kind of a—"

"Got it. But why?"

"My husband started it, the devil, said the statue looked as if she'd been on the Scarsdale diet too long. The name stuck."

Like Tramontana; the trouble this crowd goes to when they baptize children only to watch their names slide into new letters. "Bet you folding money Julian took it."

"Did you see how shocked he looked? And snapping at Valda Fairfax like that when Valda practically brought him up. Tram as a mother, not exactly—" luckily, she stops, Xavier is in no mood for a lecture on child development.

"Julian has a key. He could have come in earlier, gone out again, Shaughnessy would hardly notice him."

"It's not Julian," Emeline insists.

"You sure? Paranoid, spoiled, likes to gamble? You told me so yourself."

"And here speaks the psychologist."

"I work at a gym, tell me what about human nature don't I see." Xavier can feel Emeline shaking more than usual. He puts his arm around her. "*Pobrecita*," he murmurs. "We're almost home."

"I've never seen—except that one time, Clifford. You've seen how many dead? Stabbed. Or shot." Xavier doesn't answer. "But you, you're fearless, aren't you? Your mother is the anxious one and nothing frightens you."

Xavier hears the meter click over. Cab rides, another way to hear the minutes go by. "Until now."

"The doorman? No, you mean your . . . condition. I'm so sorry, I didn't think. You've got to get more rest, Xavier." The cab pulls to a stop. Emeline pays the meter and hands a twenty as a tip to the startled night doorman. "Glad you're keeping well, Alfredo."

"I never thought you saw your doormen as, you know, people." Xavier says in the elevator.

"Nonsense. Alfredo is putting his daughter through New York University, I help where I can."

Soon after they're home, he knocks on her bedroom door to find her still dressed and asleep on her bed. Gently he pulls off her shoes and tucks a blanket around her. September nights are turning cool.

Chapter 9

The Greek pizzeria on the corner is already exhaling onions and peppers when Xavier tiptoes out early next morning. He speed dials his gym to reschedule his one appointment, makes three more calls while he power walks to the 51st Street station, then catches the Broadway Line to Queens. In Jackson Heights he finds the street where a handful of Irish families hold their ground against the mixed accents of Central America. He talks to four people, stops for an early lunch of *empanadas,* crosses back under the East River on the F train, works his way to Chelsea, and makes a quick stop.

Uptown on the Lexington local then a block walk to Third. Outside the Cuban coffee shop a sandwich wrapper on the sidewalk draws a trio of pigeons. Detective Hill is sprawled on a banquette in the back.

"What have you got for me," barks the large man.

"How's it goin'?" Xavier counters. "Wanna join me in a coffee?"

"This ain't a date, Escudero. You called me, remember? Said you didn't feel comfortable," the detective manages to sound like Dr. Phil, "coming into the station. I'm a busy man. Let's have it."

Xavier plucks up the plastic menu leaning between salt and pepper twins, studies it for a long minute while the waitress snaps her pencil against her order pad and the detective glares. "An espresso, large. A slice of your *tres leches* cake. And separate checks," he adds, before the growl across the table can blossom into protest.

"Detective Hill, appreciate you meeting me here. Some of us are still a little, you know, sensitive about the reception we get at headquarters? Which—" he raises a hand to stop Hill's impatient snarl, "is why Shaughnessy never told anyone at 1088 Park about his private life. Yet it seems our doorman . . . no sign of a wife, right?"

"Divorced."

"Says?"

His mug halfway to his mouth, Hill pauses. "The super in his building, couple a neighbors."

"I talked to a couple a neighbors myself. None of them ever saw any women."

"A few nephews over the years, the super says, his sister's kids."

"Shaughnessy had no sisters," corrects Xavier. "Grew up in Jackson Heights, his mother drank, his father beat up on her. His older brothers," Xavier pauses to try the cake and because he can, "they got out early, one to Boston, one to Miami. Irish diaspora, you know. A gay closeted man—"

"Closeted? No one could accuse you of that. Boy-toy, my ass. You and your Mrs. Hughes, you should have stuck with 'nephew'."

"We're sorry. We were rattled. Good cake by the way, want a bite? No? An older guy like Kevin Shaughnessy, I bet he thought it would mean his job if people knew."

"Even if half the folks at 1088 are bleedin' hearts, more likely to ask him for dinner with their decorator than fire him. Seems somebody knew, though. Besides you."

"I'll take that as a compliment."

"You can take it as my wantin' to know how you found out."

"One of your men. He'd pulled back Shaughnessy's collar to check his pulse. I saw the tattoo." Xavier's thin fingers push a business card across the table, only half covering the black and white line drawing of a Phoenix. "You remember the red AIDS ribbon."

"Society ladies at a Symphony benefit," snorts the detective. "Long Island train conductors with five kids in Hempstead. Lord, I'd be on duty at some fancy party, looked like the red tide'd come in, everyone was wearing 'em."

"Everyone except older gay men worried about job security. Bound to happen, then—someone opened a club. Niche market, you might say." Xavier taps his fingers on the card. "The guy to talk to is Richie, assistant manager at the Phoenix. Do not, repeat *not*, go to the manager, who never comes in until five or six anyway. Or there'll be, what do you guys call it? A lock down. Richie liked Shaughnessy. Richie's sense of justice, for the moment, beats his discretion."

"Salvai," Hill says. Xavier looks blank. "Your name, right?"

"Xavier," he corrects, sounding the *X* like an old man clearing his throat. "My mother wanted the old-fashioned spelling." And it sounded like Flavia, but he doesn't say it.

"I wouldn't know how many clubs like this we got in the city, and you just happened to find this one."

"Happened to? Took me most of the day and I missed my gym appointment.

"Building muscle?"

"Trying to make a living. Personal trainer."

"Who killed him?"

"I don't know, Detective, I gotta do all the heavy lifting, here? I'm guessing if you start here," Xavier taps the card again, "you'll find out."

Hill reaches out two stocky fingers to pluck the card and store it in his raincoat pocket. "Listen, before you think we're puttin' you on the payroll—I haven't ruled out your pals. Mrs. Lipscomb, or that son of hers."

"Can't you see Julian Lipscomb wrestling the doorman to the ground? While his mother holds his Brooks Brothers jacket for him."

"What if Shaughnessy caught him leaving the building with, I don't know," Percy Hill stares unblinking at Xavier. "Like a thief. Any ideas on that?"

"What, the plasma TV, his mother's fur coat?" Xavier puts down his cup. "I wonder if it was a girl. His last night of freedom—"

"In his mother's apartment? You gotta be kidding me."

"Not there," Xavier concedes. "Try the fiancée, why don't you? See what time Julian really got home. What about all the rest of the people in 1088? Plenty of other stories there, I bet."

"Still digging." For the first time the detective smiles. "'Course, anything makes more sense than a hopped-up addict bangin' on the glass, persuading one of Park Avenue's guardians to unlock the front door." He slurps the last of his coffee.

"Now, I got somethin' to tell you. How did Mrs. Lipscomb know Shaughnessy had been murdered? Police had no sirens. Blue lights only, after someone in the building phoned it in. We have some respect for 'sleep deprivation' in the one-nine. Well, lemme tell you. It was the housekeeper."

"Mrs. Fairfax. She's from the Ukraine. You can't always tell from names."

"Lady says she was up in the night, saw flashing lights out the front window, and took a ride down to the lobby. By the way, Escudero, I never met your Mrs. Hughes before the other night but I've heard her name. Pal of mine in the one-ten had to give her the bad news when her husband died. You sure there's nothing else you want to tell me?"

Xavier thinks of Emeline, looking over her shoulder when they're out in the street, asking about the men in the Conservatory Garden, and to distract the detective pushes forward his plate. "Jeez, all right. The wife has me on the South Beach diet. Makin' me crazy."

What's left of the tres leches cake disappears and Hill looks hard at Xavier. "So the husband's death was an accident?"

"So she says. Julian's free to go on with his wedding, then."

"Afraid so."

"I'm with you, Detective, I don't give them great odds."

"Do I look like a marriage counselor?" Hill growls. "Point is, his fiancée, as a wife come Sunday she can't be forced to testify."

Back at the apartment Xavier finds Emeline drinking tea in the kitchen and looking tired. She listens to his report while Scaramouche purrs on her lap. "This would be what you call gay-dar, I suppose."

"Not even. Last night, when you were fainting away in the lobby—"

"Providing you with leeway to look around, you mean."

"One of the officers had opened the doorman's collar. I saw the tattoo."

"And you suspect some mysterious man, maybe a jealous lover? Sounds farfetched if you ask me."

"And here I thought you'd be relieved."

"Your theory does take the heat off Julian," Emeline admits. "In case Julian is a person of interest—stop smirking, the police on television talk like that all the time." Xavier's cell phone buzzes against his hip. He pulls it out.

"Don't mind me, Xavier, go ahead and take it."

"He's texting." Xavier moves two thumbs at warp speed and snaps the phone shut. "Interesting. The fiancée's changed her story."

"Talk about your doxies."

"Julian came home from his stag party but not at eleven thirty. Julian didn't get in until after two."

"Do you realize what you've done?" Emeline is alarmed. The cat jumps off her lap and flees. "That girl will call off the wedding. Tram will be furious!"

"Tram would probably give me a medal, but it's not gonna happen. This is one fiancée who isn't going to let a last-fling f—" Emeline winces, "a last boy's-night-out ruin her plans. The fiancée already knew, don't you see? All she did was own up." Emeline mutters under her breath, sounds like *silly cow*. "Which means," Xavier draws out his pen and makes careful, horizontal lines on Emeline's flowered paper napkin. "Julian has more than two hours unaccounted for."

Staring into the depths of her mug as if reading tea leaves, Emeline shakes her head. "I can't see where he has a motive. Kevin Shaughnessy's known Julian since he was a boy, letting Julian in or out of the building whatever the hour." Xavier shrugs, unconvinced.

"But Xavier, if it wasn't Julian we have another problem; and if Hill doesn't have to think about it, we do. If a gay lover as the killer sounds like a stretch—what are the odds of a homicidal gay lover with a taste for Ninth-Century Chinese sculpture?"

"However will we carry it off?" Tram's sitting on the edge of a rented bamboo chair, hands clenched, neck stretched forward like a gull. Lined up in a semi-circle, the chairs make her living room look more like a theatre than a church.

"Not like that," snaps Emeline. "Get off your fanny and follow me." Shoulders pulled back and down, she tucks her left hand into the arm of an imaginary usher, and glides across the living room in her blue silk sheath and dressy Ferragamos.

"You can take the girl off the runway," says Julian, looking in his black tux more pompous than usual. "But you can't take the runway out of the girl."

Asshole. She frequents charity benefits, Xavier wants to say, you don't have to make it sound like she's pole dancing.

"Such a shame dear Deborah couldn't be here," Tram says. "Or even your brother."

"I'm sure Deborah will have another chance," offers Emeline. Xavier tries not to smile; he gets it, though her true meaning goes right over Tram's head.

"You have a brother?" Xavier murmurs as Mrs. Fairfax whisks the groom off to the kitchen to stuff him with ginger cookies and unwanted advice. Emeline nods. "You never mentioned a brother. Where's he live?"

"In England."

Emeline engineers a forced retreat to the library, transporting the mother of the groom, her tea-length gown, and her brocade shoes so the fiancée and her sister can fluff and fluster in Tram's mirrored bedroom.

Musicians turn up and tune up. The minister arrives, his robe draped over one arm, his breath a heavy cloud of Chardonnay. Guests step off the elevator to swap air kisses and position themselves on the bamboo chairs. Looking for anyone he might identify as a plainclothes person, Xavier's keeping his eye on a petite, sleekly dressed woman with olive skin loitering near the door; until her preppy boyfriend comes in and lifts a circle of pale green orchids in greeting.

The ceremony moves along like expensive clockwork, ending with a kiss and a burst of applause. The bride looks triumphant, Julian dazed, Tram resigned. Efficient young men in white shirts and black pants move the chairs aside, then reappear carrying teetering flutes of champagne and hors d'oeuvres whose size has to be in inverse ratio to their price.

"Lavish," murmurs Emeline in his ear as they survey the meager buffet spread out in the dining room. Xavier's sure she's being ironic until he sees she isn't. Pigeons would starve on such a diet.

Only one suggestion of a glitch: when the time comes to cut the cake the bride look around, puzzled. Emeline by his side is all at once very still. In seconds the wait staff bustles back carrying trays heavy with small plates of cake. Mrs. Fairfax, whispering to the musicians, begins to clap. In seconds the applause catches on, competing with the accordion's vivid *brio*.

Untethered in a sea of well-heeled WASPs, still hungry, and battered by the din of voices, Xavier is edging slowly toward the door when an elegant older man in a pinstripe suit and deep maroon foulard stops him

"A word? Detective Hill wants you to know," the man coughs discretely, "that his visit to the Phoenix paid off. Richie had a name to offer in connection with the, er, trouble here. The other night," he adds in case Xavier might think he means the wedding. "Hill has him in custody. Another older man, though there seems lately to have been a young cub involved to cause tension between the two. Very sad."

"Everything all right, officer?" Gliding up, Emeline tucks her hand under Xavier's elbow.

Clifford's Ghost

"Mrs. Hughes, is it? Pleasure to meet you. If you ever need our help at all," he hands her a card, a discrete NYPD icon in the corner. "Or if you think you might be able to help us out in any way."

"This gentleman has just been thanking us for our work, Em—Mrs. Hughes."

"I am curious," the man adjusts his foulard. "The two of you, have you done this kind of work before?"

"Now and again, just to help out. A knack, really. Like ice skating. Won't you take a piece of cake with you?" Emeline holds out a miniature box wrapped with thin gold ribbon. The plainclothes man shakes his head, touches two fingers to his forehead, and slips out the door.

"You knew he was police, Emeline?"

"That ascot? Please. Noel Coward straight from central casting."

"But ice skating"

"I know. NISJ. Not in San Juan. The reception's about over. Still, I think we might keep Tram company a bit longer. And you can tell me what else Noel Coward had to say. Oh look, here they come," Emeline cries, giddy as a girl. The groom, wearing his new wife on his arm, his new wife wearing her new Armani suit, fly down the hall in a hail of paper rose petals and into the waiting elevator.

"Elevator," observes Emeline, "Perfect. Talk about starting married life with its ups and downs." The guests leave, the caterers clean up and leave. Xavier and the three women are once again sitting in Tram's kitchen.

"Tram," Emeline begins," you might be interested to know the police caught your doorman's murderer." Tram looks not a bit interested. "It seems he had no connection to the theft after all." A surprisingly large part of the cake sits in the center of the kitchen table. Deliberately, Emeline runs her finger along the top layer and licks the icing, closing her eyes with satisfaction.

"Caramel butter cream," she murmurs. "You have been at the top of your game, Mrs. Fairfax. Perhaps I will have another slice, since there still seems to be so much left." Emeline lifts a knife toward the upper layer and cuts. "Or, did you think you ought to make two cakes, just in case?

"We really muffed that one, didn't we, Xavier." Emeline picks up the wedge of cake with dainty fingers. "Not paying attention, not asking how our two friends, here, knew there'd been a murder. What were you doing up in the night, Valda, baking already? Or was it learning about the murder that gave you the idea?"

In case Xavier's mind is slowed from champagne, Emeline tilts up the outer corner of one eye, trying to look Asian while smudging caramel butter cream on her eyebrow.

"Oh, dear," sighs Tram. Mrs. Fairfax, her round cheeks turning pink, bites her lower lip.

"The Scarsdale Doxy," Xavier guesses. "She's hiding in the cake. But, why?"

"Julian's debts," Tram confesses. "Three years ago I was forced to sell the original. So I had a copy made." As consolation she helps herself to a finger scoop of butter cream icing. "After the article came out in *Art in America* and dealers started calling? I knew they'd spot the copy in a minute if they ever saw it. And when Valda found out there'd been a murder she was terrified the police would come in, turn the place upside down. It was her idea to hide the statue in the cake." Valda's lower lip trembles, remembering police in the Ukraine.

"For three years I've worried I'd die, Julian would go to sell his legacy, and find out it was gone. Now he'll never have to know.

So don't you think, in a way, poor Kevin's murder solved a big problem? You know, I think I might be able to collect on the insurance." Tram smiles around the table, quite pleased with the way it's all worked out.

Xavier is speechless. Even Emeline looks appalled. "Honestly Tramontana," Emeline scolds, "sometimes . . ."

"What?" asks Tram, genuinely puzzled.

Emeline picks up her beaded clutch and pushes back her chair. "Come along, Xavier."

Xavier waits until they're in the elevator to ask, "What did he mean, that policeman: if you could ever help them?"

"Couldn't tell you."

He makes one more try when they get home. "What the policeman said, was it connected with Clifford's death?"

"I have no idea what you're talking about."

"So it was an accident," Xavier continues when Emeline looks away, "nothing to do with the way you act when we're outdoors, looking over your shoulder."

"I really cannot have this conversation." She blows her nose on one of her embroidered handkerchiefs. "I plan to run a bath and have an early night. As for you, Xavier, you have too much imagination for your own good."

CHAPTER 10

"I suppose it's the same with your people," Emeline says the next morning, "all this fuss over a wedding."

"All Latinos in all countries, you mean, and I'm supposed to be the expert?" Xavier relents. "To begin with there's a First Communion, that's a girl's white dress number one. Some countries throw a *quincinera* when a girl turns fifteen, white dress number two. Weddings can come third with 'my people.' What about your own wedding?"

"My wedding caused nearly as much trouble as Julian's. Certainly the idea of it did."

Back in the city from East Hampton, Cliff called the next week and invited her to take a Circle Line cruise around Manhattan. She'd never been, naturally, the Circle Line being for tourists. Clifford pointed out sights she hadn't seen from this angle, if at all. As the boat zipped back to the dock, he'd put an arm around her shoulders and casually kissed her cheek.

Next, after a carriage ride in Central Park and more kissing, more serious, Emeline suggested they try spending time together without the moving scenery. Rudy's became their place, around the corner from Clifford's bachelor apartment. Since the Third Avenue

El had been torn down, letting light reach a few windows part of the day, developers were arriving in droves; in a few more years Rudy's, its mixed drinks and mixed clientele, would be replaced by Café Angelo and hordes of slick, young professionals.

Finally Emeline allowed Clifford to pick her up at the apartment and meet Aunt Mildred. Her aunt, clearly wary, proved more of a snob than Emeline had guessed.

"The Buccaneers backwards, is it—wealthy Brit coming to court a well-brought up American gel?" Aunt Mildred's accent deepened when she was upset. Yes, she hoped to marry him, Emeline said when grilled. Yes, she hoped to finish Wellesley but maybe not. No, she was not pregnant. Yes, the Junior League was a fine way to meet people if she ever moved to another city. Emeline bit her tongue so as not to say more. Those aren't the people I'd want to meet; I know enough of them already.

Emeline could have made quite a meal of the story today. Only she's pretty sure Xavier's knowledge of buccaneers is limited to an action film about eighteenth-century pirates, not nineteenth-century New York heiresses marrying English lords, the parties involved trading cash for a title or a title for cash, and risking a lifetime of misery.

Emeline persisted. Clifford charmed. Aunt Mildred relented. For the wedding Becataurus Florist did their usual handsome job with the flowers (which ended up where they belonged at St. James and not, as in the florists' only ever mix-up, two blocks north decorating Madison Avenue Presbyterian). All went well. Even if the new Mrs. Hughes, smiling in the Gabor Eder wedding photo, looked young enough to risk a call from DSS if not the DA.

"You still look young for your age, Emeline."

"You don't actually know my age." Flirting, anyone watching them would say. Not really, but safe in their own zones the two of them felt free to be more playful as the days went on.

Little by little Emeline's letting Xavier into her life. First it's the kitchen: low-hanging fruit to be sure, she's never had a sense of hegemony over her kitchen. She's given away all the clever Williams Sonoma cooking toys that guests, who didn't know her as well as they might, brought as gifts over the years. Emeline can turn out an omelet, a roast chicken if pressed, boil new red potatoes, and compose a salad. Until Xavier arrived she's subsisted much of the time on take-away. These days he shops, though if she's just taken her pills and feels peppy she'll go along to buy the occasional paté for Scaramouche.

"What's that cat's name about, Emeline?"

"Scaramouche? A character in the Italian *commedia dell'arte*."

"Whatever that is."

"It's old-fashioned Italian theatre. Scaramouche's a burlesque of a Spanish don—you know, a lord? Like, for instance, Don Xavier Escudero."

"Gimme a break, lady."

Xavier's easier to have around than she expected. When he walks he doesn't stamp, he accepts the genteel violins and winds she likes on her stereo. She's seen him practicing slow, precise tai chi moves to a Schumann nocturne, then discretely tugged the coffee table back to the center of the room on occasions when he forgot. Best of all, he's discrete. He's never asked why certain ladies snubbed her at Luca's fashion show or mentioned anything his mother may have read about Clifford in the New York *Post*.

Clifford's Ghost

In her old life Emeline always had people under foot: a cook, a caterer who came in when Clifford was expecting a crowd, a weekly cleaning service; Emeline never knew the women's names and the women seemed to change often. Hardly PC on his best days, Clifford called them all Maria, but not to their face after Emeline told him it was gauche. Thursdays, a woman with a pony tail and body piercing came to do the flowers. Clifford loved the subtle scent of freesias, if not so much the jewelry.

And, of course, an au pair when Deborah was small. Other young mothers liked to hire women with accents from Mayfair or Knightsbridge. Emeline preferred a nanny whose speech, even if more proper, did not raise echoes of sadness for the mother she'd left behind in Peckham. One au pair, a young woman from Bruges with a near-Parisian accent and the face of an angel, impressed Emeline's friends, delighted Deborah, and left abruptly after the theft. Clifford was partly to blame, he forgot to move a stack of cash out of his briefcase and into the safe in his closet.

With staff and strangers in and out of the apartment on 95th Emeline's grown used to a lock on a drawer. Remembering how one stranger, posing as a possible buyer, searched Clifford's old study, she's been tempted to create a mountain of papers to discourage any new snoopers ... file folders, files, bills paid and unpaid, unanswered notes, old invitations, papers, post-its, abandoned cups of tea trailing a tail and a tag. She couldn't, her temperament didn't allow it. Emeline keeps the key rolled up in a lacy black half-slip in her underwear drawer.

Until the day she wakes up with a cough, a fever, and the co-op check due. Xavier, bringing her tea and toast, looks concerned. "Did you sleep at all?" Choking, unable to answer, she waves him off the foot of the bed to the chair beyond. "Emeline, cancel your plans and telephone the doctor's office. You need to go in, I'll take you."

For once she doesn't argue, "but first, I need a favor." From under her pillow she draws out the Lilliputian brass key she retrieved in the night. "My checkbook is in the top drawer in the den, if you'd fetch it for me."

He looks suspicious. "Is this a test?"

"What? If you'd wanted to snoop, I'm sure you have the skills." Neither mentions the lobster picks. "Go get me the checkbook, an envelope, and a stamp, if you please. It is not my habit to pay bills late."

"Xavier?" she calls when the front door opens. Though quiet days have helped her cold, her voice is still croaky. "Telephone your mother, will you? She wants to talk to you."

"Her and I talked two days ago. Unless," he looks worried, "is she sick, too?"

"She's fine, only she says it's important, it's about her job. She wants us both to take tea with her." Emeline sees the thought alone makes him cringe: these two women in the same room.

"Forget it. Far as I know my mother's 'taken tea' twice in her life. Once when she had the flu and once after Rocio was born. Tea brewed each time by her friend Renata."

"Xavier, we must go see what your mother wants. Maybe we can lend a hand. At least we can listen, that might help her."

"I'm not your child, so don't try to make me feel guilty. If it's a problem with Mrs. Wells, let her call the civil-rights commission. You and I are not the police—"

"You think she'll need the *police?*"

"'Course not," he snorts. "We never call the police." They stare at each other like strangers, trying to understand the chance that brought them together and grasp a symmetry they can't avoid. One, fighting free of a mother by turns devoted and demanding, the other with a daughter across an ocean and not sure even that is far enough. Determined, Emeline waits. Xavier blinks first.

"You go, then, and good luck with that. Dios mio, you ever been above 96th Street?"

"How quickly we forget. After the hospital, lunch al fresco in the rose garden?"

"Believe me, 105th is no rose garden."

"Phone her," Emeline tries for patience, "tell her we'll be there at three o'clock. And do tell her not to fuss." She's borrowed his old iPod, Xavier doesn't need it anymore, his fancy cell handles his music. Deliberately, she plugs in the ear buds and humming, goes back to her book, hoping he won't remember his iPod is out of juice.

The cab driver annoys her, the Haitian chatting in patois while he steers with two fingers of his left hand. "Forget about racing the lights up Third, it won't be faster. There, don't you see? They're timed, the lights," and in loud whisper to Xavier, fidgeting beside her, "he must be new to the city."

Tall apartment buildings give way to low-rise brownstones, gentrified at first, less so once they cross 96th. Cavalier King Charles Spaniels on leashes are replaced by occasional dogs, mixed-breed and feral, who snuffle at the base of garbage cans. They enter a world Emeline's only seen from the train until now. She remembers a playground at the foot of sixteen-floor brick projects and one very old building with a water tower on top.

"Turn right at the next corner," Xavier says, the first words he's spoken, and hard to hear against a steam shovel banging and scraping. "By the Bread Corrado sign."

"A cafecita?" Flavia offers.

"Would you mind?" Emeline, trying to catch her breath from the stairs, draws a circular pod of decaf from her chain-handled bag and holds it out toward her hostess, buffed nails hovering over Flavia's deep plum, her tremor apparent and the tissue pod shuddering in the air like a moth.

Nodding, Flavia moves six steps to her kitchen where Emeline can see a gallery of photos on the fridge door. She's tempted to follow, offer to help, if only to see what Xavier looked like as a boy, but before she can make up her mind Flavia reappears with a small tray.

The decaf pod sits submerged in a cup of steaming water alongside two cups smelling richly of Café Bustelo. Making experienced small talk, Emeline admires the finely painted enamel tray, her hostess's best flowered cups, a pitcher of steamed milk, three miniature spoons, white paper napkins folded into fan shapes, and a bowl with minute squares of sugar that Flavia doles out with a lavish hand.

"You have still a leetle of the English accent," she smiles at Emeline. "Is so pleasant to hear." Flavia herself speaks with a trace from zip code 00956.

"I went back and forth after I married. Until I couldn't anymore, because—"

"Okay, Mai," interrupts Xavier, "what's this about?"

"Perhaps, Mrs. Hughes," Flavia ignores her son, "a slice of dulce con leche cake?" Emeline agrees, yes, a small slice. "Next time, I'll make you mine but this one, it's nearly as good, from the shop of Elizabeta Sanchez and I must say, even though she's from Dominica—"

"Mai?" Out of the corner of her eye, Emeline sees Xavier's head jerk up.

"Your manners, they are not improving at that gym of yours." Primly, Flavia smooths her skirt over plump knees. "Is all right, your coffee, Mrs. Hughes? A leetle more milk?" Xavier winces as his mother's accent widens. Emeline drains the tiny cup, sets it carefully on the tray, and shoots Xavier a look. He doesn't budge. It's going to have to be her show.

"When you phoned, Mrs. Escudero, you said you thought your son and I might be able to help you. Would you be so kind, tell us from the beginning? Messages, you know how they get mixed up."

"I am the nanny," Flavia makes no effort to mask her pride, "for the children of Mr. and Mrs. Wellington. Sophie and August, they are called. Sophie, she is four, and August, nine, already in the fourth grade at Dalton. Yes, a school without a number, a private school. Such very nice children. Just the other day—"

"Mai!"

"We've known each other since Sophie was born." A stern look at her son. "We are not friends. I am her employee. I do not meddle in her life, any more than I gossip in the park. But over the years Mrs. Wells, that is a nickname she uses, she and I have grown at ease. We talk about our children, our families, holidays. Things like that, until last week I was in the little laundry off the kitchen—you know?" Emeline, who no longer has a little laundry off the kitchen, only a washer-dryer in a closet, nods to the woman who never did.

"Folding the children's clothes, Sophie's in one pile, August's in another. Mrs. Wells, she comes in to tell me about their supper or the next day's plans. But no words come. She stands beside me, she picks up a little jumper of Sophie's, red checks with embroidery up here." Flavia trails a hand across her ample bosom. "And my employer, she begins to cry."

Wide-eyed, Flavia glances from her guest to her son, inviting them to picture such a scene. "I didn't think, I am not her friend. I put my arms around her." Understanding a truth common across languages and zip codes, both women nod. "Mrs. Wells wraps her arms around my neck, she has to bend, she is a tall woman. At first she only cries, and I am frightened. The children, I say? I fear a call from Dalton or Sophie's preschool.

"No, no, she say, the children fine. It's Belmont. She always calls him Belmont, so you wonder, you know?" Flavia gives a smile. "Is it always, Belmont, even when they are—?"

Xavier shrinks further into his chair. Biting back a laugh, Emeline asks, "She thinks there is, you know, another woman?"

"She doesn't know what the problem is. Only that Belmo—that is how his friends call him—he has changed. He always very suspicious but lately worse. Who was that who called, he ask her. Or if Mrs. Wells is out he ask me, where did she go, who is she with?

"I felt I had to take steps but what could I do? Then I thought about you and my son. How twice, between your brain and his muscle, he says you've solved a problem. Partners, I told her, a team." Emeline sees what that costs her. "And I said I would ask if you could help her."

No one speaks. The only sound is a battery-run clock ticking on the table. "Well, thanks for the coffee, I gotta be at the gym." Xavier stands.

Emeline does not. "What would you like us to do, Flavia—may I call you Flavia? And please, call me Emeline."

"Oh, for God's sake, there's nothing—"

"What would you like us to do?"

"Get an MBA, buy a seat on Wall Street."

"Oh, do be quiet, Xavier." Emeline, concerned, turns to his mother. "Flavia, what is it you have in mind?"

"If you could only talk to her? With me out of the way she might say more. She knows Xavier, she knows he's an honest—"

"Knows me? She's met me couple times for those holiday dinners."

"She was trying to be nice, to include us."

"Huh. Ramon and his cards, teaching August how to gamble? And don't tell me playing with 'little Sophie' didn't give Rocio ideas."

"*Hijo mio, silencio*," Flavia says so sharply Emeline has to feel sorry for the boy.

Emeline's met Wendy Wellington. They are not close, not at all; still Mrs. Wells might feel comfortable talking to an older woman. Emeline feels strangely excited, guilty almost, about the challenge put in their path. "I could have a word with her, Flavia, if you think that might make any difference."

"You would do that? I am so grateful. She seems very alone, you know. Not like our family here, so many friends we can count on, like my dear Renata; yes, I know, Italian, not Puerto Rican, but she—"

"Good, that's settled." Xavier stands up. "We're leaving."

"Your place is lovely, Flavia. You have an eye, like my daughter. I've recently moved to a smaller place myself—"

Even if Xavier's face turns red, Emeline can tell his mother doesn't mind. Flavia moves close to her so Emeline sniffs the light scent Flavia wears, a hint of jasmine. "I want to tell you, Emeline," she says quietly, "I am very sorry about your husband. And those terrible stories. Too bad, your daughter, she live so far away. England, yes?" Emeline stiffens. Flavia takes both her hands in hers. "No, do not worry, I do not ask questions. But I will pray for you."

Seriously out of sorts, Xavier steers Emeline past a building with boarded-up windows and a dumpster out front. Another reno on the way. He heads west toward Lexington but when a cab slows at the corner he flicks his fingers to wave it off.

"Xavier. Where are we going?"

"I need food." Walking as if he owns the sidewalk, he hustles Emeline around an orange traffic cone smashed flat, past an acrylic nail salon and an Evangelical church that's taken root in a store front.

"I thought you were late for the gym. Not so?"

"I was dying in there, was what I was," he says, opening the door of Bodega Boricua. He orders in rapid Spanish. Two ochre-colored bowls of black bean soup appear, with chopped eggs and whiffs of garlic and cumin.

"I don't want that stuff, take it away." Emeline raises her voice against the excited vocalist piped in over a Spanish station.

"Dabbling in business that don't concern either one of us, Emeline? It's not right. It could also be dangerous. I'm the one that got shot, remember."

"From now on we'll be more careful."

"You need a hobby, a suitable hobby. What about bridge, you play bridge? Or mah jongg," he says.

"Ah, so." Emeline folds her hands together and bows so her chin nearly touches the black beans. "But I am not Chinese lady like Scarsdale Doxy. No mah jongg. No bridge. I plan never to play bridge. Besides, I have plenty to do."

"Try the soup, it's very good. Plenty to do, like what?"

"Lately I've had to help Muffy with her benefit—oh, you're right, this soup is delicious. And then there was Tram's wedding."

"Julian's, actually. Did he even want to get married?"

"I have my doubts. That girl, vapid doesn't begin to describe her." She watches Xavier search the dictionary in his mind and come up empty.

In a way he's right, Emeline knows. These events keeping her busy, they're all superficial. What would Flavia do if she found free time on her hands? Angry as she would have been at Rocio, baby Jomar must give Flavia a new purpose, a second go at raising her children right. Emeline sees no such chance for herself on the horizon.

Anyway, since Cliff died whatever sense of adventure might have survived her carefully ordered life is gone. "It's too late for me to change, Xavier. You, on the other hand . . . you should be looking ahead."

He's quick to change the subject. "You were nice to my Mom."

"She has a heart of gold."

"*Corazon de melon* we say."

"Heart of a melon," Emeline translates. "Anyone would like her."

"Maybe not Tram."

"No, maybe not her."

When they finish their soup they both say yes to the *flan* and Xavier insists on paying the bill. Outside a man is rolling down the metal gates in front of Eastside Wireless. She realizes it's late. Xavier hails a cab and they head downtown. Xavier is woolgathering, she has to ask him twice.

"What?"

"I said, you don't think we should help your mother's employer?"

"Help Wendy Wells," Xavier is scornful, "who can hire ten private detectives and a firm of lawyers? She wants to get her nanny to help her for free, no extra compensation."

"Your mother doesn't see it that way."

"She's too proud, is her problem. 'I've known Sophie since she was a leetle baby'," he mimics in a high voice. "Makes it sound as if she was the nanny, doesn't it."

"She is the nanny."

"Now she is. Back then she was the cleaning woman." It's more than Xavier has let on about his mother, their income, the apartment. Is the place rent-controlled? A single mother raising three children, and in a neighborhood like this . . . Emeline's admiration grows.

"Was it safe, growing up here?" She asks. He shrugs. "I know you've seen dead bodies before. I could tell, at Luca's studio."

"And you? Your husband's, I suppose."

"Yes, I had to identify Clifford. But he . . . I hardly recognized him."

When Xavier puts a hand over hers, absently she pats his. "Your mother does want us to help, Xavier, even if she looked uncomfortable when she talked about us being a team."

"Partners," he corrects. "She called us partners."

"An unlikely pair perhaps."

"Emeline. She thinks we're living together."

"Of course we're living together, she phoned you at my apartment." He looks away, embarrassed.

"Oh Xavier," she giggles. "My dear, I don't know whether to be flattered or—are you telling me she doesn't *know?*" He shakes his head. "Come on. You can take the boy out of Puerto Rico…"

"San Juan."

"Okay, San Juan."

"Santurce is our old neighborhood."

Emeline sighs. "Can't catch a break, can I."

"It's more you can't take the mother out of the church. It's the same thing all across the islands. I had a friend from Barbados," his voice trails off, smile fades. Is he remembering some other man's sad face, describing how his mother, consumed with shame, swept him out of the house with a broom?

It makes sense. A strong Catholic from the islands, Flavia may have stepped over the threshold to birth control, but she's probably a long way from the high plains of alternate life styles. So, Xavier can't let his mother know who he really is. "Then she thinks you're my, I'm afraid I don't know the word in Spanish."

"*Gigolo.*"

"Terrific. Be useful for me at my next dinner party!"

Xavier brightens. "You want us to give a dinner party?"

"What about the rest of your family?"

"If one has a secret, everyone else pretends they don't know. Ramon, he knows. Needled me big time once he figured out where I was going, evenings. Until I showed him pictures I'd taken of his business associates."

"You said," Emeline guesses. "you'd show them to the police."

"Police? Hell no. I told him I'd show them to Flavia." Of course: the woman with no badge and twice the power over her children.

"Her beloved first-born," Xavier reveals, "deals in petty theft and drugs. Sooner or later he'll get arrested again, or even killed. Don't you get it? I'm supposed to be the 'good son,' the one who made it to college. And you think I should tell her I'm a *maricon*? She'll have a heart attack."

"You children, you always think your mothers will perish on the spot if you tell them news they don't want to hear. When Deborah decided to move to London she didn't tell me for a month. Why? 'I thought it would kill you,' she'd said. What about Rocio, does she know?" The sister with a baby and a fighting chance for a diploma.

"Rocio lives in a world of mirrors; if it's not about her, it doesn't exist. You know teen-agers."

She does. Except with Deborah, so thoroughly Deborah from the day she was born, it was easy to write off adolescent behavior as business as usual. "Maybe you should tell her, your mother."

"You think she'd be happier with the truth? Emeline," Xavier is close to pleading, "don't even think about it. Already she has the high blood pressure."

"We'll have to invent a beau for me then, won't we," but Xavier, preoccupied, is tapping his fingernails on the cab door. "What's the matter now?"

"There's something my mother's not telling me. And I don't know what it is."

CHAPTER 11

Apart from the differences—cumin and garlic, island accents, and fire escapes that zigzag up the fronts of buildings—for Emeline, Flavia's neighborhood brought back old memories. Alongside the lessons Aunt Mildred taught her ("say thank you, not *cheers*, and never, ever, *rubbish*") endure images of the crowded flat in Peckham, her mother's printed house dresses, beige raincoats on the street, salt cod and potatoes on the table.

Temporary, her mother assured her: a few months in New York, a year at the most, Mildred's concern offering Dora's daughter a chance for the good life in a city not wracked by war. Emeline protested, wept tears, and threw tantrums. No, she didn't want a different life, didn't want to meet new people, it was all a mistake. Her mother trotted out stories of the *kindertransport:* frightened Jewish children sent to England from Berlin and Prague in the hope they'd survive the Nazi round-ups; trainloads of English kids sent north to the countryside to find safety from the Luftwaffe's nightly bombing. Emeline should see her journey as a gift.

During their own train ride to Southampton, their walk to the docks through fog and the salty scent of the sea, Emeline tried to meet her mother's determination with a valiant spirit of her own. "Look, Ma, a line of sea gulls sitting on the boat railing."

"Ship, dear girl, this large and they call it a ship." Years later when Emeline heard Dorothy Parker's line, "You mean the whole thing goes?" the writer's quip spread a thin salve of humor over the memory of this earlier, painful good-bye.

The weary SS *Caritas* ferried American students to Europe for the summer, then home again in time for school. In between the ship offered discounts to Brits with pressing reasons to cross the Atlantic but not the money, or the nerve, to take one of the new commercial flights. With one hand gripping her mother's sleeve and the other a drooping clump of daisies, Emeline joined the line of passengers climbing the gangway. On board, her tears ready to spill, Emeline spiraled down to the lowest deck, her mother squeezing her hand in their familiar rhythm: I love you; I love you, too. How much. *This* much.

In their cubicle below the waterline, buffeted by waves and rattling like marbles in a tin, Emeline's roommate taught her ocean-crossing lesson number one: better to starve than to hurl. Even today memories of the stubborn vessel, built in Trieste, flying an Estonian flag, and manned by a work crew entirely Greek, mirror Emeline's sense of displacement. What was true? What was camouflage? Who was she, really?

Her Aunt Mildred was as kind as could be, but still Emeline found everything in New York strange: the accent, the elevator, the prosperity, the pace, the odd way Americans handled a knife and fork. Used to the chilly flat in Peckham, come fall Aunt Mildred's radiators dried Emeline's skin to paper. Her aunt applied lotion as she coached Emeline in the language, manners, bearing, and dress bred into the other girls in her new school. No cattiness. No talk about the cost of things or money. Be conspicuous by being inconspicuous. "And, Emeline dear? That means behaving on the bus."

Emeline noticed her aunt's accent had veered away from the one her mother had; Mildred had acquired a more proper English accent.

Grateful as Emeline is, to this day she can't imagine her mother's pain in sending away her only child. It would be years before she'd hear she had a little brother, Michael, living in Peckham, embedded in the life she'd left, eating the oatmeal hers by rights. And once their father mended from his injuries and returned to work, soaking up London's postwar advantages: chicken, beef, green beans, fruit for the table, coal for the furnace, and brief summer holidays spent camping in a caravan in Brighton.

Emeline reminds herself what privileges have come her way. How hard could it be to do what Flavia asks? And if Xavier won't come to Wendy Wells with her, she'll go alone.

"Cheer up." Emeline gives Xavier a sly smile as the cab ricochets toward the Lincoln Center address. "You know Mrs. Wellington's apartment. More to your taste, I imagine."

"How would you know my—"

"Because you've already added a *mariachi* shawl to your room?"

"Too much? I'll move it out."

"Leave it, leave it. Clifford and I were in Acapulco once."

"Anyway, the shawl isn't Mexican, it's—"

"Very colorful." She lifts her hand to take in the whole continent to the south.

"—a Barbados shawl."

"Just don't cover up the Corot."

"The radiator?"

"The ink drawing, very small but genuine. Clifford bought it from Ron Segal."

The Wellington's condo, Emeline knows, will be exactly what she helped Clifford avoid. Back when she and Cliff married new buildings were springing up everywhere on Madison, Lexington, and, with railroad flats torn down soon after the El, even on Third.

"Not for us, Cliffie." Emeline stood firm.

"Why not? We have friends in those buildings. The McClintocks have a splendid terrace on east 86th, didn't we have drinks outside in April? The terrace had one of those standing heaters, looked like a brolly. We watched the boats on the river." Watched the boats for ninety seconds, Emeline remembered, before the men circled up to talk real estate and finance. She shook her head.

"Okay, what about the building where the Greenberg's bought the penthouse? They can walk to Lincoln Center."

"Very convenient. At least for Rachel and Jake; I'm lucky if I get you to the symphony once a year. Take a look at the co-op for sale on Fifth and 95th, will you? We'd have a straight shot through Central Park, when and if you decide you like Rachmaninoff."

"He's the mournful one, sentimental?" Clifford recalled, "Oh, got it. You're changing the subject."

"Redirecting the conversation is all. No, no, don't think snogging will distract me. We should bid on the co-op at Fifth and 95th."

"Practically Harlem."

"At those prices? Clifford, one more time: there's old money and there's new money."

"And mine is new."

"Your wife is old."

"At twenty-six?"

"Old money, your girl."

"Who didn't have much money of her own old or new when I met her."

That was true. Aunt Mildred's generosity paid for school, college, much of the wedding. Mildred had counted on connections made in these hallways to secure a suitable marriage for Emeline. Even after Clifford Hughes replaced suitable she'd been generous. Emeline understood and perhaps Aunt Mildred did, too. If her pedigree on her mother's side was respectable, her penury from her father's injury was acute. To his credit, Clifford never promised her fortunes, only fidelity "and one hell of a lot of fun." His continuing success surprised them both.

"Try to remember why you married me, Cliff. You knew I'd give you 'classy' children, your word, not mine. And, at certain moments, steer you in the right direction. This is one of those moments. You want to represent more clients who are old money. I do not wear Prada, we are not—"

"Flash?"

"Exactly. We're tasteful, even a little staid."

"If anyone but me were to see you in bed . . ."

"Oh, do be still. Go look at the co-op, and Cliff, if you like it? You'd best bid over ask." Whether it was her English beginnings or her own granite will, back then Emeline believed a spirit forceful and irreverent had survived her family's hard luck and her aunt's relentless polishing. Only lately it seems she's misplaced that spirit.

The elevator stops at the 25th floor, elevator doors opens. Not onto a modest hallway like Emeline's, with her Chinese vase centered on a polished table. Here, guests step directly into the foyer. A modish, Asian gentleman bows once from the waist, turns smoothly on his small feet, and leads the away.

"That's not Mr. Well—" Xavier whispers.

"Don't be ridiculous." Emeline, for once, finds it easy to match the butler's short steps. Ticking off the icons of décor is like clicking the beads of a rosary. Emeline almost says so out loud but holds back, uncertain where Xavier stands with respect, or lack of, for the Catholic Diocese of New York.

In the living room, a Stark carpet, an Italian sectional covered in subtle brocade, stocky leather Hancock & Moore chairs—every shade of cream, beige, taupe, and mushroom. A scribbly, oversized painting, a Cy Twombley look alike, spans most of one wall. Glass sliders give onto a terrace looking over the green park that breathes for the city. In the spaces between concrete balustrades, Emeline glimpses shapes of curved blue sky, empty except for a vee of geese heading south, oblivious to the property values under their beating wings.

Past the piano the Asian butler makes a military turn into a smaller sitting room and stops so suddenly Xavier knocks into a side table. Emeline catches his arm, murmuring, "Do try and behave."

"*Hari-gato,* Jin." Waving away the butler, a blonde woman stands to greet them. Young and elegant, she's wearing a short-sleeved, cream-colored cashmere shell, taupe silk pants, and expensive scent. From a small speaker near her chair Peter Gabriel sings softly.

"Mrs. Wellington," Emeline says with her polite smile, "how nice to see you again. Yes, we have met, with Muffy Strawbridge, though I don't think I ran into you at the Young Yorkville Musicians benefit." Neither woman refers to the drama of that day. "So many good works, Muffy, so many chicken lunches. I believe you know my colleague, Xavier Escudero."

Wendy Wellington nods. Tall as a super model, her shoulders droop and her head bends from years of trying to fit into the world's shorter crowd. "Do sit here." She offers Emeline a chair that faces the sky, leaving Xavier to sort out his own seating on the ottoman, hands between his knees and moving nothing except his eyes.

The women sink into chairs covered in colorful Brunschwig & Fils. On a small table sits a basket with needlepoint, the canvas half filled with bargello in yellow, ochre, and red yarn. On the walls photos formal and informal of two blond children, in the bookcase volumes in uneven heights for pulling down and reading, not display.

The butler returns, burdened under the weight of a silver tray, a teapot swaying on its hinged stand; a smaller pot holding hot water; a sugar bowl, a creamer as curvaceous as a nude, and lemons sliced muslin thin. He sets the tray on the low table and bows out. Emeline studies the display the way she would view a morning shopper at Gristedes wearing satin to buy arugula. "And how are your children, Wendy?"

"Growing much too fast. Sophie is four and August nine. You have a boy and a girl, don't you?"

"One daughter, in London." Emeline accepts a china cup of Assam.

"Oh, not far then," which makes Emeline smile, as if she and Wendy share access to a secret tunnel that runs under the Atlantic, avoiding crowds and inclement air.

"We're not close, my daughter and I." Sipping tea, Emeline moves a piece forward on the game board. "Life is not always what we expect, for any of us."

"I know." Wendy Wells lowers her voice. "It must have been terrible for you when your husband died and then all those awful—"

"Tell me," Emeline interrupts, "how is it you think we might help you?"

"There they are!" says Wendy, hearing footsteps in the hall. If her greeting sounds forced, with a pinch of envy Emeline finds nothing false in the mother's affection as two blond children run in, the boy tripping over his feet on the edge of the Aubusson rug. A small dog follows. Wendy holds out skinny arms to give each child a hug, indifferent when her daughter's warm cheek leaves a smear of chocolate on her cashmere.

"August, your reading test went well? Good for you, Daddy will be proud. Sophie darling, wipe your mouth—no, no," she laughs as the girl's face rubs back and forth. "Flavia, can you find this imp a tissue? August, sweetie, go on with Flavia and you too, Sophie." Impassive in the doorway, Flavia holds out her hands.

Emeline sees the daughter, younger and more observant than her brother, eyeing Xavier.

"It's Xavier," Sophie trills. "Look, Flavie, it's—"

"Run along, you two, Flavia will make you both a snack, and then, August? You must do your homework." With barely a glance at her own son, the nanny herds her charges back through the cavernous living room and on to a distant area; their voices fade then disappear. Emeline catches the pained look on Xavier's face, imagines the infinite afternoons when other children snacked on the milk and Milano cookies he'd have liked. It is a pain she knows.

Xavier tiptoes across the room to close the sitting room door as Wendy dips a cloth napkin into her teacup and casually rubs against the stain from Sophie's homecoming. The gesture, so out of keeping with the sitting room and the woman's façade, makes Emeline draw a quick breath and remember the cat-licks she used to bestow on Deborah.

"You were starting to say?" prompts Emeline, even though Wendy wasn't.

"It's Belmont." Wendy frowns, indifferent to some beautician's advice. "He's very distracted is the word, I suppose. He actually," her eyes widen, "shouted at me the other night, can you imagine?" Imagine an evening passing without shouts? That would have been unusual in her old Peckham neighborhood; Emeline is careful not to look at Xavier who may be thinking of his.

"He's rarely here for supper on our 'home' nights. That's what we call . . . of course it's been such a busy time. He's hardly been out to East Hampton at all. We summer in East Hampton, you know. Of course once winter comes he wants to ski, even at the last moment. So I can't always get away with him." Emeline sees Xavier raise his eyebrows: told you so.

"And I know what you're thinking." For the first time Wendy looks directly at Xavier, then busies herself with cups and the sugar bowl, running her fingers along the curved edges of silver for comfort; as if Georgian-style silver ever kept trouble away. "It's not a woman. It's some man."

A man? Emeline doesn't dare look at Xavier. "What is his name?"

"I don't know his name. This man, and you can stop grinning, Xavier, it's nothing fun, believe me. He's serious, he's dangerous, he's a threat to Belmont, to me, to our little family.

Whatever sympathy briefly warmed Xavier's face, Emeline watches it ebb away. Little family? Two healthy, perfectly spaced children, a nanny, a butler, no doubt a cook, a cleaner, and a driver. Xavier stands up.

"Oh thank you, Xavier," Emeline says quickly. "It does feel a bit cool, if you could find my jacket? " She waves her hand toward the door, watching as he heads out of the room to retrieve her Burberry.

". . . and since then Belmont's been the director of the Cadmium Fund," Wendy speaks in capital letters, honoring a capital base worth millions. "It's not at all the life we were used to when we first married. Things weren't as comfortable for us then. It was hard for us, this change, hard for me, especially. The dinners, the decorator we had to hire. And the firm's chief partner, his wife actually told me to hire a stylist."

"Mrs. Wellington, I really—"

"Wendy, please call me Wendy," their hostess begs. "And your name, Emeline, so unusual, is it French?" Advance, retreat, advance, retreat.

"I really don't see how we can help. What you need is a private detective, discrete, who will respect your, ah, reticence."

"Flavia has told me about you and her son." Wendy smiles at Xavier who has returned with the tan jacket. "She says you are partners, that together you can learn things other people can't. Your mom," she assures Xavier, "said she didn't know the details and even if she did, you know she wouldn't gossip. Only what was in the paper after Luca Bevilaqua's show."

"We are quieter than the police," Emeline looks demurely into her tea. "I do know a number of people and of course Xavier has certain skills. Between the two of us . . . or perhaps we've just been lucky."

"Then you do understand. If I hire some strange man who says he is a PI no one will even speak to him. But if you were to ask a few questions, please?" Her voice trails off. Emeline turns to Xavier, lifts her eyebrows. Xavier shrugs: up to you. "I'm frightened, I tell you. The people Belmont works with, they are not always—"

"Honest?" Xavier speaks for the first time.

"Exactly, Xavier." Wendy draws a deep breath. "They are not always honest."

"Perhaps we can ask around," says Emeline. "We'd come to you with anything we learn, though it might still be necessary to call in the authorities. Because you see," hands clasped on the head of her cane, she leans forward to make her point, "if it should turn out there's a legal problem? If it were ever to come under investigation," Wendy shrinks at the word, "and it became known we knew about it and said nothing, it would put us in a very awkward position."

Walking her guests back to the elevator, Wendy tucks her hand under Emeline's elbow. Emeline finds she doesn't mind. Wendy pushes the button, then pats Xavier's shoulder. "You've grown tall since I first knew you, buddy. And strong. Flavia says you work out at a gym."

"Work at a gym, personal trainer" he corrects.

"You're practicing tai chi, too, I hear. Good for you. I still do my yoga. Makes a difference, doesn't it." The elevator doors open. "Thank you both for coming. Emeline, I really did want to call you after Clifford's accident; I just didn't know what to say."

Wendy extends her hand to Xavier and when, in a reflex of good manners he takes it for a formal good-bye, she covers his hand with both of hers. "We are lucky to have Flavia as part of our family, very lucky."

"You and me both," he says, his smile bittersweet as the doors glide shut, the elevator already returning them to pigeons underfoot, rude crowds, and the incessant blare of Manhattan streets.

On the lobby floor, a tall man with a frown and a monogrammed brief case pushes his way into the elevator, hardly waiting for them to get out of his way,

"Emeline," hisses Xavier, "that was—"

"Belmo Wellington. I know. I saw it, too, the photo on the piano. He was sitting on a dark horse."

Chapter 12

Even though shaken by the visit and resentful of the luxe surroundings, Xavier feels sympathy for his mother's employer. Bouncing them against the back seat, the cab speeds through a yellow light. As before, Emeline grips his arm to keep steady. She needs something to catch her attention and engage her mind. Everything he's suggested so far—duplicate bridge, good deeds at Lenox Hill Hospital—she's made it clear the answer is no. But Wendy's suggestion, that's just plain crazy.

Maybe Xavier can persuade her to work on her Spanish, act as her tutor, evenings. Next time he's on 105th he'll palm the pack of alphabet cards he bought for Jomar, still too young to do more than chew on the edges and chortle.

"Big mystery, Emeline? I don't think so. Belmont is getting some on the side. Sell the silver and buy off the *puta*. Case closed." Emeline is staring out the window at a worker with his cap on backwards sponging the glass window of a high-end emporium with a two-story long pole. Xavier tries a new tack. "Did I read you right when you sent me out of the sitting room?"

"You did. What did you find?"

"Bathroom is high end. Fancy dried flowers in a bowl, same as you have. Sink has a faucet like a, a," he draws a shape with his hand.

"Vase? Horse shoe? Croquet hoop?"

"What's a croquet hoop?"

"Tell me about the towels."

"Pretty paper guest towels, printed in colored stripes." Nothing like the worn terry cloth towels the family uses until, come the weekend, Flavia throws them in with a family's worth of jeans and shirts, ready for the laundromat.

"The point is they're paper."

"Like I just said, Emeline."

"In the bath for guests? And that isn't all." She counts the tally on her fingers. "Rough scratches at the foot of a slipcover where the JRT—"

"Huh?" Sounds like a subway line.

"The Jack Russell Terrier, he paws at the slipcover. The cookies came from d'Agostino's, I buy the same kind myself. The Louis XV desk, I doubt that was genuine, whoever vacuumed missed a folded store receipt underneath. And your tea cup was chipped."

"Not to be rude, Emeline, but one or two of your cups are chipped."

"Mine are Spode," she brags, "from my Aunt Mildred. I bring them out for friends."

"So we weren't friends, tell me something I don't know."

"This has nothing to do with you, Xavier. Friends, strangers, guests, business acquaintances, don't you understand? Wendy Wellington has a job."

"She goes to business?"

"She works full time, you'd call it 24/7. She creates an environment, like a stage . . . never mind, here, look at this." From her bag she unearths a ratty slip of paper. "I retrieved it when Wendy Well left the room to take a phone call."

"You didn't." Xavier pictures Emeline crawling to the desk and hoisting herself back on the couch.

"There are days my cane comes in handy. It's a receipt. She returned a lamp, pretty expensive, at least for Macy's. Macy's!"

"What? My mother shops there."

Emeline raises her eyebrows, my point exactly. "Go on, Xavier what else?"

"Down the hall there's a big study. Door was open, no one there. I didn't poke around in the drawers or anything."

"And?"

"All very impressive. Huge desk, comfortable chairs, paintings in heavy frames on the walls. You'd have seen more, it's what you see, the details." He'd never be as good at that as she was. But she'd never read people the way he could, she'd never needed to the way he had. "They'd hung the art so the tops of the frames were in a line. Is that how you're supposed to do it, all the frames in a line at the top?"

"Depends."

"One of the paintings had glass over it, the others didn't."

"Watercolor, then, not oils. Or was it a lithograph?"

"Lithograph?"

"Black and white, like a drawing."

"No. But the top of the frame didn't line up with the others, and the space around it looked kind of faded"

Emeline nods slowly. "The Wells have hung their art in the study as well as the living room and the dining room. And they've removed a piece, from the study where it's less likely guests will notice. What did it look like?"

"A woman, might have been a dancer."

"Red hair, bending over to tie on her ballet shoes?"

"How'd you know that? What's wrong, the Wellingtons can't like dancers?"

"They've mixed a Degas reproduction with original works and—"

"How do you know the dancer isn't an original."

"Even the Wellingtons couldn't afford a real Degas. Point is, they haven't had time to repaint the wall. The Wellingtons are having money problems, serious enough they're selling off assets."

"Wouldn't paintings be hard to sell?"

"Maybe. But they can hardly cart out that dining room table, can they, must be solid mahogany."

"Or they're just changing things up, haven't gotten around to repainting. Who knows, could be this weekend's project.

"Sure, Xavier, the whole place reeks of do-it-yourself." She grins. "At least Wendy didn't ask you where you summer."

"And I didn't have to say 'we summer where we winter.'"

"Questions Raised in Financier's Sale of Paintings," was the first salvo fired by the *New York Post* not long after the funeral. Someone had been talking. Emeline turned to Clifford's lawyer, Cooper, his sympathy outrun only by his hourly rates. She'd met him in enough meetings that required her signature: The day she and Cliff closed on the 95th street apartment. The spring they bought the house in Southampton—that made her wonder if Cliff's preference for property on Long Island, not in Connecticut, was to avoid adding another lawyer from another state; and again, during the 2008 recession when they sold that house to a super model.

"Let it go," advised Coop. "Getting into it at this point will only fan the fire."

"What Cliff was doing—"

Coop cut her off. "Don't want to hear it, Emeline. The gossip may die down. Maybe it's just a fishing expedition, the *Post* waiting to see who bites." Persuaded, Emeline settled for buying the notorious rag at the newsstand after dark, too embarrassed to send her doorman. Gregor made good pocket money on his breaks, running small errands for residents too preoccupied or infirm to secure newspapers, cigarettes, or a quart of milk on their own.

Ten quiet days went by. The *Post's* next blurb proved discretion had gone out the window. "Financier Clifford Hughes Involved in Irregular Art Sales," blared the black headline. The sub-head turned the blade of enquiry: "Did death cheat the law of an embezzler?"

Coop saw it before she did and picked up the phone. "This will never do," he barked. "We have to take action."

"You'll speak to the editor?"

"Speak?" A rich laugh. "We're not speaking, we're suing. It's risky, can be messy, will be expensive (Emeline could hear how he enjoyed those three syllables). "But it's our best chance." He paused. "Any chance Cliff did anything, you know, irregular?"

"What he was doing, as I tried to tell you before, was a straightforward favor for an old friend. Ron Segal was downsizing. Cliff helped him, for a commission. End of story."

"Sit tight, don't speak to reporters, don't speak to your friends either." Coop was in charge. "I'll get back to you. Deal?"

"Deal."

The next phone call was from Ron's sister. "I was in my brother's apartment when your lawyer called," she said, in the tone she'd have used if she'd had to say drug dealer. "Ron's very upset. No, you cannot speak to him. He does not want to talk to you." Two days later the sister called again. Ron had suffered a massive stroke. He wouldn't be speaking to anyone, not anymore.

Coop's legal threats, whatever they were, took effect. "No retraction from the *Post,*" he told her, "that's fine with us, a retraction would only draw more attention," but no more stories, either. Anyway, a sex scandal involving a university coach washed onto the tabloid's pages for the next ten days. Coop sent his bill. Still, the pebble had been dropped into the pond. Soon enough Emeline knew from the mumbles of sympathy, the curious looks, or the turned backs which of her acquaintances read the *Post* or at least knew someone who did.

Emeline can see her housemate's having a bad morning. He came home late, for one thing. Then Flavia telephoned Emeline, not Xavier, to ask what they'd learned from Wendy Wells. Emeline knows Xavier overheard her blending vague replies with assurances Flavia's job was not in jeopardy. Then Emeline told him her idea.

"Julian, that asshole? *Ni pa.* No way. You plan on talking to him again, you can talk to him on your own."

"He is a self-important little poser. Though, sometimes first impressions are wrong." Emeline watches Xavier realize that's what she'd thought of him once.

"You forget how he treated me? Like some spic you'd taken in off the streets."

"Don't use that word, it's vulgar. Besides, it was you took me off the streets."

"Dig out our contract, I'm adding a Julian-free clause." At least he's stopped scowling.

"I've known Julian since he was a child. His mother has been a steady friend when many others have not. And we need to take advice."

"What about Tramontana?"

"Tram?" Emeline laughs. "She has money, yes, but she doesn't know the first thing about managing money, probably thinks a 'dividend' is a refill on her martini."

"Cooper?"

"I'd rather not involve Coop. No, Julian's our best bet."

"Maybe I could—"

"Could what, Xavier, analyze a hedge fund like Cadmium, lay out the rules, the risks and financial history? I'll give you a day to cool down, and you can decide where the three of us should meet. Some place public."

"Why not here?"

"The rug is quite new and I'd rather not see blood on my Shiraz."

"Sure, Emeline," Julian says on the speaker phone, "you're practically family. Matter of fact, I've got a sweet opportunity might interest you, an IPO with significant upside potential."

"Julian, I am not looking for an investment. I need information. And while it won't compensate you the way your outrageous fee would, I can offer you lunch."

"Local McDonald's?"

"Try not to be nasty, dear. One other thing, Julian?"

"Yes?" He sounds suspicious.

"Xavier will be joining us."

"Not on your life." Julian's no more eager for a lunch *a trois* than Xavier.

"His words, pretty much, but yes, he'll be there."

"It is beyond me what you see in that—"

"Julian, I changed your diapers more than once. I've bailed you out of any number of misadventures. Which reminds me," Emeline continues in a voice you could spread on toast, "How is your dear wife, what is her name?"

"Thursday next," Julian's voice has grown quieter. "Thursday next good for you?"

"Let me check my diary. Thursday. . ." To make a noise she riffles her fingers over the *New York Times* and looks up at Xavier. He consults his cell phone calendar and, reluctant, nods. "Yes, Julian, that will do very well."

"Tell your little friend to wear a tie. He does own a tie?"

"I'll provide one of Clifford's. Shall we say Fortuna's? They do a very nice duck breast with blackberries. I so rarely find my way downtown; it will be quite the adventure. Perhaps afterward we can all take a ride on the Staten Island ferry."

Disgruntled as he is to see Julian again, when Xavier holds the door for Emeline he's glad she made him wear another of Clifford's jackets. The restaurant, abuzz, is full of important men in dark suits and striped ties, with a few striving women in dark suits and infinitesimal earrings. Several of the men are lunching with very young, very pretty women who hang on every word. Xavier raises his eyebrows to Emeline."

"Ask to be introduced," she says in a low voice, "and they always explain the girls as 'nieces.'" One of the men looks up from his 'niece's' rapt attention, sees Xavier with his elbow under an older woman's arm, and winks.

Waiters in white shirt sleeves flash past, balancing round trays above one shoulder with one arm bent. It's a pose that makes Xavier think of the baking soda box his mother uses for cleaning. Lamps hang from a distant ceiling, more for design than illumination. Good thing Emeline made a reservation, Julian hasn't bothered.

Julian hugs Emeline. Xavier takes the offensive. "How's it goin'?" Julian nods curtly and ignores him through their Caesar salads. Emeline waits until the entrées arrive to come to the point.

"Let me be frank with you, Julian. I need your help. Or rather, someone we know," she smiles in Xavier's direction, "needs your help." Julian continues to look anywhere but at Xavier, who has no trouble reading his thoughts: a drug runner looking for bail, an injured gang-banger, or, Xavier watches Julian's lip curl a millimeter, maybe the little spic is bi- and some silly girl three months gone. Julian takes a sip of Pinot Grigio as if to clear a bad taste.

"You know him, too, Julian," Emeline goes on, "Belmo Wellington."

White wine spews onto white linen, and a waiter hurries over to mop up. Astonished, Julian turns to Xavier: "*You* know Belmo?"

"Old friend of the family," Xavier answers smoothly.

"Here's the problem, and I count on your discretion, Julian," Emeline explains. "The Wellingtons have called us in. Wendy did actually. She's very concerned about her husband. As a rule she doesn't bother herself with business details—"

"Which she wouldn't understand anyway. Belmo deals in fairly esoteric vehicles."

"Precisely, dear, which is why we need you to help us make sense of what's happening."

"So you want me to lay out the details, offer a tutorial in Hedge Fund 101. There are courses on that sort of thing, Emeline." Unblinking, she stares back. "Or why don't you buy a book? If you like I can have my girl email you a few titles. One or two are fairly accessible, I suppose," a glance toward Xavier. "I simply don't have the time."

Emeline moves her lunch plate to the left to spread her hands on the table as if laying down four aces in the final trick of a card game.

"Wendy is worried that Belmo is, well, short of cash."

"Look to the horses, *cherchez la femme*." Julian waves his hand, dismissing household cash flow problems as nothing more than rounding errors.

"No. She says it's not a woman."

"What," Julian snorts, "she's confronted him? What does she expect him to say, I love her, and you will, too, when you meet her?"

"Wendy fears there may be a problem with Cadmium," Emeline says flatly.

Julian blinks once, furrows his eyebrows, fails to notice when the waiter places the dessert menu in front of him. Emeline glances at Xavier to see if he's been following the exchange so far. He answers with a faint nod. He gets it. An esoteric vehicle can't be all that different from *bolito*, the old-time gambling scheme where Puerto Ricans wrote bets on chalkboards. Until a legal state lottery wiped it out, except for a few old men who still play in the back rooms of *bodegas*.

Xavier knows Julian's not thinking about Belmo's personal debts, Wendy Well's anxiety, or the health of the marriage. A waiter passes behind Julian holding a silver tray vertically under his arm, and Xavier sees it like the thought balloon over a cartoon figure. As if written on the shiny surface, he reads Julian's thoughts: Fuck me blue. Cadmium?

"Julian?" Emeline speaks sharply. "What I'm asking you to do is to dig into the history of Cadmium. Perhaps 'your girl' can arrange it for us on a cover sheet . . ."

"Spread sheet," Xavier and Julian say in unison.

"Spread sheet. Don't worry about our taking more of your time. Xavier is a CPA, he will explain it all to me." Xavier enjoys the inflation of his semester at La Guardia before he realized: American Dream be damned, he'd make money sooner if he took the job at the gym. The waiter refills their coffee cups from a silver carafe.

"The data are a little advanced," Julian says to Xavier. "If I can clear an hour or two, I suppose I can walk you through the basics." Emeline pays a lunch bill that would feed a family of four for a week, and Xavier hails a cab to take them home—only because he talked her out of heading straight over to Wendy Wells.

"And I thought you Latins leaned toward impetuous."

"*Paso a paso*," Xavier describes the approach he uses with his overweight matrons at the gym. "Not like the 'let's get with it' we use with the young guys. See, these ladies are half-hearted at best, dressed in spandex because their doctors say they should exercise or their husbands have hired a cute secretary. Step-by-step, that's the only way, they have to see success, or they won't keep going. You and I need to understand what's happening at Cadmium before we talk to Mrs. Wells again."

After supper he brings out the alphabet cards. "See how many words you can make." To his surprise she takes him seriously, sits at the kitchen table, and spells out *plato, plata, zapata, cervesa*.

"Great, only beer—"

"Beer in Spanish is spelled with a zed, I'm not an idiot. But I already used the Z," she points the card with the lightning bolt. "for zapata. If we're going to do this we need more cards. What do you expect me to do with only one zed?"

Emeline's made strides, socially, asking friends for lunch: now, might be a good idea to branch out. She suggests they ask some of Xavier's friends over for supper, an idea he meets with scorn.

"Why not Rocio and Jomar? We'll give the kid pureed asparagus, that'll go well with your couch."

"What about the gentleman from your club?"Emeline parries.

"You talking about Gabor? You do know he's gay."

"Then he can bring—"

"Ryan. His partner's name is Ryan. Sure, why not? You can pick one to be your escort the next time we have to see Flavia together. Which I pray is never."

"My beard," she says smugly.

"You got it backwards, but nice try."

"You did say a foursome?" asks Gabor. Xavier's staring at the creature on a leash, a long-legged dog with a reddish coat. "Oh dear, I thought I should call about the little rascal but Ryan said—"

"Welcome," says Emeline, bending down and bracing one hand shoulder high on her cane to keep her balance. All three men lean forward to help her. "No, no, I'm fine. Who do we have here?"

"Diogi."

"Would that be Italian?"

"No, Hungarian actually. He's a Vizsla ."

"Emeline," suggests Xavier, "Try spelling it."

"D I O . . . my goodness, how clever." Emeline adores dogs. Her cock-a-poo Fritzy was on his last legs when Clifford died. Emeline, out of the house for a meeting with the lawyer, came home to find Deborah had snuck off to the vet and sent Fritzy to the great kennel in the sky.

"I was worried you would fall!" Deborah's excuse only added insult to injury. The day Deborah left for London Emeline hailed a cab. Venturing out of her comfort zone, she rode to the shelter on East 110th and brought home Scaramouche; a cat instead of a dog, in case Deborah did have a point.

A kindness the cat has apparently forgotten. Scaramouche surveys the crowd, hisses angrily at Emeline, and retreats to the guest room closet; later Xavier finds the animal curled up on his dirty laundry.

With pleasantries, and complements on the décor, they settle in the living room. Emeline sees Xavier staring at Ryan, frowning. As if oblivious to Ryan's illness or Xavier's expression, Gabor finds common ground.

"I know this neighborhood, Emeline. In the late '50s, I was just a kid, my family moved from Hungary to 74th and Third.

"Third Avenue." Emeline sounds dreamy. "I remember a pub called Rudy's."

"And the El, like a huge, metal jungle gym, that ran all along Third," Gabor recalls. "I thought it was magic, even if it made everyplace we lived dark."

"The photographer Gabor Eder was Hungarian, he did my wedding. Perhaps your family knew him? White wine for me, please, Xavier."

"Forty thousand people moved to the US after the war, most of them to New York." Gabor turns to Xavier. "We were the immigrants back then."

"Hungarian," says Xavier, "there's another language for you, Emeline. She's been working on her Spanish." Emeline suspects Xavier's heard her practicing in the shower, he'll be pleased she's taken his suggestion seriously.

"Not so easy to learn, Hungarian's only related to Turkish and Finnish," Gabor explains. "Hungarians and Czechs lived in the 70s, and the 80s were all Germans. Do you remember Eine Kleine Konditorei, the little café on 86th?"

Emeline nods. "When it closed fifteen years ago, there went the last of the great marzipan."

"Except," Xavier says, showing off, "a café would be French."

"Anyone notice the guy from the British Isles is the only one here with an accent?"

"Yes, Ryan darling, and you've always groomed your brogue as carefully as your beard." Gabor seems not to notice the beard is no more or worry Ryan may miss it. "French, your name, I'm guessing, Emeline. Am I right?"

"A family name, they tell me; some story about a woman who went to Paris and came home with opalines and a bun in the oven. Such beautiful, clear blue stones; I have the necklace, though I can't vouch for the story. You know how that goes." She and Xavier exchange a look; neither mentions the Chinese statue hidden inside a wedding cake.

"Not French, then?"

"Disappointed?" Is she flirting? "My parents were English, I started out in London."

"Ryan is tracking down the stories in his family," says Gabor. "Everyone has lineage, after all, even a family like Ryan's."

"Bunch of reprobates, drunkards, scalawags, and rogues," Ryan sounds quite proud. "You should give it a try, Emeline. Log on to 'ancestry' after breakfast, and the next thing you know it's suppertime."

Emeline doesn't know if Xavier's agreed to the dinner to thank Gabor for giving him a job at the gym. Or to give her a companion in case Flavia pops in. The first seems unnecessary and the second unlikely. Xavier darts back and forth, bearing a tray of miniature *empanadas,* refilling Gabor's Pinot Grigio and Ryan's Malbec. Emeline holds up her glass and, reluctantly, Xavier pours.

"We're opposites in everything," Gabor says fondly.

"Like us. Xavier finds me stuffy, and I find him quite cool." The cool one looks uncomfortable. "He should have seen me at the wheel of our friends' yacht."

Only when Xavier invites them to the table does Emeline understand: it's a chance to show off his Latino flair in the kitchen. Her compact, square teak table is nothing like the sprawling, mahogany BBC prop seating twelve she presided over on 95th Street. Determined to do her bit (if a little anxious how the meal will turn out), Emeline picks up the string of small talk she's begun with Gabor.

"Yes, Antibes. We sailed there once."

"You know, I've never been sailing?" Ryan muses. "That was in Gabor's other incarnation, with his wife." As he reaches for his wine glass, Emeline notices Ryan's hand has a tremor too. He seems much older than Gabor.

"Our friends, the Greenberg's, had a fifty footer," Emeline continues, "lovely, except for the squalls. Xavier thinks I should lead a more exciting life, only I'm pretty sure those days are behind me."

Sipping his Pinot Grigio, Gabor confesses he, too, dreads the rough seas, going on at some length and giving Emeline, behind her polite smile, a chance to hear what Ryan is saying to Xavier.

"How far didje get, then," Ryan asks in his brogue, "at La Guardia?"

"Usual beginner's classes. Programming. Some code. A semester of math and physics."

"And you did okay with those? No trouble with the math?"

"The math? God, no."

"It's always math or physics kills the dream."

"Neither killed the dream for me, only the tuition."

"Xavier," interrupts Emeline, "it's delicious, this chicken. What do you call it?"

"*Pollo con ancho.*"

"You have some lovely things, Emeline," Gabor nods appreciatively.

"Clifford, my late husband, liked to buy prints that struck his fancy, limited editions, of course. Then later," she hesitates, "a friend was breaking up his collection, and we bought a few pieces."

"Who was that?" Gabor asks. She studies his face for signs of nosiness. Seeing only polite interest, she says "Ron Segal."

"I've heard of him," Gabor nods, "one of *the* Segals."

Emeline concentrates on her dish of black beans. Gabor is right. Generations back Ron's family built the department store, the family money upgraded from off-the-rack to *couture* by passing decades and benevolent works.

"Lovely man," she says. "At Yale he was a tenor in the Whiffinpoof's." She notices the chef yawning. "But there was much more to him than a singing group, Xavier. Later on he was second chair on a case defending a chemical company accused of hazardous waste spills. He stood stony-faced when the company was cleared and quit the firm three weeks later. I've seen Ron, really excited about a new painting, lean his head back and sing out a high C. 'That's the note that got me Whiffed,' he'd say.'"

"Humble brag, we'd call it today." Ryan winks at Xavier. "What's for dessert?"

"Candied guava shells with cream cheese," Emeline answers. "A special treat."

When Gabor and Ryan stand to help clear the dishes, Xavier whispers: "Nice guy, isn't he, Gabor."

"Very."

"Anything like Clifford?"

"Not in the least."

After dinner Gabor walks around looking at the walls in the living room. "A Bridget Riley, I noticed it before; an early Diebenkorn watercolor. Were you the eye behind this collection, or your husband?"

"A team effort, I'd say. When Koerner's was going strong…"

"Ah, Koerner's," Gabor laments. "How did they get into such trouble?"

"Conners?" Xavier asks, curious.

The others laugh, but Gabor pats Xavier's hand to reassure him, "It's that difficult German 'euh.' A gallery and one of the best in the city, until they fell on what, hard times, would you call it?"

"Xavier has the right idea," insists Ryan. "Conners they turned out to be."

"But maybe conned as well, sweetheart."

"Let's call it what it was, gentlemen," Emeline stiffens. "Fraudulent action. Arguably one of the city's finest galleries until they succumbed to greed. It closed a year ago, Xavier, in a swirl of allegations and lawsuits. All because the gallery chose to accept at face value the provenance of particular pieces, all coming from one man who claimed to have a pipeline to treasures in Europe."

"A pipeline to shite, you ask me. Easy to believe some buyers might be fooled, but Koerner's? The gallery had to realize what was going on." Ryan likes to have the last word, Emeline notices. Cliff had been the same way until he met his match in her.

It isn't until the men are sipping coffee that Gabor says: "Xavier's told us a little about the agreement you've struck, Emeline."

"Between us," she manages to sound modest, "we seem to get things done. You may have read about Luca Bevilaqua's fashion show, the excitement at the end? That was one of our capers." Xavier winces. She ignores him. "Right now we're looking into another matter. It's about—" Xavier, watching her, looks worried she's a little drunk, will talk too freely. Perhaps he's right. She changes course.

"About some confusion over a project of my husband's." Xavier looks up, startled. "It's alright to talk about, Xavier, he was my husband and I can decide. Paintings were involved. Perhaps another time we can get your thoughts on the problem?"

Xavier jumps to his feet. "Another coffee, gentleman? Actually, Emeline, Gabor was talking about our other arrangement. Living here."

"Might come a time when ye could use an escort." Ryan is giving his blessing.

"Glad there's no misunderstanding." Boldly she puts her hand over Gabor's, as spotted as her own, and feels pleased when he covers her hand with his.

CHAPTER 13

Xavier finishes vacuuming and stretches out in the room he shares with Ramon. The problem is Ryan, seeing Ryan, seeing him look so much worse. Thinner, paler, and Kaposi patches around his nose and mouth. Had they been there before? No, he'd remember. Shocked but trying not to stare, Xavier focused on the silly dog instead. Surprising that Ryan has made it this far; one of the early guys infected in the '80s, Ryan has to be a superman.

Xavier knows he was lucky to get to the clinic early, thanks to Alejandro's silly postcard in the language of flowers, though not another word since. Xavier knows what Emeline would say if he had the nerve to tell her about Alejandro. "Look ahead, not back."

He owes Alejandro for the postcard. Xavier watches his CD4 count the way a stock player reads the WSJ on line. Successfully ducking bad habits like heroin, alcohol, and coke, now Xavier's addicted to HAART. The highly active antiretroviral therapy keeping AIDS from developing and prolonging the lives of millions.

Twisting to pull his cell from his rear pocket, Xavier checks into the data base. The tiny figures on the screen reporting large numbers do little to reassure him. Fifty thousand new HIV infections each year, and he's gay, Latino, and under 24: a dark trifecta. On automatic he clicks to the other link, the one he hopes will save him: "With early treatment, the development of AIDS can be stalled for decades."

Because he's anxious about Ryan—or else because they're on their way to lunch with Julian—Xavier takes it out on Emeline. "I swear, Emeline, use 'capers' one more time and I'm done. That's all our work means to you, a parlor game you can tell your friends about? It's serious business, this messing in people's lives. And what's with the drinking? I didn't think with your meds you were supposed to drink."

"I am allowed. From time to time. A bit."

"Three glasses, or was it four, you call that a bit?"

"Look who's messing about in people's lives now."

"You were—"

"A little tipsy?"

"Tipsy, my ass. You were drunk."

"For goodness sake, Xavier, I was in my home." She gives him a look he reads as *not yours*. "Relaxing with your friends."

"Nothing you'd do in front of your own friends, you mean?"

"But I did, at Julian's wedding. You were too busy stuffing yourself with shrimp to notice. And I caught my mistake, I said nothing to our guests about the Wellington's, only Clifford. Surely I can talk about my husband's affairs if I choose."

"Just as dangerous. No one keeps secrets, and you—"

"They are your friends, Xavier; don't you trust your own friends?" That shuts him up. They ride the rest of the way to Wall Street in silence.

"The original notion of a mutual fund was to protect the assets in case Company A's stock went south." Julian might be lecturing

MBA students instead of an audience of two. "If it did, investors in the company lost money, though only on paper, as long as they had the stomach to ride out the decline and wait for a brighter day. But touchy investors who sold as the stock declined, they locked in their losses."

Julian's picked their lunch venue this time, a Greek deli with framed posters of the Acropolis, blue Aegean waters, and an endless loop of zither music; an unprepossessing place where they can talk without anyone overhearing—anyone who matters, Julian means.

"Then some smart guy came up with another play. Hedge funds, private partnerships that date back to 1949," Julian glances at Emeline, the only one of the three for whom 1949 can mean more than a costume party. "The idea was to hedge against losses by managing investment risks and still deliver strong returns."

"How?" asks Xavier.

"Say a hedge fund owns stock in a company, we'll call this one Virtu." Julian smirks, virtue rarely the driving force on Wall Street. "Dude, you know what it means to short?" A straightforward enough question if Julian hadn't added an up-down gaze to call attention to Xavier's modest height.

Emeline intervenes. "Of course he does. You bet that a stock, in this case Virtu, will lose value. You may even take steps to undermine its value. A rumor here, letter writing campaign there, a public investigation."

"Or wangle seats on the board. Change the company's management. But, back to the basics, Emeline. Say a hedge fund owns 100 shares of Virtu but thinks the price will decline. So before that can happen the fund sells the shares for $1000. Let's say the hedge fund proves right and the share price of Virtu drops to $600. Now the fund buys back the 100 shares, paying only $600, making a profit of $400."

"We're with you," says Emeline. "Do you recommend the Reuben?" Xavier and Julian stare. Reuben Fund? "Clifford did like a good Reuben, sauerkraut dangling about the edges. Though I never thought of it as Greek."

"But shorting is only one strategy. There's leverage, relative value arbitrage," Julian catches the glazed look on the their faces. "Besides, because hedge funds are private they've been hampered by fewer regulations and less oversight.

"Private," echoes Emeline before Xavier can ask, "means it's not sold to the general public."

"Exactly. They are sold only to sophisticated individuals or groups with very high capital worth. More than half are institutional investors like endowments and pension funds. Lemme tell you, positions in a hedge fund are big, we're not talking a hundred shares of AT& T. Last spring?" He gulps his beer. "The industry reached a record high: over two trillion dollars under management."

"The new golden age," murmurs Emeline. "Aren't they riskier?"

"Depends. The best managers tend to be right more often than the market; but then you've got your fees: 2 percent of your assets under management plus twenty percent of your profits. Still, since hedge fund managers often invest their own capital, they have an incentive to increase risk oversight. Anyway, with new regulations in the last two years, they're reporting more information than they used to."

"Hedge funds tend to specialize in the stocks of particular kinds of companies," says Emeline. "Gold, say, or pharmaceuticals. Cadmium, what are its interests?"

"Here's the story near as I can make out. Cadmium started as a by-blow of another fund called—"

"By-blow?" Xavier interrupts. Julian looks annoyed.

"An illegitimate child," Emeline says, "it's an old English expression. In Medieval times when an earl and his mistress had a child—"

"Got it. Like Jomar."

"No, not at all, your nephew is part of a loving family—"

"And the father, whoever he is," Julian interrupts, "will hardly be an earl."

"Julian's talking about a financial fund that's a spin-off of another fund. Do go on, Julian." Irritated, Julian makes them wait while he sips his Heineken, giving the heavy glass mug a sommelier's attention.

"I dug into Cadmium. I'm seeing a blend of high-risk companies, opportunities for real players," a contemptuous look at Xavier, "and a couple of pretty safe investments. Like pharmaceuticals, candy manufacturers, or gun production."

"In other words," Emeline gives him a scathing look, "making money on addiction, health risks, and armaments."

"Be that as it may, if Cadmium weren't doing it . . ."

"Others would be. Thank you, Julian, I am familiar with Wall Street logic."

"Interesting thing is, Cadmium turns out to be more highly leveraged than I expected. The original investments, while sound, have been the basis for very creative borrowing strategies."

"Mortgaged," Emeline translates. "Like a house."

"Supposing you own a house in East Hampton." The professor's back on his podium. "But you've taken out a second mortgage on the house to realize needed dollars—for instance, to buy a ski house in Vail. You borrow cash out of your asset. Cadmium holds a few solid stocks: ores, minerals, things that come out of the ground. They're like the house. Trouble is, looks like Cadmium has borrowed against the solid stocks to buy a whole bunch of risky ones, making the fund vulnerable.

"Which means," Julian grins like a wolf, "anyone who scopes out the real situation can short shares in Cadmium. Eventually make a killing, which is exactly what I plan to do." With a smothered burp and satisfied grin, he tips his chair back so it barely balances on two legs, then spreads his jacket wide and hooks his thumbs behind his belt.

Xavier considers the precarious balance. Not Cadmium's, the chair's. Poor impulse control, that's Julian's problem. It's a phrase Xavier learned from the social worker the Union Settlement sent around, the one who insists Rocio and baby Jomar only see "the dad" when others are present. Xavier filed away the term, along with bonding (DSS-speak for cuddle the kid) and support system. Six months ago he'd have stuck his foot under a front chair leg and watched the jerk fall to the floor.

"But," Emeline asks sweetly, "doesn't that expose you to charges of insider trading?"

"If I go down, you go down," Julian growls in imitation of "The Godfather." He's chewing with his mouth open; Flavia would slap him upside the head if Julian were her son. "One other thing: I found a trail of investments that don't fit with the rest of the portfolio; I just didn't have time to track 'em down."

"Don't give it another thought, Julian dear. You've been terrific to figure out this much." Emeline wraps the untouched half of her Reuben in paper napkins as Julian's nose twitches in distaste.

Waiting for the bill, Julian's still talking. "Fashion Week only happens twice a year, thank God, or I'd be stone broke and out of closet space. Tell me, why does she have to call her mother in Coral Gables every damn day?"

Emeline looks away. While Xavier knows she has little use for Julian's bride, he can see she envies the doxy's closeness with her mother. In a generous mood, Julian grabs the bill from the waiter and pulls out his credit card.

"Thank you, Julian, that's very sweet of you." Emeline withdraws her fingers, dragging them on the white tablecloth to still the tremor.

"Come on, you're like a second mother to me. And after the mess you went through with Clifford? You'll have to come to us for supper; I'll have my little lady set it up." At the curb he ignores Xavier's outstretched hand, gives Emeline a peck on the cheek, and heads off.

"I don't get it." Xavier helps Emeline into a cab. "I thought you'd want him to keep digging."

"I've known Julian since he was born: tell him to do *this*, and he'll do *that* instead. Believe me, he'll dig into Cadmium. Be interesting to see what he comes up with."

"How long will that take?"

"Such a *very* busy man," Emeline widens her eyes. "So important, so much to do, but we'll hear from him. A week, I'm guessing, maybe ten days. Do I drop you at the gym?"

She does, but when she gets home and opens her mail she wishes Xavier were still with her. "What's happened?" Xavier asks when he gets back. Distraught, she holds out the stiff note paper and mouths the words as he reads them out loud. "Thursday, 3:00 p.m., your place. Unless you want to read more in the tabloids. Sergei Morosov."

Alarmed, Xavier kneels on the carpet and gently pulls her hands away from her face. "Who is this man with the strange name? Serge is a fabric, my Aunt Koka knows all about fabrics."

Emeline can see he's only trying to cheer her up. Her mind hopscotching, she rubs her fingers over her eyes so her diamond ring flicks the light from her desk lamp onto the wall. Off, on, off, on. Like Tinkerbell she told him, the first time he noticed. Then had to explain, Xavier thought Tinkerbell was one of her friends.

"Emeline?"

"Sir-Gay, not *serge*; he's Russian."

"A knighted homo, what next?" he laughs. She doesn't. "Then I should clean up, the place smells like cat. Do I help with the tea when he comes, this friend of yours, or stay out of the way?"

"Friend! I've never heard of him. Just listen to him. Peremptory, setting the terms, the time, even the place, my own home. What a nerve."

"So he's not coming for tea."

"He's coming to confront me. As if I have any idea what happened, or would tell him even if I knew, which I do not; I want to forget the whole business." Xavier keeps his hands tightly over hers. She finally pulls away one hand, lays it tenderly on her upper chest.

"Then we should talk to him together, don't you think? Okay, I'll be here. If you like," he gives a quick smile, "I can get a gun from Ramon."

"Really, Xavier," Emeline reaches for a tissue and blows her nose, "I hardly think that will be necessary."

"Send him up, Gregor." Relieved her voice sounds strong on the house phone, Emeline pours herself a glass of water and walks down the hall, Xavier right behind her. Good thing, too. As soon as she opens the door Emeline knows she's in trouble.

Even if he's a small, slim man with a neat moustache, Sergei Morosov has eyebrows that signal belligerence. What he lacks in bulk he will make up for in bluster. A few of Cliff's early business associates had the same manner, gave off the same attitude: Don't mess with me. I may not have your money, your connections, your standing, but wait and see, end of the day, I will.

Sitting dead center, Morosov takes over the sofa and crosses one ankle over a knee. Is providing sightlines to his crotch part of his plan to intimidate? For a long minute he stares at Emeline. Determined, she gazes back, unblinking. Morosov unbuttons his jacket, providing an expense of grey Oxford shirt stretched over a taut stomach.

"We have problem, Emeline. May I call you Emeline?"

"You may call me Mrs. Hughes." She avoids Xavier's warning look. Just don't dis him, Xavier has said, it won't help.

"Mrs. Hughes," his tone is mocking. "You may not remember me. I had business with your husband."

"As did many people, Mr. Morosov." Her impeccable pronunciation catches his attention. He lowers his offending leg to the floor, clasps both hands between his knees and tries a confidential approach.

"I am here in regard to work he did for Mr. Segal. Mr. Hughes helped him downsize to a smaller place; at least that's what was claimed."

Emeline sees Xavier stand to catch her eye. Is he about to take over? Morosov flicks a dismissive look his way. "Would we be more comfortable speaking privately?"

"No." Inspired, she adds, "my man is quite deaf." Lord, Xavier won't be happy, and I'll have two angry men to deal with. Xavier opens his mouth, closes it again, and sits down.

"Your husband was disposing of Segal paintings. Quite a few went to auction."

"I knew nothing about my husband's business affairs." She rests her left hand on her right, to grip her cane, still her tremor. And, perhaps, draw attention to her ring? "I'm unable to help you. Perhaps you should speak to Sotheby's."

"Ah! You know it was Sotheby's? Not Christie's, then, or Phillips or Doyle. No matter. I do not concern myself with pieces went to auction. Two Feininger woodcuts. A pencil sketch of the Dutch school, no attribution; a possible Chagall sketch." Morosov had gone to the auction or at least studied the catalogue; he wants her to know he's informed.

"If you say so," she lifts her left hand to cover a yawn.

"Certain buyers were approached beforehand, did you know that? Given opportunity to purchase privately half a dozen other pieces. I was one of the fortunate."

Risking a glance at Xavier, Emeline guesses he's weighing the same questions. Besides this obnoxious gentleman, who were the others treated to this rare opportunity? A commission is charged at auction. What about these private sales. Were there commissions larger than the auction's? If so, into whose pockets had they fallen? Her stomach cramps, she feels again the tension of her last days as a wife, not yet a widow, watching Clifford's favor for a friend convert to a burden, a puzzle, and eventually a worry even as he refused to tell her what was bothering him.

The Russian's accent is swelling, soon he'll sound like Valda Fairfax. "And my buyer, gentleman in England, wishes to adjust his collection. Only Mr. SinJen Pearce in Surrey comes up against difficulty, a problem with the provenance, the history of the painting, you understand?" Out of the corner of her eye she sees Xavier suppress a smile. At least hearing loss will spare him one more definition of provenance.

"Perfectly. Still, as I already said, I cannot help you."

Morosov leans back and crosses his legs again. "At the time of your husband's unfortunate accident, was there not possibility of legal charges? Questions of deceptive market practices, practices this city grows tired of and," a jerk of the head from this volunteer ombudsman, "seeks to root out."

Supposed to be hard of hearing, Xavier continues to fuss with the cushion behind his back. Emeline, to stifle a gasp, begins coughing into her monogrammed handkerchief. She's heard these words before or at least read them. Morosov is quoting from that rag, the *Post*. Emeline steels herself to refuse the bait.

"If my buyer fails to auction painting because of faulty provenance, he will come after me." Morosov's smile is a tiger's spotting a gazelle. "But before that happen I intend to come after you."

"Then I must refer you to my husband's lawyer. There is nothing I can tell you." Emeline's come prepared. From her jacket pocket she extracts one of Coop's cards.

Ignoring the card, Morosov changes direction. "I am unable to reach your husband's colleague Mr. Hueber. Can you provide me with address?"

"I am afraid we have lost touch."

"Is he in the city?"

"As I say. . ."

"I've heard you and he were quite close."

With a shaking hand Emeline deliberately spills her glass of water onto the rug. "You have been misinformed. I have nothing more to tell you. Our business here is finished."

She realizes too late she should have asked which painting concerns him. In the way of a mute Xavier does. He points to the John Sloan landscape on the wall, taps his lips, twice and lifts his eyebrows. With a great show of reluctance Morosov reaches into his maroon briefcase and brings out a four-inch by six-inch print. Miming indifference, Emeline stares out the window. It's left to Xavier to takes the glossy print and with a firm hold on the visitor's elbow, lift him from the sofa and bundle him toward the hallway.

"We are not finished," calls the Russian, trying to snatch back the print but already, except for one grasping hand, he's out the door. Xavier holds the print high over his head, Morosov's hand retreats, and Xavier slams the door shut. The muted voice from the foyer, "You hear from me more," is followed by two angry kicks at the door.

CHAPTER 14

The photo is not large so it's difficult to see details. A man in a black cloak stands against a murky background, white collar around the neck and white trim on the sleeve edges, leaning on a table with a hint of red cloth and a sword handle just visible. His is a pale face with a proud expression."

"What do you think," Emeline begins, "does Morosov believe there's a problem with the provenance?" Still playing the mute, Xavier raises his eyebrows, a mime's picture of incomprehension. "Or hope he can convince me there is so he can get his money back? Come on, Xavier. Use your words."

Deliberately he picks up the silver-framed portrait of Clifford; gestures, one palm open, and waits.

She lets out a deep breath. "I suppose you want to hear what happened."

"That would help."

"Hurray. He speaks."

"The whole truth, no more bits and pieces like you've been dealing out," then Xavier stops; if he sounds too cross she'll clam up.

"All kinds of things I don't know about you," she grumbles.

"Today is not my day to tell and tomorrow doesn't look good either. This worry you carry around, Emeline, it didn't start with Clifford's death, did it."

"I thought so. Until our old apartment was on the market and someone, as I told you, was looking through Clifford's desk."

"I'm listening."

"Ron Segal was an art collector. Earlier collectors, like the Havemayers and Peggy Guggenheim, had an eye for the contemporary art making its way into the New York mind. But Ron was different. When he got the chance he bought older works to keep what art he could from being swept into the Nazi dragnet."

"You're kidding me. Hitler?"

"Hitler fancied himself a collector or at least he saw the value. He and his minions scooped up a massive number of pieces."

"How can people fuss over canvas and paint when others are struggling to stay alive?"

"Ron bought art from Jewish families trying to escape from Europe, so they'd have some cash. His efforts were a drop in the bucket Ron used to say. Still, when he could, he bought an etching or a lithograph, an oil, an aquarelle. He had contacts in the States and in Germany. Cliff used to wonder, was Ron worried the same thing might happen here? Ron never forgot how our country turned back boatloads of Jews, people who might have been relatives for all he knew."

"I didn't . . . America turned away Jews?"

"You think Puerto Ricans are the only people picked on in America? At any rate, when Ron was getting ready to move to Florida, he asked Cliff to help him."

"Get rid of stuff," he nods.

"Valuable stuff!"

"Sorry. Go on."

"Ron was ready to sell most of his collection: antiques, paintings, sculpture. I believe there was a Brancusi."

"Not a big market for those at Goodwill." Xavier gives his bargain jeans a surreptitious hike, they'd always felt looser than he liked.

"Goodwill? Assets, Xavier, just as much as his stocks, bonds, the six-bedroom house in Tarrytown, his pied-a-terre on 71st. Ron wanted to sell up, and if the past is any guide, much of the money went to charity."

"We apologize, Goodwill and I."

"Ron could have let Sotheby's have everything. Cliff thought it would be smarter to sell some pieces in a way that was more, more . . ."

"Under the radar."

"Ron had every confidence Cliff could help him dispose of these assets properly."

"And Segal was selling because?"

"He wasn't well. He was moving to a new residence."

"A nursing home," Xavier has some idea what those cost, Segal would need every penny.

"A lovely retirement community," Emeline corrects. "In Palm Beach, his sister already lived there. Cliff arranged for an appraiser to value the furniture, rugs, lamps, and so forth. But Cliff wanted separate estimates on the art, so he brought in a man he knew—a Ph.D. in art history who'd once been a partner in a gallery. Several of the paintings were taken away for cleaning or restoration, don't ask me the details.

"Cliff arranged to have some pieces auctioned at Sotheby's, they had a nineteenth-century European auction coming up. You know, a theme?" Xavier doesn't, but he's relieved Emeline's finally getting the story off her chest—if it is the whole story, hardly the memory of a wife who knew nothing of her husband's business.

"What went wrong?"

"At auction, nothing. But not every piece went to Sotheby's. Either they weren't nineteenth century or the consultant knew one or two collectors who might pay more if they bought privately."

"You knew him, this consultant?"

"Hueber? I met him a few times. He was checking that every painting had a paper trail."

"A provenance."

"If you insist on being pompous."

"I was shooting for professional. What happened?"

"After these pieces came back from the restorer Clifford seemed to think something didn't look right."

"Your husband, not an art expert," he sees her wince, "how would he know?"

"I wish I knew, but I was worried Cliff was, that Cliff wasn't . . . don't make me say it." Emeline's eyes fill with tears.

"Wasn't being as upright as you'd like." It takes him a minute but he figures it out. Emeline wears a look he hasn't seen since the day he found her in the alley. She looks frightened. Maybe this was what she meant, back in the beginning: *You might help me look into a few things.*

"That's what been so painful for you." Xavier's voice is gentle. "Ron turned to your husband, a man he thought he could trust, and Ron's reputation—along with Clifford's—winds up tarnished."

"And now this Morosov," Emeline wipes her eyes, "he knew about the rumors and innuendos in the *Post*."

"Do you still have them, the *Post* stories?"

"You think I would keep that garbage?"

"Where is Ron Segal now?"

"Poor Ron, he had a stroke, he can't speak. Two fine men and they fell off their perch within months. I miss them both." Emeline looks mournful.

"Have you tried to talk to this consultant?"

"I haven't seen him since Cliff's funeral. Call him if you want, I've got the number somewhere. He's moved to Chicago."

Xavier hesitates and decides; in for a dime, in for a dollar, or else the moment will pass and he'll never know. "Emeline, tell me this. Are you sure the car crash was an accident?"

"Of course it was an accident!" Her face flushed, she curls into a ball on the sofa. "Ron insisted on treating Cliff and Hueber to dinner in Tarrytown. They were on their way back. It was late, and they'd both had plenty to drink so Hueber was driving. He was injured in the accident, too. But it was Cliff in the passenger seat, the most dangerous spot. No seat belt, of course, Cliff never wore a seat belt. 'I managed to break out of Brixton,' he'd say, 'I don't like to be restrained.'"

Xavier reaches out his hand but she swats it away. "Just leave me alone, Xavier. Go away and take your lurid imagination with you."

Xavier doesn't know anything about art; still his time at La Guardia taught him how to look things up. The Internet doesn't yield what he wants so his next free afternoon he heads to the public library. Sixty-seven branches in Manhattan alone, Flavia used to brag, even if she only ever took her kids to the branch on 125th Street. He remembers light stone walls, dark shelves, and many stairs. Flavia says there's a new children's room. Maybe he'll take Jomar once the kid can read.

On Fifth and 42nd two giant stone lions, Patience and Fortitude, guard the mother ship. Students with knapsacks colonize the steps, along with homeless men holding their shopping bags of meager belongings, or maybe only cups of coffee. Today a skinny model with long hair, a make-up artist, and a photographer stand for a fashion shoot.

At the reference desk a manicured dude eyes Xavier with interest. "Yes, even the *Post*," he admits; clearly he'd prefer the NYPL to microfiche only the city's more reputable publications. Xavier writes out the date of Clifford's accident and asks to see the following six weeks and, as an afterthought, the six weeks before as well. Led to a cubby and a machine, he feeds in the strips and begins winding backwards in time.

After a round of calls on his cell Xavier tracks down Detective Hill; reluctant at first, Hill agrees to meet. Xavier finds him at the same Cuban coffee shop, settled into the same banquette. Maybe Hill leases his out-of-office space by the month.

"You messing in police business again, Escudero?"

"Morning to you, too, Detective. Matter of fact, I don't know." Hill frowns. "I don't know if it's police business or not."

"Take it from the top, *amigo,* but hurry, I've only got ten." That's enough time for the eggs, fries, and cinnamon bun Xavier offers to buy.

"Mrs. Hughes' husband died back in April," Xavier lays his pile of papers on the plastic table top, "in a late-night car crash on the Henry Hudson."

Hill, chewing, squints a while at the plastic tiles overhead. "Not my turf," he says finally.

"And it took you that much time to notice."

"So?"

"So I'm guessing you remember the case."

"Not actually a case is what I remember. Two men, driving home from Westchester kinda late at night, kinda drunk. They veer, hit the barrier, the old guy dies."

"Mr. Hughes." Xavier's indignant though he never met the man.

"Mr. Hughes dies. His friend is hurt. EMTs arrive, send him to the hospital; within a week he's out."

"Why?"

"Do I look like a doc to you?"

"I mean, why did the car veer? Does the report say? I assume there is a report."

"Sure, somewhere."

"Which guy was driving? Was one of them still been behind the wheel?"

"Doesn't your Mrs. Hughes know?" Xavier looks down and stirs his coffee. "Lordy, man. Lemme guess. You haven't told her you're on this fishing expedition."

"I'm looking after her interests." Xavier reaches into his windbreaker pocket, brings out the card from the plainclothes man at the wedding. "You send this guy after us? Or was it your pal in the one-ten?"

"You are in such deep—you gonna even tell her we're talking?"

Xavier doesn't answer, only smooths out the copies he's made from the microfiche. "Financier Meets Sudden Death on Henry Hudson," mourns one headline. "More to Hughes Death Than Meets the Eye," hints another. Xavier taps the pages here, and there. Words leap out: *Investigation! Embezzlement?* Hill chews.

"Another thing, detective. Mrs. Hughes is convinced," that's a little strong but Xavier needs to bring up his heavy artillery, "she's being followed."

"Maybe she has an admirer." Neither bothers to say that absent a direct threat, the police won't be impressed. Eggs are gone, fries are gone, and half the cinnamon bun. "You read too many mysteries, Escudero. Or else she does."

"Please, Detective?"

"I suppose I could ask a couple questions."

"You'll text me?"

"Meet me here in two days. Good food and no bugs. Well, maybe the odd cockroach in the kitchen. You seein' anyone, Xavier?"

"Nice segue: cockroach, boyfriend." Hill studies him, waiting. "Matter of fact, no. Appreciate your help, sir. Only other detective I know is Flynn from the Middle South Precinct."

Hill rolls his eyes. "Him! Jesus may love him. Everyone else thinks he's an asshole."

Emeline's had no luck arranging a sit-down. Wendy Wells returned her first call and proposed a time, but Emeline couldn't confirm because she couldn't reach Xavier. Now Wendy's called again. "No, Emeline, I haven't changed my mind. I do want to meet. It's only," a forced laugh, "something's come up I have to take care of first. I'll call again in a day or two. Promise."

Fine, the Wellington's problems can wait. Emeline's got her own problems. Distraught by Morosov's intrusion, she's told Xavier way more about Clifford's affairs than she meant to. Not because she doesn't trust Xavier, it surprises her to realize. Only Cliff's business dealings with Ron Segal, she'd thought all that was a closed book. Morosov's insinuations and Xavier's curiosity, they've brought it all back, revived the unease she'd hoped she put to rest.

During their intense, early days at Rudy's, their exchange of promises in the park, Emeline made up her mind she'd trust Clifford, believe his promise: "From now on, luv, I'll stick to the straight and narrow." Together they signed onto a conspiracy of silence, agreed to draw a curtain over details of his early rise and new money. She hadn't wanted to hear, and Clifford hadn't wanted to say.

This summer, stunned by the slurs and innuendos in that tawdry rag, she's had many moments to agonize. Losing Cliff was bad enough. It was worse, somehow, not to be sure she actually knew the man she'd lost. If she'd gotten to Cliff in time, if she could have asked him, injured as he was he'd have told her the truth. By dying, he's wrapped them both in a new conspiracy and this time without her consent.

"You home?" Xavier calls out

"In the den."

"What's the matter, Wendy Wells?"

"Wendy is playing hard to get, but no. I'm worried about the painting. If there's really a problem we have to take it seriously. That means digging into Clifford's business, the last thing I want to do. And what if that dreadful Morosov comes back? Though I did direct Gregor to say I'm not at home if he does."

"Got to get ahead of the game, Emeline, not get locked into playing defense."

"If you say so. No idea what it means."

"Do you still have your husband's laptop?"

"In the closet, in your room." Lately he's noticed she's stopped saying guest room, waiting to see if he'll object and so far, he hasn't.

"Mind if I take a look?"

Emeline looks uneasy. "What do you think you'll find?"

"I thought maybe something in the files can help us." She hesitates. "No, my bad, Emeline, you should get Coop, he works for you. Call him tomorrow, he can look into it."

Emeline straightens up, looks him in the eye. "You work for me, too, Xavier; of course you can look. Cliff's password is Brixton 547."

It doesn't take Xavier long to find files marked Segal and read through them—details about the collection, the condition of pieces, all that back story to art Xavier never knew existed. The last file holds his attention. He reads the words, no trouble, only he doesn't know what to make of them. Frowning, he closes the computer and turns it off.

Meeting Emeline in the kitchen, seeing her mind's moved on to other matters, he's relieved, though not for long.

"Xavier," she says, looking serious, "I've come to a decision. You'll have to be the one to go, take care of it. Because I can't."

"What are you talking about?"

"The painting, of course. The del Mazo. We need professional help."

"You mean talk to Julian." Xavier feels his lip curl.

"What? Lord no, not his thing at all. Deborah."

"Your daughter, in London. That Deborah?"

"She's knows so much about art already, let alone getting another degree. You'll simply have to pop over and talk to her."

There must be one or two experts in New York, Emeline waits for him to say. He does not. Has he no idea art experts exist? Soccer, computer, personal training experts, those would fall into his realm.

Still, this is not news Xavier takes well. "I'm not going anywhere, Emeline, I have a job."

"It's still valid, your passport?"

"You don't need a passport to go to Puerto Rico."

"Ah, but your other trip, when your mom took you to Santa Domingo," she plays it like an ace, watching him wish he'd never brought up Santa Domingo. "You have to go on my behalf, Xavier. I am not able to."

"Air sick? Busy social schedule?" He eyes her, suspicious. "Doesn't matter, I'm not going. Our agreement says nothing about me leaving town."

"At the time it never occurred—"

"I've settled in at the gym. What happens if I tell Gabor I'm walking out?"

"Tell him you're taking, what do they call it? Family leave."

"Family leave is for a new baby. Or a death."

"There has been a death."

"Clifford's, three months back? Stretch the truth all you want, no one else will call you and me a family; like I don't have enough trouble with my own people."

"I'll speak to Gabor, he'll understand."

"Good plan. Tell him you're taking my place. Mornings you'll work with Tiffany, a little bitch, by the way, pray she lands an audition soon."

"Don't be absurd, Xavier."

"Then Mrs. 'the Countess' Palmer. Seriously overweight. She'll whine at you for forty minutes straight."

"You and I, we can talk through what you need to find out. You'll have an easier time with Deborah than I would, you don't have the same history."

"No history at all!"

"I'll make sure she meets you at Heathrow. You can follow up if she has contacts to suggest and be home by the end of next week."

"No, Emeline, you go. She's your daughter, and don't you have a brother in London? I'll take you in a cab as far as JFK. That's it."

Emeline presses her hands across her stomach and looks out the window as if sky writing may inspire her, then settles for the truth. "Xavier, this is very embarrassing, I cannot fly. Severe panic attacks, I shake, I sweat, I think it's my heart, there's nothing underneath but air, malevolent, deadly air. Then that moment when the engine slows down and the rumbles subside? I know I only have moments left to live."

"The engine slows because the plane's reached cruising altitude. Otherwise, it's heading for outer space, not Heathrow." She guesses it's a fact he learned from a pilot during cruising of a different kind.

"Very well," Emeline says, trying for the voice of a medieval martyr. "I'll have to manage on my own, then, won't I?" After a couple of tries she rocks herself up from her chair. Shoulders slumped, dragging her foot more than usual, she brushes past him and heads for the kitchen.

"Listen," Xavier follows her, "if I could help I would. I can't lose my job at the gym."

Emeline straightens. Moving slowly, hand braced against the wall, she walks into the kitchen, her mind reeling, as unsteady as her feet. Deborah is the one to turn to, much as Emeline dislikes having to ask her daughter for anything. Art savvy and discrete. There's no one else.

Airplane. London. Leaving her new place on 63rd and her recently revised, barely formed comfort zone, it's like pulling off a scab. Already she feels like throwing up.

Only she will not go on her own. "You're always saying I need to show more *chispa,* so how about this? I'll go if you go. So stop playing with your phone, get on the computer, and book us some tickets." She's scrambling through her handbag.

"I am. I'm using my cell to book."

"Oh." She flips her credit card onto the table. Like a stone skimmed over a pond, it comes to rest against the Dundee marmalade jar. "The PIN is on the back. Try Iberia."

"Spain? I thought we were going to England."

"We are, only it's easier if the flight lands late morning instead of at dawn." Is she putting off re-entering her old world?

"C'mon, Emeline, it'll be fun."

"I wouldn't count on it. Hello, Gabor? It's Emeline," and she cajoles, finishing her plea with "a week at the most, I'm sure. Oh, you are the dearest man. Thank you." She tries Wendy again, but hangs up when the machine answers. She needs to telephone Deborah next; but no, easier to send an email.

"You can sleep on the way over," Xavier assures her, squinting at schedules

"I won't sleep a wink. Awake all night and starving, too."

"It's international, Emeline. They'll have dinner and blankets." She's turns her back: now I'm getting travel tips from the son of a nanny?

She tries the Wellington's once more—bad enough to leave Wendy Wells in the lurch; worse manners not to explain why. This time it's Flavia who answers. "No, she's not here, Mrs. Hughes, she's out with the children."

"Know what time she'll be back, Flavia?"

"I've hardly seen her, and when I do she seems very anxious. Has she talked to you?"

"No. Tell her I tried to reach her, will you? I have to go out of town, so I'm afraid it's my turn to postpone."

She and Xavier spend the next day quarreling and organizing their bags. He's got his knapsack, and she's lent him Clifford's old rolling duffle. She's stopped the *New York Times* and packed what she hopes will do for a city she hasn't seen in years.

Meticulous, she's sorting her pills into the plastic box when she hears the house phone, then Xavier's loud voice.

"For God's sake, can't you see she's my *mother?*" Walking into the kitchen Emeline hears Gregor's tinny voice on the intercom, "but you told me never . . ." sees Xavier pointing to his face as if the doorman can discern matching skin tones through the house line.

Emeline snatches the receiver. "Send her up at once, Gregor. The front elevator, if you please." By the time the elevator stops and the door opens Emeline and Xavier are waiting for her. As breathless as if she's climbed the four flights, Flavia stumbles onto the black and white tiles.

Xavier catches her. "Mai, what are you doing here?"

"Xavier, for God's sake, don't be grilling her until she gets her breath."

"Wendy." Flustered, Flavia uses her employer's first name. "She left a note. She's gone away, but she doesn't say where. She's taken the children with her, and she didn't want me to worry. But I do worry, for her, for them. Something is very wrong. What should we do? Xavier, what should we do?"

Chapter 15

"No more than a few days," Emeline's promised, so they packed light: his backpack and a rolling duffle of Clifford's; her less worn matching roll-on and a sober tote. Xavier persuaded her to sit in front of Clifford's computer with him, and in the end printed out a few of Clifford's files in a folder marked Segal. Emeline left to go find her husband's leather carrying case, "I'll unlock the safe and pull out his black and white notebook, too."

About to shut down the computer, Xavier decided he'd take a look at Clifford's browsing history: theft, petty and grand, jail time for each; theft vs. embezzlement; New York statutes. Mind racing, Xavier's hand hovered over the keyboard, the erase history command a half an inch under his finger.

As the cab speeds toward the airport Xavier can see Emeline feels ill. "Should we pull over."

"No, please no. I am not comfortable in this section of Queens."

Outside the terminal he stamps out his last smoke for the next seven hours. They pass through immigration and security, make their way slowly down the jet bridge. Finally they settle in their seats, Emeline's as far inside as seating allows. When a handsome flight attendant tries to be friendly in Spanish, Xavier ignores him, and lets out a long breath.

Que dios te bendiga. Xavier's ready to believe Flavia's blessings helped. How else would they have survived finalizing tickets, deciding what to pack, and bribing Gregor to feed the cat? With his mind on all these tasks, it took Xavier a while to realize it wasn't any old art expert Emeline wanted to consult, must be plenty of those in the city. She needed to see her daughter. Anxious as she is, she's turned to her closest relative, the one she's not close to at all. Though he hasn't met the daughter, already Xavier doesn't like her.

England's ahead. In July he'd have given a kidney to be going to England. While Jomar swiped jammy fingers across the television as if it were his mother's cell, he fought daily with Rocio to win screen time for the Olympics. Mesmerized, Xavier watched the opening ceremonies at Cardiff's Millennium Stadium; the women in hijab from Saudi and Brunei competing for the first time ever; superstar Michael Phelps winning his twenty-second medal. Awed by the skill, muscle, drive, talent, and patriotism shining like sweat on the athletes. This is the top of the ladder; his work at the gym no more than the puny second rung from the bottom. At cruising altitude he closes his eyes.

When the flight attendant brightens cabin lights to rouse the passengers, Xavier sees through threads of cloud the plane banking over slices of a grey Irish Sea to begin its descent. Touching down at Heathrow, Xavier waits for the applause; skimming over palm trees and shanty houses on the outskirts of San Juan, Puerto Ricans applaud when they land on their island. Waits in vain. In London it's nearly noon as the plane speeds down a runway. Xavier resets his watch; his cell phone's done it on its own.

In the terminal PSA messages, blurred by accents, sound as loud as ever. Emeline's using her US passport so they both peel off from European passengers to stand in the much longer line with other

Americans: high-end travelers, gold bracelets clanking; students bent under backpacks, hostel-bound; tourists wearing matching sweat shirts and sweat pants. Emeline points with disdain at their clumsy sneakers. "Will you look at those ugly trainers?"

They pass five men in striped head scarves rolling out their prayer rugs, knowing by instinct or experience which way is east, dropping to their knees, and touching their heads to the floor in prayer. Xavier retrieves their bags, and they clear customs.

At an ATM Emeline's credit card lets loose a flurry of silver coins and multi-colored bills bearing the Queen's face. Looking at the screen over her shoulder, Xavier is shocked at the exchange rate: $1.61 to buy one English pound? Emeline hands him half the haul, and they move on to scan rows of drivers holding lettered signs with names from around the world—Siddiqi, Moghadan, Solmaz, Wang, Atiago; fewer than half, Gallagher, O'Connell, Campbell, and Clark, bear names from the British Isles.

"You did email your daughter?"

"I thought it . . . wiser." Of course. A request from an unknown Escudero to send a driver, the daughter would dismiss it as a scam. The line thins. Three drivers are left, shifting from foot to foot with their signs. None spell the short, essential name: Hughes.

"It will have to be a cab," Emeline sounds weary, "going to cost the moon."

Listening to music from Mumbai, they ride past commercial outskirts, under railway bridges, their line of traffic swirling on the wrong side of the M4. Emeline tells him winter air in London was thick with smoke when she was a child, everyone burned coal if they could get it. Even without the smoke today she looks weepy. Xavier risks a personal question, "Strange to be back?"

"Terrible for my dad, the smoke," Emeline says as if she hasn't heard. "He worked in an auto factory. Ma had a job in the sugar refinery on Plaistow Wharf; each one helping the war effort, they'd tell me, though mum's was the sweeter job. That's what he'd always say. Before his accident."

"And after?"

"Ma had to leave to care for him, and I moved upstairs to stay with my grandma."

"You couldn't stay with your parents?"

"Too much trouble, I guess."

Even though it's Sunday and the traffic not as bad as it can be, it's an eternity before the cab stops in front of 43 Searles Road, a block-length stone building with entrances spaced like Legos, each entrance flanked by bay windows. Emeline pays the driver. Xavier unloads the bags and when a grey-haired man steps outside, Xavier props his knapsack in the entrance. Emeline climbs the three steps to Deborah's flat, and rings the buzzer.

"Back already, you rascal—what the bloody hell?" A woman wearing a terry wrapper and ferocious scowl stands in the doorway. "Ma! You told me you would email!"

"But I did, darling."

"Never got it."

"A misunderstanding, please don't be mad."

"I'll be whatever I please, thank you very much. You used my new email? Of course you didn't, I'll wager you sent this message to my old account."

Where Emeline is as short as Xavier, Deborah is a tall, stunningly beautiful blonde. Trying to look unobtrusive, Xavier pulls out his cell but still Deborah's furious eyes find him; he might be a tardy waiter turning up to take their order. Reassured at the sight of proper technology if not the owner, she recites a rapid string of letters, " . . . uk. Got that?"

"Deborah, let me introduce—" but not waiting to hear, the daughter's turned on bare pink heels to stride inside. Since she didn't actually slam the door, Xavier decides it's safe to enter. One hand under Emeline's elbow, the other on her luggage handle, he tugs both inside the apartment, greeted only by the smell of toast. From force of habit he goes down the few steps to retrieve his knapsack and Clifford's bag; who leaves luggage unprotected in a strange doorway?

The living room's not what he expected at all. Clean white walls, light-colored woodwork, an open space minimally furnished. Across from a tightly upholstered, beige divan stand two yellow metal and leather chairs, lesser cousins of the cushy seats in Emeline's lobby on East 63rd, and one upholstered arm chair, a square dining table and four chairs, a large rug with geometric designs. No wooden paneling, oriental rugs, Victorian knick-knacks, or walls of leather-bound books, nothing antique or pretending to be.

Only the walls suggest a daughter of Emeline's lives here. Abstract watercolors mix with old-fashioned pen-and-ink prints. One might be the twin of a hunting scene on Emeline's wall; another shows the face of a bitter, old woman. On a side table sits the silver-framed photo of Clifford he already knows.

Balancing one hand on a sideboard with a tray of wine bottles, Emeline whispers: "I wasn't expecting anything so . . . small. And the mood she's in, I don't know what we should do."

"What she can do is tell us where to find a hotel."

"I'm sorry, I thought, hell, let me be the one to talk to her. I don't want you getting in her line of fire."

Xavier settles her in the single armchair. That's the trouble with flight. You step over the plane's low threshold in one country, one climate, one time zone, and deplane in another world. At least in San Juan the faces look familiar and Spanish sounds the same.

Steeling himself, Xavier follows the angry clang of pans to the kitchen. Furious, Deborah's stirring a sizeable pot of oatmeal, gonna be no sweet rolls here. The kettle throttles up. Deborah ignores the piercing sound while another minute goes by.

It's a stand-off. Lift the kettle? Deborah's anger will boil over, who does he think he is, invading her space? Do nothing, and Emeline's likely to wander in, too. While he may be the nearest target, Xavier knows it's her mother Deborah's waiting to attack.

"Your mother's taught me how to make a pot of tea," he says, "before I barely knew to pour boiling water over a paper sac with a tail like a mouse." Not amused, Deborah looks at him. Unblinking, he studies her in turn. Her strong nose and delicate lips are inherited from her mother, except arranged on a square face—a pronounced jaw inherited from Clifford, maybe, or a more distant ancestor.

First to blink, Deborah turns off the tea kettle. When she reaches into a cupboard for a blue-and-white tea pot like Emeline's, Xavier's caught by a pang of homesickness. He points to a curved canister painted in rust-red and blue in the image of an overdressed Indian elephant. "Tea's in here?"

"And you would be?"

"Xavier Escudero. Your mother, well, I've been helping her out."

"I just bet you have." Radiating contempt, Deborah returns to her oatmeal. "You'd best go back out there, then, hadn't you, I don't fancy her following me around. Besides if, God forbid, she falls and breaks something? We'll really be in the soup."

Emeline sees Xavier's done what he can. Suggested they spread out for breakfast at the table. Spaced the place mats Deborah's chucked his way so the trio makes up three sides of a square with Deborah in the middle. Seating as diplomacy, perhaps a strategy he's acquired in Flavia's cramped apartment. At least Deborah's put on proper clothes, sort of; lurid green tights, a printed tunic to her knees, and sandals constitute her statement for the day.

Time, food, and caffeine pull them through an afternoon that moves along like molasses. They've covered the flight, the cab ride, the traffic, and the weather. Emeline asks, "Been here long, have you?"

"It's a sublet from a friend." Refusing the bait, Emeline says nothing, only stirs sugar into her latest cup of tea, until Deborah concedes, "He's taken up a squat with some pals in an old warehouse."

"I see you've hung a few of our old pictures up. Like that sad woman," Emeline points to a sketch, "the Kathe Kollwitz that Clifford bought." Silence. "My fault, dropping in when you didn't know we were coming."

"Well, you're here now."

"You must be wondering what this is all about." Setting down the blue-and-white teapot, Emeline gets the ball, if not rolling, at least onto the court. Deborah looks anxious, steeling herself, maybe, for unwelcome details about an appalling romance. Emeline can't resist; playing along, she drops her eyes and looks coy. Deborah inhales with a slight hiss.

"More tea?" Xavier steps in. "We wouldn't be here disturbing your weekend, Deborah, if your mother didn't need your help. I came along. She's not so good about flying." Not, Emeline notices, you know she hates to fly, which might suggest he and Deborah share the same familiarity.

Outside, a nearby church clock strikes four. Heartened by his tact and the tea, Emeline taps her cup back onto its saucer. "A problem has come up. There seems to be some complication with your father's business," and Emeline's into the story.

At first Deborah looks relieved, a business problem, at least, not some dreadful, late-life affair of the heart. They both know Clifford's finances took a serious dive during the recent recession; even if they rarely talked about it, even when their 95th Street place was on the market. Emeline watches relief turn to confusion, then shock. Her daughter looks miserable and close to a good cry.

"Are you telling me you think Daddy was mixed up in this, this scandal?"

"Afraid so."

"Let me understand. You, not in the best of health—"

"Oh, thanks for inquiring." Emeline holds up her left hand to show off her tremor. All three register: not once has Deborah asked her mother how she is. Flushed, Deborah stands and heads into the kitchen.

"Go on," Deborah commands, returning with a glass of water for Emeline. "You take it upon yourself to look into the provenance of this painting because of a transaction that took place, when?"

"Last spring."

"If you had doubts, you should have gone to the FBI. They have an art crime team. Makes no sense at all, you waltzing over here with your little sidekick, like you're in a BBC mystery. It's real life."

"It's her real life," Xavier points out. "Your mother is trying to protect your father's reputation, can't you see? Even if she's convinced he wouldn't act dishonestly on his own. Except, what if someone put your father in a tight spot? Threatened harm to you or your mother, left him no choice?"

Emeline frowns: that thought's never crossed her mind. Deborah looks as if she's been punched. "Want to have a look at the photo?" Xavier says and pulls it out of his knapsack. Reluctantly, Deborah reaches out her hand.

"Subject against a dark background," Deborah confirms, "the muddy brown that lingered until dispelled by the Impressionists. Dressed in a black cloak, red back then was for kings and popes, though we see a corner of red cloth on the table right behind the sword handle. White collar; smaller white trim on the sleeve, it might be braid. Who's the painter?"

"Juan Bautista Martinez del Mazo."

"Might have heard of him," Deborah shrugs. "I don't pay much mind to the old Spaniards. He is old?"

"Seventeenth century."

"Won't fetch all that much, then. Nothing like the Picasso at Sotheby's last spring, a cool $106 million." Deborah sounds proud, as if she'd been the one to profit from the Sotheby's sale."

Xavier spews out his coffee. "You're kidding me! It's paint on a canvas. *Merdita sea!*"

"Damn it all you want, that's what the Picasso went for. Just think, Ma," Deborah says, too sweetly, "that would pay for all your doormen's children to go to university."

"You might be surprised to hear that my building association . . ."

"You can buy a CD of a whole symphony," says Xavier, "for twenty bucks."

"Not that you'd ever want a CD of a symphony."

"Deborah, do not start being nasty."

"It's a painting! The world's gone crazy."

"Doesn't sound to me, Xavier, like you know very much about the art market. Paintings have always commanded the highest price of any of the arts." Deborah might be giving a lecture. "Sure, we have our symphonies, operas, theatre productions, ballet. Still, fine art is special. Because these pieces, they're singular. They last. Each is a cultural artifact. And they don't depend on a corps de ballet, a conductor, equity actors, or a theatre in the West End."

"Even if sometimes ugly as hell," then Emeline bites her lip, annoyed she's taken to swearing.

"Beautiful or ugly," Deborah sounds supremely confident, "each offers insight into a time and place."

"Who gets to say?" asks Xavier. "Who decides a piece is valuable and not a picture my nephew Jomar could do with finger paints?"

"That old cliché," Deborah sniffs. "Art critics, scholars, historians, and art publications. They consider the historical importance of the artist, the date of the piece within his or her career, the decorative appeal or its lack. Eventually they agree certain works are significant."

What with the flight, and the tension, Emeline's worn out. With no stomach for more debate she suggests they find a hotel for the night.

No, no, Deborah retorts without grace, room enough here, anyway, she has to leave early next morning. "That's sorted, then. You'd best bunk down with me, Ma. I cannot rearrange my study to make room so your friend will have to make do on the divan."

"Very kind, dear. Just for tonight. Tomorrow we'll move."

"—though it is crap to sleep on, and Mother? Do try not to snore."

Whenever she and Cliff stayed in London it was always at the Savoy. Now, Emeline's back in Peckham. Soaking in the claw-foot tub with a loofah and lavender-scented soap, Emeline thinks of the Green Falcon bars of her childhood. Soap was rationed even after the war; when it came to the laundry, her mother had to make do with washing soda and Borax.

The flat seems fine, if small, and Emeline wonders about this roommate who refurbished the flat only to decamp to squatters' digs in a warehouse. Emeline suspects this visit is going to go as badly as she feared; yet in spite of Deborah's open animosity, it's not only the bath water Emeline finds soothing. Much as she hates to say it even to herself, under the same roof with her daughter she feels safer.

Emeline is startled each time she sees her daughter. Not by the blonde hair, Deborah changes hair color on a whim, and her own was once blonde. It's how much Deborah's hazel eyes are like her father's. Except where Cliff's were warm and humorous, Deborah's tend to be wary, when not downright critical. Emeline's hardly surprised at Deborah's behavior and deeply chagrined at her own stupid mistake with the email.

Emeline's done a poor job of protecting Xavier; she should have told Deborah she wasn't traveling alone. Luckily the new London won't be surprised at a Latino face, she could have said. Latino blurred national borders, leaving room to imagine a suave actor like Ricardo Montalban. Or Javier Bardem, Deborah won't have heard of Montalban.

Arty as Deborah fancies herself, she's grown into a terrible snob. Determined to dodge her mother's insecurities and uncertainties, she's absorbed her London classmates' indifferent prejudices along with their accents. In her daughter's mind *Puerto Rican* would signal a threatening youth with a boom box or a cleaning woman with too much eye-shadow.

At once Emeline regrets the thought, remembering Flavia's modest appearance, her orderly apartment in spite of the snarl of remotes and toys. She recalls Flavia's genuine alarm when she turned up on 63rd Street, worried about her employer and seeking her son's help. Emeline really needs to get this knee jerk of judgment in check. Each new day offers a budget of opportunities to deplore others and reassure yourself. Or to refrain. Emeline vows to work on refraining.

Pulling on her familiar pajamas, Emeline climbs into the unfamiliar double bed. "Ma?" Deborah calls through the closed bedroom door. "I've got reading to do. Are you settling in?"

"Yes, dear, thank you." She can't bring herself to say: come in and see for yourself. The hallway goes quiet. Sliding into the half zone before sleep, Emeline wonders. If I wanted to try harder with Deborah, where would I even begin?

CHAPTER 16

Xavier runs water in the kitchen to drown out the women's voices, whether they're quarrelling over sleeping arrangements or revisiting the past. Tonight, opting for happy ignorance, he revels in the distance, slight as it is, and feels a freedom he never feels when Flavia and Rocio spit words at each other.

Once Emeline's gone into the bedroom and Deborah into her study, he assesses the divan. Hardly the first strange mattress he's landed on, yet he's uneasy sharing close quarters with Emeline's kid, even if she's been an adult for years. And wary. Never mind she's good-looking, striking in a certain way, Deborah's tense as a tick, and given to drama.

With travel, the tension of arriving as guests unexpected and unwelcome, Xavier hopes he'll sleep until noon. Too soon, he opens his eyes to a lessening of darkness against the Roman shades and morning sounds only feet away in the kitchen. Retrieving clean briefs from his duffle, he puts on yesterday's clothes. After he folds up the blanket and sheet tossed carelessly his way the night before, he makes his way to the bathroom. Once again outnumbered by women, he has the sense to knock first. All clear.

The hot water is a relief, he feels warm for the first time since he got off the plane. *Mas limpio que sabaco de rana:* in this city it's a wonder even the armpit of a frog can be clean. Gritty and chilly, no central heating on yet; he snuck a look at the thermostat except he can't convert centigrade.

Still in her bathrobe, words evidently more than she can muster, Deborah raises eyebrows shaped like crescents then points to the bread box, the toaster, and flounces out of the kitchen. A section of Saturday's *Guardian* lies on the counter. If Xavier feels too disoriented to take in the news, taking in the English words without dealing with the accent helps calm his nerves.

Fifteen minutes later Deborah's ready for the day. She's taken a sharp left away from the upper-east-side life her father craved and her mother provided. Dressed in black tights, high boots, and a ripped tweed jacket, she's winding a silky rainbow scarf into a turban, plucking at the edges and tucking in wisps of blonde hair. Bohemian chic. She drops a pair of keys on the counter.

Though Xavier dreads circling around the dour student in her tiny kitchen, out of habit he starts to make Emeline's tea the way she's taught him: milk into the mug first, sugar, boiling water poured through the rattan tea strainer. Deborah watches, silent.

"I'll take this in, then be out of your way," he expects no thanks.

"Did it occur to you I might want to take her tea myself, my mother?" Xavier glances at the one half-empty mug Deborah's left on the counter. Caught out, she scowls. "I was about to, when you barged in. I have to say I don't get it. What are the two of you doing together, anyway?"

Xavier has the sense to know there's no answer she'll like. With a nod he walks out, taps on the bedroom door, and sets the mug on the end table beside the rumpled double bed. Little chance Emeline has slept through Deborah's outburst; tactfully, she makes no sound.

The only place to be alone is the bathroom and Deborah will want to commandeer that to get busy with her make-up. Putting on his black leather jacket, he grabs the spare keys from the counter and heads out.

The air feels familiar, a hint of cool that will fade as soon as the sun climbs. Happily, Xavier lights up and inhales; sneaking out for a smoke yesterday had been murder. A few blocks later he hears the thunder of overhead trains. If he closes his eyes he's back in El Barrio. As the sound slinks into the distance he passes two workmen hauling wheeled bags of tools: "then she goes and posts the fookin' snaps on Instagram."

Cars play tag driving on the left side of the paint striped roadways. Passengers form an orderly line at a bus stop. Xavier crosses Old Kent Road and turns down Albany Street. Swimming against the tide of people on their way to work, he sees faces from Africa, Asia, the Middle East, and Caribbean.

Past the New Peckham Mosque, he comes across a café and the aroma of serious coffee. He orders a large dark roast and a bun, struggling to manage the unfamiliar money gleaned at Heathrow. Taking pity, the cashier plucks the proper coins from the palm of his hand and drops them in her drawer. A few, reviving sips and Xavier's ready to think about Deborah's question, blunt as it was.

His friendship with Emeline, did it begin with an impulse of charity or the glimpse of an opportunity? Either way, it hardly rose to the level of a scam, only giving up one cab to the gym in exchange for a couple extra bucks in his pocket. Brother Ramon would have labeled Emeline a snob or a target. Xavier saw her as a way to know a different world. Besides, he was curious. Her frosty manner, how deep did that go, was she always like that or merely scared that afternoon?

It was Emeline who tracked him down, to apologize, she claimed. First time inside the apartment and he got to see Emeline's sense of humor after the plumber called on the house phone. When she telephoned next to ask for his help, a note in her voice suggested a choice: he could say yes or no. Given the freedom to choose, he said yes. Money changed hands, cash for services rendered. She offered her guest room, and he was seduced. Not by the woman, of course, and old enough to be his grandmother: by the shimmer of a life so foreign he couldn't resist.

He knows Emeline better now, gets glimpses of her struggle for, what's that social worker's word, the one she uses with Rocio? *Agency*. Not a social service, another meaning: running your own life. Emeline's trying to figure out how to run her own life now that the center of her old one is gone.

The islands have a saying: *Ay que ver como combate la cobra.* In London, how the cobra fights surprises him again, Emeline's frosty front dissolving as she faces the daughter whose manner is more snub than welcome.

All too complicated to explain to Deborah, he won't even try. Concentrating on the practical, Xavier decides tomorrow he'll ignore the café's lure of coffee until he knows what he's doing with pounds, shillings, and pence. To scope out next morning's early walk he heads toward the bank of the river. The "tems" they call it, dispensing with the "h."

Heading back, he crosses Southwark Street twice, dodging red buses marked #38. At home he depends on the east-west, north-south grid; here, in two minutes he's lost. Guessing, he takes Munton Road to Rodney and circles an unfamiliar park. With each wrong turn he worries Emeline will fall or fail to make herself breakfast. He's winding past three-story buildings when like a miracle John Maurice

Close changes its name and turns into Searles. To his relief he sees the familiar bay windows of Deborah's building. He walks into what Emeline will later call, in understatement, "quite the brouhaha."

Emeline's waking up to another country, another time zone, a strange flat, and a hostile daughter. Hoping to stay calm, she dresses carefully. In her tortoise shell head band, her pearls, her half-buttoned cardigan, her flats, she looks nothing the way her own mother Dora would look, if she'd lived to the same age. Dora, her sweet, determined Ma, Emeline doubts her own daughter will ever think of her in the same way.

Deborah did cut straight to the heart of the matter. Emeline always knew some of Clifford's business dealings were dodgy, in the years before they met, certain transactions that brought Cliff his sizable portfolio, murky. Emeline didn't ask questions. She didn't want to know. Because from the start she sensed this man—earthy, direct, brash, smart, and funny—was the bloke she'd wind up wanting. Besides, if she did ask questions and heard the answers, Aunt Mildred might winkle the details out of her and arm herself with new objections. As it was, she already referred to Cliff as "that man."

It was enough, Emeline believed, that Cliff assured her all the dodgy parts were in the past. He'd opened his heart to her and, if it would make her feel better, he'd happily open his books. Standing close to Cliff that afternoon in Central Park, looking into his hazel eyes, she said no, not necessary, her answer given less from trust than awareness of her own ignorance. What would she learn, looking at pages of entries and in longhand, back then? Soon as he could Cliff would switch to a desk-top computer, then a laptop small as a Pomeranian, and on to some program called Quicken, a noun for managing finances, evidently, not a verb reserved for the pulse of a maiden in Jane Austen.

Standing in Central Park at Fifth and 104th, the rose garden giving off attar of Amber Queen and Heathcliff, Cliff put two fingers under her chin and solemn as a judge, nodded. They'd reached an understanding. On her side, her one condition for marrying him; on his, consent. And while he lived she never doubted him; although his manner in the few, fast weeks before he died had raised questions in her mind.

"So you are convinced," Deborah says, though Emeline's barely started on her tea, "this horrible little man thinks Daddy was mixed up in crooked dealings? Daddy was only helping out this client."

"His name is Ron Segal."

"You cannot believe Daddy was copying paintings to cheat him."

"I never said Daddy was copying anything. The point is questions have been raised and he's no longer here to answer."

"And that's the reason you're in London." Watching her daughter, Emeline sees Deborah manage to sound hurt for ten seconds, then draw breath to fuel her default emotion, anger.

"Yes," agrees Emeline to head her off, "and you're right, if you were reading law or literature I doubt I'd be asking for your help. Your world is art history, and I am asking. Because," Emeline's tea cup surfs slightly so tea splashes onto the rug, "don't you see, if there's a problem about this painting, what about the others from Ron Segal?"

The door to the flat opens. "Morning, ladies," Xavier slips off his jacket and drapes it around Emeline's shoulders. Briefly Emeline touches his hand, glad he's back; otherwise who knows how long she and Deborah would have been at it? "Everyone sleep well? Nice day out there in South-wark."

"It's South-uk," Deb corrects, swinging her anger his way. "Where have you been? If you're here to help my mother, you could at least help her get up. On her own in the kitchen, reaching for more Assam," she makes the Indian tea sound like crack cocaine, "when she hasn't even taken her pills? You're here now, you take over. I've got to get to Courtauld."

"I'm curious, Debby." Emeline watches as Xavier tries to divert Deborah and take down the tension.

"It's Deborah." Her voice is cold.

"What are you studying at Corto, computer science?" Lord, he's referencing the LaGuardia catalogue; at least he didn't suggest automotive technology or probation. "Corto, it's like a technical school?" Emeline waits for Deborah to explode. When her daughter replies it's with one sharp bark Emeline recognizes as the laugh like her own.

"If that isn't you all over, Ma, leaving out a few crucial details." Deborah wipes her eyes, transferring a smear of lipstick to the side of her nose. "C O U R T A U L D," she spells with pride, "is the pre-eminent art history program in the country. Afterward, assuming I graduate, *what* with all these distractions," she turns toward Emeline, "where'd you find this guy?"

"He found me. Downtown. I'd been mugged. He put me in a cab and brought me home." Deborah stares. Count the silver when he left, did you?

"And he doesn't have a mother of his own?"

"A very nice mother. We've had tea. She's a nanny."

"Really."

"Yes, really," Xavier says, and straightens his shoulders. "She used to clean houses and now she is a nanny."

Nonplussed, Deborah retreats. "I'm leaving. You'll still be here this evening, I dare say?"

"I wonder, dear, if it wouldn't be better . . . there must be a small hotel nearby."

"Another night shouldn't kill us. After that, if you want to move, Ma? Fine, move."

"One other thing: we'll need to use your computer to open a couple of discs." Deborah looks horrified. "For heaven's sake, we're not the least interested in your files. Your father's will keep us busy enough. I imagine we'll need the password. Xavier, here's a piece of paper."

"Even you, Xavier, won't need a piece of paper. It's Scottie." Deborah spells it. "What about supper? I don't actually cook much. I suppose I can pick up a take-away."

"We'll go out later," Xavier volunteers, "let me make supper." Deborah looks doubtful. "You'll like it. Right, Emeline? *Saborosa*, I promise."

"If you must, and given the way Ma walks, make sure you use the pedestrian pen when you cross the intersection."

After Deborah leaves Emeline turns up the thermostat. Spirits revive as the heat climbs (in centigrade steps, another vocabulary she'll have to translate for Xavier). She pronounces the dry cereal "cardboard," steps on the trash can pedal to toss it, and begins cracking eggs. Putting the omelet on the table, she counts silently to three; then smiles when Xavier gets up on "three" to check in the fridge for a small bottle of hot sauce.

"*Nada*," she laughs.

"Scottie," Xavier's reaches for the pepper shaker. "Is that a boyfriend from Scotland?"

"A terrier we took care of on Shelter Island one summer. Deborah was six."

Emeline watches Xavier rinse the dishes and stack them in the dollhouse dishwasher, pretty sure Deborah will rearrange every one later. Emeline retrieves the soft leather carrying case from her roller bag. "I guess we'll have to work on this little table of hers," and laughs at his expression. Flavia manages a family with a table the same size.

"You sure you want me looking through your husband's business files?"

"I thought you were here to help." With Deborah out of the way Emeline feels more like her bossy self. "So let's see what we've got." From the carrying case she pulls out typed pages of notes stapled together, hands them to Xavier, then takes out a small notebook and her pack of cards, both wedged in the bottom of the big envelope.

"You didn't bring those along?"

"Of course. What better place to study Spanish than South London?" She points to a pad of paper next to the phone. Was it there yesterday, or overcome with helpfulness, did Deborah leave it for them?

"Look like notes from sales documents. Good. If you can prove Segal sold the the *Duke* to Morosov, then none of Segal's heirs can lay claim."

"Hardly my biggest worry. Three files in all. You've got the one for Ron. I've got one for Dan McCormick, don't know who that is, and one for Tuck Bradley. I didn't know him, either. Cliffie, Cliffie. Colleagues, contacts, prospects, he attracted people the way Scottie attracted fleas."

"Let's each read one," he hands her the file marked Segal, "then swap and compare what we find. We'll chart the steps."

"Why?" She hands him the file for McCormick. "All that's in the files."

"Not the same way each time. A chart makes it easier to compare."

"And your learned this where?"

"LaGuardia. Buyer," he says, turning the pad of paper horizontal and starting a grid. "Date of contact. Follow-up phone calls, meetings, payments made, memos attached." Emeline remembers his embarrassment in New York, describing his campus of minority students after Emeline told him about Wellesley. He looks embarrassed again, applying lessons he got to learn in one semester.

"Name of each painting, any description," he adds boxes to his graph, "asking price, selling price, date sold." Quickly he draws a second chart for her. They work in silence; Emeline avoids looking at him as she moves entries from Clifford's print-outs onto her chart.

"Any extra notes that don't fit in the boxes?" Xavier asks when she stretches her shoulders and puts down her pencil.

"A few. I've circled them in red on the pages."

"Could the snoops who went through Cliff's desk have been after these files?"

"I think they were after this." Emeline picks up the small notebook. "Cliff kept one of these every year."

"All about computers, your husband, what's he doing writing notes by hand in a notebook?"

"Odd, innit. Deborah'd tease him, said he was like a teenage girl with a diary. On the computer Cliff said he had to be organized. The notebook let him jot whatever crossed his mind. It's quite the mess," she thumbs through the pages, "would take Bletchley Park to decode the notes. You know: hush-hush place during the war. Huh. Here's something," she spells it out, "CAD."

"Computer assisted design? A person? Or could it be 'Cadmium Fund?'"

"Cliff didn't have anything to do with Cadmium."

"How do you know?"

"He was in charge of our finances."

"Of course he was."

"Though he'd always tell me what he was doing. 'Took a position in Qualcom,' he'd announce, or 'we've decided to short NatureLife.' I couldn't always tell if he was sharing or boasting, but I was pleased, it made me feel useful. Beyond being, you know, the hostess."

"And you remember all these companies?"

"I wouldn't say that. I know when Wendy Wells said 'Cadmium' I'd never heard the name. January. That's when Segal called him, right after the New Year."

"Two more notes: one in April, one in June."

In Deborah's quiet flat they review the files, discuss, argue, and come to terms. Data points on *The Duke of Abrantes* are transferred to a sheet of their own, a set of boxes on a single page.

"We going to tell your daughter, we're working on this together?"

Emeline imagines the scene that will cause. "Not sure, yet, let's see how—what's that expression of yours?"

"Let's see how the cobra fights."

Land south of the Thames, once owned by King Henry I, over time morphed into a prosperous residential area. Nineteenth-century local roads acquired curious names from Turkey like Marmora and Scutari. In the twentieth century prosperity ebbed. Mid-century redevelopment shifted families from dilapidated buildings into more modern digs. As blocks of ten-story buildings went up thousands moved into new flats

"Not my family, though." Emeline seems glad to be outside in the air. "My ma used to write she was relieved they'd stayed in their terrace house, tiny as it was."

"Flavia's the same, she loves her apartment. Too much crime in the projects, she says."

"Like crime in the North Peckham Estate."

"Estate? Sounds like the Hamptons on Long Island." Emeline has the sense not to ask how he knows about the Hamptons. Maybe the Wellingtons took his mother there.

"Not by a long shot, these are council houses. You know, social housing? Trust me, the names are what's grand, nothing else."

Bicycles and cars, red double-decker buses, and boxy, black cabs crowd the main streets. Pedestrians from Wapping, Shoreditch, Cairo, and Kenya fill the sidewalks, women in silk saris called Pakis, even if Indian; women in hijab called Arab, even if Kurds. Emeline begins to see how the new faces might distract the English from their perennial preoccupation with class.

Walking along, they come to a pop-up market under a railway arch, where Xavier explains he's looking for rice, garbanzos, fresh plantains, spices like adobo powder and cumin. "We're going to make *sofrito*."

"Sofrito?" echoes the owner in a strong, unfamiliar accent.

"Peppers, tomatoes, onions, garlic. Stuffed olives if you have them."

"Ah. In Turkish we call it *ezme*." The Turk is filling paper sacks and weighing them on his portable scale. "What else you need?"

"Chicken."

"Go two blocks," says the owner, "on the corner, you'll find chickens."

"Fresh?" queries Emeline.

"Very fresh, better than Sainsbury's. *Afiyet Olsun!* Enjoy your meal."

"Interesting, my neighborhood?" Deborah says, putting air quotes around the word. Xavier was merely trying to make conversation. "Well, sure, but deeper into Peckham . . . once upon a time it was brothels and bear-baiting, now it's all auto repair shops and nail salons. Hardly bloody posh Belgravia."

Now who's doing the baiting? Before Deborah can expand on her rant Emeline describes the pop-up market. She's excited by the changes she's seen in Peckham compared to her childhood, "and nearby used to be a greengrocer. We were still on rationing after the war, and no one ate well, not much meat or sugar. The Russians sent us fish."

"Is that why," asks Xavier, "you're kind of on the small side?"

"No smaller than you," Deborah comes to her mother's defense.

"It doesn't count," says Xavier.

"Why not?"

"Because," he stands up, "I am Puerto Rican."

"We played outdoors all the time," Emeline goes on. "No telly or video games, no cell phones."

"You love my cell phone," Xavier teases her, "you're jealous."

"Like Ma could figure out what to do with a mobile."

"We had peculiar grey stuff instead of flour. If Ma ever got her hands on eggs and butter for a cake she'd sieve this wheat meal through old nylons to make it white, and then give the left-overs to her neighbor for the chickens."

"Later, though," Xavier's showing off new knowledge, "they built these estates of yours, right?"

"Like North Peckham Estate?" Deborah snorts. "One of the most deprived areas in Europe, vandalism, muggings, robberies, murders. Working-class folks blamed changes on the newcomers, naturally. Aylesbury Estate, remember that one, Ma? Thousands lived in Aylesbury."

"What good are new buildings when there aren't enough jobs?" Xavier says. "Poverty, regeneration, decay, it's a cycle, over and over. Today it seemed safe enough. At least your mother seemed relaxed, back in New York she thought she was being followed. Might have been her imagination.

"Ma, imagination," Deborah scoffs, "the most practical woman in the world?"

"I'm right here, you two!"

"Leaving aside these ominous followers, what facts, if any, do we have about this business problem?"

Emeline lays one piece of paper on the table. "Xavier helped me put it together, he writes faster than I can. *The Duke of Abrantes* was in Ron Segal's collection. A client of Clifford's and later a friend, you remember how your Dad was. Ron was getting ready to sell his large house in Tarrytown. He asked for Clifford's help in disposing of some of his possessions."

"De-accessioning," says Deborah. "That's what museums call it. Sounds more dignified than having a good clear-out." De-accessioning, Xavier repeats to himself. The fancy word might persuade Ramon to off load his collection of dated electronics and suspiciously new Nikes.

"Xavier, let me see the portrait again." She studies it, frowning. "It's a three-quarter portrait, though not full length, that was usually for kings. No wonder the Duke looks proud."

"Proud," adds Xavier, "because this Portuguese nobleman, Mar-quiss of Porto Seguro, was duked by King Philip IV of Spain because of Mr. Alfonso's fidelity to the Spanish monarchy."

Astonished, Deborah looks as if her tea kettle started delivering data. "You know this how?"

"Everything's on the Internet," Xavier taps his cell phone.

"And we say *Mar-key*," corrects Emeline. "And we don't say *duked*—"

"Honored, then, that better?"

Deborah's studying the photograph. "We clearly see the metal handle of his sword. I wonder if there's a market for antique swords."

"Here's a sword," Xavier's tapping at his cell phone, "a Spanish cup hilt rapier c.1650. Going for, dios mio, $9,100. That starts to look like money."

"Where'd you get this photo?"

"From Sergei Morosov," Emeline says, "the man who came to see me. Quite the bully, wasn't he, Xavier. Morosov claims he's acting for a Mr. SinJen Pearce who lives in Surrey. If what he says is true, ten days ago Mr. Pearce telephoned his dealer because he decided to sell the painting."

"And whilst getting it appraised here, questions were raised." Whilst? Deborah talks like she formed her baby words in London.

"He says Sotheby's wasn't satisfied with the provenance."

"Not our problem, then, palm him off on Southeby's. Plenty of old paintings turn up," she turns to Xavier, ready to lecture, "without an adequate provenance. That means without—"

"History, paper trail, proof of ownership—got it."

Emeline's handing over another paper. "Ron Segal's father bought the *Duke* in 1938. From a Jewish collector, is my guess, wanting to finance the family's escape from Germany."

"We see a lot of that," Deborah nodded, "art from Europe carrying no early paper trail. Doesn't mean there wasn't a trail; only that it's lost. Like the way we have ancestors whether we know who they are or not. Okay. I'll call the owner. I can take tomorrow off, go see him in Surrey."

"We'll all go." Emeline is adamant. "Maybe Pearce will have papers of some sort even if he thinks they won't hold up to scrutiny. Want me to bring this one?" Emeline waves the photo in the air.

"Hell no. We're not to compare anything on site. Understood?"

Chapter 17

Deborah needn't act so haughty, Xavier thinks, out walking again. Clifford's father was a dock worker. For a while Emeline's mother took in laundry. Whatever's going on with this mother-daughter duo has to be different from his dance with Flavia. Back home Xavier concentrates on keeping a secret his mother shows no interest in knowing. On Searles Road Deborah flaunts how far she's sailed from her mother's careful upbringing. Huge round sunglasses, striped menswear jacket, "not one petal of Liberty floral," as Emeline says.

Seeing Deborah tighten the belt around her terry robe the day they arrived, it made Xavier wonder if she was concealing a shine of navel piercing. This morning, though the weather's barely cooled, Deborah's changed her Doc Martens for knee-high black boots, luminous purple tights between boot top and skirt hem, and a skirt so short Flavia would have slapped her.

"In a non-European art class," Deborah's sipping coffee, "I saw slides on Day of the Dead."

"That's Mexican. Puerto Ricans don't do Day of the Dead, though we do make Christmas last to January 6th," Xavier adds when she looks disappointed. "Three Kings day."

"Why?"

"Because the Magi, traveling to see—"

"I mean, why so late after Christmas?"

"Took them longer to get there."

"Of course, when did men ever ask for directions?"

"My turn, Deborah, if you don't mind?" She looks wary. "What made you leave the city to live in London?"

"You New Yorkers, you can't imagine life anywhere—"

"Okay, forget I asked."

"I came over for my junior year abroad, looking for a wider world, one that didn't center on sailing, tennis, and boy bankers who brag. In London I saw there was; only I wasn't confident I could find it in the states. It didn't help, frankly, that Ma and I were growing farther apart."

"You should have tried my neighborhood, ten blocks up from 95th and very few bankers."

"I came back here to attend uni. Made a marriage I shouldn't have, worked jobs I didn't like, then began teaching. With dual citizenship I can work over here.

"Lucky you. And Courtauld?"

"Courtauld was out of reach for me, and after 2008 Daddy's business wasn't doing so well. Ma was worried about him."

"Why 'Ma'? Sounds a little . . ."

"Working class?"

"Ya think?"

"Ma said it was what she called her mother, my Grandma Dora. Anyway, life being the crapshoot it is," Deborah sounds bitter, "Daddy dies, and I get to go to Courtauld. His estate went to Ma, rightly so after all she'd done for him. He left me a neat sum as well, in a trust." Estate. Trust. Words Xavier's heard at the gym along with Vail or MOMA, nothing to do with him.

"Daddy knew I wanted to move on from teaching. He came over quite often, you know. Didn't like to fly herself, Ma always said. I ask you, how smart is that, letting your handsome husband ramble around Europe without you? That's when temptation—"

"Tiptoes in?"

"Tiptoes? Try stomps in with lumbering great boots."

"Even your revered Daddy?"

"Not as such." Seems Deborah has said more than she meant to and may know more than she's saying; maybe from, and more than once, being the temptation for another woman's husband.

"Daddy knew about my dreams, he supported my ambitions, nothing Emeline could get behind or even understand."

"Why you so sure, did you ever tell her?"

"And watch her try to sabotage any plan that didn't include the Colony Club and Ferragamo's with a nice stacked heel?"

He gets it. Deborah reacts to her mother's stuffy side, doesn't see, or doesn't choose to, the funny, clever, even defiant side. Probably Deborah likes to think she has the monopoly on defiant. "That's harsh. Probably all Aunt Mildred's doing."

"Oh, yes, Aunt Mildred groomed her well. You notice where my mother's mind goes with any situation, is this person well-spoken? Properly dressed? One of the 'nice people'? Or, one of *them?*"

Xavier thinks of Emeline drinking tea with Flavia. Polite, of course, antsy as he was he'd have settled for polite, but much more: gracious, genuine, *simpatico*. He's tempted to tell Deborah, but decides against it since she is, for the first time, not talking to him as if he were the help.

"Daddy knew I wanted to do more than teach art to young bohemians in public schools." Xavier tries to picture young bohemians in rag-tag skirts and colorful head scarfs among his classmates in

Central Park East High. They'd have been beaten into *masa* the first day.

"They have art in public schools?"

"Words here don't always mean . . . in the UK, public school means private school."

"Mind the gap."

"Very good."

"When a ship docks, the sign says mind the gap, not watch your step."

"I thought you meant—"

"I know what you thought, Deborah. The gap between your school and mine, between your family and mine, between the chances you've had—"

"Lay off it, fella. I'm sorry. And I'm sorry about scrapping with Ma."

"It's not me you need to tell."

Emeline appears, serene in a twin set, iconic pearls, and a polite smile; oblivious to what's she's overheard, or at least pretending to be. Deborah manages a brief hug, then produces a serious breakfast: poached eggs, grilled tomatoes, toast in the metal rack, more bitter marmalade, and a pot of strong tea. She even asks Xavier if he'd sooner drink coffee and brews it ebony-black in her French press. It's all quite congenial.

Until Emeline asks, "When are we going?"

"Listen, Ma, better if I go alone. You stay here and rest. This Mr. Pearce, he's way out in Surrey. The motorway can be a horror."

"Can't be any worse than the traffic in New York. I'm coming."

"She's right," says Xavier. "She has to come."

"Man, it's like having a bossy brother. That's what I needed, Ma, a brother?" It's hard to tell if Deborah's joking.

"I came to ask your help, Deborah, not have you take over. Xavier, are you sulking?"

"Only wishing I had a license"

"You're taking the piss, right?"

"Deborah, that is extremely rude. Will you be going dressed like that?"

"I will, yes. Come on, Xavier, don't go all macho on me." Deborah slaps his shoulder, jostling his arm so his coffee splatters. "Hello, traffic pattern? We drive on the left, in case you haven't noticed, and the roundabouts can be murder. Actually I don't see why you have to come at all."

"Of course I am coming." Xavier uses a paper napkin to sponge at his black jeans. "We know nothing about this man. And as you say, he's way out in Surrey."

They make their way through Peckham, past blocks of row houses ("terrace houses, we call them") and shop signs in Hindi, Urdu, and Arabic. Men loitering on the sidewalk remind Xavier of jobless men outside the corner bodegas in El Barrio. Suddenly anxious, Xavier longs for New York, for his job, and worries Gabor will replace him.

So much looks strange. Aside from the islands, he's seen little outside Manhattan other than the yearly train ride to visit Flavia's sister. Grateful to escape El Barrio for Holyoke, Tia Carmen thinks she's died and gone to heaven. Xavier finds the Massachusetts mill city's housing ratty and unsafe streets little improvement. At least in Manhattan a few subway stops put you in another universe.

"No chance of going by the old house, I suppose," Emeline asks from the back seat; maybe he's not the only one homesick.

Emeline's working-class accent is getting more noticeable each day, Xavier notices, and Deborah's, more lordly.

"Not in this direction. Another day we'll go."

Thickets of chimney pots start to thin against the skyline. Terraced rows give way to semi-detached houses and small yards. Unused to sitting on the left, Xavier feels dizzy as the car spins clockwise through the rotaries Deborah calls roundabouts.

"Why couldn't Pearce live around here?" grumbles Xavier, who needs a pee.

"Not a chance," Deborah laughs. "This part of Kent is stick in the mud."

Trying to translate, he's rescued. "Staid," Emeline says, "boring."

Not Surrey. It offers wide patches of greenery, with rivers and canals snaking through marshes and fields. "Such ancient land and still they've kept waves of hills," says Deborah. *They* are the rich ones, Xavier supposes, landowners like the man they're going to visit.

Deborah's turned on her GPS though she hardly seems to need it. Off the motorway, rounding corners, turning onto narrow roads, she has no trouble finding her way through a green, clipped, area where owners maintain the appearance of country on their own terms.

"You seem to know your way around here pretty well, dear."

"Had a friend out here, one time," Deborah makes a hard right. Black iron gates lead onto a gravel drive that takes them in graceful swirls past lawns with trees arching overhead.

Xavier is in awe. "Mr. Pearce lives in a park?"

An imposing pile near the top of a small rise, Sandley Hall is a large, two-story, yellow-stone manor house with dormers peering out of the roof and two, maybe three chimneys; it's hard to tell from where they stand. A hunched, grey-haired servant opens a front door framed on either side with mullioned windows.

As they're ushered inside, Emeline sees two long wings that stretch toward the back. The balcony built on one of the wings must offer views across the Wey Valley. The garden is in late bloom with asters, chrysanthemums, dahlias, and zinnias, all flowers she recognizes from the house she and Cliff used to own on Long Island. She catches a glimpse of a pergola and croquet lawn, wire hoops standing at attention.

Inside, iconic period elements prevail: high ceilings, wood-paneled walls, parquet floors, and in the reception room where the servant settles them, a strikingly large fireplace. A short, pudgy, beardless gentleman with a florid face enters. No ascot, not even a tie, an open-front, yellow polo shirt tucked into grey pleated pants and held in, barely, by a brown leather belt. If Xavier's expecting any version of James Bond, Emeline knows he'll be disappointed.

"SinJen Pearce." He shakes Xavier's hand. "Mrs. Hughes, how'd you do," he says to Emeline. "Deborah Hughes? It is you; I think we met at a party out here a while ago."

"I really couldn't say." Emeline's not sure what she means. *I go to so many parties out here? You won't catch me dead partying out here?*

"Let me offer tea, perhaps a sherry. It is after noon already, heh, heh." All charm, Pearce, they might have merely dropped by to pick up tickets for the local Chamber Choir.

"Why, that would be—"

But Deborah's taking charge. "Thank you, sir, no. We won't take up too much of your time. You understand why we're here, Mr. Pearce?"

"My dear, you were quite clear on the line. You wanted to know about my interest in buying the painting." Silence. He looks from one face to another.

"Or, perhaps you thought it was already mine? No, I'm merely holding it. I've grown fond of it, you see. Now and again I take on new pieces, and I'm looking into the possibility of purchase. That's why I drove the portrait up to Sotheby's myself. Weren't you wise to come today, the weekend traffic lately is horrid. Congestion fees, I'm afraid, have done little to relieve the flow."

Emeline steps in, "So Sotheby's—"

"All done and dusted, I'd have said. Then Sotheby's came up with one or two questions about the old fellow, and I mentioned them to Sergei Morosov. Let's see, did they have to do with the provenance? That means," he turns to Xavier.

"Historical record of ownership. Sir, if you would you be so good as to show us the way?"

"Of course, of course," Mr. Pearce gestures down the hall. "We'll step into the music room off here to the right."

When Xavier lingers in the hall, Emeline knows he plans a quick look around. She doubts he'll spot frayed rugs, uneven frames on walls, or lighter squares where a picture might once have hung. Sandley Hall is the picture of old money. She sees Xavier lean forward, whisper to the small servant. Pearce, for all his place and possessions, must prefer not to look upward at the help on a daily basis.

The servant points, "Show you the way, sir?"

"Thanks, I've got it." Xavier strides past the old man.

Only slightly smaller than the reception room, his music room serves as Pearce's main gallery. Paintings hang on every wall. One large canvas stands off the floor on a plinth. Groupings of small sculptures perch on tables. Nothing arranged by era or style as far as Emeline can see. Deborah pauses before a glass case.

Pearce looks interested. "You know about objects from the China Trade?"

"A bit. Once the market opened between Salem and Canton, Chinese artisans painted on every possible material: ceramic snuff boxes, trays, tiles. Even sheets of glass, reverse painting—isn't this an example?" She walks around to the other side of the case. "You have to look through the wrong side to see the scene . . . but I'm afraid we're holding you up."

"No, no, a pleasure, my dear," happy to have an audience, Mr. Pearce shows none of Serge Morosov's nervous energy. He puts his hand on the small of Deborah's back. Emeline watches her step away.

"You know how they copied portraits from lockets and amulets," Pearce goes on, "made little miniatures. See over here, this trio of porcelain cranes each in a different pose. Come, madam, sir," Xavier's rejoined them, "have a look—each one has wings painted different to the other, very Chinese."

"Very lovely," agrees Deborah. "Now, may we see the portrait?" Proudly, Pearce leads his little tour toward a distant wall. Emeline draws a silent breath. *The Duke of Abrantes* reads the small metal plaque tacked to the lower edge of the frame.

Deborah steps in to study the canvas. "The brush marks on the dark coat," she murmurs, "the folds of the cloth." Some detail catches her eye. Emeline, a foot or two back, hears her daughter whisper words she can't catch.

"Might we have a look," Deborah's voice is professional and polite, "at the papers you have for the *Duke*?"

"Ah, had I but known. I keep them in an office in London. We could meet there one day, if you'd like, perhaps for lunch?"

"Why don't I give you a call?" She brings out her mobile and taps the office number into her contacts. Again Pearce offers tea, sherry, "or something stronger if you'd like?" Deborah turns him down. Thanking their host for his time and assuring him they'll meet again, she neatly hustles everyone toward the door.

"Mrs. Hughes?" Pearce is standing in the doorway to see them off. "I was indeed sorry to hear about the death of your husband." Emeline inhales sharply. What tangled grapevine brought the *New York Times* obit to his attention? She's taken him for a jolly, middle-aged county gentleman. In this moment she sees a man nothing like as slow-witted as she'd assumed, exceptionally pleased with himself, and thoroughly steeped in the belief that the wishes of others can be waved away, or if not, bought.

The county road feels like satin after the gravel of Sandley Hall. This time Emeline sits in front, and Xavier behind Deborah. Twice Emeline turns to ask if he is all right.

"Fine. Don't fuss."

"That name, SinJen." Emeline changes the subject. "Left over from the China trade, the opium wars?"

"How come you don't know—"

"Deborah, please don't begin sentences with 'how come you don't know.' My Peckham school failed to teach highborn English names."

"Okay, Ma. Maybe we could all use some tea."

Coming into Guildford, Deborah rattles off highlights of the county seat: its own Shakespeare Company, a philharmonic, music festivals, the theatre, "with try-outs often hosted here before new plays brave the West End." Crossing a pedestrian way paved with cobbles and lined with shops, Deborah pulls in at a restaurant called The White House.

"Lewis Carrol lived in this town," says Deborah, climbing out.

Xavier whispers to Emeline, "Who?"

"You remember," Deborah's hearing is excellent, "Winnie the Pooh?" Emeline sees Xavier's face. Winnie the Pooh. Lewis Carrol. Who are these people?

"Come on, you two." Forgetting her mother's limitations, Deborah scampers up the outside circular staircase. By the time Emeline and Xavier make it to the balcony Deborah's selected a table and, like a painter who's captured the scene, says: "Will you look at that!"

Past masses of flowers in the balcony boxes and beyond a stand of weeping willows a tiny bridge with gingerbread balustrades arches over a flow of water. Sweet, graceful, narrow, the River Wey gives a sense of enduring tranquility, nothing at all like the busy Thames. London might exist on another planet.

"Norman," Deborah says, as the waiter delivers menus; Emeline wonders if she's here so often she knows the waiter. "Pearce's first name. After the invasion French names got mixed in with English. St. Clair became Sinclair. St. John turned into SinJen, though you rarely hear it outside the theatre."

"Pretentious," sniffs Emeline, her working-class roots edging closer to the surface.

As if scratching an itch, Xavier's searching on his fancy cell. "St. John, sorry, SinJen Pearce."

"His cousin," Deborah says with a straight face, "he's likely an ink artist."

"While Pearce does the ear lobes," Xavier says, quick as can be, and wins a smile from the daughter. "Says here SinJen is his father's middle name. Refer to Debrett. What's a Debrett?"

"Peerage registry."

The waiter is back. "We do a nice bangers and mash."

"No, we'll have only tea," Deborah is ordering for everyone. "Well, perhaps a biscuit."

"And scones," directs Emeline. Orders taken, she puts her hand on Deborah's. "I admit it was a thrill watching you today, all that knowledge."

"Come on, Ma, your elegant East Side manner is what got us in the door." In spite of your clothes, Emeline wants to say.

"You two," Xavier observes, "are more alike than you think."

"Me and Ma? Don't play at silly buggers." Silly buggers? Emeline can see Xavier adding more new slang to his inventory.

"Come on, I never even finished Wellesley."

"But think of all you've learned since, Mum."

"Don't call me Mum, I'm—"

"—not the bloody Queen,'" chorus the women.

"BBC, you know," explains Deborah.

Looking pleased, Xavier mimics her accent. "What's that when it's at home?" As he explains about Rocio, her infatuation with the BBC, the biscuits, scones, and tea arrive. A few sips and Deborah's ready to talk about their visit.

"Often collectors concentrate on a particular category—Old Masters, Impressionists, American painting before 1950 or British after. One collector loves faces, so he buys portraits. Another buys only African-American work. Not all are so precise of course; we call that kind of collecting cross-over. Pearce though, he's beyond cross-over." Emeline wants to ask Deborah what it was she'd noticed in the *Duke,* but decides to wait.

Driving home, Deborah turns up the radio. In the city they slow to a crawl in the sludge of traffic. They're deep into South London when Deborah says, "I need to make a quick stop." She double-parks, then changes her mind, makes an illegal U, and parks on the other side. Unkempt men, a full rainbow of the most diverse community in Britain, form a queue in front of an old stone building.

"Won't be a minute," and Deborah swings her legs through the car door. Emeline wants to turn and see what's up, except she's feeling too stiff. It's past time for pills. Back in the car Deborah offers no explanation. Half a dozen dizzying turns and they're back on Searles Road. "Hop out here, you two. I'll park where I can and be right up."

"You should be proud, she's a wonder, she is," Xavier puts a hand under Emeline's arm and helps her through the lobby door.

"Listen to you, more Brit by the minute. That old building where we stopped, did you see what Deborah was up to?"

"Carrying in groceries, looked like."

"My daughter, doing good deeds . . . did someone meet her at the door?"

"A nun, I think, tall woman in long clothes; hard to see, really. Does it matter?"

"Yes, because Deborah went out of her way to repark the car when it would have been easier to stay where she was. Why didn't she want me to see what she was doing?"

Chapter 18

Next morning Xavier and Deborah circle in the narrow kitchen like rooky diplomats. "Xavier, any chance yesterday you got a photo—"

"And good morning to you, too, Deborah," adding, as he feels familiarity if not comfort settle around them, "I'm glad to see you're being nicer to your mother."

"Not that it's any of your business. However do you put up with her?"

Xavier steals half her toast, unimproved by bitter marmalade. "If you met my mother, you'd understand quick enough. Your mother, she's formal—"

"Abrupt and distant—"

"Snooty when uneasy, all true; yet underneath I find her sweet, funny, much smarter than she realizes. Besides, she doesn't radiate hidden demands."

"You're having me on, right? Don't scowl, it means you're kidding. The way you'd say 'pulling someone's leg.'"

"No, we'd say *tomar el pelo*, to take someone's—"

"Growing up I felt nothing but demands. Dress like a lady. Don't laugh out loud on the crosstown bus. Be conspicuous by being inconspicuous."

"All down to the famous Aunt Mildred, I suppose."

"Worlds apart, the two of you, however do you manage?"

"A signed agreement," Deborah snorts, a sure sign caffeine is spinning through her system. "Don't laugh, it's true."

"Maybe that's what we needed," Deborah sounds wistful. "Mothers and daughters, they should all have signed agreements."

"Renegotiated yearly, like the baseball contracts."

"I get it, Xavier, I do. She tried to balance my dad, offset some of his more boisterous ways. Like when they'd meet someone new and he'd talk in cockney."

"You had a question?"

"Right, do you have a picture of the *Duke* on your mobile? Because I need to see a close-up, if you can send it to my computer and print it out for me. Cheers."

"What did you mean yesterday," Xavier's hoping he won't sound the fool again, 'Corto' was bad enough, "when you whispered 'children's bees'?"

"Not children's," Deborah corrects, if without her usual bile. "Childeric's." She spells it; he arranges the letters in his mind, gets nowhere. "Listen, I'll explain tonight, I gotta run. Treat Ma out to lunch someplace, okay? Fresh air will do her good, and she needs to keep walking." She digs into her bag for cash. "Take this, I'll stop at the cash point and pick up more."

Too fast for her, Xavier flicks his own bills on the table. "I've got it. Queen, queen, queen."

"Five pounds, tenner, twenty pounds."

"And this copper coin?"

"One pee." She grins.

"Watch it, lady, lack of manners doesn't cure inequality. Your mother's said that more than once."

"*My* mother?"

"She voted to let Black women into the Junior League."

"Black women from Smith or Barnard, you mean. Like earlier when the League let in Jews, Brandeis Jews, not *shtetl* Jews," she sees Xavier's puzzled look. "Shtetls, the villages in Europe where Jews were allowed to live, before they moved into ghettos? That's exactly what I mean. Hanging around Ma you'd learn about the Junior League, never the shtetls."

"You telling me there were Jews in the ghetto?"

Deborah looks shocked, then laughs like her mother, *Haw Haw*. Trying to keep a straight face, Xavier says, "I did take a spot of history in high school, *señora*."

A dozen years earlier the world's largest Ferris wheel was named the Millennium Wheel; now everyone calls it the "Eye." Tall from a distance, it looms higher against the sky as they walk from the Embankment tube station, Emeline having no intention of taking a cab unless she must.

While Xavier queues to buy tickets, she tips her head back to see the glass-walled capsules slowly undulating, as if wafting on unseen currents. Is it the clouds scurrying behind or is the Eye sliding to the left? Dizzy, Emeline looks down, and Xavier grips her arm, steadying her as the doors open.

She realizes the wheel doesn't stop for them, merely slows. How very like life. Once inside Emeline stands toward the center and grips a pole, not sure she trusts the transparent sides to hold. Not Xavier, he's leaning on the rail that runs around the edge, pressing his forehead against the glass. Uneasy, she closes her eyes, then opens them to risk a view of the serpentine Thames. The north bank is laid out like an ancient jigsaw, the pieces growing smaller as the wheel turns. Nudging Xavier with the end of her cane, she points out Canary Wharf and the Tower of London.

At the top of the loop Emeline feels a trembling balance before the capsule begins its measured descent. Buildings grow in size: St. Paul's Cathedral, Cleopatra's Needle, the new, tall building Londoners call the Shard. She feels like Alice-in-Wonderland eating the mushroom. Xavier takes her arm, and they're back on solid ground. Trembling, relieved, and unwilling after all to walk, she waves her cane at a cab.

On their way into the Swan at Shakespeare's Globe Theatre they pass iconic photos and follow the maître d' to a table with a view of the river through a wall of windows. Emeline sinks into a chair that, thankfully, does not move.

"I could do that every day," Xavier says. She envies him, exhilarated by the ride. "Better than the Coney Island Ferris wheel."

"Never been." Emeline isn't going to confess the Eye frightened her.

"Lady, you lead a sheltered life. We're starting a list of things to do when we get home."

Oh, God. No. Maybe? Yes, while I still can.

Xavier can tell the Eye scared the hell out of her. After sole with grapes and a lovely sauce for her, lamb chops and potatoes for him, he's not surprised when Emeline consents to cab. At home, when she says she needs a lie-down Xavier says he has an errand to run.

Peeling an orange for breakfast, Emeline announced she wanted "a mobile of my own. Nothing too fancy but I want to be able to text." So, after a fast walk down Old Kent Road, Xavier queues up for the bus to Rye Lane and finds his way to Fone4U. Proud he's managing English money and unfamiliar buses, he's back at the flat before Deborah gets home.

"We went on the Eye," brags Emeline as Deborah unpacks dinner from Curry in a Hurry. "Saw the Shard, had lunch at the Swan, and went by the construction at the Tate Modern."

"The Tate Modern used to be a power plant," Deb says for Xavier's benefit, "and now they're building a new addition. With a façade of perforated bricks, if you please, the papers say it's going to look like knitwear." Working their way through *dal, chicken tikka, raita,* and *sag paneer,* Xavier is waiting for one of them to bring up the visit to Surrey.

It's Emeline who begins, raving about Sandley Hall: the facade, hallway, rooms, garden with croquet hoops. The woman must have a photographic memory. "Though weren't you surprised? Xavier, I was certain that Mr. Morosov said Mr. Pearce wanted to—"

"Buy the painting," finishes Deborah.

"Deborah, you weren't even there. Morosovv said sell, not buy."

"It would help, wouldn't it," Xavier wants to head off an argument, "if paintings could speak for themselves. Too bad they don't have ghosts."

"They can. They do. Occasionally an earlier painting seeps through the one on the surface, it's called *pentimento*." Deborah stops, stares at her plate. Curry too spicy? No, she's thinking.

"Even if the original doesn't seep through, it doesn't mean it isn't there. Listen, I don't want you laughing at me—especially you, Xavier—but I think the *Duke* we saw yesterday may be trying to tell us a thing or two." She sweeps a piece of *naan* around her plate. "Have either of you heard of Clovis?"

"Prescription drug?" guesses Xavier.

"Clovis was the king who united all the Frankish tribes under one rule. We're back in the fifth century BCE, of course."

"Of course." Emeline can sound as sarcastic as her daughter when she wants.

"And we care about this because?"

"Because, *señor,* Childeric was the father of Clovis."

"Ah," says Xavier. "Enter Childeric's bees. Don't look at me like that, Deborah, I can find things out, I googled it after you left. They're gold, by the way."

"You are an encyclopedia of information, Xavier." Emeline looks proud of him. Still, *encyclopedia*? How old is she, anyway?

Deborah looks deflated. Xavier's feeling generous. "You'd have much better sources at Courtauld. Deborah, you explain."

"It goes back to ancient burial custom." Deborah pours herself more wine. "In the mid-seventeenth century, a workman was reconstructing a church on the continent and discovered a tomb with a cache of golden bees. The bees disappeared again, for centuries, and the next time they turn up is in Napoleon's era. Napoleon turns them into sort of an emblem of his new empire."

Emeline shakes her head, amazed. "How do you know about this?"

"We had a lecture on excavated art. Makes a great story, yes? Now in the painting yesterday I'm pretty sure I saw a line of tiny gold bees running along the edge of the Duke's cloak. Xavier, did you run off prints? We can take a look."

Xavier retrieves the print-outs, pushes aside the white cardboard boxes, and lays out the photos he took at Sandley Hall: three cranes in the glass case. Dutch landscapes hung four square on a wall, several pictures of the *Duke*.

"There, see?" Deborah's tapping one of the close-ups. "Xavier, can you use—" but he's already brought out his cell, shining its little spotlight onto the print. "My God. That's the problem."

"Deborah, I don't understand."

"A painter in seventeenth-century Spain, Ma, why would his painting show a row of golden bees? The bees were barely out of the earth in Belgium. No faxing back then, no internet, images didn't go darting around the continent like they do now. It looks to me like the clumsy forger didn't do his homework."

Xavier picks up a different print. "Emeline? Look at this one."

"Xavier, do you mind? We need to find out the date the bees were unearthed, where they were transferred—"

"You don't think . . ." taking a good look at the second photo, Emeline's hand trembles more than usual. "Could it be?"

"Focus, you two, damn it. We have to get the exact date—"

"Deborah, in this other picture—"

"Is anyone paying attention to me? This will take research, and I'm slammed with work of my own. If, Xavier, you're up for more hunting, you and your mobile."

Another favor for Deborah, that would put credit in his account. Besides he's curious: ancient gold bees turning up when they shouldn't. "Why not?"

"Okay, here's how to go about it. Start with—"

"Childeric," Xavier says firmly, "the tomb, the transfers, the theft, and the dates."

"Oh. Okay. Pretty much."

After making herself a Chamomile tea, Emeline shows Deborah the second photo: an Asian statue, a pale stone woman with cloth in sharp folds. And tells her, briefly, what happened with Tram.

Deborah isn't buying any of it. "These Chinese pieces, they're all over the place, Ma, you can't know it's the Scarsdale Doxy. Go into any antique store and you'll see—"

"I'm sure that's true, dear. Still, Xavier, do you have a photo of Tram's statue?" Xavier shakes her head.

Deborah scowls as if the negligence is his. "Even supposing it is the same statue, what's it have to do with the *Duke*? I say we get back to our problem—Pearce's painting is likely a forgery."

"And you know so much about forgery."

"Don't say it like that, Ma, the Courtauld fees came from Daddy."

"Give us the basics anyway," Xavier's trying to forestall conflict, "if you can?"

Taking it as a dare, Deborah does. "Fine. You can make a direct copy of a painting. You can create a brilliant oil copy, right canvas, paint that will pass inspection, bake the finished painting in an oven to get the *craqualure*—"

"Which is?"

"Tiny cracks on the surface of old paintings. It's kind of an obscure term." She sounds more kindly than patronizing; maybe Deborah's getting used to having him around. "Though you'll still have a problem if the original is out there somewhere.

"Or, you can create a different work, 'in the style of.' Now you have another problem: if the painter's well-known, there's bound to be a *catalogue raisonnée,* a complete list of the artist's work with all the info about each piece. These days it may even be on a website."

"And everybody knows to look?"

"Not everybody, no, but you can be sure someone will, what with the publicity if the forgery's put up for auction. That's where he was clever, the dealer who offered painting after painting to Koerner's.

He stayed away from public auctions and transacted directly with the gallery."

"Shouldn't the gallery have known better? Or, did it?"

"Am I in Koerner's confidence? Don't ask me."

Next evening, over take-away from Kam Foh, Xavier borrows Deborah's lecture style to report on Childeric's Bees. "In 1853 a mason was working on the reconstruction of the Church of Saint-Brice in Belgium." He pauses. "He discovered a Mero, a Mero—"

"Mer-o-vingian," then Deborah claps her hand over her mouth. "Sorry."

"A Merovingian tomb from the fifth century and found various objects, including a signet ring inscribed *Childeric Regis*.

"Identifying the tomb," Deborah crows. "Of Childeric, father of Clovis."

"Bits made of iron, gold coins, a gold bracelet, numerous items of gold called clo-zone," he stumbles and stops to chew on a Honey Spare Rib, "studded with garnet. And 300 small gold bees. These land in the hands of the governor of the Netherlands, Archduke Leopold William."

"I thought you said Belgium."

"Probably all one empire, Ma, let him talk."

"The archduke put his personal physician in charge of studying and publishing the finds." Xavier frowns, "His physician?"

Deborah nods. "Makes sense, doctors were the scientists back then."

"Luckily this Dr. Chifflet wrote detailed descriptions and even made engravings of the missing pieces. He published his work, Anas-tas-is Childe—do I gotta tackle the Latin?"

"No," Emeline steps in. "Keep going."

"Later, the bees belong to the Emperor of Austria. He gives the treasure to Louis XIV to thank the French who helped him against the Turks." Xavier pokes at a glutinous lump on his plate. "What's this stuff?"

"Jellied eel, try it. So now the bees are in France."

"Yes, but not for long, the French king isn't much interested in the gift."

"I've had gifts like that." Deborah winks at Xavier.

"Anyway, the collection is stolen; the thieves melt the bigger gold pieces, but smaller, less easily melted pieces like the clo-zone—"

"Cloisonée."

"Ma!" Deborah runs two fingers across her lips, zip it. "Xavier's doing fine."

"—they hid in the Seine. A few pieces were retrieved."

"Very thorough," Deborah says, impressed.

"Here's the interesting thing. In 1804 Napoleon is declared emperor by the Snot."

"The *what?*"

"It's French," says her mother. "S E N A T, like our Senate."

"Here's a portrait of Napoleon." Xavier enlarges the photo on his cell phone. "You can see bees embroidered all over the red velvet."

"That's it!" Deborah claps her hands. "Nobody's talking about golden bees before 1853. And our painter Juan Bautista Martínez del Mazo died in Spain nearly two hundred years earlier."

"Here's the other thing," Xavier waves his cell phone like a flag at a parade. "Napoleon needs a symbol of his new France. Not the eagle, not the fleur-de-liss." Mesmerized, neither woman corrects him. With a gracious bow he hands his cell to Deborah.

"Napoleon chose the bee," Deborah reads, squinting at the tiny screen, "*because* it traced back to Clovis, to Childeric, and to ancient France."

Deborah hands back his phone. "No way would del Mazo paint an emblem of France on the cloak of an Iberian aristocrat. Good work, my friend."

To Xavier's astonishment, Deborah gets up to give him a hug. "Be like a Manchester United fan wearing an Arsenal shirt," he says, laughing.

Emeline isn't laughing. "And there's me, hoping we had no skin in the game. Clifford used to say that, some foolish football expression."

"Even if the *Duke* is a forgery," Deborah sends Xavier's a look: let's don't get her worked up. "It could have happened years ago. Before Daddy came on the scene, or even before Mr. Segal bought the *Duke*. Maybe no skin in the game, Ma."

"Yes we do," insists Emeline. "If the painting is a forgery, what about the other paintings Clifford arranged to sell for Ron?"

Chapter 19

"Believe me, Ma, Tate Modern doesn't half tell the story." By morning Emeline's still worrying and Deborah's making an effort to distract her, insisting they take a look at Peckham's new art scene. "We have pop-up galleries in arches beneath the over-ground trains; one important gallery is in a renovated meatpacking factory. We have a sculpture display in a multi-level car park—original venues to bring original art closer to the people." She spreads her arms as if to embrace all South London.

"Trendy." Emeline does not intend it as a compliment.

"Banksy, of course, the graffiti artist and no one knows who he is. Performance art, too, one woman works body paint into dancers' skin and then poses them. Art is not just about what you like or don't like."

"Is that so." Emeline's not impressed.

"We need to see what the artist reacts against, imitates, inches toward."

What Emeline sees is Xavier's eyes tracking the debate. It's time to draw a line in the sand.

"Very well, my dear, we'll visit one or two of your venues and I will judge for myself."

Deborah unfolds her South London Culture Map, admitting the art is a bit spread out. At first, reassuring her, "don't worry, Xavier will find a cab, " Emeline is dismayed if not shocked to see Tate Modern on the same map as a venue called the Asylum, offering a multi-light installation in a derelict chapel. At this rate she will need an asylum of her own.

Deborah leaves for Cortauld. Xavier finds a cab, and through the window Emeline studies the Peckham streets sliding by, a pastiche of familiar and strange. Their first stop is the South London Gallery.

Comforted by the ordinary architecture, Emeline still braces for the "art" she expects she'll find inside. To her surprise it's not so different from the last exhibition she'd seen at MOMA: huge paintings with erratic splashes of color along with canvases cold and geometric. She quite enjoys it all, paying close attention to the artists' names. Middle Eastern, Latin American, South Asian, names to match South London's new faces. Let Sir Joshua Reynolds turn in his grave—Emeline feels a tug of understanding close to kinship.

Less so at their second stop. A store-front exhibit offers political posters on butcher's wrapping paper, drawn in furious black lettering and described as cutting-edge. Certainly charm has been excised.

"I know," agrees Xavier. "Why do people get so worked up? Art's nothing but things to look at, innit."

"Innit," she echoes his adopted slang. "Let's sit, shall we? If we don't mind balancing on stools it appears they also offer tea. Pray it's of a better grade than those posters."

Tired, musing over what they've seen, Emeline is ready to get a cab and ride home. Once on Searles, though, instead of going straight inside she makes a slow detour up the street looking closely at the parked cars, at license plates. Walking back, she refuses to catch Xavier's eye.

Xavier doesn't ask, he doesn't have to: in London Emeline is still afraid she's being followed. Crazy, of course, who even knows they're in London—Deborah, SinJen Pearce, and a couple nameless cab drivers? He spends a few minutes in the kitchen, making a sandwich ("not for me, Xavier, I'm not hungry"). Other women might behave like this to get attention. That is so not Emeline. Maybe she was always an anxious soul and finding herself alone has sharpened her antennae.

Emeline is napping when the buzzer rings. Xavier goes down three steps to the tiny foyer, sees only the shadow of a figure through the clouded glass. Years in El Barrio breed distrust, and he's ready to retreat. Except whoever it is presses a face close to the glass and waves.

When he opens the heavy door, right away wishes he hadn't. This unknown visitor is a woman, middle-aged and stocky, her navy suit tight across the shoulders, her matching skirt wrinkled from sitting in a car. With a nose for coppers, he's prepared for the flash of her identification. Even so, he's about to close the door before she can insert the toe of her sturdy, shoe when he hears Emeline behind him at the door to Deborah's flat. "Who's there, Xavier?"

No one, he's getting ready to say. The woman, surprisingly strong, pushes her way in, slipping her warrant card back in her pocket. "I need to talk to Miss Deborah Hughes."

"Wrong address," says Xavier

"Better if we talk upstairs," then to Emeline: "Hello. Might you be Mrs. Hughes? I was hoping to speak with Deborah but since your man says—"

"Deborah is not at home," Emeline's voice is sharp, "and he is not my man. What is it you want?"

"Detective Sergeant Kelsey, Art and Antiquities Unit, New Scotland Yard," the smile is gone and before Xavier can stop her, Kelsey shoulders her way into the flat.

"How did you find us?" Emeline's frostiest manner's back. Xavier guesses she will not be offering tea.

"Why don't you both sit down?" The intruder tilts her head toward the two metal and leather chairs. Xavier doesn't budge. Something about this feels off, unless it's one of those Brit subtleties he doesn't understand.

"I am here in connection with several paintings that have surfaced in our inquiries. We believe you may have information than can help us." Kelsey pulls out three four-by-six-inch photos. Fanning them like playing cards, she holds them at arm's length. Two, Xavier has never seen. He recognizes *The Duke of Abrantes,* but can't see whether there are bees and decides he will not walk closer to look.

Emeline, not even glancing at them, seems more than a match for the Detective Sergeant. "I have no information that can help you."

"Kindly take a closer look." Kelsey moves toward her. "Have you seen any of these before?"

Giving the photos a New York nano-second, Emeline returns her gaze to the woman. "The photographs?"

"The paintings themselves."

"I see many paintings. The other day Xavier and I—excuse my manners—let me present my friend Xavier Escudero. And you are Careless, was it?" Xavier suppresses a smile.

"Kelsey." Again she flicks out her warrant card and looks annoyed when Emeline shows no interest in it. "Mrs. Hughes, this is not a game. Our unit is tasked with investigating paintings whose history is, shall we say, uncertain. Since I am sure you may have seen these paintings before," Emeline remains still as a stone, "are you aware that Mr. SinJen Pearce is putting one of them up for auction?"

"Who?"

"Don't waste my time! The gentleman in Surrey, you went to see him two days ago."

"Let's see, Tuesday that would be." Xavier worries she'll actually start counting on her fingers. "We did take a drive to Guildford. Charming town, my daughter wanted us to have a look."

"Perhaps you'd be more forthcoming if you came with me to—"

That's it. Xavier is beside her in a flash. Too many times he's met this woman, a bully from the park, the school yard, the street. "Do you have a warrant?" he snaps. "Otherwise you may leave. You came looking for Deborah Hughes, and Deborah Hughes is not here. This is an unjustified intrusion."

Knowing well the line between rudeness and assault, Xavier presses close enough that she steps back. Without taking her arm, he herds her toward the door and down the steps. Opening the door to Searles Road, he is so close they are nearly nose to nose. When she retreats he closes the door behind her with a clash. He half expects to hear pounding on the clouded glass, possibly a mobile calling for back up. He waits until he hears a car start halfway down the block before he goes upstairs.

"*Bien hecho,* my good man," Emeline gives him a sly smile. "Well done. You learned those maneuvers on the telly?"

"I wish, call it real-life practice. You didn't seem all that surprised, Emeline. Were you expecting her?"

"Not specifically. Resembled a badger, didn't she. Look up the Art Squad."

"New Scotland Yard," Xavier is punching at his cell, "Art and Antiques Squad founded in 1969 after a series of—ha, you'll love this, Emeline."

"Stolen paintings?"

"Holdups of stamp dealers."

After Xavier gets a text from Deborah: *out for dinner, home late,* Emeline says, "We'll have to wait until morning to tell her about the Badger," and forages in the fridge. After warmed-up Chinese food and a limited conversation she insists on carrying on in Spanish, she retreats to the bedroom to relax with her pack of Spanish cards, leaving Xavier to wonder if there's a nightclub anywhere nearby.

Morning comes and Xavier leaves early. At the café, making friends with the cashier, he shows off is dexterity with English coins. The day is sunny, the air no worse than New York's. Back at the flat his mellow mood evaporates.

Deborah's up; more accurately she's back, wearing yesterday's clothes. Xavier's done that often enough, he knows what it means. He suspects Emeline knows, too, which may explain why the two are arguing over another matter entirely.

"With Daddy, it was all about money, I get that, Ma. The man grew up in Brixton. You should have a look at Brixton these days, by the way, all juice bars and vegan cupcakes. Thing is, I don't care about money for money's sake. Art, that's what matters to me."

"Lofty goal, my dear."

"The beauty of it, the experiments, the way one intention grows into another." Man, talk about pompous, Xavier's glad he's taken on caffeine. "Look at Kandinsky's work, advancing the viewer's understanding, presenting abstracts independent of visual references—"

"Advancing? Like that painter Ofili, paints with elephant shit?"

"Ma!"

"Dung, then, you prefer feces? How about urine, if we call it piss will it sound cool?"

"You think *I'm* frivolous, Ma. What did you do with your life besides cater to Daddy and prance around with friends at the Colony Club?"

"Very little prancing on my part from here on, you can count on that."

"Yes, and you have the perfect excuse, don't you."

"Now hang on a minute, Deborah," Xavier interrupts, alarmed.

"This has nothing to do with you, Xavier, so butt out."

"Really, Deborah? I've been living with her for weeks, which is more than you can say. Don't you try telling me how difficult she can be—"

"Oh, thank you very much, Xavier!"

"—that doesn't mean you get to throw shade on her entire life."

"Three weeks? Huh, new kid on the block. You didn't see how she pampered Daddy when he didn't need it, ran her impeccable household to impress his clients when she could have been making something of herself. She does have a brain, after all."

"Of course I have a brain," Emeline shouts, "so kind of you to notice."

"Even Ma's help has more purpose. At least they work for a living, they have skills—"

"Children! This is getting out of hand."

"—even if it's only scrubbing toilets." Catching the stunned look on both their faces, Deborah stops

"Scrubbing toilets, yes," Xavier speaks very slowly, watches Deborah realize, too late, what she's said. "Keeping a family together, food on the table, making sure we went to school. Trying to bring up good Americans. Facing struggles you can't begin to imagine."

"Xavier, I'm sure Deborah didn't mean . . ."

"I am not at all ashamed. My mother started by cleaning toilets, yes, and these days she's a nanny, a well-paid, well-dressed nanny with beautiful manners. Yes?" He whirls on Emeline, who nods weakly.

"Manners she brought with her from Puerto Rico, nothing you'd learn in New York where you're pushed out of the way on the subway, talked about behind your back in fancy apartments. 'My dear,' Xavier squeaks, 'my new girl seems a gem, we'll have to see if she is honest as well.' Not even waiting until the new girl is out of the room to bad-mouth her."

Deborah's lip trembles. Xavier wishes he hadn't gone so far.

Not Emeline. "We'll leave my faulty behavior for another day. Tell me this." Emeline takes a step closer to look her daughter in the eye. "If you have grown such a tender conscience, why are you spending your inheritance on a path to take you straight to an art gallery? Not to mention catting around at night like a wanton teenager."

"Ma, I never—"

"But I forget. You're part of a revolution and Peckham is the new Soho: galleries, cafes, watering places for London's idle yuppies. The city pulled down Aylsebury Estate, displacing thousands. Now you, with your exotic clothes and high-flown ideas? You are going to be part of the new SoHo. I'm only glad your Grandma Dora isn't here to see what you're making of her old neighborhood."

Crying, Deborah runs into the bedroom, and the door crashes shut. Emeline avoids Xavier, stalks into the kitchen, and having no door to slam, resorts to banging cupboards open and closed. In minutes she's whisking eggs. Alone in the living room and helpless to mend the rift, Xavier sinks onto the divan he's grown used to thinking of as his own.

Deborah flounces out for a day at Courtauld, leaving Emeline miserable. Mostly she's recognized her calling: not to finish her degree, Clifford needed her at his side, she knew she was much more than decoration.

Though she might have worked on her degree, too. Smith, a Seven Sister college like Wellesley, started the Ada Comstock program for women—"Ada's," they were called—who'd earlier been too caught up in the exigencies of their lives to go to college. Emeline met an Ada when they worked together on one board. A large, gentle woman, she ran a children's welfare non-profit with brilliance, a sure hand, and connections everywhere Emeline had none.

Emeline's growing envy came close to propelling her into action. Then Clifford came home with a new project of his own, it would require her cooperation. Her husband's executive assistant, diplomatic hostess, whispering muse, not to mention lover: she'd been all those and more, most of the time finding it enough. Until the focus of her efforts was no longer there.

"What does she know?" Emeline is fighting back tears. "My role was in place before Deborah was old enough to notice. She knows nothing. Did she ever ask what else I might like to have done, what else I might have been? If, if, oh, never mind."

Xavier hands her a tissue and takes her thin, bony hand. "I'm asking. Tell me."

"You'll laugh."

"Try me."

"I wanted to be a counselor, or maybe a social worker, a professional who helps people." Xavier coughs. "See? I knew you'd laugh."

"I am not laughing, Emeline. I am what you'd say, gob-smacked. You're not even that curious about people."

"You don't think? You think you're the only one who's had to learn to hide behind a front?"

"Until this morning you and Deborah were doing better. You still have time to change thinks with your daughter."

"This is your approach, is it, trying to see both sides when Flavia and your sister fight?"

"You kidding? Lace up my Nikes and book out fast as I can, that's my approach."

"Just look who's doling out advice. The man who won't tell his own mother—"

"Pull this off with Deborah," Xavier says, "and I promise, I will. When we get home I'll level with Flavia." She wonders if he notices he's saying Flavia more often than Mai, as if widening by centimeters the distance between them. Emeline blows her nose.

"Know what, Emeline? Let's go be tourists for the day. We could visit the Barbary lions in Trafalgar Square."

"You do realize the Barbary lions are not alive? Stone, like Patience and Fortitude at the NYPL."

"Did you know foreign monarchs used to send exotic animals to the king's menagerie?"

"You've been googling."

"It said people could get in free if they brought a cat or dog to feed the lions. Is that true?"

"I really can't say, Xavier. It was before my time."

"We had a visitor," Emeline begins that evening, and gives a focused review of the Badger while Deborah unpacks little boxes from Five Star Fish Bar. Furious or frightened, Deborah turns on Xavier. He should have known better, he should never have opened the door, he's meant to be looking after her mother, if he isn't up to the job he can jolly well head back to SpaHa where he belongs.

"El Barrio," Xavier corrects with dignity.

"Deborah, don't be an ass, Xavier's the one who got her to leave. Anyway, it's you she was looking for."

"Me? My name isn't on the lease."

"It's on the mailbox inside. Anyone could have stepped into the foyer on the heels of another tenant. And what about your landline, is it in your name?"

"Well, yes, it plays 'Greensleeves,' actually, though I seldom use it."

"Or, suppose someone did follow us from Surrey."

"You think they tailed us through the traffic from *Surrey?* Xavier, tell me she isn't like this all the time."

"You have no idea."

"Preposterous." Deborah folds her arms against her chest.

"Look, I know, your mother has been a bit . . ."

"Paranoid?"

"Watchful," Xavier amends.

"My dears, if the paranoid can get a word in edgewise? I did see a car as we left Mr. Pearce's house, a dark blue sedan with several antennas and two people in the front. I couldn't see their faces. Once we got onto the motorway I didn't see it again, until yesterday. There was a car like it parked on the street."

"My goodness. In greater London, a dark blue sedan, how distinctive. It makes no sense. No one," Deborah glares at Xavier, "knew we were going to Surrey save the three of us."

"Right," Xavier says, "and me with my close ties to the London fuzz—"

"I didn't mean—"

"Of course you did, Deborah," Emeline says, "but never mind. If we don't know when they got on our trail we do know why: it's the *Duke*. Nobody was paying the least attention to us before."

"Whoever 'they' are. I suppose you mean the Art Squad."

"I'm not so certain; does the Art Squad have the manpower to watch a respectable house in Surrey?"

"You think it wasn't the Art Squad? Ma, you're being weird."

"Make fun of me all you want. But remember, please, it's my husband who died suddenly, I'm the one who can't be sure . . ." her voice trails off.

"If," Deborah's voice is small, "it was an accident or not?"

"Precisely."

"Ladies, can we remember I have a job, and if we don't get back soon, I won't."

Emeline sees what he's up to: distracting her from unwelcome thoughts under the guise of self-interest. Clever. He's got a point, too. If he loses his gym job and has to get another, it could upset their convenient arrangement. Or if, God forbid, he gets a full-time job?

"Why don't I text Gabor," Emeline suggests casually.

"Who the hell—"

"He's Xavier's boss, Deborah."

Only when Emeline pulls out her cell, does it dawn on Deborah. "What do you mean—you'll text him? You don't text."

"She does," Xavier says. "She wanted me to get her the new mobile so she could text." He scribbles Gabor's number and hands it to her. Deb blinks pulls out her own phone, and gives a dozen rapid taps. Her mother's cell pings. Emeline opens it, smiles, passes it over so Xavier can see. *Ma U amaze me*.

"Thank you, dear."

Xavier feels his role as middleman is wearing thin. Emeline still talks with him as she had in New York, if guarded any time the subject of Clifford comes up. Deborah, who doesn't do guarded, can't always manage polite. The tension between the two of them, for this he could be home on 105th. Lately he feels he doesn't give a fig who wins. Xavier likes that one, maybe fig is the polite way of saying . . .

"I'm off to visit a friend," announces Deborah, reappearing. "Why don't you come with me, Ma? You, too, Xavier, show you I know another side of London, it's not all Courtauld and art collections. I'll get the car. Be outside in fifteen minutes."

The neighborhood where she stops doesn't look all that different from East Harlem. As many dark faces as white, as many bodies hunched in doorways as standing upright. The gutters run with crushed cigarette packs, bottle caps, and worrisome debris. Xavier and Emeline follow Deborah, walking swiftly. A voice reaches them from a doorway. "I could murder a doughnut, mate, you wouldn't have a—"

"Sod off, buster," says Deborah. "Xavier, take Ma's arm, will you, or we'll be late." He tries. Emeline shakes him off and ploughs on, her cane clicking. They round a corner.

Deborah's leading them to the run-down stone building where she parked on Tuesday. Pediments once proud are over the doorway, the windows clouded with dust. Nearby a church bell tolls: one, two . . .

Deborah sprints ahead. They pass a line of bent, bedraggled people, mostly men, huddled against the wall as if for warmth, and up stone steps curved from centuries of footsteps. Once a monastery or a barracks, Xavier can't tell.

Three, four . . . "Hurry, will you?" Deborah pounds the outsize brass knocker on the door. His arm around Emeline's waist, Xavier half guides, half lifts her up the stairs, intimidated by Deborah's voice and in the dark about why they're here.

"Hey! It's a queue, Sunshine," snarls a man near the front. "You don't follow Sister proper like, none of us get in." The queue shuffles forward, the first few men tossing cigarettes into the gutter to hiss and die, and starting up the steps.

A tall woman dressed like a nun opens the door. "Not open yet," she growls, "you lot need to remember . . ." her voice fades as she stares at the trio on her doorstep, swinging her gaze between the older woman and the younger. Five, six, tolls the bell . . .

She lifts a chapped hand to her lips, her eyes fixed on the woman with the cane. "Emmy?" she asks in a rough voice. "Emmy?" No answer. Doubling his grip, Xavier barely manages to catch Emeline as she slumps against the door jam and faints dead away.

Chapter 20

It's the same dream she's found herself in many times. Leaving the doctor's office, stepping on air, Emeline decides to walk the twenty blocks home to 95th. Past brownstone houses where plane trees grow in squares of soil hewn out of the sidewalk, she shuffles through a few leaves fallen early off the trees. An observer in the dream as well, she's aware shuffling then was optional.

Still dreaming, at Park she crosses carefully with the light and turns north on Madison to take advantage of the shop windows. Not to see embroidered pillow cases in one, African statues in another: it's her reflection that interests her. She calculates the months before her stomach curves out. Will she be able to button her winter coat? Maybe she'll borrow Tram's. Oat, brown, and black plaid with a tunnel belt, Tram's coat will allow more room as more room's needed. Emeline promises herself she'll walk this way often so as not to miss a moment.

Clifford's going to be thrilled. Deborah? They'll figure out how to present the new addition to Deborah. They can spin it as a present for her. Only three, she may like the idea. Deborah and the new little one, they'll be a better version of herself and the London brother Emeline's barely met. For once Emeline feels her usual jealousy of the much younger boy dissolve.

Clifford's Ghost

How the memory of that afternoon has lived on: Clifford's glee at the news; down on the floor, coloring with her rump in the air, Deborah is happy, ignorant. Over their daughter's head she and Clifford make plans and play with names.

As always, the observer tries to push this iconic walk from her mind. Forever sad if later less so, young Emeline will avoid the storefronts on Madison, reminding her as they do of her brief, futile joy. Emeline never does borrow Tram's plaid coat once she understands she will not, after all, be needing it.

Normally the dream ends there, yet still finds herself in a fog, hearing voices she knows, Deborah's, Xavier's . . . where is she? Not New York. Peckham, that's it, she's having a dream about being back in Peckham. The voice again, that would be her daughter, not coloring on the floor but grown up. The room is too warm, she feels nauseous. That's the problem, that's why she's imagining things that make no sense, why she saw a face she knew in a person she'd never met: the strange, nun-like person with the low voice and familiar eyes.

Saint Bertie's keeps to a strict schedule and stricter policies. Three evenings a week the meal starts at 5:30 p.m.; anyone who tries to cut into the line or set so much as a foot on the steps before the bell tolls is sent to the back of the queue. Not that in London cutting in line is common. Xavier's seen the same docile behavior in people lining up for the bus or picking up fish and chips at a take-away window.

The nun, if that's what she is, helps Xavier move Emeline into a small office and make her comfortable on the narrow day bed. Deborah hovers. When Emeline resists, moves uneasily, Deborah gently strokes her shoulder and pulls up a folded afghan, seeming not to mind its musty, charity-shop smell, kinder with her hands than any words spoken since Sunday. Tender feelings lie somewhere in Emeline's estranged, glamorous, independent daughter.

Sweeping her veil to one side, the other woman kneels beside the day bed and takes Emeline's hand in her own large one. Her face catches the light from the bare bulb overhead Xavier has a glimpse of a rough cheek. Is that a shadow near the handsome cheekbones? Xavier thinks he's being discreet until the nun sends Xavier the trace of a smile, and yes, a wink.

"We see this here from hunger. Deb, when did she last eat?"

"Oh, very nice, you think I'd trot my mother onto the bus without—"

"Don't be getting fresh with me, girl." Too familiar, Xavier thinks as a hand ruffles Deborah's hair; though she doesn't mind, she lays her palm over the nun's chapped hand and leans with a sigh against her shoulder.

"We've got this, Deb. Why don't you go help with the food?"

"You sure?"

"Yep. She's coming around, we'll let her rest a bit."

"What is this place," Xavier asks the woman as Deborah leaves, "an abandoned church?"

"Shh, let's keep our voices low." Where Emeline's accent has smoothed out over the years, Sister's blue-collar speech is a legacy of South London.

"Nah," she explains, "our building never harbored clerics. Mostly it was office clerks worked here, perched on high benches to scribble away in paper ledgers. Then later, what with immigrants pouring in from all parts and computers taking over, the area sank in popularity as a business center.

"Did they tell you South-uk has the most council housing of any borough in London? Even so, people are sleeping rough. Nearest tube station is a busy dot in the great London underground until night arrives, then it turns into a haven for the unsheltered. A while back we took over the building, chose a most unlikely saint's name, and today we have St. Bertie's."

On guard, Xavier watches Sister run her eyes over the large rock Emeline wears on her left hand. Nun or not, is such a stone safe in this low-rent corner of London? The woman's gaze doesn't rest on the ring, though. She's staring at Emeline's face, the eyes flickering.

"Kitchen, chapel, our dining hall," a calloused hand waves toward the door, "used clothing room, my office here. Living quarters: one for me and two for emergencies. You hear it all over South London: have a go at St. Bertie's, St. Bertie's will have a 'butty and a cuppa.'" The nun gives a low laugh. "Folks make St. Bertie sound like some strapping bloke from the Midlands, ladling out the mash."

"You wanna tell me," Xavier demands, "what we're doing here?" Now Emeline's eyes do open, blink at the patched plaster ceiling. Afterward Xavier likes to think it's his voice broke the spell.

"Come on, compra." Anxious, Xavier grips her hand and feels a faint squeeze in reply. "Come on, now, you're going to be fine."

"Michael," Emeline croaks, "is that you?"

Abruptly, the nun stands, "I'm after getting a drop of brandy," and walks out. Emeline clings to Xavier's hand. "What happened?"

"You fainted."

"Figured that much out for myself."

"We were standing at the door of the refuge, the door opened, and you collapsed."

"Deborah?"

"She's gone to help with the evening meal."

"So glad my daughter has her priorities."

"Your daughter did not run away, Emeline. She was very upset. The nun was trying to keep her busy, she thought the two of us could manage."

"Did she, now. What is this place, anyway?"

Xavier watches her look around. A modest cross hangs on one wall. A desk, battered and scuffed, is piled with folders, bills, mail. On a little table a box of tissues bent at one corner, a tattered Bible, books by Eckart Tolle and Carl Jung, whoever they are.

"It seems to be the sister's office."

The nun comes back with an empty jam jar and a bottle of brandy. Sensing Emeline's dismay, she hands them both to Xavier, then settles on a chair as far away as possible in the stuffy space. Xavier pours an inch of amber. Emeline takes two sips and coughs furiously. Not used to alcohol, Xavier remembers. To help her out he reaches for the jam jar and finishes the brandy.

"You okay, Emmy?" Sister's husky voice is calm.

Emeline coughs, as if clearing her mouth of a bad taste. "You look . . . I thought . . ."

"And so I am. Or I was. Our meeting like this is down to that girl of yours, Em. Deb's been after me since you turned up in London, wanting to bring us together. I did think I'd get a heads up, maybe she'd invite me to her flat. Not drop in at our busiest time." Emeline is shaking her head: over her daughter's casual ways or this unlikely encounter?

Xavier sees the similarities between the two: eyes set slightly close together, heart-shaped faces. Except the sister's forehead, her overbite, her skin close to the color of his own, these seem shaped by different genes.

"Ask me anything you want," says the sister.

"Are you," asks Emeline, "Catholic?" Xavier can't help himself, he breaks out laughing and Sister joins in, the two eying each other as if suspecting a kindred spirit.

Sister recovers first. "And that would be your main question, would it?"

"No one in my family," Emeline sounds prim, "has ever been Catholic."

"Bit lower class, Ma used to say. Not Catholic, as it happens. I did live a while in a retreat center. Common dress, this was, so I stayed with it as I made other changes."

"Ma mentioned something about changes but I never imagined . . . What do I call you?"

"People around here call me Sister." Xavier sees Emeline's shoulders stiffen. But I am the sister!

"Or for family it's Mary-Margaret." Unruffled, Sister turns to Xavier, "How about a proper introduction, then? You must be Xavier." Curious, merely, not outraged the way Deborah had been, was it only last Sunday?

"Xavier Escudero, friend of the family. And this is—"

"I've known her a long time, dearie, if never well. Emeline Hughes, née Emeline Dimock. I am—"

"He is—he used to be my brother Michael Dimock, little Mikie. Frankly I have no idea, who he is now." Emeline sits up, puts a trembling hand to her head. "Xavier, I think it's time we left."

"She's not supposed to drink, Sister."

"C'mon, a sip of brandy never hurt. I'll get Deborah, she'll see you both home." Sister lifts a large hand as if attempting a blessing. "I do want to meet up with you again, Emmy. Or Emeline, if that makes you happier? Get to know you. Be friends, if we can. Try to explain."

"We aren't long in London, I'm afraid."

"I see." A look of disappointment quickly covered.

Emeline manages to stand, leaning heavily on her friend of the family. "One more question: how is it you know my daughter?"

"Your daughter," Sister reminds her, gently, "is my niece. With no other family in London, she made the effort to look me up. It wasn't difficult, not so many Dimocks in the directory. Though she could have asked around," modestly Sister lowers her eyes. "I had a bit of a reputation in some circles. Ask her to tell you about Melody, if you don't wish to ask me. Emeline, I want to hear how you've been doing since Clifford died, how you're handling the trouble." Emeline inhales, stiffens.

"Yes, Deborah's told me. It's fine, I'm no gossip. I am tired of family secrets, I truly am, they bring nothing but harm. When can we meet? We will meet, won't we?"

Emeline reaches for her cane, waving Xavier away when he moves to help, and at the door turns back to send Sister an unreadable look.

"I really don't think so."

The reunion not having gone to plan, Emeline can tell her daughter's furious. Driving back to the flat Deborah delivers a few well-chosen barbs and in a huff drops them both on Searles Road. Growing dark though it is, Emeline persuades Xavier to walk with her up the block and back, claiming she needs fresh air and hoping he won't notice her eyeing the number plates. Xavier thinks she's good at details? Fine, it may come in handy. Back in the flat, feeling off balance, Emeline retreats to the bedroom and lets her thoughts return to Michael, as once was.

Clifford, what would he make of this Sister? He'd never mind, Emeline admits, he'd made his packet by embracing all comers and many became friends; as long as they weren't under indictment, openly rude, or pretentious. People pretending to be something they weren't, that's what Clifford hated most, for sure he'd have had no use for Luca Bevilaqua. More than once Emeline's wondered how she made the cut herself. By now she knows her doubts were a remnant of the Peckham girl, feeling out of place in the world Aunt Mildred offered her.

Lately life's gotten confusing enough with Xavier and her daughter getting on like a house afire, Xavier speaking as if she and Deborah are his family when it no longer feels like hers. Last thing she needs is this half-brother turning up—if she can even call him a brother. Unbidden, come thoughts of the baby boy she'd almost had, and then lost.

Maybe she should try reminding Deborah of the baby brother her daughter never got to know, saying they'd each lost . . . no, she can't imagine how that conversation could go well.

Ridiculous to feel jealous of the London boy who had a tenth the advantages rained on her in Manhattan. Yet ten times the affection. Mikie got to stay in London with Ma, sit down to her meatloaf every Thursday, her salt cod every Friday. Ride the bike with her Saturdays to the library. Thinking of the years she missed at home brings tears to her eyes, for the moment obscuring her better schooling, prosperous life, darling husband. She'd loved Clifford many ways, how smart he was, adventurous, successful, funny; and, she'd recognized early on, the particular ease of living with a fella who might have grown up in Peckham.

It's after eight when Xavier calls through the door. "No idea when Deborah will be back, I'm going to find food." In a while

Emeline's drawn to the kitchen by the smell of frying onions. On the counter sits a jar of Bovril. Squinting at a recipe he's found on his mobile, Xavier's putting together a proper English supper—beef, cabbage, carrots, potatoes—even if it won't be ready until the Spanish dinner hour.

When Deborah finally turns up, having walked off much of her fury, she digs in with delight. "Good job, Xavier, cheers."

"Comfort food, I thought it might be welcome."

"Though as a rule" Deborah can't resist, "I don't use so much of the Bovril."

"I don't suppose," Emeline says in a small voice, "I'll ever find out why."

Deborah shoots her a look. "I guess, we're no longer talking about Bovril. We're on to your brother being different."

"Different?" Emeline protests. "A girl at school loving horses and not the boys at Buckley—that was being different. Not this."

"It's not so uncommon," Xavier's trying to smooth things out. "Native Americans, they call people like Sister 'two-spirit' and in Samoa—"

"What was wrong with being a boy? Everyone wants a boy."

"Gosh, thanks Ma."

"I didn't mean your father and I. He doted on you, so did I. But you know, society . . ."

"Mary-Margaret told me about it," Deborah refills her wine glass, "if you want, I can tell you. Or Xavier," she invites, "you two had quite the long chat, you want to explain?"

"What it's like to grow up thinking you're someone else?" he says. "No idea." Emeline raises an eyebrow. "Emeline, come on, being gay's totally different. Not feeling at home in your own body, I can't imagine it; I feel fine in mine."

"To say nothing of other men's—" Emeline glares at her daughter. "You want the history, Ma? Okay. First of all," Deborah pours her third glass of wine, "when he was fourteen and still called Michael, Grandma found the money to get him singing lessons."

"She never!"

"Hard to believe, salt of the earth, Grandma Dora. You and Mary-Margaret can agree on that much, anyway. Michael wanted to dance, too, except that was—"

"A bridge too far," Emeline nods.

"Even voice lessons," says Xavier. "Back when Sister was a teen?" Emeline watches him fall silent, remembering his own years, the cruelty and jeers, the assaults.

"How terrible for him," Emeline's careful her voice shows sympathy, not sarcasm. "Did he realize early on that he wasn't who everyone thought he was?"

"Some kids do, very young, but Sister says no. It wouldn't have mattered if he had, no puberty-blocking drugs in Peckham back then."

Puberty-blocking drugs? Out of her depth, Emeline is grateful when Xavier jumps in, "Sister says she wasn't a great student, anyway, then when your dad died, your mom needed Michael to go to work."

"People around here were poor. Even now," Deborah says, "if you walk deep into Peckham—"

"I have," Xavier says. "Poverty like that, you people must hate the royal family, those horses and diamonds; hate the Queen."

"Hate the *Queen?*" Emeline choruses with her daughter.

"Listen, buster." Outrage colors the art student's cheeks. "We love our Queen, everyone does. Old, young, Labor, Conservative—"

"Not quite, dear. There's a percent—"

"Yes, Ma, I know. But over seventy-five percent in favor? American presidents would kill for ratings like that."

"Why?" Xavier looks baffled.

"History lives on in England, we have a sense of tradition." Deborah sounds reverent. "You should see the hats at Ascot, or the clothes at Glimmerglass."

It amuses Emeline, one minute her daughter's against all things aristocratic and the next she's in awe of their ways. "She's talking about the horse races, Xavier, and the opera." Emeline doesn't mention that Clifford once took her to Ascot.

"And truthfully, money comes into it as well. No more British Empire, that sun has set. We need the tourists. Without our royal family," Deborah's apparently forgotten she is an American, "our writers buried in Westminster Cathedral, the Tower of London, the guards wearing their bearskins. What kind of a crime is that anyway, killing a black bear for a tall fur hat? Without our famous sights, our traditions, what would draw the tourists? Not the weather, God knows. It's not Ibiza."

"Off topic, Deb," Xavier says, frowning over words he can't place: Ibiza, bearskins.

"Right. Your parents needed money, Ma, and they didn't want to ask you."

"Cliff and I, we'd have—"

"Or," Deborah's voice rises, "if you'd gotten yourself over here more often?"

"Ladies! Can we get back to Mary-Margaret?"

"Your brother went to work in a West End club," Deborah goes on, "called himself Melody. Handsome was made up into pretty, he was svelte, lithe, and he had a terrific voice. Sultry. Melody became quite the star. Sister has a poster, she keeps it in her private room.

Melody's holding the mike and singing. In drag, back then. Sister's proud of the poster. Though drag isn't necessarily a step toward changing a cis-man into a—"

"Sis man?" Emeline frowns.

"With a *C*, not an *S*, it's a biological term." Emeline shakes her head, unwilling to delve further into biology. "There are CDs in the stores, in case you ever want to hear the music."

"Then presto, one day she's a Sufi or whatever she is, and runs a soup kitchen." Emeline, abruptly standing to clear away the dishes, realizes she's switched pronouns. "Michael, Melody, Mary-Margaret. What's with all the M's?"

"Don't you get it? Em. Mary-Margaret says it's the name she grew up hearing all the time."

"Em," echoes Xavier.

"Exactly." Deborah nods, "Em, the girl who left Peckham to build a successful life in New York. Em, the woman who—"

It's too much for Emeline. For the second time that day Deborah and Xavier reach out to catch her as the plate she's holding drops and shatters, as she bends forward, tears streaming through her fingers, and cries as if her heart will break. Steering her into the bedroom, taking off her shoes, tucking her under the bed spread, one on each side of her holds a hand until she falls asleep.

Chapter 21

By morning Emeline's pulled herself together. She lifts her chin, and opts for the practical. "I've been thinking about this woman, the Badger." Skeptical, the other two eye her: that's what she's been thinking about?

Determined, and who does Sister suppose Deborah got that from, Emeline goes on. "If the Badger thinks the painting is a forgery—"

"She never said forgery, Emeline."

"No, she was very careful, though after what you two learned about Childeric's bees, we can be pretty sure the painting's a copy. If so I see four possibilities." Now she has their attention.

"First: when Ron Segal bought the *Duke* it was already a forgery. If so did Ron know?" She sees Xavier and Deborah exchange a look; had they not thought of that before? "Second: later on Ron, or someone close to him, substituted a forgery. Third: Clifford handed the original to his consultant for conservation and that's when the switch was made. Fourth: the switch was made in England before or after the painting arrived at Pearce's."

Holding her breath, she waits. No one brings up a hypothetical fifth: that Clifford orchestrated the switch.

"On top of that," Emeline goes on, "I'm not convinced the Art Squad sent the Badger. How would they have the resources to keep watch on a house out in Surrey? If the Badger were really from the Art Squad and wanted information, why bother us, why not flash her credentials at Pearce and walk into his house? If she wasn't from the Art Squad—I think she came here to find out what we know."

Xavier asks: "Why do you call her the Badger?"

"*Wind in the Willows.*"

"Ah," he sighs, "and here we go again."

Never a fast learner when it comes to technology, Emeline is catching on with her phone; even if Deborah says her mother texts "like a snail," and sees no point in trying to teach her new tricks,

More patient, Xavier stretches an arm over her shoulder to help, but Emeline swivels away. She gets up with surprising speed, holding the phone to her chest, and moves across the room. She gives a few more taps on the keypad and hits send. Then looks up, startled, when Xavier's phone gives a single honk. Reading, Xavier flushes a deep red.

"Somebody's got a message," Deborah says in her once-a-teacher singsong. "You made a friend here already?"

"Oh my God!"

Helpful, Emeline translates: "OMG."

"Ye-es, Xavier?" Deborah persists.

Xavier stuffs the phone into his back pocket and, head in his hands, drops into the arm chair. Sensing this is no joking matter, Emeline moves to put a reassuring hand on his shoulder. She can feel the tension in his muscles.

"Your new boyfriend?" taunts Deborah. Emeline shakes her head at her: leave him alone.

"My mother." Xavier's voice is muffled, he won't look up.

"What's happened. Is she ill or," Emeline's suddenly fearful, "in an accident?"

Deborah moves toward the kitchen. "I'll make tea. No, coffee, Xavier, I'll make you coffee."

"Is she—" Emeline can't finish. Unreality is billowing its way in, stronger than fog through an open window, it's happening again. "We can go home. If Flavia's sick or . . . or anything, we'll go right home."

"She's not sick." Xavier looks up. "She's not hurt. She's in London."

Coffee tin in hand, Deborah slumps against the door jamb. "Your mother Flavia, she's here?"

"At Elephant and Castle. She wants me to pick them up." Them? Emeline pictures the Escudero clan shivering in the wind outside the tube station, not one of them dressed for the cool London day. "She has Wendy Wells with her, Sophie and August, too, poor kids. They've been awake most of the night."

"Does everyone think," mutters Deborah, "I'm running a doss house here?"

"They can't stay, of course." Xavier frowns, "but maybe crash for an hour or two until I can figure out something? And find out why they're in London at all."

"Call a cab at once," Emeline directs Deborah, "a large cab. And bring me a couple of sweaters."

"Who the hell," Deborah mutters, "is Wendy Wells?"

"Yes, flight okay," Flavia says. "Long as the pilot don't say 'Flight attendants take your seats' I'm good."

"Flavia," Emeline says gently, "I think what Xavier wants to know is, why are you here?"

Wendy was frightened after Belmo told her to leave town, Flavia explains. She didn't know where to go, couldn't pack on her own, she begged Flavia to come with her. The helpless, presently mute young mother looks haggard and close to tears. Pounds have dropped from her thin frame. Her persimmon Dolce & Gabbana bag looks scuffed.

"Wendy has relatives in Omaha, so I say why don't you go there? That's when she tell me—" Wendy starts to interrupt, Flavia lifts her hand like a traffic cop. "We're here now, in their home. If we want their help we have to tell the truth."

Anxious, Wendy eyes her children, and Emeline steps in. "Sophie? August? Let's take your mom into the kitchen and see what we can find to eat. Those rides across the ocean, they're long, aren't they." As if Emeline flew the Atlantic twice a month, when before this week she hasn't in years. She heads toward the kitchen, her cane tapping out determined clicks.

"Toasted cheese, you'd like that? We'll do a nice toasted cheese." Shooting her a grateful look, Wendy takes the children by the hand and follows her.

"*Entonces—*"

"English, please," commands Deborah.

"I'll show you where the bedroom is," Xavier keeps his voice low. "In case the children want to rest." Xavier herds his mother into the bedroom, it's as far from the kitchen as they can get, and right behind him Deborah closes the door with a click.

"What's this all about, Mai?

"Go to Omaha, I say, until you hear from Belmo again. Wendy tell me her lawyer Mr. Cunningham say no. He is very respected, well known—"

"Don't need his resume." Unfamiliar lawyers get the courtesy of their last name, Xavier notices, his mother's employer no longer does.

"Belmo is in trouble, big trouble," Flavia frowns. "He leave for a business trip, like often. Then he call Wendy."

"Where was he?"

"He not say, he use his cell. We never know where he is."

"When was this?" Deborah prompts.

"Deborah, stop interrupting or we'll never get the story."

"Three days ago in the evening. Several weeks now he's upset, even I can tell. This night, she say he sound frightened. She didn't even want to tell me. Until," Flavia shoots her son a look: work with me, here, "I told her you would help."

"Enter the El Barrio Detective Agency!"

"Deborah, will you please—"

"Don't call the police, Belmo beg her. You need to go somewhere safe with the children. He afraid," Flavia chokes, "Belmo told her to run, he afraid she be used as—"

"Hostage?" says Deborah, "leverage?"

"Those, yes. Belmo don't want to know where they're going, they can call the lawyer to get in touch with him once they're safe. First I thought I take her to Puerto Rico, we hide there. Then I thought you, my son, would be more help." Xavier catches Deborah's expression. Xavier, helpful, in London? "No one is looking for you there, I tell her. Not yet."

"Is that true?" Xavier asks gently.

"I don't know," Flavia admits. "I say London a big city, you can hide there. Not by myself, she say, you have to come. Me?" Flavia spreads her arms wide. "What you talking about, they speak English over there. I'm afraid on my own, she say. I tell her, I am not going, have my own family to see to."

"And yet, Mai, here you are."

Opening the bedroom door, Emeline sizes up the situation. "Maybe we could put pillows on the floor."

"Hold on, sounds to me like we're one step ahead of big trouble ourselves, not planning a jolly sleep over." Deborah's sharp voice startles Sophie and August who've trailed in, too, toasted cheese in hand.

"We'll leave soon," Wendy promises.

"If I had a shilling for every time I've heard those words lately—"

"Deborah dear, get a grip, you're frightening the children."

Sophie whispers to August, who leans into his mother. "Can we have more?" Emeline leads the kids back to the kitchen to make more cheese sandwiches and pour the last of the tomato soup from the pan.

"Better help yourself while you can, children," Deborah calls, rolling her eyes at Xavier. "Tomorrow's likely to be all *tostones* and *pastelon*."

Lunch over, Wendy and the children curl up on the only bed in the flat. Emeline stretches out on the divan for a few minutes. Xavier joins Flavia in the kitchen, drying dishes as she hands them to him. Avoiding his gaze, she remains silent.

"So just like that," he prompts, "you pick up and leave New York?"

"They have their passports, last winter they went skiing in Switzerland. I have mine, from when I went to the Dominican Republic with my friend Dolores, she'd been wanting to take—"

"Remember me, your son? Not a travel writer."

"I'm trying to explain to you, we didn't need to prepare much."

"Rocio, little Jomar, Ramon—who needs more supervision than the baby, you say so yourself—you leave them all and fly across the Atlantic."

Flavia pulls her hands out of the sink and dries them on a towel with images of lavender from Provence. "Come and sit down with me. Better yet, we go for a walk. Fresh air."

"In London? Good luck with that."

"I am your mother. I am telling you, Xavier. We go for a walk."

Outside a trio of mothers in their teens pushes strollers that block their way. Bending to look into the little faces, Flavia coos. Crossing the intersection at the pedestrian pen, Xavier leads her at a near a trot to his familiar café. He pushes open the glass door, relaxing into the aroma of serious coffee.

Xavier orders café con leche for Flavia and himself, then gets down to business. "Stop stirring and talk to me: why are you really here?"

Stunned, his coffee growing cold, he listens while she tells him. Xavier had no idea what she earned, none of the family did. Or how much, *paso a paso,* she'd been able to put away. No idea his father, in spite of repeated wrongdoings and a new family, occasionally sent her money for his children. "Not regularly. When he can." Xavier sniffs with contempt.

Certainly he had no idea Flavia, charmed by Belmo Wellington's sympathy, the respect he'd always shown her, his earnest manner as a big man of finance, six months ago took her deposit book to the bank and withdrew almost the total sum. His mother packed the cash into her Kohl's faux-leather bag, tucked it firmly under her arm, rode the bus downtown to her employer's grand office and handed over her hard-won bills in exchange for promises of a more secure future plus a thin packet of papers. Even now Flavia refuses to tell him how much, keeping one secret to veil her alarm.

"All your savings?" Desperately Xavier waves at the waiter to bring a new cup.

"Nearly."

"So whatever big trouble Belmo is in, it affects our family, too."

"Ramon, he always make out somehow." Xavier sees his mother's prepared her defense on the flight over. "You, two jobs, I'm not worried about you." Great, thanks. "Rocio, though . . ." Yes, pampered little Rocio and her son, Flavia's escape hatch to the life she's most comfortable with, blocking the life she was on her way to having.

"What the hell kind of investment?" Xavier can hear how angry he sounds.

"How would I know?"

"Well, did you bring the papers with you?"

"On a trip, you crazy? Papers might get lost."

Xavier's laughter burns away his anger. "Ma," he reaches across the zinc table and puts his hands over hers. "Stop worrying. None of your kids ever gonna kick you to the curb."

"I'm going down the shops," Deborah announces when Xavier and his mother come back, "we're out of milk." Xavier doesn't blame her. Too many people in her flat, too much confusion in her life.

Sophie and August are curled together on the nest Deborah's made in one corner. Flavia's slept in a chair before, she says, when island visitors crowded in. Wendy can have the divan. Xavier does a quick pillow count in case he has to manage a night on the floor, too, then catches himself. Even in a situation as bizarre as this he's catering to Wendy Wells. Emeline hands him a shopping list, "plain, basic food. And toilet tissue," adds the practical Emeline. Xavier goes out, too.

He sees nothing untoward on the darkening street when he leaves. When he returns, he sees a dark sedan parked down the block, lights off, and a shadow behind the windshield. Watchful, Xavier waits for the driver to climb out or start the engine.

Shuffling the grocery bags to get a better purchase and whistling loudly, he climbs the steps and checks the street door locks behind him. And thanks the sixth sense that's saved his ass many times on the night streets between his subway stop and home.

Back in the flat they could almost be mother and daughter with their chairs pulled close, Emeline's respect for Flavia growing into affection. If his earlier anxiety about Emeline and Flavia meeting has faded, he's not sure how he feels with these two becoming so *cercana*. Tonight he has a bigger worry. Anxious about the car, he steps into the bedroom to call Deborah wherever she is.

"What's up, buddy?"

"There's a sedan parked down the block, no lights, with one person, maybe two inside."

"Was it there when you went out?"

"Didn't notice it."

"You sound worried."

"Concerned," he admits.

"I'm on my way back, I'll have a look."

"Definitely two people," Deborah reports minutes later, keeping her voice low as she bolts the apartment door behind her, "and no one's shagging. Are they after them?" She tilts her head toward the figures strewn around the living room? "Or us?"

Hungry again, the children fall on Xavier's take-away: chicken nuggets and fries. Brits may complain about the fast-food invasion;

tonight everyone's grateful, even Wendy though she eats very little. Casually Xavier goes to the window, comes back. "Gone?" Deborah mouths. He shakes his head.

Preoccupied as she may be with symbolism, provenance, her grades, and her day's outfit, Deborah is a realist like her mother. She beckons Xavier into the only empty room, the bathroom, and closes the door. "If it is about them, if Flavia and her group were followed, whoever is watching may find them in a hotel even in a city as big as London."

"What about St. Bertie's? No one would look for them there."

"Good idea." Deborah slaps him on the shoulder, "you call Mary Margaret, let me deal with Wendy and your mom."

"Sure, mate," says Sister Mary-Margaret. "Our two emergency rooms are free and it sounds to me like this is an emergency. And no problem about the kids, they can help out in the morning."

Getting the nod from Xavier, Deborah puts a hand on Flavia's shoulder. "I wish you could all stay here—"

"I know. We are too much for you. We go to a hotel. Mrs. Well has cash, is how she paid for our flights."

"Money's not the problem, Flavia. Someone's outside in a car. They may be watching the street."

"The police?" Flavia panics.

"Probably," better to stick with police than scare her more, "and since police can check hotels we have another idea." Flavia looks alarmed, Wendy, sitting up on the divan, as if moving a centimeter is beyond her.

"Where?" asks Emeline.

"Sister Mary Margaret's." Deborah provides the full title.

"Sister?" Flavia is curious. "She is a nun, your friend?"

An awkward silence until Deborah says, "It won't be the Savoy, but safe."

"And my children?"

Xavier's relieved to hear Wendy finally speak. "Of course, but first we have to get you there. Your car won't fit us all, Deborah, and cabs keep records."

Deborah checks her watch. "Bus is still running if we can get to Old Kent Road. We'll go through the basement to the alley in back. From there it's a short walk to the bus stop."

"St. Bertie's, though," Emeline murmurs, "it's in such a sketchy neighborhood."

"Sister says she'll meet us at the corner stop, we'll be safe if she's with us. Ma, will you be alright here alone?"

"Fine. Anyway, someone needs to switch lights on and off, draw the shade, pass in front of the window from time to time. Like Mrs. Hudson in Sherlock Holmes." This time Xavier's too preoccupied to inquire.

"We can't take all your bags," says Deborah. "Pick out the things you need and put them in your totes. We'll get the others to you tomorrow. We're just a family, riding home late. Wife, husband," a glint of mischief as Deborah looks at Xavier, "the children."

"I," says Flavia without a trace of irony, "will be the nanny."

Emeline is pulling down shades in the bay window. Wendy, disoriented and exhausted, goes to her, lays a chipped, manicured hand on her shoulder. "I don't know what to say, Mrs. Hughes."

"Emeline, dear girl; it is past time you call me Emeline." She hugs the distraught mother.

They rouse the children. Xavier tries to pick up August. Too big for coddling, the boy insists on standing on his own, still throwing anxious glances at his mother. Flavia struggles to push Sophie's stubborn arms into her jacket.

"Shoulders together, Craigie Gallagher," Emeline says to Wendy, "it's an old expression of my mother's. Now blow your nose, my dear. Flavia needs your help with Sophie."

Deborah pulls a pack of chewing gum from her bag and instructs her mother to lock the back door behind them.

"Gosh, Deborah. I'd never have thought of that!"

"I'm serious—lock it. I'll text you when we get back to the basement. Keep your mobile on."

They go down the stairs, dusty and dark except for the cone of light from Deborah's phone. Move along a warren of cement walkways, past washers and dryers, past ghostly storage cells barred with chicken wire. Xavier sees a broken pram in one, cartons stacked in another. He drops his hand on August's shoulder. "Want to guess what's in the next stall, dude? Think it's going to be a live horse?"

Deborah opens a creaking door to the alley, pressing her wad of gum against the lock so it won't close after them. "Haven't got the key. Wendy, wrap this scarf around your head."

Only a silent African carrying a lunchbox is queuing at the corner. When the bus lumbers to a stop they climb in, join a trio of tipsy youths and an elderly woman asleep with her head against the window, all at first indifferent to the new passengers.

Even so Wendy tightens her scarf over and over. When Flavia notices one of the drunken boys eyeing Wendy's spectacular diamond she pushes Wendy's hands into her lap and holds her own over them. At the next stop the merrymakers stumble off. Near a block of council estates, the silent man descends with his lunch box, followed by the elderly woman with her large bundle and a bad limp. Xavier, Deborah, and their people are alone on the bus with the driver.

Waiting at the corner as the bus pulls away, Mary-Margaret claps Xavier on the shoulder and nods to the newcomers, then leads the way down a few deserted blocks to the refuge.

"We can come in and help them get settled," Deborah offers.

"Since you've left my sister on her own, you better get on back. See that lorry over there?" In the street lamp's light Deborah reads the lettering: Grimwood's Produce.

"That's not the St. Bertie's van," she says, confused.

"You and Xavier are the only link between here and Searles Road, you really want that advertised? Lakshmi's driving, so hop in."

Xavier helps Deborah into the front seat and settles himself in the back on a crate of onions. Deborah gives Lakshmi directions, and when they arrive back at the alley, tries to hand her a five-pound note. Insulted and still silent, Lakshmi drives off.

They're almost into the alley when a police car with spiraling blue lights starts down the street behind them. Unnerved, Xavier turns to Deborah and draws a quick breath; good thing too, before he can speak she's pulled him toward her, wrapped her arms around his neck, is kissing him on his mouth, her unfamiliar lips whispering, "Shh, shh." The police treat them to a knowing honk and cruise on by. Xavier reaches up to pull away her arms.

"Come on, bro," Deborah gives a wicked chuckle. "Wasn't so bad, was it?"

CHAPTER 22

Emeline confesses she's come down with a cold. She'll spend the day in bed, "So bloody damp, this city." Spoken from memory, apparently; back from a morning walk Xavier knows better than to tell Emeline it's sunny outside and 70.

Deborah's already dressed. "Ma, we have to take these bags to the refuge. After that I need him to go to Courtauld. If the library has books on Martinez del Mazo they'll likely be in Spanish."

"You both run along," Emeline sneezes twice, "I'll be fine."

"Okay to leave her?" Xavier asks once they're outside with the luggage. "She's rattled."

"Probably best if she spends time alone, gives her a chance to get her mask back on."

"That's a little harsh."

"Trust me, Xavier, I've known her longer than you have."

"We really going to Courtauld?"

"After we see how your mother and her other little family are getting along." Getting a good grip on the bags, Xavier hails a cab and says nothing.

At the refuge Sister seems glad to take a break from her pile of papers and help them roll in the bags.

"New arrivals settling in?" Deborah asks before Xavier can.

"Give 'em time. It would help if I had a bit more background."

"Ask Xavier," generously, Deborah nods his way, "he knows the story better than I do."

Leaving out Flavia's money worries, it doesn't take long for Xavier to explain: Flavia's job, the meeting with Wendy Wells, her worries about Belmo—overall a short story to cause so much turmoil.

"That may help explain," Mary-Margaret suggests," my sister's reaction to meeting me again."

"Actually, there's more to it." Using her hands with drama, Deborah launches into her mother's problem with *The Duke of Abrantes*. All goes smoothly until Xavier, happy to let Deborah be the center of attention, interrupts: "What's the difference between selling through a gallery and at auction?"

"If you think I know everything about art," snaps Deborah.

"Your mother thinks you do." Xavier sees her flash of pleasure, quickly gone.

"Goes to show how much she knows."

"Listen to the two of you having at it," Mary-Margaret laughs. "You might be a younger brother and older sister." Her smile fades, "I'd have liked that chance, m'self."

"Ma may come around. She hasn't seen you, even heard from you in—how long?"

"Point taken, Debbie. Meantime, if I can make a suggestion? I know someone you should talk to about your *Duke*. Milo Graves. I'll make a call; he owes me a favor."

"What about my mother," Xavier aks, "and the others?"

"Honestly, man, rest is what they need. I'd lay odds they're not up yet. I'll tell them you stopped by?"

"My mother used to talk about going back to school." Deborah has to raise her voice against the noise of the tube as they sway their way to Courtauld

"Why didn't she?"

"Probably right then Daddy needed her to plan three dinners for ten people each and the idea kind of slipped away. She did a lot of reading; she had her boards, her friends. She loved to walk the few blocks to the Metropolitan or the Frick, the Frick was her favorite. You been there?

"No. She talks about it, though." Maybe back home they'll trade: he'll take her to Coney Island, and Emeline can take him to the Frick.

"The whole idea of studying art history, it came from watching Ma."

"Have you ever told her that?"

"I haven't. I was afraid it would seem like bragging,"

"Depends how you do it, lady. It's all about tone of voice."

The Courtauld Institute of Art in Somerset House sits proudly on the Thames' north bank. Deborah nods to the guard, escorts Xavier downstairs to the library, points out Romanesque arches and pillars in brick, the modern white metal stacks and art-deco stair rails.

"Want at least to head me in the right direction, Deborah?" Impatiently, she shows him the computer catalogue, and heads for the stairs. "Be back in an hour, do the best you can."

She obviously thinks that won't be much; certainly Xavier feels out of place. A balding, blond man, chin resting on his hand, is absorbed in his reading. Across the way a young man gives him a curious look, then adjusts his glasses and goes back to his books. To prove her wrong, by the time she's back Xavier's leafed through five books (three in Spanish) and made notes in the notebook she's donated to the cause.

"Buy you lunch?" he offers, pulling out his wallet to count the bills. "Queen, queen, queen."

"Cheers. How are you on Indian?"

"Did alright the other time, didn't I? Lentils, rice, chick peas—almost like home."

"At least you've learned not to order vindaloo. Worse even than, what do you call it, your people's hot spice?"

"*Aji Caballero.*"

The DePuy Gallery on Cork Street is a sleek, white space divided into cubes. High-design ceiling lights illuminate framed pieces on the walls. A slender man with a mass of dark curls and a thin moustache jumps up from his desk and comes toward them. Dressed in black pants, an unlined grey jacket, an off-white shirt, with a scarf of taupes and tans, he heads straight toward Xavier, who for once does not feel ignored.

"Sister said I'd know you when you walked in. The clothes, my dear. All black. If we were in summer when it's all white for me, wouldn't we be the negative and positive."

To forestall an embrace Xavier holds out his hand. *What's happened to British reserve?* "How's it going? This is Deborah Hughes, she is—"

"I know, Sister's lovely niece. And isn't your mother having the time of it, finding the brother's now a—"

"We have a little problem, Milo," Deborah interrupts. "Mary-Margaret said you might help us."

"Yes, Sister explained to me about the portrait." Taking each by an arm, Milo heads for an office with bitterly spare metal and leather chairs and seats them around a low, round, glass table centered under a miniature chandelier. "So we're talking about found art, not excavated. Because if it's excavated or part of a national cultural heritage, the 1970 UNESCO Convention forbids—"

"Found art," Deborah assures him. "Anything you can tell us about costs, sales, though we know you're primarily interested in the beauty."

Milo's laugh threatens to shatter the crystal overhead. "Art hasn't been 'primarily' about beauty since the Medicis and probably not then. Hard-core collectors have such a hunger: paintings equal profit equal power. Most have an eye out for value, even if they plan never to sell. My mother inherited a bit of stock, kept it her whole life. Didn't keep her from checking the price every day, was it up, was it down, was she poorer than yesterday or richer? Beauty, heh, that's a good one.

"For a long time sales were mostly primary sales: that means art bought directly from the artist, or art bought through a gallery. These days we've moved beyond bricks-and-mortar. Think about Basel." Xavier thinks about Basel and frowns.

"The art fair in Switzerland," Milo explains. "and its spin-off, Basel-Miami. Emerging artists even use websites to promote their work. Of course there's eBay; though you'd hardly put your Helen Frankenthaler on eBay. I've even heard," he turns to Xavier, "about art cruises down your Mississippi."

"Though not necessarily with good art," Deborah guesses, "and rarely great."

"Doesn't matter. These days half the big-ticket buyers wouldn't know a Hockney from a Homer." Xavier, who doesn't know either, doesn't let on. "Buyers rely on experts to tell them what's valuable, what's hot, what's, how do you Americans say it, trending. Right now most buyers want modern, postwar art. If you want to see specific prices—"

"Go to Mei-Moses," Deborah's not to be out done. "It's the biggest index."

"Galleries are still responsible for much of the pricing. Though, if a spectacular piece comes our way, before we even show it we've likely offered it to a major client like a museum or a collector."

"Of course, not all are serious collectors like Henry Frick," there's a name Xavier knows, "or Peggy Guggenheim. Art is big business. An owner of one of your major auction houses shifted the whole way we—my goodness, good afternoon!" Milo leaps up to bend his dancer's body toward a short, plump woman in tweed walking toward him.

"Peggy Guggenheim?" whispers Xavier.

"Dead for decades, but maybe as important to Milo." They watch the owner position the woman in front of a small Richard Hamilton collage, then dance back to them.

"My apologies," he gives Xavier a long look and a business card, "I really must . . . call me so you and I can liaise."

Outside Deborah gives way, giggling, "So you and I can *liaise*."

"What about you?" Xavier's deliberately dense. "Will your studies allow the time?"

"Don't be daft, he doesn't want me. It's you he's after. And in the interest of helping out," she elbows him in the ribs, "honestly, you are obligated—"

"Oh, shut up, Deborah."

Next morning Emeline thinks she'll stay in for another day until Deborah, leaving for Courtauld, throws down the gauntlet. "I've done what I can, Mother. Do what you want. She's your sister."

Stung by the challenge, Emeline bristles, aware she's at a crossroad. Deborah is right, it is up to her. Emeline finds she's flirting with a new possibility, not seriously at all, more the way she might try on a bright, flowered Bergdorf's sundress instead of her usual striped seersucker. If Mary-Margaret can change so much about her life, why can't she? With a touch of smugness, Emeline reminds herself: she will always be the Big Sister.

She only wishes she'd started earlier when she had better health, more energy, less time behind and more ahead. How often she's balked, hesitated, demurred, and declined. She thinks of Tram's dry wit: "I'll wear my tennis shorts next summer . . . when my legs look better."

If Xavier's surprised, he doesn't say so. They hail a cab and set off, neither saying much. Vaguely Emeline remembers the face if not the name of the South Asian woman who comes to meet them at St. Bertie's. "Lakshmi," she reminds them, unsmiling. While Xavier heads off to look for his mother, Lakshmi leads Emeline into the dining hall.

Emeline's first glimpse of the crowd takes her aback. In the hungry throng, a few guests look as if they slept under a roof. One man swings a helmet, suggesting an expensive, if second-hand, scooter parked outside. Another, on his mobile, is setting up work for the day.

Most, though, must sleep rough—men, red-eyed and shivering; women with teeth missing; more than a few folks bent over a beat-up metal walking frame. Nearly all shamble across the linoleum floor in ripped shoes or sandals.

Yet all queue up properly for the meal. Slowly the guests shuffle by the cold table where cereal, milk, juice, and baked goods are on offer. The hot table holds large casserole pans: turkey and noodles;

ham, rice and beans; sliced pork and stuffing; eggs with green peppers and onions. Wearing baseball caps, plastic gloves, and aprons laundered to thin muslin, volunteers serve the food. Emeline watches one gloved hand reach across the table to smack a newcomer who's reached grubby fingers into the toast tray.

Embarrassed, Emeline looks away and finds she's facing a dozen portraits on the wall. With muted backgrounds and highlights of startling color, each captures a distinct personality in a few, bold brush strokes. No dukes in this collection, these are worn looking men and women, whether born in the British Isles or immigrants from around the old empire. Two show the tender face of a child.

"One of our volunteers is an artist." Lakshmi says. "Maria's memorialized many of our guests and done it while they're still alive to feel pleased, proud. She's had her sorrows, Maria, and now she uses her special gifts. We count her a blessing."

Leading Emeline toward a table of women, Lakshmi greets each by name. Kyana, a stalwart Jamaican in a print headscarf and shoes too holed to keep out the London damp, says: "Lakshmi, *wagwan?*" Amazingly, Lakshmi seems to understand and replies in patois. Izzy, a tall Scot with red hair and blank eyes, Emeline recognizes her from the portrait wall, holds her paper plate carefully with two hands and limps toward the table. Sitting in a wheelchair Dolores, a stocky woman with a straw hat and the face of an angel, balances a pyramid of buns on her lap. Laughing, Lakshmi slaps her hand: 'Cheeky cow, I'm running a tab on you." The women both caw in amusement.

A bedraggled old dame, head shaking, pushes in front of Emeline to snag a seat at the table. Alcohol, or perhaps a fellow traveler with Parkinson's? Lakshmi makes the introductions.

"How d'ja do?" Carla shouts. "Where the fook's the jam?"

Lakshmi points out Flavia sitting at a low table and ranged around her, hunched over their plates, a dozen ragamuffins with faces from Dickens and several continents. Two, looking dazed, sit up straight: Sophie and August.

Emeline watches a young boy knuckle August in the ribs: "Hey kid, pass me the mash." August, uncertain, lifts a bowl of orange squash.

"No," Flavia says, "the other one, we call it mashed potatoes." When the boy jerks his thumb twice in a universal language, August answers with the first smile Emeline has seen since he arrived.

"They seem well enough," she admits. "What about Wendy?"

"We'll try the loo." Emeline follows Lakshmi down a corridor, dismayed to think traveler's stomach has added to Wendy's troubles.

Emeline barely recognizes the woman bent over a row of sinks, brandishing a spray bottle of Dettol Power and Pure. She wears a bandana, loose cargo pants, and a sweatshirt three sizes too big, gleaned, Emeline guesses, from the St. Bertie's clothes room. Doing likely the dirtiest job in the refuge, Wendy's hard at it.

Emeline's stunned. "Why, Lakshmi?"

"She volunteered, didn't she."

Wendy straightens up, one hand pressed against the small of her back. Seeing Emeline's startled face, the socialite laughs. "How do you think I worked my way through four years at State? Cleaning's in my DNA."

Impetuously, Emeline wraps her arms around Wendy's thin shoulders. "Did you get any sleep?"

"August and Sophie did, that's more important."

"I saw them. Flavia seems to have organized a play group."

"She sent me away, told me it was best to keep busy."

"Also best," Lakshmi urges, "to get some food in you."

"You go. I'll finish up here and meet you in a minute."

"No skiving from her." Lakshmi sounds proud as they walk back to the hall, "I told her already she should take a break, wouldn't hear of it. You go get something to eat, too, I'm due in the clothes room. Unless you want to help me sort?"

Emeline feels no appetite for sorting used clothes or eating. "Could I work in the kitchen instead?"

At first the beating heart of the refuge looks like the final word in chaos. Then again, as Emeline pauses to catch her breath and her bearings, she picks out signs of a plan. A Sikh in a turban is refilling a giant urn for coffee. A pale woman unloads a box of donated pastries onto a metal tray. At the large double sink, working with a man in a Manchester United cap up to his elbows in suds, a tiny woman like a beautiful elf with a Peter Pan haircut does the drying, the two of them managing to stay ahead of the steady flow of dirty pans, lids, bowls, and serving spoons. Lakshmi hands an apron to Emeline, then pulls off her own cap and holds it out.

Emeline hesitates. "No, that's okay."

"Take it." Understanding, Lakshmi gives the cap a quick shake. "Don't worry, it's my own, lice-free. We get drop-in visits from the health inspectors. Whether our volunteers have a roof over their heads or not, we have to follow the same rules."

A half-blind woman, "call me Kat'leen," stops chopping onions, green peppers and possibly her thumb to ask Emeline where she's from. Emeline says only: "Lakshmi brought me," then after an anxious minute watching the wayward knife, "know what, Kat'leen? Let's switch. I'll cut the onions and peppers, you take your knife and slice it through this big bowl of eggs. Right, like that, keep going back and forth until they're mixed. Faster than beating, innit?"

While Lakshmi's been taking charge of Emeline, Xavier hails an ex-boxer passing with a mop, his nose broken more than once. When Xavier asks where to find Mary Margaret, the man, limping, leads him up a staircase to a row of cramped rooms.

Mary-Margaret calls it her cell, but a woman's touch has turned the space into a comfortable cave. A faded paisley duvet covers the narrow bed. A plain pine desk holds a goose-neck lamp, a laptop, and two framed photos—one, an older couple, probably the Peckham parents Xavier never met; the other, the same young mother holding a baby girl that Emeline has in New York. Take away the chubby cheeks and keep the forthright stare and Xavier has no trouble seeing a little Deborah. Indian cloth hangs over the window, "too bloody cold to open, come winter, and there's newspaper behind besides. I've always been a Trib . . ." Sister catches herself before she says "man."

"What are you working on?" Xavier points to the monitor; Mary-Margaret doesn't seem one to waste time on idle games.

"You see the Hunger Summit last day of the Olympics?" No such luck, by then Rocio had reclaimed the TV. "Prime Minister Cameron, delegates from the UN, NGOs, the private sector—all trying to leverage the moment and focus on hunger. Cameron works at a global level, see; I work in one tiny corner. Others do as well. This website here, it's a network of soup kitchens. You ever gone hungry?"

"Not really." Sparse times, sure, black bean and sugar sandwiches, but never real hunger. "And that other window you've got open?"

"Geneology," Xavier waits. "Trying to figure out where I came from."

"Trying to trace the past, find the story. Like a provenance," Xavier says. "Except you can fake a provenance, until some expert tests the paint and it turns out to be twentieth century." Now who's the expert on provenance?

"There you go. DNA tells the truth the first time."

"Emeline says some of your family was Welsh."

"Yeah, well," Mary-Margaret hits Save and closes out. "Emeline come along with you?"

"She's with Lakshmi." Sad, Sister stares down at her clasped hands. "Be patient, she'll come around."

"Obstinate old trout," Mary-Margaret says fondly. "I only met her the once, I thought she was an angel from heaven. Except not my angel because she never came back."

"Nothing to do with you, Sister; it's a phobia she has about flying,"

"That's always the way. We think it's all about us, and most of the time it's not. Will you look at me, crying in my beer when there's a bright young lad in front of me with stories of his own; yes, I can see, young as you are you've had your losses."

"Your story's the more interesting. What happened to the blonde nightclub star?" Xavier points to the poster on the wall, the stunning drag singer in sapphire blue satin, the face, if younger, not hard to recognize. In scrawled hand-writing across the bottom, Peacock Lounge.

"Couldn't face becoming an aging, out-of-work singer, could I; enough has-beens in my past as it was. I thought it was time I reclaimed the real person. And you, what happened to the good Catholic boy?"

Xavier tells her about his father, his father's new family in Puerto Rico, even about Alejandro, "appearing like my own angel for a time before leaving for stardom in L.A."

"Leaving you with a little more than you bargained for, am I right?"

"How do ya know that?"

"Living years longer than you, my friend, I've lost many a dear one. I can always tell, healthy as you seem, and myself as well, thanks to cocktails I never dreamed of in my days of pints and whiskey. Without the national health—"

The ex-boxer's face appears around the open door, "Sister? Another visitor for you, you're drenched in 'em today."

Emeline's unsure she's done the right thing. Like a gentleman Mary-Margaret gets up to offer her the single chair then sits on the bed beside Xavier. "Feeling better, are we?"

"Good night's sleep, that's the thing."

"Ma used to say, 'Take a hot bath.' Remember? Her cure for every ill."

Emeline smooths her navy blue skirt, looks around, notices the framed photo: Deborah as a baby, sitting on her lap.

"I asked if she had a picture of you," Mary-Margaret confesses. "She made me a copy.

"Not that young anymore, either of us and—" Emeline sees the poster, the blond singer, her smiling mouth open in song. Flustered, she blinks and stares down at her hands.

"Emmy, we don't have to talk about that, we can move forward from here. Unless there's anything you want to ask me."

"I do, yes. Where did you get the money to buy this building? Our parents never had any."

"Sold the old house."

And whatever they had *you* got. Mortified, Emeline covers her face with her hands; as if she ever needed their parents' money.

"I know," Sister cuts into the silence. "I know."

"It isn't about their house, it's—"

"It's about the cake, m'dear, about who got the bigger piece. I did try to talk them out of it, didn't find it fair. They wouldn't listen; they said you didn't need anything."

Didn't need *them* her parents meant. Betrayals like German Stukas are diving at her from everywhere. Emeline pulls her hands from her face, then all at once recognizes the worn, fake Oriental rug and drops to her knees. She crawls to one corner, a second corner, at the third she finds what she's looking for. Rubbing her fingers over the rip she made with her child's stubby scissors, she feels again the miniature round handles against her thumb and finger. Tears rain down her face.

"Ah, the old rug," Sister says. "Take it if you want, you're welcome to it."

"Not the rug," Emeline crawls a few feet to lay her head on Sister's lap, rubbing her cheek against the soft folds of cloth. "Not the rug," she sobs. "I want my brother back, my little brother. I never knew him, and I want him back."

"He's gone, darlin,' along with the parents; you'll have to make do with me."

Apart from her Ma it had been the old house Emeline longed for most. After disembarking from the boat and riding in a cab to Aunt Mildred's large, sunny Park Avenue apartment, Emeline cried herself to sleep nights in a row. She missed the hallway smell of cabbage and onions, her family's bric-a-brac and family photos; missed her father, coughing on the sofa in their cramped living room. She longed for the voice of her Grandma, waiting after school with biscuits for her tea.

"Accept, adapt, move along," Grandma used to tell her. Proud to live in the little house her husband managed to buy, even if he was long dead. Because of Grandma, Ma could go to work at the sugar factory and add income to the family when her husband was working. And after he was injured, her earnings added to his state compensation.

Emeline desperately missed her tiny room, her single window facing a wall of brick across the alley. Missed her dolls lined up on her faded sprigged coverlet. Missed her street, close and communal, the women leaning on their elbows in front windows to look out for one another's kids: "Oi! Freddie! You stop that, hear? Or your Pa's gonna give you such a lickin'."

Dressed in the requisite plaid uniform and white shirt, Emeline started her New York school. Girls mocked her accent, poked fun when she said she'd lived in a terrace house. "Terraces, in the middle of a city? You have to drive to Connecticut for terraces."

The first day one girl, who sat catty-corner from her, kept turning to smile, trying to make the newcomer welcome. Climbing the steep steps onto their school bus that afternoon, Emeline was glad to see the girl had an empty seat beside her. Sitting, she tried to talk. Rebuffed, she felt miserable. It was two days before Emeline realized they were different girls, the friendly one, and the other one; and more than a month before Emeline understood: she, the new girl, was the "other one."

Soon she invited Emeline to her Connecticut weekend house; no terraces, though between two parts of the house was a screened passage called a breezeway. Trees, a swing, and a happy, blunt-faced Boxer named Tigger, a name from Emeline's own world.

Has Emeline driven by the old house, Mary-Margaret asks? No. Well, doesn't she want to? Not really; except in her heart Emeline knows if she leaves London without even a glimpse she'll regret it. That's one thing age teaches you: don't casually add to your list of regrets. Mary-Margaret herds her outside and into the St. Bertie's van.

Seeing her off, Xavier leans in the open door, "Can we boost the heat?" The weather's taken a turn.

"Heat, what heat?" Sister reaches into the back and pulls a disreputable afghan over Emeline's knees. "We'll have a bit of a mooch around South-uk. You getting in, too?"

"Nah, I'll take the tube, do a few errands. Keep her warm, will you? She chills easily."

Not begging, Emeline remembers. Brits say mooch when they mean have a slow look around. They drive past houses with brick walls that need mending, trim with paint peeling, and the odd porch with flowers in pots. Emeline can't believe her ears when Mary-Margaret says, "On the rebound, this area, young people come from all over London especially at night. See that club over there, and in the storefront next to it, the gallery?"

Emeline's attention, though, is on a corner shop, the windows, the awning. There used to be a shop with wrinkled carrots and potatoes, scrawny chicken legs. Coinneach was the owner. "Means handsome," he'd tell her mum with a wink and an accent; nothing to it, men were always playing up to Dora. The new owner steps outside, Indian, not the old Scot she remembers.

"Emmy, look over here," Mary-Margaret says, "that building with the café on the first floor. Recognize it?" Sister's voice is urgent, as if counting on Emeline to affirm a memory she holds in her own heart.

Emeline studies the café, trying to see beyond the green and white striped awning, the green metal chairs on the sidewalk to tempt passers-by on a warmer day. She stares at the clean brick and new windows. "It's not."

"It is. At least it was, new owner's made a few changes. You should see what he's done to the top floor, all skylights."

"How do you know?"

"Twice he's let me in, after I woke up and suddenly needed to be there again. First time I was afraid he'd think me mad, but he seemed to understand. I could ring, if you like, see if he's home."

"No, keep going." Emeline feels an odd elation. This is no dream. The building looks little like their old home yet once it was, and again she's here to see it, thanks to Mary-Margaret. She should venture out more, Emeline decides. One day soon she'll take the tube on her own and visit other London sights.

"You sold our old house," she laughs, "bought that grotty building you live in now, and turned it into the refuge. Have I got it right?"

"Mind, it's more than a home to me. Keeps me working, self-employed you might say. An advantage, face it, for an old gal like me."

Emeline's cheery mood lasts until they pull into Searles Road. Seeing a man holding his roller bag with one hand, his face a study in exasperation, she feels her energy drain. "Good Lord. What's *he* doing here?"

"Who is that?"

"Julian, the son of my friend Tramontana. Drop me off, will you? I'm not up to explaining you to each other."

"Oh, very nice."

"It's not you, Mary Margaret. It's Julian. Bit of a tosser."

"Emeline." Sister's voice sounds urgent. "Will I see you again while you're here?"

"Yes, I rather think so. Don't you?"

Chapter 23

Xavier watches the St. Bertie's van pull away. Emeline could use time alone with her new sister; not that he feels sidelined or anything, and this gives him a few hours on his own. That leaves him with two choices.

Worry about Flavia's savings gone up in smoke? Claw back comes to mind, a phrase he's read in the *Post*. Sounds to him like a shout from the rooster-fight crowd in El Barrio, rooster fighting being as illegal as Belmo's dealings. Since Xavier hasn't a clue how to claw back Flavia's money, he might as well work on the problem that brought him to London.

Pulling out the silver-bordered card, he sends Milo a text, less intrusive than a call, in case the gallery owner is charming yet another matron in tweeds. In seconds comes a reply: "Brilliant. Free in 1 hr."

At the tube station Xavier steps into a car with women on their way to clean houses and working girls ready for a bed to themselves. A family is speaking patois, from Trinidad, maybe, or Jamaica. Makes him homesick for El Barrio; homesick even for Puerto Rico, the island where he never thinks he feels at home. Rattling underground on this foreign, ancient island Xavier sees how wrong he's been.

Today Milo is wearing shades along the spectrum of grey; Xavier imagines a closet arranged by day of the week and hue. "It will be quieter in the office," Milo promises, "come through, we'll have a coffee." Coffee, as it turns out, is a dark roast. Xavier's happy

"So you have a painting." In the comfort of his own cave Milo seems more straightforward.

"Us, no. We're interested in a portrait hanging in the mansion of an old guy out in Sussex, SinJen Pearce. *The Duke of Abrantes* passed through Clifford's hands."

"Clifford?"

"Deborah Hughes' father, he died in June. The painting's seventeenth century."

"Ah, the Golden Age of Spanish painting, de Ribera, Velazquez, Goya, royal portraits, reflections of paintings in mirrors . . . whose is it?"

"Like I said, Pearce has it hanging—"

"The artist, Xavier."

Embarrassed, Xavier takes a sip of coffee, "Juan Bautista Martinez del Mazo. Heard of him?"

"Maybe," Milo studies a dissolute Germanic face on his office wall. "Before my time, really; I'm like a laptop that goes to sleep, I only wake up around 1920 or possibly earlier for a really nice Kazimir Malevich." Sounds like a pastry to Xavier. He explains how Deborah found the bees.

"Experts argue all the time," nods Milo, "ask to be indemnified by the owner before they'll give an opinion, one person afraid to be sued by the next. If Deborah's right, if your Duke's not authentic and Pearce wants to sell it, he'll have to fake the provenance. That means—"

"Thanks, Milo. Up to speed."

"Unless he has an accomplice working with him."

"Accomplice? You're making Pearce sound like the crook."

"Isn't that what you're thinking? It is odd. We hear of paintings coming out of old country houses—lost for generations in a cluttered attic, then discovered by an eager estate agent or a greedy heir. We don't hear about paintings going in."

"His agent in New York claims Pearce wants to sell it, Pearce says he wants to buy it. Supposing his agent is right: how would you go about faking the provenance?"

"My dear, I would never dream—"

"Of course not, Milo."

"In a perfect world you trace the history back to the time the work was created only often that's not possible. So we look for exhibition catalogues, sales receipts; even a gallery label on the back can help."

"And these can be forged successfully."

"Forged, yes. Successfully? Depends. I have a couple of books on forgery if you want."

"What do you mean," Deborah gives Julian a glacial look; they've been out of touch for years and here he is, "do I know anything about the art market?"

Emeline lets out a breath. Watching their children flirt and fight through their teens put paid to any hopes she or Tram had that these two would make a blissful pair. Even before Julian waited for wife #1 to walk up the aisle at St. Bartholomew's, wreathed in white silk and impractical expectations.

It's been a long quarter hour since Emeline ushered Julian into the flat to find Deborah home early; the two have been at it ever since and Emeline's relieved to hear Xavier's key in the door. She watches him set down a paper bag and take in the scene.

Feeling fortified when he slides onto the divan beside her, Emeline says: "Need I remind you, Julian, she's getting a graduate degree at Courtauld?"

"Possibly you know," Deborah comes in on cue, "the 1980s brought a tsunami in art as an asset, and even since 2008—"

"—the art market's gone up. Though the recession did slow down sales, shook out plenty of high-flying speculators. Not the true-value collectors. The super-rich have been investing in art, monetizing—"

"Not all buyers—"

"—so for the last five years as an asset class, including stocks and bonds—"

"Julian," says Deborah, "if you'd let me finish? Not all art buyers are multi-millionaires."

Emeline tries to keep a straight face as Xavier tosses in his newfound factoid: "You got that right. Seventy percent of artwork sold at auction is priced at five thousand dollars or less."

Finally Julian acknowledges him. "How's it going, man?" Xavier gives a non-committal grunt.

"Astounding, really," Julian resumes, "how this paint thing, begun centuries ago to tell Bible stories, has morphed into a commodity with almost no ceiling." Emeline isn't sure if Julian means to honor painting's history or the chance for profits. "When you have a duplex on Park, and your private jet leaves Teterboro on your schedule, what else can you buy to show—"

"It's not just Americans," interrupts Emeline, Julian does wear on her nerves. "Think of the Manhattan condos bought by Chinese, Russians, Arabs. Don't look so surprised," she says to her daughter, "your father knew a good deal about real estate."

"Irony is," Julian's never one to cede the floor, "it all started when Giotto painted a few trees with no perspective in back of the Virgin Mary."

Deborah turns to Julian. "Giotto?"

"Babe, I did go to Princeton."

"Earlier, actually," counters Emeline. "The Lascaux caves in France, Tassili frescoes in Algeria." Deborah looks surprised. "What, I've done some reading on art on my own."

"Okay, if Xavier's right," Julian concedes, "five thousand is small potatoes. Though a couple multi-million dollar sales—"

"Like the Picasso, *'Nude, Green Leaves, and Bust,'*" says Deborah.

"Went for $106 mill," Xavier finishes, happy he can help.

"There you go, man." Julian appears impressed. "Returns in the art market have been higher than bonds, no surprise there, some years even higher than the DJIA."

Xavier looks toward Emeline, who murmurs, "Dow Jones Industrial Average."

"Making art higher in value than any other asset class except gold. Therefore," Julian clears his throat, "art is an excellent candidate for portfolio diversification."

Oscar Wilde got it right, a man who knows the price of everything and the value of nothing. Emeline knows Julian can't help himself, his world view is fixed on the fluid dynamics of finance. "Julian. Try to remember you're not here to give me a sales pitch."

"Actually," says Xavier, "why are you here?"

"Because Emeline asked me to look into Cadmium?" Julian sounds smug.

Deborah is fidgety, "Fine. Let's have it."

"No more foreplay, Deb? Okay, here goes. You have your main Cadmium fund with the usual suspects: growth oriented, secondary private equity, structured portfolio solutions, yada, yada."

"That we could learn on our own," brags Xavier, "with a little digging."

"Maybe, maybe not, hedge funds can be pretty opaque."

"Anything else, Julian?" Emeline's growing impatient, it's like watching ten-year-olds see who can pee higher on a board fence.

"An odd little venture. Hidden under a name that escapes attention because it looks like another part of the Cadmium portfolio and not what it really is."

Deborah starts pacing, "Spit it out, Julian."

"An art fund. Called Ochre."

"Art fund?" Xavier starts tapping on his keypad. "Milo mentioned art funds, he said they'd come and gone."

Julian pulls from his monogrammed, maroon briefcase three sheets of paper stapled together. "Don't bother, man," he says, reaching across Xavier to hand the information directly to Emeline. "I've got it all here."

Emeline's not surprised Julian followed up, only that he's flown over instead of faxing. Flicking past the pages of financial data, she finds the names. "Here they are, the directors. Xavier, would you mind—"already he's heading for the bedroom. He's back in a minute with Clifford's folder and lays it on the table. Julian, over there like a shot, turns the folder upside down so files and papers fall onto the table. A box of cards lands on the floor.

Julian picks up the pack of cards as if he's caught a dead rat. "What the hell is this?"

"Ma's been working on her Spanish."

Emeline notices Xavier reach casually for a small black box and pocket it. "Julian," she commands to give Xavier cover, "come back and sit down," then lying for good measure, "we had a filing system going."

Chastened, Julian retreats to his chair. Xavier finds the file they need and hands her the list. Slowly she reads the names to herself

"Notice the accents these gals have?" Julian asks Xavier. "Deborah's talking like a lord in Parliament, and Emeline's taken on a, I don't know, what would you call it?"

"Working class," Deborah says proudly, in her best Lord-in-Parliament tone. "Folks below stairs call it apples and pears." Julian looks flummoxed. "Princeton didn't cover Cockney rhyming scheme? You take a word like stairs, substitute a word that rhymes, pears, it's like a code. The old trouble and strife . . . you can figure that one out, Julian."

Xavier's studying a text that's pinged.

"If that's more of your family," Deborah says, "tell them we're fully booked." Xavier looks toward Julian, then Deb, and raises his eyebrows.

"No worries about me," Julian stands, ready to breeze off with his four-way roller, "I always stop at the Savoy. You're looking fab, Deb, how about meeting me across the river? We'll have dinner at Kaspar's."

Once Julian's out the door with his roll-on and ego, the atmosphere lightens. In no rush to do what Julian tells her, Deborah goes to the kitchen and pours herself a glass of Merlot. Armed with wine and tea, the women clear important papers off the table while Xavier unpacks the Korean take-away he's brought in.

"Who was your text from?" Deborah asks, sweet as honey.

"Milo." Deborah smirks, Xavier ignores her. "He was very helpful, and it's like you said. Unregulated, the art market operates more like a Middle Eastern bazaar. A fixed price may be a suggestion, not final, whether gallery owner to dealer, dealer to customer, but you know all this already, right?"

"Keep going," with a pair of chopsticks she picks up a string of *kimchi*.

"Hey! You're eating out. Dealers are offered paintings all the time. Most are genuine. If not necessarily very good, at least they're what they claim to be."

"Don't suppose your Milo has any idea who the forger is."

"Deborah, he's not *my*—"

"Sorry. Can I have one shrimp?"

"The forger's the last person we'll find, Milo says. Forgers live in the shadows, proud of their knowledge, their skill, what they've gotten away with."

"Even if, in the *Duke's* case," Emeline adds, "his knowledge is nothing to write home about."

"He—"

"Or she."

"Or she," admits Xavier. "Leave me a couple shrimp, will you? Let Julian buy you dinner."

"This forger," Emeline speculates, "likely as not buries a bee in every painting, in a ruff, a cuff, or the shadow of an orange. Like Al Hirschfeld, remember, Deborah? For years we looked in his cartoons for his daughter's name hidden somewhere in his swirly lines."

"Yes," Deborah's smile might almost be nostalgic, "Nina. That was her name."

"What caught Milo's interest," Xavier goes on, "was the *Duke* hanging in a house out in Surrey. You hear about paintings coming out of old houses, Milo says, not going in. Unless, he said, any chance Pearce's house could be part of a storage scheme?" Xavier waits. The silence grows. "I don't know, I thought one of you would."

Deborah puts her hand, sticky from sauce, onto Xavier's. "Storage scheme? Ask him, will you?" She winks, "if you get a chance."

Deciding she's kept Julian waiting long enough, Deborah changes into a close-fitting black sheath, a teal pashmina, and departs. Emeline says she needs an early night, and Xavier heads out to meet Milo for dinner.

It's Xavier's first dinner out in London, yet posters on the walls beckon to Bordeaux and Tuscany. Gentlemen's-club curtains are striped moss green, yellow, and orange. Over the bar, chains hung from the ceiling hold thin zinc strips with slots for glasses parked upside down. Mahogany shelves on either side of the fireplace are filled with wine bottles instead of books. Milo orders them Asti Spumante.

"How come you Brits handle the knife and fork like you do?" Xavier's making small talk

"While you Yanks brandish your fork around like a weapon? So awkward. My sister tells me you knit the same way, swinging around."

"Your sister won't catch me knitting."

"Tradition," Milo answers. "You ever hear how the handshake started? Shows you're not carrying a weapon. Rest your wrists on the dinner table? Shows you're not squirreling away the silverware, but come on, I'll wager you didn't meet me to talk about table manners."

"We're concerned about this particular painting."

"We?"

"A group of investigators."

"Who are?"

"A team assembled when we formed the business," Xavier says with impressive cool. "We prefer to work behind the scenes. What can you tell me about art theft?"

Milo laughs. "Starting when? The Romans scooping up Greek Art? Or Lord Elgin 'rescuing' Greek marbles now at home in the British Museum?"

"Not that far back."

"There's the 1990 Gardner Museum heist in Boston, clumsiest robbery of all time, and they still can't find the paintings. You could check INTERPOL; it keeps a data base of stolen art. Then there's IFAR."

"How far?"

"International Foundation for Art Research, they have a stolen-art alert section. Buyers can check it if they have suspicions about a work they're considering; though if a piece isn't listed that's no guarantee it hasn't been stolen. After drug smuggling and weapons dealing, art crime's the most profitable criminal activity. And remember, art these days is more than paintings, prints, and sculpture. Grayson Perry won the Turner prize a few years back, and he's a potter. You can make a fortune in art."

"That's what Emeline's friend says. So why doesn't everyone invest in art?"

"Difficult to sell in a pinch, for one thing, you don't ring up your broker and say 'Let's get rid of the Hirst by close of business.' Contemporary art's been the hot commodity lately: David Hockney, Lucien Freud, Francis Bacon, to mention a few of the modern Brits. Even the Old Masters 100 index can't keep up with the moderns. How's your sole?"

"Excellent. Your veal?"

"Delish. Other problem is the art market's faddish. Take Indian contemporary art. Five, six years ago it saw a seven hundred percent gain, then after the recession, prices tanked."

Impressed, Xavier files away the stat, hoping he can trot it out for Julian's benefit. "How did you learn all this?"

"A bloke I was seeing for a while; he couldn't afford to buy Hussain or Reddi, yet he followed them in the news like a doting father." Milo signals for another bottle of wine. "What else does this Julian have to say?"

Sipping his third glass, Xavier describes what he's learned about Ochre.

"Huh." Milo sounds skeptical. "Art funds never really made the grade, though one with a portfolio of high-end artwork has been going for ten years or more. Open to investors worth at least $2 and a half mill. You got that, you can invest a minimum of $250 grand into the fund. Could buy a piece of Manchester United for that."

"Soccer!" Xavier brightens. "I bet you got to go to the new Olympic Park this summer."

"You watched the Olympics?"

"Didn't I. How about that Michael Phelps, taking home his twenty-second medal?"

"Listen to the two of us. Anyone eavesdropping will hear two blokes trying to prove they're straight."

Xavier laughs, holding Milo's gaze for a long minute. "The art fund this idiot Julian uncovered, would it buy actual paintings? Not shares or anything, the paint on canvas kind. Where would they be keeping 'em all, for God's sake?"

Milo stretches his hand across the table to clink his glass against Xavier's. "Want dessert, do you?"

"Not here."

CHAPTER 24

The sun is edging up when Xavier lets himself into the apartment minutes before Deborah tiptoes in. "You, too?" she asks.

"Don't be naff," he bluffs, "I'm going for a walk, didn't sleep." That much is true.

Deborah has shadows under her eyes and doesn't look happy. "You won't tell Ma. Please?"

"Listen to yourself, you sound like a teenager."

"She makes me feel like one. You have no idea—"

"Save it for your girlfriends." Even if Xavier sees her as a troublesome older sister, Julian on the scene, capturing a whole other level of her attention, makes him irritable.

"Testy," she accuses. "Is it because your mother turned up like that? Flavia's terrific, you must be proud of her."

Searching for sarcasm and finding none, he says truthfully, "There isn't nobody like her."

"Whereas my mom," Deborah sighs. "I do try to remember what her life was like, moving to another country, another life, no matter how privileged. It left her a little insecure. Mind you, took me years to figure that much out."

"Privilege wasn't one of our problems. Even if my grandfather was the mayor of Aguas Buenas before he fell on hard times."

"Ma would understand if you told her."

"Sure," says Xavier, "Emeline knows first-hand about falling income and falling down drunks."

"I know Ma has a doorman and Flavia has, what, three flights of stairs?"

"Four, but who's counting."

"Ma's income's dropped plenty this year. What did you think the move this summer was about?" Deborah's debating whether to say more. "What's worse, she suspects Daddy was involved in dishonest business. She lives under a shadow, waiting for criminal charges against him."

"How'd you learn all this? I knew there was something . . ."

"Julian told me. He heard it from Tramontana. Don't let on I said anything, promise?"

"Cross my heart."

"Looks to me like Flavia came out the stronger of the two; maybe that's your trouble," Deborah's eyeing him, curious. "You worry you may not live up to Flavia. What do you think?"

"I think you should drop out of Courtauld and hang out a shingle."

"I didn't mean . . . you've been really good for Ma."

"If not for you."

"Me?" Deborah grins. "I'd love to have you stick around, help with my research, cook *arroz con pollo*—hey, hey, no hitting!"

"You've got, tops, half an hour to shower and change before your Ma wakes up." Too late, Emeline steps out of the bedroom, wrapped in one of Deborah's frilly robes. "Morning, Emeline," Xavier says brightly, and to divert her attention from her daughter: "I found out about storage schemes."

She holds up a hand. "Wait until I get my tea."

"Most often it means a free port," Xavier explains, sitting with her at the table. "Usually they're built in tax-friendly cities like Luxembourg, Singapore, or Monaco. Milo says a developer's even building one in Delaware. Warehouses, we're talking about, with climate control, confidential record-keeping, even viewing rooms."

"In case you don't have enough wall space in the penthouse," says Deborah, coming out of the bathroom in a robe and a towel wound around her head.

"This is not about displaying art, dear; this is about making investments."

"And avoiding taxes, Ma, don't forget. Pearce's house has none of the features of a free port, unless it was kind of an informal station."

Insisting she feels better, Emeline declares she wants to step outside to see the real London instead of lying around watching it on UKTV. Xavier, too, if he's free.

"First, though," Emeline's voice says she means business, "I must visit the refuge."

"Ma worried about you," Mary-Margaret says. Emeline's taken up Sister's offer of another ride around Peckham. "What Ma had gotten you into. She used to fret the Big Apple might turn you into someone you weren't meant to be. Even when I was a kid, before . . ." Mary-Margaret's voice trails off.

"I've wondered that myself," Emeline admits, giving him space. "What I traded away, leaving college early and marrying Cliff; what I might have accomplished if I'd been more independent. More like Deborah."

"Goes right after what she wants, that girl, no dithering."

"She knows what she wants. You both do, you're lucky that way." Tentatively she pats the knee next to her.

Briefly the driver puts a hand over hers. "I'm glad you decided we could have a wee visit."

"I've no right to judge anyone. There's you, successful singer, financial support for my parents in their old age, can you imagine how that makes me feel? So caught up in my own life I didn't come back to see them, or you. I met you just the one time."

"Brilliant, me in my short pants scared you away." Emeline's happy, hearing the low laugh over the van's rough motor. "At any rate Deborah tells me you have an airplane phobia."

"I should have tried harder. There's treatment for phobias."

"Not everything can be treated away, Emmy."

"I didn't mean . . ."

"I know you didn't."

"No wonder Deborah's disgusted with me."

"Your daughter's angry, that's all. You don't fly here to visit her, but for some business problem you pop a pill and take a plane. And bring along a buff, gorgeous guy. How do you suppose that made her feel?"

"Xavier? It's not as if he's my gorgeous guy. At my age, too, what was she thinking, the silly girl."

"You don't get it, Emmy. She's not angry because she thought he was your lover. She's angry because you treat him like your kid."

Startled by Sister's perception, and more than a little uncomfortable, Emeline looks out the window for anything familiar. The old library, she remembers riding there Saturdays on the bike behind her mother, it's gone. The library these days is a modern, copper-clad structure with a startling overhang.

"Tell me about naming the refuge, will you?" Emeline noticed the carved sign at the door the first day, *St. Bertie's House*.

"No easy job, for sure. Anglican or Catholic, we have churches named for saints from St. Agnes to St. Wilfred. I could have named it St. Michael's, I suppose," again the low laugh, "except you'll find a St. Michael's on every corner of the city."

"What you needed was a Xavier."

"Had I but known."

"Instead you thought well enough of Bertie to give his name to your big project."

"Very good to me always in his own way until the day he died."

"Why not?" Emeline can't help sounding bitter, remembering the morose, injured man she tiptoed around as a child.

"Aye, about that, Emeline? I know a place does a nice tea, we'll have us a little talk. First we got to invoke the parking gods."

On a street crowded with foreign signs and storefronts, Mary-Margaret finds a place for the van and rolls her eyes skyward in thanks. Inside Tariq's, the plump owner himself greets them with delight, "*Salaam alaikum,* Sister, Salaam, madam." Shaking hands with Mary-Margaret and flashing white teeth at Emeline, he leads them to a plastic-covered table in a corner.

Nervous for some reason, Emeline presses her spine against the wooden back to stop her trembling. "You were telling me how you named the refuge after our father."

Mary-Margaret still studies the menu even though she's already ordered; waits until Tariq is back with two sturdy brown pots of tea, brown mugs, and plates with sugary buns, then looks up with an uneasy expression.

"Your father's name, m'dear. Not mine, not really."

"You're not suggesting . . ." Emeline, attempting to keep the urgency out of her voice, presses her hands flat on the table to keep them still. Mary-Margaret raises hers, palms inward, so the edges of her fingers touch her face. As if Emeline hasn't seen for herself since the first day, Sister's skin is almost the color of Xavier's. Sister shakes her head.

"I've no idea who the bloke was. I couldn't imagine there'd been anyone other than our Bertie; then once Ma grew sick I knew I could never ask." Emeline feels another piece of her old reality chip away. So many bits flaking off in one year, soon there'll be nothing left her but memories and illusions.

In the quiet café Mary-Margaret waits for her to speak, to admit how she feels or declare she's changed her mind about being friends.

"Our Ma," Emeline clears her throat, "who would have thought it?"

"London was full of new faces after the war. Brits had their fingers in pies in countries all over the world so no surprise former colonials would move here and soon have their—"

"Do you mind?" Emeline says to stop impending images.

"I was going to say have their way with the local girls. After Ma died I sent away my DNA." There's a pause, each sipping slowly, avoiding the other's eyes. "Turns out I'm a mix of English, Scandinavian—"

"Scandinavian?" Emeline raises her eyes.

"Sure, and you must be, too; centuries back the Danes lived all up and down England's east coast. Didn't they teach you anything in your fancy school? I'm English, Scandinavian, and South Asian, with a little percent of Chinese. I picture an adventurous trader."

"Or," Emeline muses, "a traveling Buddhist."

"Could be, and since I met Lakshmi," Emeline waits, she's wondered about the relationship with Lakshmi, "I've favored the notion we might be distant cousins. Though," waggling her head side to side, Mary-Margaret switches to a mock Indian voice, "I'm afraid I'll never be knowing where it is I am coming from. Want a bite of my baklava?"

Not hungry in the least, Emeline says yes; to refuse might seem to reject more than a corner of pastry.

"It needn't have been anything long-term, Emmy, just an old-fashioned, off-the-books shag. Our Ma was pretty devoted to Bertie."

Peering through the grey shades of the past, Emeline tries to catch a glimpse of anything she might have noticed as a child. Had her mother married the man she'd wanted? Had Bertie changed too much after his accident? Had her mother fallen in love with someone else, or merely gone down the pub, one evening, and walked home one time with another fellow?

"I wrote to Aunt Mildred on her Virginia horse farm," Mary-Margaret is saying. "I figured if anyone knew the truth she would, and where would be the harm, with Ma and Bertie both gone."

"That must have put her on a fast canter. Aunt Mildred have a heart attack?"

"Not at all. I was right, she wrote back, Ma had written her that much, though nothing about my real dad. Funny phrase, that; like anyone could have been more real to me than Bertie. He'd wanted to enlist, you know, be a hero; he was turned down because of his eyes."

Dour before his accident, Emeline remembers, and bad-tempered after, no matter what her mother offered—a bus ride to see the flowers at Kew Gardens, a cream tart, a rare fresh peach from the costermonger—nothing cheered him up for long.

"A hero to you, anyway. Did Dad know?"

"That's one of life's little mysteries. Was he merely glad to have another child and," Mary-Margaret grins, "a son at that?" Emeline balls up her paper napkin and throws it at him.

"I know about this ancestry business. My friend Muffy sent DNA away. Not her own, she wanted to learn more about her stuffy, taciturn husband. She was convinced his ancestors had to be crooks and scallywags out to scam others and the stuffy old dear was trying to make up for them."

"While me," says Mary Margaret, "I've spent less energy trying to fool others and more trying to stop fooling myself."

"So, even with this DNA testing you don't have any idea . . ."

"No. I'm what the ancestry business calls an NPE."

"Don't keep me guessing."

"A Non-Parental Event."

"Huh. We used to call it a CITN."

"What's that?" Mary-Margaret looks puzzled.

"Cuckoo in the nest."

Mary-Margaret laughs, puts her hand on the table top, palm up. Emeline, brushing away crumbs, lays her own next to hers. Pointing opposite ways, their hands do look alike, the ring fingers nearly as long as the middle fingers, the short pinkies.My sister, and a whole life time together, wasted. Emeline doesn't realize she's spoken out loud.

"Nah, girlie. You and me? We'll be living a long time yet. For the moment I'm thinking I should try this silver nail polish of yours."

Xavier walks in with tonight's take-away. Daughter and mother are studying the papers Julian flew over to deliver and Deborah's saying, "What are we going to tell Wendy?"

"Tell Wendy what?" Miffed at being left out, Xavier saunters over to look. It's the list of Ochre directors.

"We're checking to see if any of these names sound familiar," Emeline explains. "Belmo's, of course; Bradley, the big developer, Clifford knew him. Douglas Fleisch no, not McCormick, either. You look knackered, Xavier, you feeling okay?"

"Maybe a cold."

By nightfall his head aches ferociously, even his skin aches. "We should get you to a doctor," frowns Emeline. Xavier's anxious himself. He knows he has a fever, even if Deborah has nothing on hand as bourgeois as a thermometer. "Nah, I'll talk to Mary-Margaret in the morning."

"What kind of a fever?" asks Mary Margaret when he telephones after a sleepless night.

"104 anyway is my guess."

"Crikey! Any glands, rash?"

A dozen times already Xavier's felt around his neck, his groin, "maybe a few."

"What's going on?" asks Deborah, stumbling out of the bedroom. "Ma? What are you doing up so early?"

"Shh, he's talking to Mary-Margaret."

"For heaven's sake, the guy's got a cold, why are you all carrying on—" Emeline pulls her aside and whispers in her ear. "Oi!" Deborah turns pale. "I had no idea."

"Right, then, cheers." Xavier rings off. No one's laughing now but he feels too sick to gloat. "Sister's gonna come by and take me to her clinic."

It's over sixty out and still the women fuss, Emeline pushing his arms into his black leather jacket, Deborah tenderly wrapping her orange and purple scarf around his neck.

Twenty minutes later Mary-Margaret arrives, dressed today in boots, dungarees, a denim jacket, and her hair caught up under a wool cap. She practically carries Xavier into the van.

"Wow," says Xavier, teeth chattering, "rocking the workman look, aren't we."

"Costume when required. You should have seen me as Melody. Tight-fitting satin, except for a peplum I found useful to cover—"

"Your junk."

"If you must."

"Personally, I don't give a fig . . . you won't be talking about this with Emeline, will you?"

"Man! She's my *sister*. What do you take me for?" Mary-Margaret barely misses a cyclist as they duck under the arches of a viaduct.

"Melody's clothes, you have them hidden in your closet?"

"Don't have the room, do I. Passed on most of my lovely threads to Delight, champion drag queen. We'll go hear him one evening if you want a night out. Here's the plan so listen up. We go to the clinic, we sign in, and we sit in the waiting room until they call my name."

"I'm using your card?"

"National Health did away with cards. Memorize the number: 943 681 4243."

"Memorize the number," Xavier complains, "now I'm in a spy movie."

"They call my name, you go in, say ahh. They look at your throat, feel around. Better if you don't talk much, your accent may confuse them."

"Accent? I don't have an accent. My English is fine."

"Your English is not *English*. Roll up your sleeve, they draw a little blood, the test results come back to me. It will work, I'm due for a test; they'll see it on my record."

"What about your own test?"

"It can wait a bit."

"God. Mary-Margaret, you sure?"

"Sure. But don't tell Emeline, it'll throw her into a right tizzy."

CHAPTER 25

"It's nothing," Xavier flicks a hand. "Gave me antibiotics, in a day or two I'll be," what is that expression about the English weather? Emeline looks relieved, Julian, hanging around again, indifferent. Xavier keeps quiet about the test he took under Mary-Margaret's name.

"I've been thinking about the statue," says Emeline. "The Chinese statue Pearce had in Surrey. Xavier, you took a picture, let me have another look."

Xavier, wrapped in a blanket, taps on his phone to bring up the image, and Emeline squints at the tiny screen. "Can't be sure, can we."

"Might help," Deborah says, "if we could find out who Tram used to sell the Scarsdale Doxy."

An English heir learning his future acreage was forfeit could not have looked more appalled. "My God! My mother *sold* her?"

"Tram never wanted you to find out," Emeline glares at her daughter.

"Sorry," mumbles Deborah.

"Sold the statue," Julian slaps a hand to his forehead. "What was she thinking?"

"I believe," Xavier enjoys watching Emeline muster her matter-of-fact voice, "there was a shortfall at work you needed to cover. Three years ago. Anything come to mind?" Julian's face turns red.

"Ma, we could call her, I suppose"

"Why doesn't Julian call?"

"Probably," Deborah shakes her head, "because Tram doesn't know he's in London. Am I right?" Julian answers with a defeated sigh. "When he gets home, if he's calmed down, he can ask her."

"Mothers," for once Julian turns to Xavier, "drive you crazy. So the statue at home, it's a fake?"

"A copy, yes. After your wedding we found it hiding in plain sight, once you got through Valda's butter cream frosting." The Doxy makes a good story and Emeline doesn't underplay it. "Listen, Julian?" she finishes. "You have a chance for once in your life to be very generous. Don't let your mother know you found out."

"Crap, Xavier," Julian says to his new ally, "do you know what the original was worth?"

"C'mon, dude. Do I look like an appraiser to you?"

It being that kind of a day, Emeline's hardly surprised when Deborah's land line rings and it's SinJen Pearce.

"Yes, of course I remember." Deborah says, politely. "No, we've found out very little. Oh, really. Have you? Actually, that's not convenient for me today—" without catching the words Xavier can hear the rising voice on the other end interrupt. "And you don't feel you can tell me over the phone? No, I understand, we have to be careful. This afternoon then."

Deborah hangs up. "He's found out something about the *Duke*; he wants to tell me before he goes out of town tomorrow. I don't mind, what's one more class missed? Ma, you look unhappy, I thought you'd be pleased. You did come here for my help."

"I don't entirely trust Sinjen Pearce."

"I thought you liked the old guy, Ma."

"Not my type at all."

"At your time of life you have a type?"

"Ladies, if we can get back to business? We should all go."

"Nonsense. You stay here and work on this," Deborah gestures toward the table, cluttered with file folders and papers. "Believe me, I can handle men like Pearce. Julian, you can come, too, see the countryside." Julian smirks. "Actually, I might move into Julian's hotel for a couple days. Leave you both here to sleuth in peace."

Biting her lip, Emeline says nothing. Deborah's trying to help. Julian, too: ferreting out details of Ochre, adding what he calls data points.

Certainly the room feels larger, the air lighter, once occupancy is down by two. Good thing: it's past time she and Xavier figure out how the pieces fit. The challenge brings back her visit to Muffy's East Hampton house, the time she watched her hostess struggle to put together parts of the hummingbird feeder. Baffled, in the end Muffy had to call in her quiet engineer husband. His quick maneuvers produced two hummingbird feeders. No wonder Muffy kept finding bits left over.

"What have we got so far?" Xavier begins

Emeline leads off. "Certain hedge fund managers set up an art fund called Ochre, camouflaged inside a standard hedge fund. Ochre managers purchase art then store it somewhere. Select investors buy shares in the fund and when the time is ripe and a painting sold, they all reap a profit."

"A profit, plus an administrative fee," adds Xavier. "Ochre isn't going to research, buy, insure, and store art without charging a fee."

"Suppose one of the managers is less than honest. A go-between outside the fund approaches him—"

"Belmo?"

"What's your guess? Let's say the go-between lends money at an easy rate so Ochre can buy more paintings. After that the go-between has clout, demands Ochre wave the fee, even influences the pricing. If it's Belmo he's in a bind. If he wants to stop cooperating or go to the authorities, he's implicated, too, and the whole, sordid story will come out."

Xavier nods, then adds, "Couldn't this go-between, or his hidden boss, be behind setting up the art fund in the first place? Anyone holding a stack of dirty money needs to keep in the shadows, needs a middleman."

"You found this out how, Xavier?" Xavier waves his cell phone from side to side. "So the dirty money stays hidden."

"Exactly. Like the pentimento under a painting."

"You amaze me, Don Xavier. You remember pentimento?"

"Sure. It made me think of people, live people, not portraits. What's happened to them before—they think it's buried, but it's affected who they are—and sometimes it breaks through. Emeline, we have to see if any names on Clifford's documents match names on Ochre's list."

He wonders if she'll refuse, watches her steel herself. Clifford's money problems, she wants to keep those hidden; even more, hide her fear he was somehow involved in Ochre.

Emeline nods. He retrieves the soft leather carrying case from the bedroom and, taking turns, they scrutinize the names to see if any match. To her evident relief, and Xavier's as well, they don't.

She hands the carrying case back to Xavier. He feels a bulge in an inside pocket and takes out a small oblong box. Inside is an old-fashioned cassette. "We missed this before," he's bouncing it up and down in his hand as if testing the weight, "unless you've listened to it?"

"What are you talking about? I've never even seen it."

"We need a player," and bravely he punches in Deborah's mobile number.

"Now what, fella? I'm busy, here," but Deborah tells him where to look and in a corner of her study he locates her dusty black machine.

Scarcely breathing, they listen to a conversation: scratchy, excited, foreign, until it's overtaken, or underwritten, by electronic guitar.

"Did Clifford like electronic guitar?"

"Lord, no," she laughs.

"Then the tape wasn't his, someone else used an old tape to record this."

"I'm pretty sure they're speaking Russian. Do you suppose . . . Sergei?"

"All Russians sound alike to me, Emeline. What do we do now?"

"There's this guest of Mary-Margaret's. Strange lady, you'd probably call her a few tacos short of a fiesta. It might be worth a try. Let me call my sister and see if she can set up a meeting."

By now feeling at home on the streets, Emeline insists they go by bus, "if you remember the bus number, Xavier." Walking all around to the corner takes longer than going through the alley, and today there's a crowd in a queue. On the bus a Jamaican woman in a bright head scarf asks a question in patois. Xavier, not understanding, shakes his head and she stands up to give Emeline her seat.

"How long," Emeline asks as they jog along, "do you think Wendy and the kids can lie low at the refuge?"

"Now I'm an expert on British immigration?"

"I'm worried about her, that's all, living in limbo like this."

"Me, too, though at least she'll be safe."

Lakshmi meets them at the door and leads them into the hall. It's nearly deserted at this hour; only a cluster of older women who, chatter fading, eye the newcomers. "Yana's thinking is not very good," Lakshmi warns Emeline.

Yana's either very old or life's been very hard. A tiny, frail woman, her prominent forehead, skimpy grey hair glued flat to her scalp, and bony cheekbones suggest years of privation. Her etched face brightens when Lakshmi explains: these friends of Sister's need her help, if she will be so good as to translate?

Xavier takes the recorder from his backpack and pushes play. Tears fill Yana's eyes as she hears her language, listens intently, circles her hand in a gesture, *again,* this time moving her head from side to side. A third time through, and she chops her hand down: *enough.*

"Two men," she says. "Not happy." She mimics a clown's frown. "One, he want picture back, he say—"

"What pic—" but Lakshmi shakes her head: let her tell it her in her own time.

"Other say he cannot give, is gone. First guy say big trouble, second guy say not his problem; first guy ask where it is, second guy say England." Yana smiles proudly.

After a glance to Lakshmi, Emeline asks: "Any idea what the picture is?"

Yana frowns, reflecting. "I think big man in picture, he called, called, can't think. He like," she spreads her arms and lifts her sunken chest like a pigeon, puffs out her cheeks. "Like old Czar." Emeline sighs deeply and nods to Lakshmi.

"*Cpaciba,* Yana," Lakshmi says and, to Emeline's surprise (since Lakshmi's barely civil to her), hugs the old lady. To end your days like that . . .

"What do you know about her, Lakshmi?"

"We don't ask many questions, maybe a Soviet camp. Did she help?"

"Oh, yes. Wait, I want to give her some money." Emeline reaches into her bag but Lakshmi stops her.

"Please, don't. You've given the best gift possible to the old dear. You've made her feel useful."

Wendy's curled up on a narrow mattress with her children, reading out loud from a battered copy of *Wind in the Willows;* Emeline wonders if it used to be Michael's, or hers. Excited, August and Sophie run to Xavier and in a minute he has a kid swinging from each arm. Wendy looks thinner than before, even paler, and very anxious.

"When can we leave? My children are happy enough, a playdate every mealtime. Though some of the other kids," Wendy lowers her voice, "have *nits.*" Emeline remembers the word, her mother combing through her hair looking for lice after school.

"Sister's been so good to us, Lakshmi, too. But we can't stay hidden forever, we need to go home." Wendy straightens her back. Emeline hears Xavier's words echo: hard to erase the person you once were. Years before her husband made it to the pinnacle of New York finance this young woman cleaned her way through college.

"Thing is, Wendy," Emeline keeps her voice soothing, "your passport's been flagged by now, and if they catch up with you out there? Next thing you know you're being grilled by the local

Bobbies or Scotland Yard. It's better if you stay here another day maybe, or two." Emeline doesn't say what could happen if forces other than the law find Wendy first. Whoever they are, they'll want to use Wendy for bait to lure her husband out of hiding. Rattled by the voices on the tape, Emeline knows there's more to the story than one sketchy *Duke*.

Flavia, joining them, says she's been away from her real family too long. No one can argue with that, so Emeline nudges Xavier, and he pulls out his cell phone to book a seat for a flight late that evening.

Flavia protests, "Last minute? Will cost a fortune."

Handing Xavier her credit card, Emeline insists. "Better if we move one piece safely off the game board." This investigation—their third and last, she vows—is making her anxious, and just when she'd been regaining some of the ginger she's lost over the years.

As for Wendy and her children, Mary-Margaret agrees, they should sit tight at St. Bertie's. Captured by some lucky street paparazzi, various photos of the fashionable wife scooped up by the press, even photos of her "charming" boy and girl now flood the news. The hunt for the Wellington family is eclipsing the Kardashians.

"Yes, Wendy, we're off the radar," promises Mary-Margaret. Anyway, who would recognize in the woman cleaning the kitchen, in the pack of playful, South London rogues, the missing socialite and her children?

Wendy and her children give their Flavie long, tearful hugs, then slip back to the main hall. Xavier, his mother, and Emeline stand awkwardly near the front door. Working up to another round of good-byes, the women sniffle.

"Flavia," Emeline hands over a piece of paper with her cramped handwriting, "call Mr. Cooper when you get home, my lawyer. I'll text him today, so he'll expect to hear from you. The press, the feds, when they find you're back, you're going to need his help."

"And, Xavier," next to her, an unconvincing blend of innocence and confusion, Xavier squirms, "wouldn't you like to say good-bye to your mother in private?"

Puzzled, Flavia eyes them both. "Xavier, he's my son, we can hug each other in Times Square if we want, why do we need private?" Xavier shoots Emeline a desperate look. Emeline presses her lips together and stares him down.

Flavia moves forward, arms outstretched, then taking in Emeline's discomfort and Xavier's dismay, lowers her arms. Unsmiling, she grabs Xavier by the shoulders, gives him a rough shake. One hand swings out, back toward his face—he cringes—and lands an angel's pat on his cheek.

"Some things are private, yes. That is why I say nothing all this time. When you want to tell me, I say to myself, you will tell me. *M'hija,* you imagine I be proud of you less, love you less?" She gives a dismissive sound. "And you, supposed to be the smart one in the family."

Converting chagrin into relief, then anger, Xavier growls, "Ramon, he told you!"

"You think I need Ramon? You do not think I have eyes in my own head? He told me nothing. More loyal than you realize, your brother." She turns to Emeline. "Children, I ask you, do they not make you crazy"

"Often," Emeline agrees with feeling.

"Emeline, you sure you be okay in London?" Flavia asks with an anxious frown. "Tell me if you need me to stay, I stay."

"I'll be fine." Emeline wraps her arms around Flavia's stocky shoulders. "I'll have your Xavier with me, won't I. Que dios te bendiga, Flavia."

"Come on." Sister's voice sounds more hoarse than usual as a large, calloused hand settles on one shoulder of each woman. "Man up, both of you."

"I envy her," sadly, Emeline watches Flavia walk inside with Mary-Margaret.

"Going home?"

"Having a family to go home to."

"Would you change places with her, Emeline?"

"Well . . ."

"Right. The devil you know."

"I was going to say: only if it brought me you as a son."

"You flatter yourself, señora," he chucks her under her chin as if she were a baby, "grandson possibly."

Just the two of them for supper, to Xavier it feels like old times. After they finish the left-over curry, Emeline brings out her alphabet cards probably, he guesses, to keep his mind off his mother on her way out to Heathrow. She challenges him to toss her words and with the cards spells *embarazada, confusa, tijeras, tarjetas*—pregnant, confused, scissors, cards. After a while she gives him a quick hug good night and heads into the bedroom."

Absently, Xavier shuffles the cards. To capture the names circling in his mind he spells out Dan McCormick (using the Cs from both decks and X as a stand-in for the third). Shuffle. Tuck Bradley. Shuffle. Douglas Fleisch. Thirsty, he gets up to find a soda in the fridge. Gulping from the can and burping, he picks up a handful of cards again, fanning them in his hand. Stunned, he slowly he begins to lay them down, one after another.

"Dios mio!"

CHAPTER 26

The door opens wide, hitting the wall, and Deborah steps in. The crash brings Emeline out of the bedroom. "Darling, you alright?"

"He's he's—" Deborah breaks down, dropping into Xavier's arms before her mother can reach her. "Tea," he commands over the heaving shoulders. "Wait, I saw whisky in the second cupboard." Awkwardly he strokes Deborah's back.

"Deborah, sit down and drink this," Emeline uses the calm voice of a mother sizing up a scraped knee.

Her daughter slides out of Xavier's arms and onto the divan, face in her hands, while he murmurs to her mother, "such a bastard, that Julian, what's he done now?"

Deborah's head snaps up: "Julian? No. Well, maybe. But SinJen Pearce—" she has a fit of coughing.

"Take your time, dear."

"When we drove out to Sandley Hall the gates were open like before, only this time half a dozen uniformed coppers are standing around outside, as well as that funny butler. A few neighbors, too, though how they'd have seen anything happening, out in the country the way they all are, I don't know."

Deborah takes a shuddering breath and the glass from her mother. "An ambulance pulls in. The neighbors tell us there's been a break-in, whoever it was tied up the poor, old butler and locked him in the hall closet. All the butler can say is men came in a van, made off with paintings, maybe a sculpture: the butler said he heard men dragging out a heavy object—unless that was Pearce, he wasn't anywhere around." Swallowing the whiskey in three gulps, she coughs again. "What was the *Duke* doing there anyway, in that insecure country house?"

"Not so insecure," says Xavier. "Once the gates were closed and the alarm system set, Pearce would be quite safe."

"He wasn't safe today, though, was he," her voice rises, "and the *Duke*? I bet you anything he's gone, too."

Emeline raps her spoon sharply against her water glass. She's seen her daughter gear up for hysterics before and learned to divert her. "You do realize you're talking about him as if he were alive and running late for Christmas dinner. It's a painting!"

It works. Deborah says more slowly, "I talked to the butler myself, to see if I could find out what was taken. He was so shaken he couldn't say. Was the ambulance for Pearce, is he dead, has he disappeared?"

Emeline's thinking fast: the *Duke* hardly seems worth a murder, but if SinJen Pearce wanted to buy the painting and whoever lent it to him wanted it back . . ."Someone was hurt?"

"How do I know? One of the cops wanted our names, asked what we were doing there. Julian said we were engaged, having a day in the country."

"Engaged?" asks Emeline in a small voice.

"Just wait, it gets better. Julian showed his passport, the guy looked at it and told us to scram."

"Then Julian got you out of there, good for him."

"Stop saying his name!" Deborah breaks into a new round of tears. "I never want to hear his name again. In the car he announced he had to leave, he had a meeting in New York. Made me drive back to London, the coward, said the round-abouts 'concerned' him. Even though I couldn't stop crying. Straight to his hotel, then he hustled me into a cab. "And, if you can believe it," Deborah blinks rapidly, "this morning he was talking about a long-distance relationship? I told him he can run along home to his little darling."

"Tosser," mutters Xavier.

"And my car's still parked at the Savoy, running up a monster parking bill."

"Tomorrow," Emeline assures her. "We'll take care of all that tomorrow."

Come morning, Deborah still asleep in the bedroom and Xavier on the divan, Emeline decides instead she'll head out on her own for a while. Walking to Elephant and Castle, she catches the tube, rides under the Thames, and ruminates. Obsessing, Deborah would call it. Why the fuss about this unimportant painting? Once north of the river she finds a small restaurant and treats herself to a proper London breakfast—broiled tomatoes, even, if never as good as her mother used to make. Then she plans her morning.

Awake, Xavier sees Emeline has gone out on her own again, "only to mooch around," says her note; before Xavier's even started the coffee, Deborah's up, too. Stumbling around each other whichever way they turn, Xavier says finally: "Let's get out of here. I'll buy you breakfast."

"Grilled tomatoes, sardines, cold toast?" Deborah's trying to be funny though she looks dreadful; shadows under eyes, unwashed hair dragged into a pony tail.

"Better than that."

"Ma's where?"

"Out and about."

"Exercising?"

"Exercising her independence, anyway. She'll be fine, she'll call if she needs us. Come on, get dressed. The walk will do you good."

At his café Xavier orders two large con leches, pastry for himself, and for Deb, a bowl of yogurt. After her yogurt's gone down, half a mug of coffee, and a bite of his apple tart, Xavier begins. "How about we line up what we've got?"

"Be logical," she nods, "make Ma proud." She takes another bite of pastry. He waits. "You start, bro."

"No, you. This all began before I met your Ma. Tell me what you remember about last spring."

"Ron Segal was downsizing, getting ready to move near his sister in Florida. Daddy helped him sell a few valuable pieces. I think Daddy even brought home a couple paintings, parked them against the walls."

"Did your Dad tell you he'd brought them home? Or did your Ma?"

Deborah closes her eyes. "Can I remember? A phone call, I think, it was Ma mentioned conservation or cleaning."

"Remember when?"

"June. I'm pretty sure it was June. I had the paper in front of me, there were headlines: US territory Puerto Rico votes to become a US State. You have an opinion on that?" Xavier shrugs. "I don't think the paintings were there long. After that, Ma and I got into one of our spats. So for a while we weren't," she looks pained, "communicating."

And even when you thought you were, you barely were. He cuts a piece of his pastry, slides it onto her plate, "Water under the dam."

"Over."

"Huh?"

"Over the bridge, under—forget it. Next thing I remember she's calling, hysterical—"

"When was that?"

"June 28th. Like, I'll ever forget that day."

"No, never. Emeline didn't say anything about your Dad being worried or depressed?"

"I asked her. Because, like I told you, when I'd seen Daddy he seemed . . . preoccupied. Perfectly fine, Ma told me. I figured that was Ma being Ma, seeing only what she wanted. Like the time I told her I was going out with this one guy? Admittedly he was married but—"

"Story for another time. Getting back to June?"

"I flew home. We planned the memorial service; I did mostly, Ma was a wreck. The church was full, some people I knew, many I didn't. The service was short, the reception at the Cos Club, tasteful, Ma kept it together somehow."

"Why did she move?"

"Ah, that. You know what everyone says, after a death make no big decisions for a year. She kept saying she didn't need so much space, but something seemed fishy to me. So I asked Muffy. You've met Muffy?"

"Oh, yeah," Xavier laughs.

"Sworn to secrecy, of course, but Muffy told me about Daddy's debts, the bad press in the papers. Ma had to hire lawyers. She called

Coop first, the nice old gent managing Daddy's estate, but he steered her toward some other guy. If it hadn't been for Muffy I'd have never found out. Any idea what that's about?"

"Yes," Deborah, looking hurt, frowns, "but no, your mother never told me, either. I had to go the library, wade thru microfiche. The *Post* dropped hints about embezzlement—"

"No° way!"

"Good thing the internet has nothing on your Daddy's early days in the states."

"How do you know?"

"Because I looked. You know me, curious." Relieved, he sees her smile.

"Their famous carriage ride, their 'contract' in Central Park, Ma gives it quite the romantic spin."

"The stories ran for less than a week. The new lawyer did his job or else the gossip got pushed out by other news—some corruption scandal in the Department of Housing.

"Xavier," Deborah is looking at him with awe, "it occurs to me you're wasting your talents at that gym. These clippings: you have them here?"

"Didn't bring them with me, but you get the idea." She stops smiling. "I am *not* holding out on you, Deborah, promise. It's gotta be cards on the table for us from now on. And speaking of cards—"

"Lord, will you look at the time. I'll barely make it to class if I dash. Cheers for breakfast, buddy." She leans over to kiss his cheek, smearing sugar on him. "I feel better, I really do."

Back at the apartment in a splendid mood, Emeline finds Deborah gone for the day and Xavier brooding over his cell phone.

"You look chipper," he says.

"Went to the Portrait Gallery, looked at faces, trying to decide who were the honest men and who the crooks. Just like Dorothy Sayres' inspector. What are you doing?"

"Looking for signs of our *Duke*."

"We don't know for sure he's left Surrey."

"Do you remember if any of Segal's paintings spent a few days in your old apartment?"

"Your point, Xavier?"

"Trouble around this painting began months ago. Yesterday there's a break-in at Pearce's, and we're meant to believe the *Duke* is still hanging at Sandley Hall collecting dust?"

"To answer your question, no, I don't remember the Duke in my apartment."

"Suppose these people—"

"Whoever they are," Emeline mumbles.

"Suppose they stored the painting at Pearce's; in transit, maybe. It could be on its way to a gallery or an auction anywhere."

"Which is more likely?"

"Milo says a seller might take a piece around to the galleries if there's not the time to place it in auction. Auction houses tend to add a buyer's premium to the hammer price so the buyer pays more. However, an auction house might get away with uncertainty about where the work came from if they sell it 'as is.'"

"Like," Xavier waves his cell phone, "here's an auction house in Dallas. 'Largest auction house south and west of New York.' Coins, paintings, maps, manuscripts. Look, magnificent wines from the Dumond collection. Think we'd get a sample pour before we bid?"

No use, Emeline's good mood has evaporated, and she turns testy. "Xavier, we cannot be haring all over the world." She sees

Clifford's Ghost

his frown. "It means, oh never mind. Do you honestly imagine the painting is in Texas?"

"Honestly, I don't. Why go to the trouble to bring it to England only to send it back? I do think you're hungry, though, lemme make you some lunch."

"Never mind," she says stiffly, "I can manage."

Back with a cheese and pickle sandwich and a mug of tea, Emeline says, "If you want to sell, quietly, a Spanish painting by an obscure Old Master, where would you go? Not a major art center like Paris or London."

"Terrific, that's two capital cities down. What about Spain? Bring the old boy back home. A collector might view him with nostalgia or a buyer hope to impress a relative."

"Could be," she sips her tea, waiting for her drug of choice to take hold. "Spain still has royals, King Juan Carlos who married that pretty lady from Greece."

"You missed your calling, Emeline. You should be writing gossip for a Manhattan paper."

"Or maybe a rich Spanish wanna be," Emeline ignores him, "trying to establish links to one of the old families."

"Would that work?"

"Not our problem," she says. "All we care is: would he try, or she?"

"Wait until I tell your daughter you're EEO-ing Spanish women, she'll be impressed. Contemporary, contemporary," Xavier's scrolling through listings.

"Wait, stop," Emeline leans over his shoulder. "Look, an auction house sold a Ribera study in ink a few months back."

"Okay, *subastas,* auction houses: says here Madrid is the place to go for wider selections of Spanish Art."

"Madrid will be the center but our seller might like to keep a lower profile. Try Barcelona."

"Barcelona mostly auctions Catalan painters, so it's back to Madrid—"

"No, wait. While you're in Barcelona, scroll down."

"You're not being logical."

"I'm being alphabetical, so scroll! Joan Miro, Antoni Pitxot, Salvador Dali; all Catalan and contemporary."

"What did I tell you?"

"Hold it, here's one: Spanish treasures across the centuries."

"Coming up in, merdita, four days."

"Click on the link, let's see what they have on offer. Crystal, carpets, hell's bells, it's all home furnishings. Okay, back to Madrid. Xavier, go back!"

But Xavier, as stubborn as she is, persists, scrolling past standing lamps and tables, china sets and kilim rugs on the Barcelona website, and several paintings. In a minute he wipes two fingers across the screen to enlarge the image of a familiar face.

"Good for you, dear boy. You are a whiz."

"One problem, dear madam, we can't see the whole painting. Which portrait is it going be?"

"Clever guy! Ma, does Xavier ever remind you of Daddy?" Deborah slings one arm around his shoulders. "Xavier, you better move in here for the term, I've got a major research paper. You'd be such a help and," she grins, "give you plenty of free hours to cement other connections here."

Xavier, who can feel his face turning red, tries to swat her. She ducks, saying: "The catalogue didn't materialize overnight; this auction had to be set up in advance."

"Is it possible," Emeline's feeling much better, "Pearce took the Duke with him—even organized the whole scene? Here's what's bothered me since the day we went to Surrey: why would a gentleman out in the English countryside have heard about Clifford's death? He had, you know. He spoke to me about it as we were leaving."

"Ma, why didn't you say something sooner?"

"And listen to you two carry on about my overwrought imagination? No, thank you."

Over supper the three stay away from tricky topics—the *Duke*, Julian, men in general—keeping the conversation light, until Deborah asks: "Who did either of you talk to who might have started asking around, upsetting the status quo?"

"Could have been Milo," muses Emeline.

"Or Julian," snaps Deborah.

"You would say that, dear."

"Oh? It's you who brought Julian over here, Ma."

"I certainly did not bring him over here, I asked him to—"

"Ladies! Who has more to gain? The gallery owner who depends on inside information? Or the tosser with an ego needs feeding more regularly than a newborn?"

"Nobody was paying attention to us until we went to Surrey," argues Deborah.

"Nobody in England, maybe. Don't forget the 'prospective buyer' at our old apartment."

"Ma, you cannot believe your realtor's nosy parker had anything to do with this."

"What about the men in New York I saw later, following—?

"We can say this for sure," Xavier interrupts, "whoever was watching Pearce got curious about who we were and what we were doing. That rules out Milo, we only just met him and anyway," he turns to Deborah, "can you see him staking out Sandley Hall when he could be—"

"Clothes shopping? And," Deborah sounds bitter, "it can't be Julian."

"Because he says he was in New York until he showed up on our doorstep?"

"Because driving on the left terrifies him."

"Whatever is going on didn't start with us," says Xavier. "There's a group with massive amounts of money that's working in the shadows. And we got in their way."

Easy enough to book Spanair from Heathrow, London, to El Prat, Barcelona; who will go is another story. When they call Mary-Margaret about their plan, she volunteers to take Emeline's place, play the part, and keep her new-found sister safe. Give up her role at the center of this drama? Emeline will have none of it. Anyway, Wendy and her children need to sit tight at the refuge with Mary-Margaret keeping watch.

Emeline knows what Deborah will say: count me out; you don't think I've lost enough time with the two of you here? Not at all, Deborah wants to come, "I know I haven't been much of a help, Ma, let me at least—"

"Darling, you've been a huge help, I knew I could count on you. I think you should focus on your studies."

"Like I'm back in the seventh grade, for God's sake," Deborah mutters.

"Besides, someone has to talk to the Art Squad and find out more about the Badger; who better than a Courtauld student?"

So, in the end Xavier makes reservations for just the two of them.

Emeline heads into the bedroom to watch reruns on the telly, leaving Xavier and Deborah to clean up. "You have to feel sorry for Wendy," Deborah wipes her hands on a dish towel and hangs it on the oven handle. "Her husband up to his neck in this mess, everyone in New York and back home, wherever that is—"

"Omaha," Xavier heads for the dining table. "Come here, will you? I want to show you something."

"Whispering, all whispering, did Wendy realize or didn't she. Xavier, are you listening to me? Stop fooling around with those stupid cards."

"*Cara*." He tries to keep his voice calm. "Come sit."

"Don't cara me. Won't it keep until morning? I'm tired." Shaking his head, he pats the chair next to him. Acting deeply put upon, Deborah sits. "Something tells me I'm not going to like this."

"Probably not. Now, watch." He swipes the alphabet cards into a stack face up and fans them on the table in a half circle.

"Really, Xavier. Card tricks?

"Pay attention." One by one he arranges fourteen cards in a straight line to spell a name. Douglas Fleisch.

"Don't know him, never heard of him, good night," Deborah rises. Xavier puts a hand on her shoulder to pull her back down.

"You have. He's one of the Ochre names on Julian's list. Who is he?

"Haven't a clue."

Frowning, Xavier scoops up the fourteen cards and begins to select one, then another, laying them on the table in a new order. Even before he's put down five cards Deborah inhales sharply and covers her mouth. He adds the rest quickly until all together they spell *CLIFODUGHES*.

"Who," he asks quietly, "identified your Dad after the crash?"

"Ma. Tram offered to go, to spare her. Of course she insisted on going herself."

"Any chance she could have made a mistake?"

"You think he's alive?" Deborah claps both hands to her face. "You honestly think Daddy would do this to us? Disappear, put Ma and me through this pain? Leave me, leave Ma, his beloved wife," she seems unaware she's quoting his obituary, "in shock and grief, facing lawyers, scandal, money problems while he goes on to another life? It's impossible. He wouldn't, he wouldn't." She covers her face with her hands.

"Unless," Xavier pats her gently on her shoulder, "your dad got pulled into trouble over his head, unless he wanted to protect you both."

She looks up, stricken. "You mean people might have threatened to hurt us? Please, you can't tell Ma about this, you can't."

"Not planning to. Not until we find out more about this Douglas Fleisch."

"And how in hell are we going to do that?"

Too many questions, not enough answers. His last night in London, tossing on the couch in Deborah's darkened living room, Xavier sees a blurred image come in and out of focus: giant shears like Tia Koka's. Art thieves are after Emeline and the *Duke*. Persons unknown are after Belmo. Two problems, he's always assumed, but what if they aren't separate? Xavier needs Emeline's mind on this, except he can't tell her about Fleisch, not yet. He finally he falls asleep around three in the morning.

Up first the next morning, Xavier slides a handful of Deborah's washed "smalls" down the shower rail and treats himself to a long hot steam. He dries off and opens the bathroom door wrapped in a towel.

"Sorry," Deborah says, embarrassed, "about to knock."

"No worries. I live with two women."

Once Deborah's dried and dressed, the two of them sit at the table with their coffee, Xavier says, "Deborah, there's something else . . ." he describes how he looked through Clifford's computer file "the one marked *Segal,* not any of your household things or regular business. Promise."

"Scrupulous being your middle name," but Deborah sounds more frightened than sarcastic.

"Nope, didn't have the time," he admits. "Here's what I found." Best as he can remember, he describes the searches on theft, fraud, embezzlement that Clifford had opened on his computer.

"So we have questions about criminal action," Deborah's twisting her paper napkin into strings, "Ma denying any such thing, and an Ochre director with a name that converts to my dad's."

"Let's look at what we do know. Traded cleverly, art can be an asset that grows in value over time. Ochre, an art fund, is camouflaged inside a hedge fund. And," he's counting on his fingers, "there's gotta be a person or persons who buy actual art."

"Right, and sells it, in a field less regulated and more opaque than stocks or bonds. Otherwise, where's the profit? There has to be a human being selling or at least recommending the sale. What do you think, a dealer, maybe more than one?"

"You're asking me?" Xavier remembers the poster of the nude Greek he'd been studying a few weeks back before he heard a moan in the alley. "Until I met your mother my idea of art was . . . never mind."

"Banks have to report deposits in cash of more than ten thousand dollars," Xavier's busy tapping on his cell, "so cash is often invested in casinos or nightclubs. Cash often wrapped in vacuum sealed bags, by the way."

Swirling her spoon through her coffee, Deborah asks, 'Who takes in huge amounts of money and has to launder it so it doesn't flag attention?"

"Businesses that traffic in drugs, arms, human beings," answers Xavier. "Organized crime lords."

"Italians?" Deborah suggests. "The mafia?"

"You ever come face-to-face with a mafia don? Flavia's friend Renata in the building, her uncle's what the mafia call a 'made man,' I've passed him on the stairs couple a times."

"And these made men, they're likely to think about an art fund, even know what an art fund is—why are you frowning?"

"Because, Deborah, Italians aren't the only Mafia anymore. How about the Russians, that crowd out in Brighton Beach? Italians or Russians, maybe an outsider suggested it, a go-between." She looks horrified, afraid he's going to name her father. "Like, someone connected to a secret art fund."

"Please," Deborah's not even trying to keep the urgency out of her voice, "don't tell my mother about these files you found."

"You don't think she suspects?

"I think she wonders what her husband was involved in. That's what's keeping her spirits down, not merely the grief. She suspects he broke their precious contract. Bad enough he's dead, but if he cheated on her in the only way that really matters to her . . ."

Has Deborah forgotten the hints she'd thrown out when they first met? "The other ways don't matter?"

"Oh, those, I don't know. If so, he'd be very careful she never found out. Because honestly," Deborah looks wistful, "Ma was his world."

"But you were the one he'd talk to, girl." Xavier sees her face brighten. "I didn't know Clifford, but he sounds real smart, too smart to get mixed up in Ochre to make money." She gives him a shaky smile. "What if we look at the files another way? Suppose your dad stumbled on something he wasn't supposed to know. If he was going to spill the beans, go to the newspapers, or the authorities—"

Deborah's phone pings once. She reaches into her bag. Looking at her phone she turns pale. Her hand trembling, she passes him the phone. On the tiny screen Xavier reads Julian's text. *Belmo found dead this AM roadway Central Park.*

Chapter 27

"Belmo *killed?* Over a mid-list, seventeenth-century painting? You're out of your minds, both of you. It's has to be a coincidence." Sounding certain if feeling anything but, Emeline clasps her hands together. Sharper tremors signal stress, and these two are sure to notice.

"Emeline," Xavier says gently, "if Belmo was tied to the painting it could explain why he left Wendy and the kids, why he didn't tell anyone where he was—so they couldn't be used as hostages."

"Family man to the end," Deborah sounds bitter.

"When Flavia asked if we'd help Wendy—"

"Exactly! Flavia asked us, nothing to do with Sergei and the Duke."

"Until," Deborah steps in, "Julian turns up and we learn Belmo was managing a secret art fund. Ma, any idea if the *Duke* went into the art fund's collection?"

"I never heard of art funds before Julian arrived. You said it yourself, around the world there a thousand art transactions a week and you're asking me to imagine a link between Ron's painting and this Ochre? Preposterous." Firmly Emeline shuts her mouth, afraid one of them will sniff her anxiety, think she's protesting too much. The secrets we keep, the lies we imply.

"Ma, there's another thing," but Xavier shakes his head to cut her off. "Okay, have it your own way. I'm out of here. Guess that leaves you and Xavier to go tell Wendy."

"Deborah," Emeline hates to beg but now she does, "couldn't you come, too?"

"I have a paper due, I told you yesterday." It's the persuasive voice her high-school daughter used to adopt to extend her curfew. "I told you both. Remember Xavier?"

"You did not tell me, Deborah, and you can leave Xavier out of it. He does not speak for me."

"Actually," says Xavier, "I may have been in the bathroom when—"

"Xavier, I know what I heard, I don't need you as state witness."

Too much, it's all too much. Emeline feels hot tears running down her cheeks. Ever since Clifford died, she's been living on a chasm, clinging to the edge. She feels herself falling, falling into the abyss.

"Xavier's the one to go with you," Deborah says, more quietly. "I've only just met the poor woman. Xavier and Wendy have history."

"A couple strained holiday dinners, hardly history. But fine, I'll go. Emeline, you want to come with?" Roughly Emeline wipes her cheeks and shakes her head, no, no, undone at the thought—the old widow breaking the news to the young one.

"Then I'll call Sister. She and I can tell Wendy together, if you'll be alright by yourself?"

"Of course, I'll be fine. Stop treating me like an invalid!"

"We're only trying to look out for you, Ma."

"You know what? I've had it up to my back teeth with the two of you. I hate it, *hate* it, when you make me feel old and helpless, when you act like my wits are going." Hands pressed on the table to still the tremor, Emeline stands. "I am going to the bathroom, and when I come back, I want you both gone. Do I make myself clear?"

Deborah and Xavier swap startled looks while Emeline stalks to the bathroom and slams the door, but not before she hears her daughter say, "Blimey!"

Really, who do they think they are? Emeline paces into to the kitchen. Missing out on all the good stuff, I am. She stalks to the front window, peers out, her anger and fear taking their sweet time to subside. Clouds have come in. Against the outline of the building opposite she can see the faint shadow of an old woman: bent, hesitant, uncertain. Emeline keeps still. The shadow moves. So not a reflection, thank God.

These kids are not the problem. She is, flying to London after so many years and afraid now she'll return home the same person who left.

In her mind she sees Wendy cleaning the refuge bathroom. Doesn't matter what's brought Emeline to this state, what matters is finding a way to go forward. She straightens her body. Perhaps she'll go out, sit in Xavier's café and look at faces; better yet, take the tube and go across the river, visit the Portrait Gallery again. That's the place to study faces, to imagine what each person was hiding or projecting when the portrait was painted.

Deborah's landline rings. Emeline snatches up the receiver on the first peal of Greensleeves. "Deborah?"

"Mrs. Hughes?" a man's voice, unfamiliar and the accent not quite English.

"Who is this?"

"I understand you have taken interest in a Spanish painting. I wonder if we might meet to discuss next steps."

"Who are you?" she demands, gripping the phone."

"Blaine Russell. We—"

"I have no interest in any painting nor do your next steps interest me." Her voice sounds calm, if ridiculously formal.

"If you google for Russell and Spitz, Ltd., you'll see our business: tracking down paintings that have gone missing."

You're talking to the wrong person. It's not my painting. I don't give a fig. Sensible sentences or she could just hang up. Her mulish friend Tram simply lays the phone down on her kitchen counter, "Let them waste their time, not mine."

Emeline hears herself say: "Where shall we meet?"

"What part of London are you in?"

Oh no you don't. Regaining her wits, she has no intention of telling him, if he doesn't know already, where she, where her daughter lives. Someplace public, she needs to suggest an obscure address in a part of London she doesn't know; though honestly, how many parts of London does she know?

"Why don't I meet you," Emeline makes her voice sound compliant, "at a café?"

It turns quiet on the other end, as if the voice is consulting with a second party. "Yes," the voice replies, "what would you suggest?"

The one Xavier frequents is too close to home. The tea bar in the off-beat Peckham gallery? She has no idea how to get there. Wait. There's the café where she and Mary-Margaret went to talk.

"Mrs. Hughes?"

"Will 3:00 p.m. be handy for you? We'll meet at Tariq's."

"Where is—"

"Look it up."

With her hand shaking more than usual, Emeline replaces the phone. Back a few weeks, back in New York, she'd have sent Xavier.

But he's not here and she's not there; even if he were she knows she wouldn't dispatch him on this run. This one's down to her.

She searches for Tariq's address on her mobile and looks up the bus route. She'll need to be there at least an hour early, take up a position in nearby doorway, see the lay of the land. Bring her cane? Without it she tends to wobble; but the cane will only make her look older, more vulnerable, so no cane.

Emeline double locks the door behind her as Deborah always tells her to. She's halfway to Elephant and Castle before she realizes she's left no note and, while she's brought her mobile, the battery bars are down to one. To preserve what power remains, Emeline holds her finger on the button until the little wizard subsides into sleep.

Banished from the apartment, Xavier decides to check up on Wendy's family. He finds Mary-Margaret in her office on the phone so when she raises her fingers—five minutes—Xavier heads on his own to the dining hall.

Half a dozen kids sit at a low table with Wendy in charge now that Flavia's gone. When August splits off from the group and runs to throw his arms around his pal's waist, Xavier hardly recognizes him. Flavia must have tousled the Wellington hair to remove any signs of sleek or style and, he sniffs, is that coffee grounds she's rubbed in?

Wendy comes over and to his surprise, hugs him as well; evidently any Escudero in a storm will do. "August is tutoring a few kids," proudly, she hugs her son. "His father has the math abilities, not me."

Let's hope he doesn't share his father's character. Xavier says only: "Wendy? Come sit with me a minute, we have to talk." He leads her to a row of chairs and as gently as he can, begins. The recent headlines, wife and children vanished, Belmo missing. "Your friends, your parents, they must be worrying, and you're tempted to text them. Honestly, it's better if you don't. Mary-Margaret says you're safe here."

"I don't." Wendy studies him, her lovely face growing pale. "There's more, isn't there."

"Yes. Julian, he—"

"Julian?" Right, they've never told Wendy who Julian is, what they've learned about Ochre, how evidence against Belmo is mounting, all news for another day.

"A friend of Emeline's in New York. Julian sent me a text. It's bad news, I'm afraid." He reaches for her hand, "Very bad."

"Belmont." It's somber statement, not a question.

"I'm afraid so." Xavier won't forget the agony on her face as word-for-word he quotes Julian's news. Or the regret. To protect her children she's afraid she sacrificed her husband. "I am so sorry, Wendy, so sorry."

"Too young," a whisper only. He nods, understanding. Not her Belmont, not herself, it's her children she thinks of first.

Any hysterics Xavier dodged with Wendy seem to have flown through the London skies to erupt on Searles Road minutes after he walks in.

"Good for Ma," Deborah says, "she decided to go with you after all."

"I...I left her here, in the bathroom. She said didn't want to come."

"Well, she's not here!" Deborah's voice rises.

"Did you look for a note?" That sends Deborah scurrying from table to counter, to the small stand that holds the landline.

"Don't see one."

"I'll try the bedroom," he offers, but Deborah pushes past him, riffles through the tissues, ear plugs, paperback books, and Post-It notes on the table on her mother's side.

"My God, they've found her," Deborah is hyperventilating. "They've taken her—"

"Will you calm down? Nobody's taken her. Was the door unlocked when you got here? Broken in?"

"No. No."

"Then she's gone for an outing on her own. You know, lately—" he's talking to the air. She's headed for the bathroom.

"You better be right, Xavier. Because," she's rattling her mother's pillbox, "*these* are still here, and if she doesn't take them when—"

"Hello?" says a quiet voice.

Like children playing statues, they freeze. Emeline stands in the doorway, spare keys in hand and Mary-Margaret behind her.

Xavier blinks first. "Hi there, how's it going?" He was right all along; powerfully relieved, he makes up his mind he won't gloat.

"So after I answered your landline, dear," Emeline explains, "and heard what this man had to say, I agreed to meet him at three." Mary-Margaret, who's heard the story, heads for the kitchen.

"Because?" Deborah demands.

"Because I was tired of sitting here, waiting for messengers from the outside world to bring me news." Emeline is frankly very glad to be sitting in the flat again but refuses to show it. "I can still get around, you know, I'm not feeble."

"Of course you're not. Go on, Ma."

"I picked the place Mary-Margaret took me to, Tariq's, with that nice Nigerian? I got there an hour early. There's a dry cleaners across the way so I sat inside to wait. I saw them when the car pulled up, they'd arrived, too."

"Was it the—" Xavier's having a hard time getting a word in.

"Yes. At least it looked like the car we both noticed, a big, heavy, dark number—think what the petrol costs must be. I took pictures." Like a traveler returning from Arabia's Empty Quarter, Emeline pulls out her phone.

"Stupid, stupid woman," mutters Deborah, close to tears.

"I may have been a bit impetuous."

"Ma, since when are you impetuous?"

"I'm trying to help out, here."

"So am I," Xavier's as angry as Deborah, "to keep you safe."

"I know that. But—"

"And there it is: always a contradiction!"

Looking on, Deborah seems aware Xavier and her mom, this new family duo she's resented, admired, and envied in turn, isn't always so cozy after all. "Listen, Ma, we thought you were taken, so excuse us if we're a little—"

"Overwrought?" suggests Mary-Margaret, returning with mugs of tea. Emeline glares at him. Just like a man. Maybe still a little too much testosterone circulating?

Emeline has another thought: when she looks back on the afternoon later in life—however much later she still has— she wonders if it will appear like a proper memory or another dream sequence? She'd found her way on the route she planned and gotten to Tariq's well before two o'clock. Scanning the block she settled across the street at the dry cleaners on the narrow bench, the owner too busy to mind or even notice.

The old dame advantage, Tram calls it. We go from objects of interest, attention, flattery, to invisible objects. She'd laughed when

Tram described the theory. At close to six feet Tram would be the last of all their friends to fade from notice. Today, Emeline was grateful to feel inconspicuous and wouldn't Aunt Mildred applaud.

Truthfully, in spite of showing the finesse of Lewis and Clark in finding her way, she felt plenty nervous. If she hadn't been so angry at her daughter and Xavier, she'd never have done it; she'd have hung up after the man's first sentence, or at least waited until she had someone to go with her. Practical, they call her? It seemed every practical synapse she possessed fell asleep like her mobile.

She sees Tariq's café across the street, a still life except for people passing in or out the door: Middle-Easterners, mostly men; one woman, picking up food to take home, in minutes she's outside again, holding a brown sac. Tariq himself steps outside to smoke a thin, dark cigarette. On the street, bike messengers, buses, lorries and cars cruise past.

Closer to her, others from the neighborhood walk past, each one slightly larger than the people across the street, offering Emeline a living lesson in perspective. She'll have to tell Deborah. A woman in hijab pushes a baby stroller while managing to shepherd her three other children. A posse of older boys with backpacks rushes by, their school just letting out.

A heavy, dark sedan drives slowly up the block. Crikey! It's barely half after two. Squinting through the foreground of boys and backpacks she tries to see the number plate. Twice, the sedan fails to stop. It drives around the block and a few minutes later reappears. Emeline stretches, her back stiff.

The third time it circles around, with the sedan moving out of sight, Emeline sees an English-looking woman with a cane walk into Tarik's. In minutes the English woman is coming out, and Emeline hears the sedan speed up. Engine racing, it swoops forward. Brakes screech, two men jump out, seize the woman, and stuff her in back. Emeline, shaking all over, watches them take the woman away.

"So your Ma was never taken, Deborah," reminds Mary-Margaret, handing out the mugs. So upset he forgets the house rules, Xavier taps a cigarette between his lips and strikes a match.

Deborah's the first to recover. "We have to call the police."

"Already did," says Mary-Margaret. "We even have the number plate. Your mother was taking pictures while she waited."

Emeline pretends to notice neither cigarette nor smoke. "One of you will have to get the pictures onto the computer. You know me. All thumbs."

Xavier inhales deeply, "How many?"

"Half a dozen? I didn't want to risk them noticing if they looked into the cleaner's window."

"He means, Ma: how many people in the car?"

"A woman. No longer young," she sees Deborah wince, "but not the Badger. More like a woman with a high-powered job and monthly dry cleaning, and these two men? You won't believe me, Xavier, but I've seen one of them before. In New York."

"Lemme guess. When we were sitting in the Rose Garden?"

"No, earlier, one of the prospectives the realtor brought; it was the man hunting through papers on Clifford's desk."

"You told me you never met prospective buyers, Ma."

"I didn't meet him. When I was on my way out, he and the realtor were in the lobby." Emeline can see Xavier doesn't believe her, can hear him thinking: can we believe any of this? "Mary-Margaret, I could murder another cuppa."

"And you didn't call one of us?" Deborah's fists are clenched.

"How could I, my mobile was out of juice. Then Hue, the dear man who owns the cleaners, he came over: a woman sitting on his bench for over an hour, no cleaning to leave, no book to read? I explained the situation to him; though I was a bit afraid he'd think I was batty."

Xavier and Deborah exchange a look. Batty? Why would anyone think that?

"I said I knew Tariq, Hue phoned Tariq, and Tariq phoned Mary-Margaret."

"I came over fast as I could," says Mary Margaret, "with some clothes I had around. In case the men came back when they saw they'd made a mistake. Good thing, because as we walked out—"

"Melody's?" Deborah sounds close to hysterics. "Please don't tell me you spirited my mother away dressed as Melody, that would be too *Cage au Folles*."

"Deborah," Xavier scolds, "it's your Ma we're talking about, not Lady Gaga."

Emeline ignores them. "Mary-Margaret brought one of her draped robes and sort of a cape thingy. We walked out the front. Who looks twice at two Sisters of Mercy?"

"Jesus." Deb looks at her mother as if seeing her for the first time.

"Do stop swearing, dear. It's rude."

"But you took pictures? The people, the car's number plate?"

"I did," Emeline tries not to look smug as she hands her phone to her daughter. "You'll want to get them onto your computer."

"They didn't twig," says Mary-Margaret, "didn't look twice when we walked out of the cleaners."

"I don't suppose the sedan came back."

"It did, Xavier, and deposited the other woman on the street." Mary-Margaret's trying not to smile. "I couldn't see more than their silhouettes, but before we walked out Emeline was careful to tell me where to look, because she didn't want to point."

Xavier's sigh of exasperation would have launched a sailboat, until Deborah whoops with laughter and he has to give in, too. Arms spread wide, he repeats: "She. Didn't. Want To Point—is our new agent field-ready, or what?"

Wrung out, the four say little over the supper Deborah pulls together: warmed-over pork pot stickers, fried rice, green salad. "As long as you're okay with the pork, Mary-Margaret?"

"I am, and neither does our order forbid chocolate," she points to the frozen eclairs Deborah's left to thaw on the counter.

"I do try to respect other practices," Mary-Margaret sounds quite righteous, "vegetarian for Hindus, halal for Muslims, but I say food is food. We see enough real hunger at St. Bertie's: men, many Mondays, who ask for a second potato, because they haven't eaten since Friday; women putting rolls in their pockets for their children. Tabloids are hungry for scandal; celebrities for status. Everybody forgets where the word comes from."

"Not you," Emeline says. Mary-Margaret puts her arm around Emeline's shoulder and holds her close. Emeline, happy, closes her eyes—a sister. I crossed an ocean and gained a sister.

"Mary-Margaret," Deborah's back to being bossy, "soon as you finish eating, if you'll go get the van? I'll help bring down their bags. These two can still make their flight."

"I'll need a few minutes, dear. What's the matter, Xavier?"

"What if the Badger comes here again when Deborah's alone?"

"Let me worry about the Badger," says Deborah. "You have a plane to catch."

Dear Wendy, Emeline begins, then wrinkles the paper into a ball. In New York Emeline would have put money on it: any free-fall from privilege would turn Wendy into, what does Xavier call it? A train wreck. How wrong she'd have been. Even today, Emeline doubts she'd have the nerve to speak in person, to tell the young mother what she wants to. Emeline takes a fresh sheet of paper

My dear friend Wendy, For that is how I feel about you. Not only for what has happened to you in the past weeks, but for what lies ahead. This is a terrible time for you. I understand. Though you were tactful when we met at your apartment, I'm sure you know from the newspapers or your friends what happened to my husband Clifford last June: the "accident," his sudden death, the rumors. Yes, horrible, all of it. Still, today I see better than I could in June, my job is to move forward, as is yours, and you will be propelled by all you must do for your children. They tell me you put yourself through college cleaning. What stamina and determination that took, let alone hand lotion. As a bystander, I believe—I see—that however grim the days look to you now, your stamina and determination are intact.

"Emeline, it's getting late."

"In a minute, Xavier."

I've come to believe the kind of crisis you and I have faced does not erase the person we once were. It chips away at some edges, yes. I like to tell myself that is where new strengths will grow, as if we were plants who've endured drastic pruning. We have to figure out who else we want to be from here on. I must admit, seeing you these days has strengthened my own resolve. I hope this letter will strengthen yours.

"Ma! Mary-Margaret's out front."

"I'm coming." Emeline reads over what she's written, debates about the hand lotion and leaves it in, but scratches out the quotes around *accident*. Belmo's widow will have enough speculation to deal with about her own husband's death.

Clifford's Ghost

Wherever life next takes you, I hope you'll count on me as your friend. This is the number for my new mobile. I hope we will stay in touch, though I cannot promise to learn to Skype.
Very fondly, Emeline D. Hughes.

Chapter 28

Spanair's Barcelona flight takes off and Emeline hears the throaty whir of wheels retracting. Vigilant, she waits for the pilot to cut back the throttle, the engine growl to drop, her anxious heart to skip a beat. As if to remind her about cruising altitude, Xavier pats her hand: the engines are still doing their job, propelling them south to Spain, not outer space. Thanking him with a sleepy smile, she bunches her Burberry raincoat into a pillow and leans against the window. A window seat, and she chose it herself. Will wonders never cease?

Emeline's reminded things aren't always what they seem. She's not heading for outer space, the *Duke* in Barcelona may not be the original . . . she dozes. When the plane banks sharply, she opens her eyes and see clouds, canted at an angle. It's a minute before she remembers where she is.

"Landing in a few," Xavier pushes the button on her seat to prop her upright, just as he's already held her up in so many ways. As the plane levels into its approach, glimpses of tiny buildings alternate with the wide expense of marine blue that can only be the Mediterranean. How long has it been since she's seen the Mediterranean? She and Clifford went to Italy for their honeymoon. Emeline feels an unfamiliar joy at the memory.

Clifford's Ghost

By the luggage carousel she studies other passengers. "Look for descendants of the Moors," Mary-Margaret's told her, "Spain used to be their home. If you see a woman with a face grill she can only be a Saudi, though when Persian women travel they go all out." Emeline notices two Iranian couples, the women dressed for a red carpet, hair covered in bright silk hijab and bling flashing on their wrists. Next to them, the British men and women look like as dull as London sparrows.

"Don't worry about calling Deborah," Emeline tells Xavier, who's tapping on his cell. "We've never been a family to call at the end of a trip to say we're safe." Even if there'd been times she wished they were, reimagining the phone call as a loving link rather than a signal of disaster averted.

"Looking for a hotel."

"But you booked already."

"What's the point of losing your guys in London if we go straight to—?"

"You can't think they've—"

"Here's one, we'll stay near the Old Quarter."

"I'd prefer hot running water."

"Barcelona's a major tourist center, you won't be drawing water from a well. Bet they'll have lovely soap."

He's right. "La Chinata Olive Oil Soap," she calls through the open door; Xavier's insisted on adjoining rooms. Since he's again her sole watcher, he's probably anxious after her expedition the day before.

"Heno de Pravia shower gel," he calls back. "One thing I love about Puerto Rico, they believe in shower gel, not that lumpy block you Americans like." Emeline laughs. In Spain the Nuyorican is suddenly a Puertorriqueño.

Xavier guesses it's a dream deferred to find herself in this ancient city when Emeline insists they go out and explore. Steps into the Old Quarter a handful of people sip beer and read *el periodico* under red umbrellas advertising Cruzcampo. Emeline studies the endless list of *tapas, vegetariano, pescados y camarones, puerco y beef* and enlists Xavier's help in translating. He orders for them, by now he's starving, too, and a Cruzcampo for himself. They pick their way through the tapas, each delivered on its own small plate ("that's what a tapa is, a lid"), and finish off with flan.

Music, traditional if secular, draws them toward the city's basilica: the Cathedral of the Holy Cross and Saint Eulalia. Several dozen people have come together to dance singly, in couples, or with friends. New arrivals push through the lopsided circle beginning to form, and drop their handbags and backpacks out of the way in the center. As the music ends there's a moment of quiet, broken only by the murmuring pigeons high on the spires of the basilica.

Musicians strike up a new dance. Holding a lover's hand or a stranger's, each dancer seems to know the steps; each adapts to the rhythm as they move clockwise. In minutes Xavier is watching a joyful, deliberate community in motion.

Not everyone celebrates the day by dancing. To one side Xavier sees a clown blowing gigantic bubbles with a hoop. A small Chinese girl steps forward, following the balloon ahead of her while her parents laugh and clap their hands. So Emeline can enjoy it with him, Xavier turns to point out this delicate side show. Only, Emeline is not there.

Blind panic chokes Xavier as he swings this way and that, standing on his toes to survey the onlookers and find his charge. If he's lost Emeline in Barcelona . . . he feels a tap on his shoulder.

"If you look for your friend?" The Chinese father is pointing. On the far side of the circle Emeline is dancing between a young American hippy and a Spanish *abuelita* whose bosom rises and falls like an ocean wave as she steps nimbly in the dance. Fear turns to its close companion, anger, and Xavier moves, ready to drag her away.

"No," says the father. "Step in here, you see her fine." Reaching out he breaks the grasp of two old men and thrusts Xavier into the circle.

Two people concentrating on their feet can miss seeing each other for a long time. It is a while before Emeline notices him, before Xavier has the dance steps down and looks up. Across the mound of shopping bags and backpacks, her wooden cane parked on top at a rakish angle, Emeline sends him a glorious smile

Getting a late start next morning, they find the breakfast buffet closed and walk two blocks to a café. "Too cold?" asks the waiter, waving his menu toward the door.

"Not at all," Emeline assures him. "We are British." Skeptical, the waiter catches Xavier's eye.

"She is," Xavier answers in Spanish, "not me. *Vale,* we'll be fine out here. Hot tea for the señora, *por favor,* and coffee for me." Thankfully, coffee everywhere in this city means the real thing, along with classic Spanish tortilla, its eggs and potatoes tasty and filling, and at last sugary buns.

To please Emeline (and take her mind off the auction), Xavier organizes a walking tour of Barrio Gotica, the Old Quarter. After tuning their headsets to English, the Catalan guide walks backward to see his group is following him into the labyrinth: Roman wall remnants, medieval landmarks, houses closely packed, and streets so breathtakingly narrow that when a motorcycle intrudes, everyone leaps onto the foot-wide sidewalk to press their backs against the ancient stone.

Old buildings, thinks Xavier, turning his headset to Spanish. Maybe you have to be rolling in it to get such a thrill from old buildings. Walking past one for sale in Old San Juan, all his family can think about is what new plumbing and wiring would cost to make such a place livable, let alone a modern kitchen or bathroom. He wonders how his mother is getting along back in El Barrio.

Curious to see how much he can understand, Xavier switches his audio to Catalan. Not much. Had he expected he'd feel at home here, where faces are mostly pale, where they say "z" as if spitting? It's another foreign country, even with plazas and buildings that remind him of San Juan. So what, they're here for a purpose. Locate the auction house, be sure they know how to get there when they need to, and keep an eye out for trouble.

The group walks under a stone bridge connecting two buildings and past balconies with colored tiles and window boxes of red Geraniums. Not everything is so pretty. Acknowledging a tragic moment, the guide leads them toward the convent used as a school for evacuated children during Spain's civil war, and he points out holes in the courtyard wall where a bomb killed three dozen children. The tour leader is proud: instead of patching the holes, city fathers leave them as a reminder of the past. Kind of like pentimento thinks Xavier, the past pushing into the present.

Far from tiring her, the tour's energized Emeline. "History gives you a sense of perspective. And an appetite, is it too early for lunch?"

Once they're sitting under a green-and-white striped umbrella, Xavier asks casually, "This Ochre director, the one with the European name, where's his family from?"

"Fleisch? German descent. I'd guess. Why?"

"Just curious," he says, nibbling on an olive. "After we eat let's check out Subasta Oriel."

"Where to, señor?" the driver asks in his best English. In Spanish Xavier rattles off the auction house address. Hearing an invite to chat, the driver ("I am Feran") draws him into an exchange about local weather, Spanish politics, American politics, and the state of tourism in the city.

"Franco, Picasso, Gaudi, it's we old men bring the tourists," claims Feran. "It's we," he takes one hand off the wheel to pound his chest, "who know the good bars and flamenco clubs, the real Barcelona. I can show you. Take you up to Montjuic." Steering sharply around a bus with one finger, he reaches his other hand back to give Xavier his card.

The Eixample district is old and magnificent, with six-story stone buildings, black wrought-iron balconies, and prosperous commerce on the ground floors. Part way along Carrer del Rosseló, brakes shriek and Feran shudders to a stop.

In a block of expensive dress shops, menswear shops, and a gallery or two, the building's larger than Xavier expected, he'd been thinking along the lines of a thrift shop. "Subasta Oriel" reads a sign in gold-on-black letters. One front window displays a matched set of antique chairs, the other an easel with a famed scene of the Spanish countryside—objects anyone can own for a price.

"You go in, look around," Feran says, "I wait for you."

"Not today, it's closed; we just needed to know the route. Emeline, you ready to go back?"

"Not at all," Emeline sits up straight: who's tired, says her back? Though she's been listening Xavier can't believe she's grasped any of their rapid-fire chatter. Until she says in careful Spanish: "We would like to drive by Sagrada Familia."

After lunch, a rest for her, a walk around the neighborhood for him, and just as Emeline announces she's ready to go out again, Xavier's cell rings.

"Got it. Right. Okay, we'll keep an eye out. No, nothing, not yet," he hangs up. "Deborah. She paid a visit to the Art Squad. They've heard nothing about a missing del Mazo. Never heard of Detective Sergeant Kelsey, either, the one you call the Badger."

"Why'd she phone you and not me?"

"She says your ringer's off, also your notifications. What were you saying?"

"Let's have supper at my usual bedtime," Emeline smiles, game. Intrigued by the chance to practice with another menu, Emeline talks him into walking downhill to the seaside barrio of La Barceloneta. To start them off the waiter brings two dishes of fried potato pieces, sprinkled with garlic and paprika. From the menu Emeline orders tapas in simple phrases and, for a cup of tea with sugar, an impeccable "th" accent for *taza* and *azucar,*

Xavier sees Emeline scan the crowd, checking out anyone coming in the door. Has something alarmed her? He's getting ready to ask when a man wearing a country cap walks in and heads to the bar. Emeline, for the moment focused on her potatoes, doesn't look up until the man has settled himself on a stool with his back to them. Xavier watches her give a little start.

"Emeline? What's the matter, you look as if you've seen a—"

"It's nothing. Only, for a moment . . ."

So that's what he looked like in motion, Clifford. Medium height, lanky, with a slight limp. Xavier only knows him from the framed head shots, one at Emeline's, one at Deborah's.

"See anyone there you want to go talk to?"

"Talk to a stranger? Of course not. Excuse me, I must run to the loo." Cane in hand, Emeline heads toward the corner beyond the bar, glancing at the wall mirror behind the row of bottles to check the faces. Xavier watches to see if Emeline stops, if her cane connects more slowly with the floor tiles. If so, he can't tell.

Soon as the door marked *Damas* swings closed behind her, Xavier stands to stretch himself, jostling the waiter delivering half a dozen small plates. Scanning the faces in the mirror, Xavier tries to see if one looks like the photo in the frame or even like Deborah. The man in the country cap has pulled the brim farther down, so it's hard to see his face. Xavier gives up and goes back to his seat.

By the time Emeline returns he's holding a shrimp on a tiny fork, nibbling around the tail. They finish their tapas, not trying to talk over the flamenco guitar. Emeline orders two flans, but only takes a bite of hers before she pushes her ramekin across the table for him to finish. Worry and fatigue are breaking through her excitement in being in Barcelona.

At the hotel Emeline decides to turn in. Xavier spends another hour on his cell, looking at the *Barcelona Guia Telefonica* and the local maps he brings up on his small phone screen, spreading his fingers to make the details large enough to read. Before he goes to bed he checks he still has Feran's card.

Next morning Xavier says, "Hey, how about a drive? We could go out into the countryside."

"Love the idea," she admits, quite pleased. Stiff from yesterday's exertions, today she'd rather ride than walk. Xavier calls Feran.

"*Vale, vale,* I be there twenty minutes."

Feran settles Emeline in the back while Xavier sits in front to talk with their new best friend.

"Today we drive up to Montjuic?" asks Feran.

"Maybe later," Xavier says. "Today we want to go out to Girona."

We do? Emeline has no idea why he's picked Girona. She watches Barcelona streets slide by, giving way to suburbs with leafy trees and houses with red tile roofs.

On a mission that began with a mistake on 41st Street, here in Spain Emeline fiercely misses her husband, wishes he were in Feran's cab with her, leaning against the cracked plastic beside her. Yet under the grief moves a soothing sense of relief. The man in the bar, his face half hidden, whoever he was, is a stranger. Still, the sight of him brought back small flickers of memory—a man back in New York, brushing too close to her at a party, touching her shoulder when he passed her in the hall, gripping her hand a few seconds too long. A man who seemed to want whatever Clifford had, his money, his bravado . . . his marriage?

Their paths crossed no more than a few times. Yet he turned up at St. James for the service. Afterward he offered an awkward, unwelcome kiss, imposing not consoling, and wearing clothes that might have come out of Clifford's closet. They had not, of course. Emeline was weeks away from tackling Clifford's closet with its aroma of spicy clove, only pushing past the empty jackets' sleeves when she needed to open the safe.

Fifty minutes later Feran turns down the main street of Girona, past a café, a church, a train station, a *pasado* of couples taking the October air. Even though she nets quite a few words from the burbling rapids, Emeline can't understand what the men are chatting about in Spanish all this time. Will she and Xavier be getting out, ordering a coffee on the café's outdoor patio? Seems not. Checking a map on his mobile every couple of minutes, Xavier gives Feran directions. Left at the crossroads where the road leads to Besalú, up a dirt road.

"Why are we here?" Emeline finally asks. Xavier has not picked this town at random from a list of Catalan outposts, she knows that much.

"You don't think I might be curious, want to know where my family came from?" Like a lawyer he's answered a question with a question.

Emeline's taken European history even if Xavier hasn't. Spain's explorers set off from Seville, the ships sailing down the Guadalquivir River to the Atlantic. Wherever his ancestors sailed from, she doubts it was this northeastern Catalonian province. Farmers or sheepherders, unsuccessful, or why leave home, they'd lived many kilometers to the west.

"I guess Mary-Margaret got you interested in genealogy, Xavier. Where we off to next, Senegal?"

Xavier turns to face her. "You know about Mary-Margaret's background?"

"Indian, I'm guessing. People with your coloring have trace DNA from Africa—"

"Tell me something I don't know."

"—while those with freckles like me," she leans forward to hold her spotted forearm against his café-colored skin, "have traces of Neanderthal."

"Neanderthal?"

"Yes, they developed later on in Europe. Amazing I don't walk with my knuckles on the ground. You must, too, my friend, since you're part Spanish—"

"Señor?" asks Feran, "left or right?"

"Left up the hill a little way, then you can park." All business, Xavier might be looking to buy a weekend place. "Let's stroll," he directs Emeline when the car stops. "Feran, we won't be long. Have a smoke, why don't you."

Xavier is up to something, Emeline doesn't know what. They climb a stretch of hillside, Xavier holding her arm with a steady hand. Under a clump of trees he stops to pull a pair of binoculars from his black leather jacket. "Borrowed them from the concierge," he explains, "told him we were looking at real estate, planning to develop an old people's home."

"You didn't!"

Laughing, he hands her the glasses. "Take a look."

Across the meadow sits a large, lovely *hacienda,* a restored stone farmhouse with second floor balconies. A driveway curves in from another part of the road they've left. A patio is settled with wooden chairs and colorful cushions, while a stone barn and two or three other small buildings lie beyond. "Who owns it?" she asks.

"It's a rental." How does he know that? Why is Xavier interested in this place?

"You want to tell me—look, someone has come outside, he's having a smoke. Want to see?" But Xavier makes no move to take the glasses. "Think he can see us?" she asks, still fussing to get the glasses in focus.

"Not if we hold still. Lower the binoculars, or better yet give them to me." He's careful to shade them, so the sun has no chance of catching a lens.

As they wait, motionless, it dawns on her: this man is why they're out in the middle of nowhere. "Xavier, he's turned to look this way. Do you know who he is, this man?" Xavier shakes his head.

Then she has a new worry: what if Feran gets impatient, decides to honk the horn?

"He's going back inside," reports Xavier. She squints, trying to decide if the man is limping. "We'll just slip away. No hurry, we're only out for a stroll."

A mile after they turn off the dirt road and on to pavement again, Feran says: "Compra? I think someone is following us."

"Merdita!"

"Now look what you've done." Emeline's suddenly anxious. "We go for a drive and come home with a tail."

"No worry, señora," Speaking English, Feran speeds up. "He know country roads but wait we get into city. I lose him in no time." Feran's right. Once back on the highway, even before Feran maneuvers through half a dozen fast turns on the outskirts of Barcelona, Xavier assures her no one is following them.

Chapter 29

Excited, hopeful, scared, and ready to go home, Emeline can't decide which gets top billing. What started as a grand adventure in New York has worn her down, what with a brother she didn't recognize and a worry she can't shake. She's too old for all this. Time to accept it: change no longer brings promise. At least the trip is almost over. Today is the auction.

On Xavier's mobile the portrait in the auction catalogue is too small, impossible to tell whether the *Duke* sports tiny gold bees on his dark cloak. She and Xavier may have hared off to Barcelona for no good reason, just to feel they were taking steps to wind up this mystery; which, she admits now, began before Sergei Morosov confronted her in her apartment. Whatever Clifford has done or hasn't, the trouble started before he died.

Emeline feels shaky. She need her pills, food, and maybe a wheelchair. The concierge, able to provide binoculars at a moment's notice, surely for a paying guest he could—.

"You ready?" Xavier knocks and walks in.

Good thing Deborah isn't here, she'd give him a real razzing. He's dressed in grey and black, imitating Milo, she guesses, and isn't that a new jacket? No wonder he urged her to nap the day before, the man went shopping.

He twirls once, arms up like a dancer, "You like?"

"Mighty fine. What do you think about a wheelchair?"

"For you or for me?" he teases her. "Forget it, Em, all you need is food. I'll find something from the buffet and bring it back. Take your time, get dressed—be sure you wear your pearls and your gold earrings."

On time, Feran collects them in the familiar cab. Feeling really jumpy, Emeline has an awful thought. Any chance Xavier brought her real coffee from the buffet? Xavier, fidgety himself, keeps checking his watch.

In spite of the traffic they arrive early at Subasta Oriel. Good thing they have Feran to drive, there's not a parking place in sight. Gentleman that he is, Feran double parks and, ignoring the honking horns, hustles around to open Emeline's door and hand her out.

"What time I pick you up, señor?"

Studying his phone, Xavier says, "We don't know yet; I'll text you."

Understanding this exchange with no trouble, Emeline points across the street and says, "Feran, park the car where you can, then wait in that café, *esta bien*? My friend will feel much better knowing you're close by."

For a weekday auction in a lesser venue, a surprising number of people are coming through the door. Gallery owners, clients, dealers, and collectors; some look ostentatious and greedy, others nondescript and shrewd. As always, a good number arrive just to enjoy the show. Inside a young woman, elegant in red silk and tiny, glittering earrings, gives them each a catalogue and a paddle as if they've arrived to play Ping-Pong.

Itself a work of art, the auction room is. Underfoot is a crimson, wall-to-wall carpet. The walls are white, the better to show off paintings hanging at eye level along the right hand side and the left-hand wall is mirrored: its entire length reflects the paintings opposite. A dizzying number of reflections, and not only of paintings: the mirrors make it appear that twice as many guests are moving in to take seats in the rows of chrome and black leather chairs.

To better study each sales lot as it appears, Emeline brings out the borrowed binoculars. "Next time I leave home I'm bringing Aunt Mildred's mother-of-pearl pair, so much easier to carry around." A promise, she realizes too late, that's unrealistic. Once she gets home, she's staying home from now on.

Xavier notices the number on his paddle and looks, delighted. "It's my birthday. Must be good luck."

"This is not a horse race, Xavier."

"You don't think?" Rhythmically, he trills his fingers on the back of his paddle, canter tempo. "You know how this game's gonna end?"

"Got a point there, Don Xavier. Who've you been talking to?"

"Deborah." He keeps his voice low, even though a buzz is building in the room. "The Art Squad called her, said they might be sending someone down for the auction." He's scanning the room. "Who are those two women at that table?"

"Staff, they're here to take bids on the phone. It's not only the person behind the paddle who bids," she coaches Xavier, "it's the disembodied voice on the phone; who could be anyone, anywhere in the world or right down the street. Interested parties who won't necessarily let on when they win, either."

At major auction houses half a dozen assistants sit poised to receive call-in bids from buyers preferring a low profile. Sotheby's and Christies offer a digital display showing the progress of each piece as it's auctioned: on the left, the lot number; on the right, rippling with each bid, the latest figure, in currencies from seven countries, USD to Hong Kong D. There's no digital board at Subasta Oriel.

Xavier's trying to ask another question except the room's getting loud; shaking her head, Emeline concentrates on her catalogue. More interested in the people, Xavier doesn't bother to study his.

Xavier leans over to speak into her ear, something about "people popping up," but the auctioneer is walking toward his podium. Wearing a wand mike strapped to his head, a black suit, and white shirt punctuated by a crimson necktie, he stretches out a welcoming palm. As the auctioneer bangs his mallet to quiet the room Emeline feels a hard jab in her ribs.

Looking past Xavier, and not as surprised as she should be, she sees Sergei Morosov, standing with others against the mirrored wall, and as the crowd's chatter fades, Xavier's clear voice: " . . . a regular commedia del arte, I'd call it." If Morosov didn't notice them before he does now. As stillness descends he's staring in direction. Pretending indifference, Emeline sweeps her gaze to his left and sees a few feet farther on SinJen Pearce, his arms crossed over his chest. Well, well, the gang's all here. At least Pearce is in the land of the living. What's he doing at the auction, hoping to pick up the *Duke* at a bargain?

"Ladies and gentlemen, welcome to Subasta Oriel. Today we offer fine Catalan pieces as well as several works from the wider world of Spain."

A man wearing a country cap sidles in. Emeline draws a sharp breath and watches him settle against the wall some distance from Pearce and Sergei, not looking their way. And why should he, why would they even know each other?

"What's up?" asks Xavier.

The man in the cap is looking around, he's spotted her, he's starting to push his way toward her. To Emeline's immense relief he can't get through because, all at once, it's show time.

Settling behind his podium, the young auctioneer holds up the wooden mallet he's used to silence the room. Two young men appear, dressed in black clothes, white gloves, and black aprons with white lettering: Subasta Oriel. From the wings they carry out a pair of painted fans, each man holding one as delicately as if it were a live dove.

"Lot #1," intones the auctioneer in Spanish. "A pair of painted fan leaves, by the late nineteenth-century Catalan artist Luis Aguirre. Believed to be painted at—"

"Five hundred euros," interrupts a voice up front.

"I have five hundred in the front," says the auctioneer. "Do I hear six hundred?"

Five rows up Xavier catches a glimpse of a hand, veined and manicured, lifting a paddle inches off an unseen lap, adding to a conversation carried on in code.

"I have six hundred euros," confirms the auctioneer. "Do I have seven hundred?"

"Eight hundred," offers a new voice. The auctioneer smiles, his game is picking up. As Xavier strains to find the latest entry he notices nearby a familiar figure; though today, instead of British tweeds, the stocky woman is dressed in fashionable black shantung and jewelry. He reaches for his cell. In her hand bag Emeline's phone pings once. She pulls out the phone and reads his text: *"OMG. Badger's here."*

"Where?"

"Ur left. Want me to translate bids?" Emeline shakes her head.

"Nine hundred euros," calls out a man's voice. Up front, the unseen woman counters.

As Xavier looks, the Badger raises her beaded clutch.

"Nine hundred euros," affirms the auctioneer.

The man counters: "One thousand euros."

Xavier follows two or three more volleys. Intent on her pursuit, the Badger seems not to have noticed them. In the end the man drops out, and she wins painted fans for eight thousand euros. Whether they're worth it or not, the Badger's established herself as a serious player.

More people arrive to standing room only. One looks British, with a regimental tie and a small, sandy moustache. Catching Xavier looking his way, the man gives a slight nod. One by one, three Catalan landscapes take their place on the plinth: oil, oil, watercolor; Xavier like the watercolor, "showing Andalusian olive groves baking in the sun," the auctioneer says fondly.

Next he veers away from paintings to offer lots that include a Tiffany lamp ("obvious copy," murmurs Emeline), several kilim rugs, and a twelve-piece place setting of Dresden china. "Missing only the odd salad plate or two," the auctioneer apologizes, as if he himself dropped them in the pantry and heard them shatter.

People with no interest in paintings for their clients' walls, or their own, begin raising their paddles to acquire objects to put on floors, bureaus, dinner tables, and bookcases. A five-piece sterling silver tea service set goes for twelve thousand euros.

Up next is a small sketch of a grand lady and a peasant on a donkey. Could be he and Emeline in an earlier era, Xavier thinks; it would be fun to bid on it; he toys with the idea of buying it as a present for her. Until the auctioneer announces the reserve: "Seven hundred fifty euros." That's close to a thousand dollars, Xavier realizes, briskly doing the math on his phone's calculator. The manicured lady up front wins this time, but only after the Badger gives her a run for her money. The action returns to a series of paintings, a few more decorative bits bought for Catalan houses near or interested parties far, and the auctioneer comes to the last offering of the day.

"And finally we come to Lot #26." Xavier sees Emeline bring up the binoculars; she turns to him and mouths: *bees*. "A fine, seventeenth-century Spanish painting, recently brought out of hiding in England. This oil is a portrait of the Duke of Abrantes. The Spanish title was created by King Philip IV in 1642 to reward a Portuguese nobleman for supporting the Spanish Crown. And still today the Abrantes live on, such an honorable family," the auctioneer bows with ceremony toward the front row where a very elderly gentleman struggles to his feet to acknowledge the honor.

"Get on with it," mutters Xavier. He's pulled his calculator up on his screen again

"This portrait was painted by Juan Bautista Martinez del Mazo. The reserve on this painting is four thousand euros. Del Mazo became the court painter—yes, sir?" The auctioneer points to a paddle already in the air, in a man's hand toward the front. Is he, perhaps, the companion, son, cousin, or personal assistant of the elderly gentleman?

While Emeline seems transfixed by the charismatic auctioneer, Xavier's focusing on the men standing at the mirrored side of the room. Pearce and Morosov, if still not speaking, look like they've narrowed the distance between them. Pearce fiddles with his paddle.

"Pearce isn't bidding. Why isn't—"

"Shh, Xavier. Wait."

Pearce finally bids, "six thousand euros." Legitimate try to purchase the painting he said he wanted or a ploy to push up the hammer price?

"I have six thousand euros on my right. Do I hear seven thousand?"

Acting as if uninterested, the man in the cap is watching Pearce. Pearce bids again: "Seven thousand."

The man reaches up to adjust his cap, and Xavier sees Pearce lower his paddle. A signal?

"I have seven thousand euros, do I hear eight thousand? No? Going at seven thousand euros. . ." Emeline raises her paddle.

"Emeline," Xavier hisses, "it's the fake!" The pretty assistant on the telephone raises one finger.

"I have eight thousand euros. So back to you, señora. Do I hear eight thousand, five hundred?" Emeline raises her paddle again.

"Jesus, Emeline!"

"I have eight thousand, five hundred euros on my left. And we have?" The auctioneer looks toward the pretty assistant and raises one eyebrow. Xavier holds his breath; beside him, Emeline does, too. The assistant murmurs into the phone, and then lifts a languid hand.

"Nine thousand euros. Señora." To Xavier's profound relief Emeline, exhaling, lays her paddle on her lap. The auctioneer looks around the room "Anyone else? No? Going, going," he pauses for a final look toward the assistant, who bids no further, "gone, for nine thousand euros." His hammer falls.

The elder Abrantes gentleman will not be going home with, as he thinks, his ancestor. The *Duke*, bees and all, has been picked up by a faceless buyer. The auction is over.

Around them people are gathering up their briefcases and catalogues, chatting with friends they know, making small talk with people they don't..

"What in hell were you thinking?" Xavier scolds. She tries to shrug him off. She knows it was a close call, her whole body still trembles. "Talk about impetuous—you almost got stuck with the fake del Mazo for over ten thousand dollars. It's something to do with that guy in the cap, over there, isn't it." Emeline knows he's only guessing, and knows it's hard to stay ahead of Xavier for long. She's glad all this is over. "Tell me. Is he the man you saw in the bar?"

"Or maybe," Emeline fires back, "the man you drove me to Girona to inspect?"

Xavier frowns. "This man, whoever he is—"

"I know who he is. I met him a couple of times." The pretentious little man who seemed always to want whatever Cliff had. Was he actually gay or like Luca, merely playing the part? She remembers Hueber's hands on her shoulders, remembers fighting her way clear of a long embrace hello or good-bye any time he found her alone.

"His name is Hueber. He is the art consultant Clifford brought in to—"

Just then several things happen at once. "Oi! Stop!" calls a loud British voice. Pearce is slinking toward the front door, with the Brit in the regimental tie after him. Two Spanish *guardia* in navy uniforms follow close at his heels shouting, "*Pare. Pare.*" One manages to seize Pearce, the other grabs a second man, knocking off his country cap as the man struggles.

"Emeline!" Stunned, shivering, she recognizes the voice, it's Hueber; he's reaching toward her. "Thank God. I tried to get to you before, to warn you. This man . . ." he turns his face toward Pearce, then back to her. "You have to help me; this has nothing to do with me, a misunderstanding, Please. Emeline, tell them."

Emeline's aware Xavier, puzzled, is watching her closely, along with the regimental tie and the two *guardia*. She has no need at all to pretend. They will see nothing in her eyes, see nothing on her face to recall a pleasing memory. Only what she truly feels—shock, sadness, disappointment, and relief."

"This, misunderstanding?" Emeline's voice is strong. "It is yours, Hueber, all yours."

"I thought, I hoped, with Clifford gone—"

"You were mistaken. There is nothing between us. There never was." Abruptly she turns and stalks toward the front door.

"Mrs. Hughes. You are sure?" asks the gentleman in the regimental tie.

"Quite. Take him. He is all yours."

The British gentleman nods to the *guardia*, who lead Pearce and Hueber away. Turning back to Emeline, he flashes his ID. "Mrs. Hughes? Carter Ramsey, Art Squad, Scotland Yard. I met with your daughter Deborah. She seemed very concerned about you, and of course, the painting . . ."

"Then, tell me, who is that?" Emeline points to the Badger in her blue shantung; in minutes she's struggling in the arms of two more *guardia*. The room seems all at once full of uniformed men, unless Emeline's fooled by the reflections?

"Thank you for pointing her out; we couldn't decide between her and the eager woman in the front row." He raises his arm, gestures to more *guardia* who immediately release a very irate, Spanish lady who lets loose a stream of angry words.

"And you must be Xavier Escudero. Carter Ramsey," the Brit repeats reaching out a hand.

Instead of shaking it, Xavier points. "See that man there, the Russian? Sergei Morosov, calls himself a dealer. You want him, too. There he is, he's heading for the emergency door." Ramsey signals to two more *guardia* who run, closing in on Morosov. One on each side, they start to hustle him toward the front door.

Around them, strangely silent, spectators are taking in more of a show than they bargained for. As the *guardia* step onto the sidewalk, removing the game they've bagged, the buzz begins again, quickly rising to a din.

Xavier hands Ramsey the hotel card he's carrying. "Come by later, then. Right now Mrs. Hughes needs to get back to her room."

Emeline begins to tap her cane toward the car where Feran, double parked, is opening the door. Almost there, and a rough-looking man in the street pushes forward. If the man had been more careful—if he hadn't brushed against Xavier's shoulder—he might have succeeded. Already his arm is raised, the pistol pointed across the crowd.

In three steps Xavier tackles the gunman and knocks him to the ground just as the gun goes off. The shot misses Emeline, it misses everyone. It does shatter one front vitrine, setting off a piercing alarm and causing shards of glass to fall out of the ornate frame that's led to views of fine Spanish art for the last hundred years.

CHAPTER 30

"You didn't think I, of all people, should be told?" Emeline's still shaking; even though she's learned she wasn't the gunman's target, her body is slow to get the memo. And she's furious. "I wish you'd never bought me those stupid alphabet cards!"

The room service waiter interrupts to bring dinner, then leaves fast. Pausing to catch her breath, Emeline sees Xavier look with longing at the tray: Spanish tortilla, grilled shrimp, tomatoes, sweet rolls, flan.

"And what if I was wrong?" he says. "An amalgam—"

"An anagram!" Emeline's having little luck reining in her temper.

"Sounds like you're stuttering, but okay, an-an-a-gram."

"Think you're so bloody clever."

"I don't think I'm clever at all. Pure chance I stumbled across the name. Alphabet cards fell on the floor, I picked them up. Or even worse, Emeline, if I'd been right, if Fleisch had turned out to be your—"

Emeline gives him such a look he cringes. *We will never speak about that,* she's trying to say without words. *Never acknowledge how she's worried Clifford might be involved, never hint that she is thankful, if not completely certain, that her husband is in the clear.*

"Besides, Emeline, it's not like you ever suggested Hueber. Isn't today the first time I'm hearing his name? Secrets on both sides, I'd say."

"Because Hueber never crossed my mind—"

"Because he was such a charmer?" Emeline shudders. "Then it has to be because he was in the accident himself," Xavier says, putting the last piece into the puzzle.

"Exactly." She's always found Hueber annoying; barely managed to pity him when the officer who came to see her described Hueber in the hospital: his face battered, collar bone fractured, leg in a cast and hung from a metal contraption. Today she's very glad she never went to visit him. Another old dame advantage, she must suggest it Tram: save your energy for what really matters.

"Sorry, Xavier, what?"

"I was asking: you won't feel badly if Hueber spends time in jail."

"I don't give a damn about Hueber, I never did!"

"Glad to hear it. I wouldn't be surprised if he's the one who put Morosov and Belmo together in the first place. "And," Xavier pauses, "how do we know the accident wasn't his idea? He just expected he'd walk away whole. If Clifford found out something; if Hueber suspected, shared his fears with Morosov, and it got back to the Brighton Beach Russians—the guy's gonna wind up charged with more than fraud."

"If Clifford had only told me," tears are running through her fingers, "he should have told me."

"I know, I know. It's okay now." Xavier hands her a tissue and puts his arms around, then tacks another way. "Tell me this, Emeline: what was this impulse to bid?"

"Ryan wanted me to buy the painting," Emeline blows her nose, "he texted me. Ryan knows he is dying, he was worried how Gabor would manage."

"Sinn Fein," snorts Xavier, "possibly ex-IRA terrorist, he's texting estate plans? How'd he know about the fake painting? I don't get the problem, anyway. Gabor owns the gym, he'll manage.

"Your friend Alejandro wasn't exactly truthful. Gabor owns only a small interest in the gym." Dodging his other question, she's relieved when Xavier decides to let it go.

"Ryan couldn't draw up a will like ordinary people?"

"I think Ryan wasn't sure about invoking the law if he didn't have to. He owns the house. He was looking for a separate asset, lodged somewhere his 'cheatin' relatives' wouldn't find it."

"So he decides to trust a woman he's met once," Xavier says. She can see he wishes he hadn't, remembering they've had their own issues with trust.

"Of course I had to turn him down," she says. "Think of it, a fake del Mazo propped against my living room wall while IFAR sniffs around."

"Then why in God's name were you bidding?

"I was conducting a test," Emeline explains. "I recognized Hueber; I wanted to see what he would do. If he'd bid even a few thousand, I'd have been left uncertain. But he didn't bid, not once. And why would he, when the painting was already his? The forgery happened on his watch," Emeline still finds it hard to believe, "under the guise of getting Segal's painting cleaned up."

"Hueber thought he'd be the one cleaning up. Not anymore, Hueber's doing time, even if he plea bargains. You plan on eating all your shrimp?" Xavier reaches over to spear one of hers with his fork.

"Take the rest," she pushes the plate toward him. "Honestly, all this trouble, over a not very important Old Master."

"Maybe," with his free hand Xavier pulls out his cell phone, "del Mazo was more important in his own day, part of the Golden Age of Spanish Painting along with Zurburăn, Goya, Murillo—"

"Crap, Xavier!" She jumps up from her chair, Xavier's so shocked he drops the shrimp on the glass table.

"That's it! God, I should have thought of it weeks ago, only we got fixated on the *Duke*, was it the original or was it a forgery—" Excited, she inhales crumbs and chokes, Xavier has to whack her on the back to clear her airway. She's lost weight, Emeline worries he'll feel the back of her rib cage right under her skin, try to hustle her off to her doctor the minute they get home.

Still, after half a dozen tentative coughs, she relaxes into a broad smile. "I'm fine, Xavier. I'm really fine."

"You were saying, señora?"

"This auction was a feint, a very clever feint, and they almost got away with it, too. *The Duke of Abrantes* by Juan Bautista Martinez del Mazo," for once she honors the painter with his full name, "has been sold. The sale's on record, that charade today at Subasta Oriol is now part of the old *Duke's* provenance.

"Go on."

"Let's say the *Duke* that left Ron Segal's house last May was the original. So where is the original now? They still have it, and Hueber knows where the real one is, he has to. Except when Ron's *Duke* reappears, I'd put money on it, he won't be a del Mazo.

"What's he gonna be," Xavier's drawing out this moment, "a really nice Kazimir Malevich?"

"A right one, you are," Emeline laughs. "When we get home I should set you up in your own gallery."

"Where's the *Duke* going to turn up? And who are *they?*"

"The original *Duke* will surface at auction or a gallery sale. Or not surface at all, if they can manage to arrange a private sale. Hong Kong, maybe, Singapore, one of the financial centers far away from the sharpest minds of Western experts. Not New York, London, Paris—"

"Or Spain."

"Definitely not Spain. They have no problems to worry about like paint chips or radiography. The paint is authentic, the canvas is authentic. They'll have to write up a convincing provenance; with a few holes in it, sure, but you'd expect that after more than three centuries. Only this time our *Duke*, the one from Ron Segal's house, will be credited to a different painter and that will be—why are your grinning, Xavier?"

"Better than the Oscars, this is. Envelope, please, Emeline." Xavier puts his hand out. "And the winner is—Diego Rodriguez de Silva Velazquez!"

She stares, open-mouthed, then raises her arm, closes her fist, and pumps like a triumphant athlete. "Yes! But how did you—"

"Del Mazo was Velazquez's student, then later his son-in-law. I googled, Emeline. It's all out there in the cloud if you keep looking."

"I knew it the moment I met you, Xavier. Between your brain and my brawn, what couldn't we accomplish?" She can see he's trying to hide how much that small phrase pleases him: your brain. Once they're back in New York she'll have to give serious thought to Xavier's future.

"Liar, you thought I was the mugger," Xavier says. "Hueber hid the original in the Ochre fund to 'monetize' it, Belmo would have told him. Wonder how long they've working together? They'd hold the real del Mazo for a couple years, then sell it and make a fortune for the both of them. Man, I bet the original's been sitting in some free port all this time while you and I go—"

"Haring around Europe," Emeline laughs. She hasn't done much laughing lately and now two victories in one day. It's not just the painting problem they've solved; it is, she hopes, also the other one; her real worry, about Clifford.

Xavier chews happily, wipes his mouth. "If you pass off one seventeenth-century painting as another, is it still a forgery?"

"Not my field," Emeline says, airily. "I'm sure we can safely call it criminal."

"Too bad you didn't know this while Segal's *Duke* was propped against your wall."

"If it ever was."

"If it was," Xavier suggests, "you could have called it a Velazquez and sold tickets."

"Or donated it to Muffy for her benefit."

"Emeline, who are *they?* Unless . . is that going above your pay grade?"

"We've got to get in touch with Carter," Emeline is fumbling in her purse. "Hell, what did I do with his card?"

"Got it," Xavier pulls Ramsey's card out of the pocket of his black leather jacket. "Think it's too late to call him?"

"Oh, please. We're In Barcelona. Carter Ramsey's not even sitting down to dinner."

"It wasn't you the gunman was after, Mrs. Hughes," Ramsey apologizes. "His name is Chuprov, by the way. He was after Sergei Morosov."

"If I'd known," Xavier's still feeling bruised from his fall, "I'd have let Chuprov just get on with it."

"Lucky for us you tackled Chuprov in time. You saved Morosov's life, which gives us a chance to question Morosov. We know Chuprov's tied to the Brighton Beach crowd, but INTERPOL says he's been hard to nail down." Ramsey smiles the way a wolf might. "Chuprov's small beer, anyway. We can extradite him to the States, or turn him loose here in Barcelona. Within a month, he's a dead man. Morosov, on the other hand . . ."

"And," Emeline tries to keep her voice casual, "the other man?"

"You mean Fleisch? He's been living in Girona the last few months, claims to be a professor on sabbatical. We're holding him overnight."

"He is no professor. His name is Karl Hueber," Emeline takes a shaky breath, "and he's an art consultant who did some work for my husband. Hueber's involved in two crimes we know about."

"That so? Chuprov didn't seem interested in him."

"You will be. The first is fraud, concerning Lot #26 at the auction tonight and an art fund, Ochre, in New York City."

"An art fund?" Ramsey looks interested. "This have anything to do with the reason your daughter came to see us about the painting?"

"The second crime," Emeline begins, and then she's crying again. Ramsey, puzzled, looks to Xavier.

""Mrs Hughes is not crying over a painting," Xavier assures him. "Last June, in New York, Mrs. Hughes' husband was killed in a car crash. Hueber was driving the car. He was injured, too, but that may have been because the plan wasn't perfect. It's possible Hueber's looking at an indictment for murder, at least manslaughter, as well as charges relating to his connection with this art fund, Ochre. If," Xavier cannot resist, "there's a proper investigation this time."

"Really. I'll pass that along. For sure Morosov could cause the Brighton Beach fellows a good deal of trouble if he talked. You think he knew about this art fund?"

"You bet," says Xavier.

"Brighton Beach," murmurs Emeline, wiping her eyes. "You know, Xavier, I'm pretty sure Valda Fairfax is Russian, and all she was ever guilty of—"

"So you see, Ramsey," Xavier interrupts, worried he'll be back home, learn Fairfax has been picked up for questioning, and have to listen to Tram complain how hard it is to get good help. "There's more to the story, and it's complicated. Emeline's figured it out."

"No, Xavier, we figured it out together, you were the one who—"

Ramsey, curious, leans forward. "Please. Do tell, both of you."

"You gotta be kidding me," Deborah's shrill voice comes through the speaker phone. Emeline's trying out another feature on her new mobile.

"Velazquez was del Mazo's teacher and later his father-in-law. Xavier looked it up. Velazquez married his teacher's daughter—"

"Which," says Xavier, "if you remember, Deborah, I did try to tell you in London. Only you cut me off."

"Then his student del Mazo," Emeline resumes, "does the same thing. He marries Francisca de Silva Velazquez and Pacheco."

"Ochre's holding Ron Segal's *Duke*," says Emeline. "The people Belmo was working for, Morosov or at least his colleagues, plan to pass it off as a Velazquez."

"Crikey," breathes Deborah, "You sure about this?"

"I'd bet your inheritance on it, dear."

Long silence from the London end until Xavier says, "She's *joking,* Deborah. But the rest of it is no joke. We think the *Duke*, the original del Mazo, will some day reappear, passed off as a Velazquez. Whether the rest of the world ever hears about the sale or not."

"God," says Deborah. "The 245th Velazquez, we have 244 at last count. The press will be all over this, everyone's going to want to talk to you. When will you two get back?"

Emeline's had enough of the press to last her lifetime, what's left of it. But for now that's not the point. "Darling, I have to ask you not to talk about this. Not at Courtauld. Not in London. Not anywhere."

"Ma, honestly, you are so—"

"This is not about me. It's about, well, protecting your father."

"Daddy had nothing to do with this!"

"I don't think so either. But why stir up the past? It's a request, more than a request actually. Carter Ramsey from the Art Squad, that nice man you found for us? Yes, he made it to the auction. So pleasant. Handsome, too. I wonder if he's taken?"

"Ma!"

"Carter says INTERPOL has their eye on a group of businessmen, Russian businessmen."

"You talking about the mafia?"

"If what happened at the auction gets out, INTERPOL loses its best chance of catching, them, these dudes?"

"Dudes? Really? You know who you're starting to sound like. Let me talk to him."

"Speaker phone?"

"No."

Has Emeline managed to distract her daughter? Arriving at the hotel, Carter Ramsey asked way too many questions about Clifford. Without directly saying so, he made it clear: absolute silence on their part was the price for dropping enquiries into any hand Clifford might have had in this sorry tale. Xavier understands; he sat close to her while the three of them talked. She can trust Xavier. She hopes she can trust daughter.

Phone to his ear, Xavier is mumbling: "Uh huh. Probably. Huh huh . . . No, I think she's ready to go home." He looks up, raises his eyebrows. Emeline lays a hand across her heart and nods. Yes. Home. Yes.

Chapter 31

More than Central Park or her aunt's spacious apartment, the Frick Museum's inside courtyard felt like home to Emeline when she first arrived in New York. Only a few days into the city's heat and her new life, Aunt Mildred introduced her to the steel baron's mansion, its galleries and paintings, its statues and gardens. The sheltering inner courtyard touched a chord in Emeline's heart. She knows it's no coincidence her new place is a short walk from the Frick.

Leaving JFK, keeping her company as far as 63rd Street, Xavier insisted on seeing her safely up to the seventh floor and into 7B before continuing on his own way uptown to stay with his family. Her night doorman's "Good-evening, ma'am," as if Emeline had been away only an hour; the plants Gregor watered in her absence; the resentful Scaramouche; and the light blinking on her answering machine were all enough to convince her Barcelona had been an off-Broadway play, London a dream. Only the brown edges of the lettuce in the fridge drawer persuaded her otherwise.

Emeline is alone when she makes herself an omelet, alone when she goes to bed, and alone when she wakes up. She expects in a day or two Xavier will be back, if only collect his things. If she's changed over the days in Europe, she knows he has, too

This morning, for comfort, she's walked to the Frick. Sitting in the courtyard, she drinks in the rows of double columns, the Ionic capitals curled like Aunt Mildred's pageboy haircut. Around her, in leaf not stone, grow ferns, elephant leaf plants, chrysanthemums.

Deborah's doing what she wants with her inheritance, her life — Mary-Margaret certainly is. Amazing that the old Peckham house fetched such a sum. Even more remarkable is the way her new sister chose to spend it.

Closing her eyes and hearing the water's melodic fall in the fountain's three basins, Emeline recognizes the ways she's changed, if not as dramatically as Mary-Margaret: certain attitudes she's ready to leave behind, old habits that now seem frivolous, or selfish.

Take Xavier. Emeline needed help and offered Xavier money to get it. Young man like that, tied down to an old woman, what was she thinking? She'd roped him in once, then done it again when she made him go to London. Soon she needs to find a way to set him free.

Emeline has a few other ideas on ways she can to move forward, herself. Still, she knows her limits, accepts that these will close in on her more as time goes on. There's no way she could do what Wendy's planning. Wendy called from London last evening. Her omelet growing cold, Emeline listened to the dear woman, buzzing with energy well after midnight in England. Wendy, her socialite patina stripped away, not so much changed as revealed.

"Yes, I'll be back in a couple of days. Deal with it all: Belmo's death, the Ochre art fund, the lawyers, the lawsuits. What? Oh, Deborah told me, she was kind enough to break that news. No, Emeline, I am not being sarcastic. I had to find out sometime, and she was very gentle. What a lovely daughter you have, I hope my Sofie will grow up to be like her." Emeline, speechless, said nothing.

"And, besides," Wendy went on, "I have to face dear Flavia. Did you know she put her savings into Ochre because Belmo charmed her into it?" Emeline did not know; Xavier's kept that to himself. "I'm determined to see her right. One good thing, anyway: Belmo put the penthouse in my name and believe me, I can't sell it fast enough."

"I've wanted to help Flavia, too," Emeline began. "I've given her the name of a good lawyer, for starters."

"Great. Text me your lawyer's number, will you? He can help me find me the right lawyer in Omaha."

"Why—?"

"Because, Emeline, I'm going to start a shelter back home. How could I face myself, keeping strangers safe, if I let down the woman closest to me? I suppose," Wendy actually giggled, "she'd throw a fit if I called it St. Flavia's?"

"I'd say so."

"And I owe you, too, Emeline. Your letter . . ."

"How are the children?" Emeline managed, swallowing tears.

"Oh. You know, losing a parent. You and I, we'll have a quiet tea together soon as I get back. Your place this time, not mine. You can tell me your plans for what's ahead. Love you! Bye."

Emeline feels such gratitude, appreciation, and, she admits it, envy. To have the years left to mark a new path, the energy to keep to it. It is what it is. Wendy has to live with the public shame of her husband's dirty dealings; Emeline only lives with her few remaining suspicions about Clifford.

If Flavia is Wendy's responsibility, Xavier is hers. Should she help him apply to Columbia, or would he be happier going back to La Guardia? She muses on what areas of study might bridge the world Xavier grew up in and the world he's come to know: Sports medicine? Sociology? Psychology?

She knows it has to be up to Xavier. Emeline remembers excellent advice from one of Deborah's teachers: "Prepare the child for the path, not the path for the child." Flavia had done the first for her son. At this point, Emeline can lay down a little tarmac herself.

And wouldn't Clifford just love it, Emeline drawing on his assets to further the education of another working-class bloke. She stares overhead where the Frick's curved-glass ceiling panes, lit from behind, bring brightness into the courtyard. Emeline straightens her back, she has things to take care of. She makes a mental list, 1, 2, 3, pulls out her mobile and before she loses her nerve begins the first text. Clever little thing, this mobile. Email is so yesterday.

The IRT train speeds uptown. Swaying, Xavier sits between a Nuyorican teen with an MP3 player and an old *abuelita,* cradling Kohl's shopping bags on her knees. Already Xavier's missing the routine he's grown used to: the grocery runs to D'Agostino's, their quiet suppers, Gregor's haughty ways, and the cat's highly conditional affection.

Unnerved by her son's cryptic texts from Barcelona, Flavia demanded he come straight home when he landed. So Xavier refused Emeline's offer of the car service, though he did choose a local train, not an express, as if trying to slow his return to 105th.

Flavia, hugging him, is tearful. Ramon is looking at him with new respect. Rocio, whining as usual, complains he'd "gotten a vacation in Spain while I'm stuck here with a teething kid and a dead-end job."

"Hardly a vacation," Xavier replies. Flavia is silent, Xavier suspects she's given up trying to score points moral or practical. Even if she has at considerable cost hired a tutor to improve her daughter's chances of graduating.

Cluttered as ever and thick with the undercurrents of family life, the apartment smells of sofrito; the tomatoes, onions, garlic, and cilantro he'd cooked in Deborah's kitchen couldn't match sofrito made by his mother. When Jomar crawls over to wrap his arms around his uncle's ankles, Xavier feels the tug of longing for a family of some kind, if not exactly this one. Patting Jomar on his tiny shoulders and agreeing to stay for dinner, Xavier feels he is coming home and knows he can't stay long.

Starchy as ever, Gregor the guardian dragon opens the lobby door a few days later. Xavier steps aside as a harried woman pushes past him. When the elevator door opens, she reaches in to loop two plastic sacs of groceries around the brass handrail and press her floor number. Xavier just makes it into the elevator before the door closes on her instructing Gregor: "Call up and tell my kids I've left them supper, will you? Then get me a cab."

Xavier rings the doorbell at 7B, even though he still has his key. A familiar, ringed hand swings open the door. To his surprise, a leggy, reddish-brown dog steps out to sniff at him, quivering with delight.

"Emeline. Who is—?"

"Diogi, of course." Emeline's ringed hand smooths the short hair.

"Ryan's dog, sure. They here, Ryan and Gabor?"

There's the sound of slow footsteps and a stoop-shouldered Hungarian with a sad face appears in the hallway. "I am here," says Gabor. "Diogi, he is here also. Only Ryan . . ." tears fill Gabor's eyes, drip down his wrinkled cheeks, he look older than he did a few weeks ago. "I am afraid," he chokes, unable to go on.

"Dear Ryan has left us, Xavier." Emeline straightens up, gripping the door frame for support. "It happened while we were gone, quite sudden toward the end, and painless. Mostly painless." Gabor gives a single sob and walks back down the hallway.

"All that texting in London, Emeline. and I thought you were setting up lunch plans with your ladies."

"Gabor," Emeline, serene, looks quite pleased with herself, "could not keep the house on his own. It will sell soon, the realtor says, but everywhere Gabor could afford to rent he ran into a problem."

"Diogi," Xavier guesses.

"Diogi. I suggested he stay here for a while."

"In *my* room?"

"No, dear. In mine."

"Activist queer for five decades—Gabor's sharing a bed with you?"

"Oh, don't be so bloody-minded, Xavier, not everything is about sex. We're good friends, that's all. Wash up, will you? Gabor is making dinner."

"So he's in my kitchen, too." Ignoring the dog (Scaramouche, of course, is nowhere to be seen, and for once Xavier feels a bond with the cat). "For how long?"

Taking the crucial first step, Emeline wraps her arms tightly around Xavier. "Who's to say?" Her voice is muffled against his shoulder. "Deborah seems able to shift her houseguests out in a couple of weeks. With me, they tend to hang about."

Even in grief Gabor is a remarkable cook. The bistro table in the kitchen too small for the trio, they sit in the dining room. Diogi contents himself with curling up on the rug beneath. Even though Emeline keeps up a happy patter, Xavier worries she's feeling a pain in her leg; until he realizes she is secretly handing off sticky bits of goulash and spetzle to the other Hungarian at, or at least under, the table.

As Gabor is clearing away Xavier whispers to Emeline: "I thought you had all kinds of grand plans." He knows he sounds mean but he can't stop, "that after London, you expected to change, do something new, something different. What happened?"

"My dear, I'm an old woman." Briefly she touches her hair; maybe so he'll notice that, barely home, she's gone and gotten herself a new look. "I don't think it is the moment to throw myself at the New School. do you?"

"I thought . . ."

"That our time away brought an epiphany? It did. And I expect to make changes in the world yet, if measured in ripples, not tsunami."

It feels like a tsunami to Xavier as he faces a dessert far too rich and an express train back up town. Filled with apple torte and regret, he stands.

"Great meal, Gabor, thanks," he says heartily. "See you around."

"Xavier?" Emeline looks genuinely surprised. "Where are you off to?"

"I'm pretty tired," he draws a breath, opts for being up front, "and I figure you don't need me here anymore."

"Whatever gave you that idea? Go to bed, Xavier, you're exhausted. The time change is murder."

"Maybe I'll check out the roof garden first."

"Sure, have a smoke." Emeline reaches out one hand. "We'll clean up."

Gabor, studying Xavier's face, laughs for the first time that evening. "She can accomplish many things, our Emeline. But persuading a gay leopard to change his spots?"

Gabor heads into the kitchen. Xavier murmurs to Emeline: "If anything, I thought you quite liked that lawyer, Coop."

"Coop? God, no! He's handsome, sure, but try to talk to him? It's just Yale, Yale, Yale."

Xavier takes the elevator to the top floor and climbs the stairs to check on the roof garden. The pots need watering, he'll get to it tomorrow. He stares out at one thousand and one lights, he's back in his own city at last, and it feels like a homecoming with no home.

Alone, his thoughts turn to Clifford. Like Xavier himself, Clifford may have needed Emeline's help with the array of forks and spoons at a formal dinner. But his parents were proud people, Emeline says, honest people. At heart Clifford knew right from wrong, and he'd promised Emeline his wild days in business were over. Xavier wishes he were here, he'd ask him straight out, man-to-man: What happened? What did you know? What did you plan to do?

Xavier snuffs out his cigarette. Back in the apartment, he heads into the den. Helping Gabor load the dishwasher, Emeline doesn't even see him come in.

Xavier blows a thin layer of dust off the keyboard and boots up. Easy enough to find the folder he'd seen before. He clicks on the draft Clifford started, saves it as a new document, fusses around so he can backdate it in the system, not just in the document footer, and gets to work.

Addressing it to the District Attorney of New York (he googles for the address) he rewrites—*finishes* is the word he prefers—the letter so it's perfectly clear. Once Clifford realized what Hueber was up to, he was ready to blow the whistle, would have blown the whistle if not for his sudden death on the Henry Hudson.

Was Clifford meant to die that night, or was it Hueber they were after? While Xavier suspects they'll never know the answer, he can take care of Emeline's other grave doubt. Carefully, Xavier checks the new draft, no place here for rookie mistakes or barrio slang. He uses Spell Check to correct *testeimony* and *fradulent*.

Should he tell Emeline what he's "found"? No, better if her daughter's the one, Deborah's already booked a flight to New York for the following week. Emeline's waited this long, she can wait a while longer. Shutting down the computer, Xavier texts Deborah, keeping it vague, *Noticed letter on ur dad's computer. Go to Recent, take a look.*

About to head uptown, Xavier's standing in his old room for a quick look around when the front door bell rings. Emeline calls from the kitchen: "Can you get that, Xavier?"

It's a policeman. No wonder Gregor let him upstairs without calling. God, what's the woman gone and done now? Two days home, and already Emeline's embroiled in some escapade.

The officer, in uniform, is young and black, smooth shaven and not too tall. With a crisp haircut, a stud in his ear, and the smile of a charmer, he has the eyes of a young man who's seen much of the world and knows what he wants.

"Xavier Escudero?"

"And you would be?"

"Pierre Hill, they call me Perry." Putting out his hand, he holds Xavier's gaze an extra moment. "You've met my Uncle, right, Detective Hill? Uncle Percy told me to come look you up. Said I should meet you. So I thought I'd come and see for myself why."

Absently, Xavier puts out his hand. *Commedia d'el arte*, it's everywhere. Diogi is thrilled: a person with a pulse, a new friend. He dances forward, puts his front paws on the shoulders of the man in front of him. Soon as one hand reaches to pat him and the other keeps hold of Xavier's hand, Diogi barks happily.

In the kitchen Gabor and Emeline are laughing, until Emeline says, "Oh my God!" A plate shatters and the laughing stops. Emeline practically trots into the hall, cell phone in hand.

"Hey, Perry, how's it going? Good thing you're here, too. Xavier, you are not going to believe this. We have to talk."

"You bet we do, lady! This meddling of yours—"

"Shhh!" Emeline waves her phone, dismissing such social trivia. "Deborah just texted me. The Kunsthal Museum in Rotterdam, you know, in the Netherlands? There's been a heist. They got away with a Matisse, a Picasso, *two* Manets . . . seven paintings in all, worth $25 million. Xavier, Perry," out of breath, she pauses, though not for long, "I don't suppose either of you happen to speak Dutch?"

THE END

Acknowledgments

For a story that explores what's real and what's not, I thought I ought to clear up a few questions. The Duke of Abrantes was honored by King Philip IV of Spain in 1642. Juan Bautista Martinez del Mazo was a painter in Spain, but *The Duke of Abrantes* portrait exists only in my mind, as does the Cadmium Fund.

Background details on Manhattan's Upper East Side, El Barrio, South London, Barcelona, the 2012 Olympics, hedge funds, subway and bus routes, are as accurate as I could make them; if inaccuracies exist the fault is mine. St. Bertie's House draws on my experience in Cross Streets, the program at Tucson's Southside Presbyterian Church that serves the homeless. Other volunteers may think they recognize themselves. I salute you all for your fidelity and service.

Many thanks to my invaluable critics, Christine Gross and Elizabeth Berlin. Also thanks to Rhona Bross, John Culp, Abigail Adams, Michael Urquart, Carl Kantor, Paula Vesely, Martha O'Brien, and Maude Brown who contributed their expertise from worlds they know: from art and medicine to personal training, fashion, finance, and Childeric's bees.

I especially thank my mother Sylvia T. Grebe, daughter of American Art Nouveau designer B.B. Thresher and a fine and prolific painter in her own right. She opened my eyes and my daughters' to art and design in its many forms, traveling through her life with a valiant spirit.

ABOUT THE AUTHOR

Cynthia Lang graduated from Smith College, won a *Vogue* Prix de Paris, and worked as a staff writer on *Glamour*. After free-lancing (*Glamour, Parents, Mademoiselle, Vogue Children,* and *New York Times Magazine*), she wrote publications for the Education Development Center, Inc. (EDC) and taught at the College of Communications, Boston University. Author of *Sarah Carlisle's River and Other Stories,* she is co-author with Jerome Kagan of *Psychology and Education: An Introduction* (Harcourt Brace Jovanovich) and with Harry Levinson, *Executive* (Harvard University Press). She's traveled in Europe, Latin America, and Africa and lived in Manhattan, Cambridge, Gloucester, and Maine. With her husband John, a photographer, she lives in Tucson.

www.cynthialang.com

About Preservation

Lee Baldwin moves to Maine to revel in a tide of solitude and brood about her missing husband. Instead she's pulled into the daily dramas of Dolly, her flighty landlady; Maxine, the small town's store proprietor; a welder at Bath Iron works; a trio of boys running wild; and their mother, who may or may not have heard a saint speak. Lee feels especially the fierce grace of Hazel, an elderly woman whose grip on life breathes energy into her own. Evoking the lives of northern New Englanders who struggle in the shadow side of prosperity, Preservation explores the isolation— and possibilities—of a time before electronics linked us nonstop through the cloud.

CPSIA information can be obtained
at www.ICGtesting.com
Printed in the USA
LVHW050833040619
620063LV00004B/622/P